CW00867963

Dasvidaniya

Dasvidaniya

W.L. Liberman

Prologue

A seventeen-year-old crack addict named Beulah Robinson lay strapped to a cot in my second floor bedroom. She'd crawled to my back door earlier that day, mewling. I'd heard a weak scratching on the screen and thought it had been a sick animal; a dog or cat from the alley out back. Beulah was the granddaughter of my neighbors, Fred and Alma Robinson. I'd watched her grow up, a beautiful girl, full of wonder and light. Then the crack dealers got to her and her life plummeted faster and deeper than anyone could imagine.

I wanted to take her to the hospital but she fought me, saying she wouldn't go, that she'd rather die on my floor.

I carried her upstairs, just a bundle of bones, and laid her on the cot.

"Tie my wrists," she said. "You'll need to tie my wrists and my ankles."

I didn't argue. I cut some strips out of a pillow sheet and bound her to the metal frame. I gave her some water. She closed her eyes and I waited for the inevitable to happen.

I knew they would come for her and I wondered if she had considered that. Whether she had wanted them to come to me? I didn't know.

Beulah passed in and out of consciousness. I fed her chicken soup one sip at a time and waited patiently while she swallowed. It had been six hours since she'd arrived. Her hair had a bright henna rinse and it contrasted garishly with the ghastly pallor of her light skin. Her mother had been a white woman.

Beulah jerked at the straps, writhed in the cot, gnashed her teeth and shrieked. She begged me for money. Begged me to buy her drugs, told me I could have sex with her, called me dirty, foul names...but I didn't answer. I just wondered how such a fine girl could fall so far and whether she'd find her way back.

Finally, she lay back, exhausted. I hoped she'd find some peace and fall asleep, even for a few minutes.

Just as I was about to leave, she stopped me.

"What is it?" I asked.

"Talk to me," she whispered.

"About what?"

"Tell me a story... tell me your story...please...don't go. I...need...you...to...talk to me...just keep talking...don't stop..."

I got up to leave the room but again she stopped me.

"Don't run out on me now, Mr. Goldman, please. Tell me...tell me about your life...so I can forget my own for awhile...please...tell me...I got time...not going nowhere..."

I considered her request. I too had nowhere to go. Everyone who mattered was dead. What else did I have to do?

And so, I began.

Chapter 1

One fine day in May, my eight year-old brother, Simmy, staggered home crying, a knife blade sticking out of his left shoulder blade. Simmy collapsed, crumbling to the ground, his pitiful wail piercing my heart.

I burst through the screen door like a maniac. Then I saw the knife and froze, feeling sick and suddenly weak-kneed.

"Oh my God...Shit...shit," I lifted his limp body and half-carried, half-dragged him inside the house.

"Katya! Katya! Come quickly!"

I heard the thump on the ceiling as Katya dropped the book she was reading and flew down the stairs to the kitchen.

I struggled with his weight. My hands slipped on his blood. Katya ran forward and looped Simmy's good arm around her shoulders. "I've got him," she said, then barked, "Table."

I looked at the oak table and in one motion swept the heavy ceramic dishes and silver cutlery to the floor.

Between us, we lay Simmy face down on the polished surface.

"We need hot water, alcohol, a scissors and bandages," Katya ordered firmly. "The blade is stuck in the bone."

I ran toward the medicine closet.

I returned and watched Katya fill a pot and set it on the stove. Simmy moaned. Katya pushed back her sleeves, took some soap and scrubbed her hands. "Get me a sponge," she said. I reached. "No, not that one. The new one." I found it and handed it to her. She turned to me. "You must pull the knife out quickly," she said and the meaning of her words sunk in. I rolled a dishtowel up tightly and forced it between Simmy's teeth.

"Bite on it," I said. He took it, whimpering like a wounded puppy.

Katya scissored away the bits of shredded fabric around the wound. I was terrified of hurting Simmy even more but took a deep breath to steady myself. I didn't want to think about slipping or making a mistake. I placed both hands around the wooden hasp of the knife. I could feel the tip of it embedded deep in the bone, speared in the pulpy mass. My fingers trembled. No mistakes, I told myself. I placed my right knee against the edge of the table, braced my body and yanked.

"Yyyeeeaaaahhhh..."

Simmy flopped and twisted and groaned.

The blade pulled free and I tumbled over backwards, arms and legs flung wide. Katya sponged the wound. "Here," she beckoned as I got to my feet. "Hold this and apply pressure."

"Mama," Simmy cried, writhing in pain. "Mama...mama..."

"Don't worry, Simmy," I said. "Katya knows what she is doing." I hoped with all my heart that I was right. After a moment, Katya touched my hand and I lifted the sponge. A slug of blood oozed out.

"I need to disinfect," she said looking distracted for a moment. "There's some sulfa powder in Mama's room, by the sink, and the thick tape. Go fetch them." I ran off again, scrabbled around in the lavatory adjacent to my parents' room, then brought them to her.

"This will sting, Simmy, but not for long." She doused the wound. Simmy yelped, arching his back, flailing his spindly legs.

"Mama," he cried again, his skinny body shivering with pain.

"Hush, hush, dear Simmy. We're almost done."

Quickly, she rolled out the bandages, cutting a section cleanly. She covered the wound, then held it fast with two bands of tape against his pale skin.

"There," she said. "It's finished now."

Katya brushed dank hair off his forehead and murmured to him, stroking his cheek. "Help me get him up to his room."

We managed to hoist Simmy up the stairs and lay him on his bed. I eased him out of his clothes, then covered him up. He'd passed out.

Katya looked frazzled, her eyes glinting with fear.

"The danger will be infection from the knife blade. I think we got it in time, but I can't be totally sure. The next few hours will tell."

"I hope you're right," I said.

"I am right," she replied.

"When Simmy wakes up I'm going to ask him for their names," I told her.

"What will you do?" she said, worriedly.

"Little sister. You leave that to me."

"What about Mama and Papa?"

I shook my head. "We won't tell them. Don't worry, I'll take care of it."

I glanced at Beulah. She listened, eyes half-lidded but awake. I couldn't escape, not yet. "Keep talking, Mr. Goldman. Sounds good so far. A real family soap opera." She gave me a faint smile.

Simmy awoke later that evening, his shoulder throbbing. He slurped some soup that Katya insisted on feeding him.

I sat and watched them. "You scared me, Simmy. Seeing you like that. I didn't know what to think."

Simmy looked ashen, his face sweaty.

"I was scared too," he said, "I've lost my spectacles."

He began to cry. Katya stroked his face, shushing him.

I felt in my pants pocket. "It's okay...I found them. No need to cry." I blew on the lenses, then rubbed them with the bed sheet. "Here. They're clean now."

Simmy took them from me, unfolded the wire frames carefully and slipped them on.

"Now Katya, you need to leave us alone for a minute."

She glared at me. "This is a mistake, Mordecai. No good can come of it."

She stalked out, slamming the door.

When we were alone, Simmy looked at me with a sheepish expression.

"Who was it?" I asked. "Who attacked you?"

"Let it go. It was nothing."

I spoke quietly and insistently.

"Tell me, Simmy. I won't leave until you do. You know I won't."

I knew Simmy would give in. We stared at each other for a good long while until he broke away.

He sighed. "Vladimir. Kolya. Ivan," he muttered.

"I'll make them pay for what they've done to you," I said. "That's a promise."

Simmy stared back at me through the grimy spectacles.

"I thought we were friends. Why did they hurt me when I did nothing to them? I don't understand." More tears rolled down his cheeks.

I leaned in and touched my little brother on his good shoulder, then cupped his chin. "Jews and Polacks don't mix. It's as simple as that. They went after you instead of me, those bastards. I'll get them back, don't you worry."

"It isn't right, Mordecai. Mama and Papa don't like it when you do these things."

I stood up and smiled. "That's why they mustn't know, little brother. Revenge is mine saith the Lord."

"You twist the Torah for your own purposes." Simmy took his Torah studies seriously. He'd taken to it, enjoyed the stories he read, loved the philosophical discussions. For me, religious school was boring. All the talk made me edgy and restless. I'd rather be doing something, preferably with my hands. Religion was the first ideology Simmy encountered and it influenced him because he was young and didn't know anything else. In many ways, he was an idealist. When he grew older, he became enamoured of Zionism and longed to move to Palestine to build a Jewish homeland.

"Get some sleep now. I have things to do," I said and looked at him fondly. "You need to rest." He nodded and slunk down under the covers, pulling them up to his chin.

I went downstairs to the kitchen and wolfed some lentil soup, dipping in hunks of black bread. I stared ahead, seeing my fists at work and smiled grimly. It was happening again. Rage bit at me.

I removed my coat and cap from the closet and went out, closing the door after me. I heard a noise and turned. Katya pressed herself against the upstairs window. She banged her palms on the pane, yelling something that I couldn't hear. I turned my back on her, hunched my shoulders and strode away into the darkness.

I marched along, passing no one.

I approached the trestle bridge, walking in the shadows. At Simmy's age, a gang of young Polacks grabbed me and hoisted me over the side by the seat of my pants. They threatened to drop me into the swirling waters of the Volga. The water looked dark and cold and so far down below my dangling feet. Once again, I felt the sting of humiliation. I'd wet my pants and they laughed at me. I heard their jeers echoing in my mind as they hauled me back and dumped me face first in the dirty road. I should have protected Simmy. I should have prevented this from happening.

The storefronts sat silent in Polish town. Gas lamps lit the streets. The deep shadows embraced me. Out of sight, I peered around the corner at Ivan's house. After his dinner, he'd meet up with his friends and they'd wander the town getting into mischief. I waited. After a moment, Ivan emerged. I heard the soft patter of his shoes on the cobblestones and counted the steps under my breath. Five...six...seven...eight... As the unsuspecting boy drew abreast, I stuck out my foot. He fell forward. Before Ivan could make a sound,

I hauled the young Polack up, clapped a hand over his mouth and dragged him into the laneway. I pressed him against the filthy wall.

"You know who I am?"

The boy nodded, his blue eyes wide and fearful. He was my age and size but gangly. He struggled, trying to free his arms, but I had him pinned tightly. I kneed him in the stomach repeatedly, getting in good shots, and he bent over and gagged.

"You tell your friends that I know who they are and what they've done and I'll come looking for them. And now, you rotten bastard, it's your turn," I hissed.

I hit the boy with my fists, measuring each blow carefully until the blood ran from his nose and mouth and each eye went puffy. I loosened my grip and Ivan slumped to the ground. I gave him a kick and he toppled on to his side.

"You will never touch a Jew again, Polack, do you hear? Or I will come back for you. Tell your friends." I looked at the huddled form and spat, then turned on my heel and walked away. As I walked, I felt the heat drain out of me and I began to shiver. Dirty, rotten, Polack bastard had it coming, I told myself. I had to do it. I walked briskly home, but felt the cold seep into my bones.

"That was harsh, Mr. G," she said in a quiet voice.

I shrugged. "Maybe, but he'd just stuck a knife into my little brother. I wasn't worried about how he felt."

"So, I see. Playing the bad boy," she said.

I snorted a little. "I was the bad boy."

Arriving back at the villa, I slipped in the back door. My sister found me at the kitchen sink, rinsing blood from my knuckles.

"I took care of him but his front teeth were sharp." I held up my damaged hand.

"Oh Mordecai, that won't undo what has been done to Simmy."

I turned off the tap. "I know that, but they'll think twice before trying it again. Little Jewish kids won't have to be afraid. Simmy won't have to be afraid."

"Let me look," she said, taking my hand and examining the chafed, broken skin. "You can't always protect him. You can't always protect everyone," she said.

"I have to try," I replied.

"I'll get the iodine and bandages," Katya said quietly.

"Yes, little doctor."

"Mama and Papa will wonder what has been going on here in their absence. Everyone is wounded."

"Except for you."

"In my heart, Mordecai," she said quietly. "Wait here. Don't move."

I clenched and unclenched my fist as I waited for her, stretching the skin, rekindling the pain I'd inflicted.

In a moment, she was back, carrying the brown bottle and the bandages. I held out my hand to her. She cleaned it with iodine, then wrapped the bandage roughly over the knuckles and across the palm.

"You'll live," she pronounced.

"I'm glad, because I need to take care of you and Simmy."

"Who is taking care of who?" she retorted.

I shrugged. I didn't want to concede anything, not even to Katya.

"You can't win every battle, Mordecai, or win every war."

"We'll see."

I went to embrace her but she stiffened. She tried to turn away but I held her close.

"Let's see how he's doing," I said.

She smiled sadly. "Yes...let's..."

I led the way to Simmy's room. He lay fast asleep, spectacles perched on his stubby nose.

I pointed. "Look...he snores."

Katya crept up to the bed and carefully removed the glasses. She touched his forehead.

"No fever. That's a good sign."

"Good work, little doctor."

Early the next morning, I ate an egg and sipped tea in the kitchen as Amalija, the Polish house servant, refilled the samovar. The rising steam wet her cheeks and brow. Katya came in wearing her robe and slippers.

"Tea, Miss?" Amalija asked.

"Yes, please." Amalija poured a cup from the samovar and placed some fresh black bread before Katya.

"How is Simmy?" I asked.

"Sleeping."

"Mama and Papa will be home soon. Pyotr is picking them up from the station."

"What are we going to tell them? What will we say?" she asked.

I looked at her. "We say nothing. Why worry them needlessly? Simmy is recovering thanks to you and the problem is solved. No one will bother him again."

Katya frowned. "This can't go on Mordecai. You must stop this before you hurt yourself and Mama and Papa. Things can only get worse. I can't stand all of this anger...this hatred..."

I pushed my chair back, heavily. Katya flinched.

"You don't know what you're talking about, little sister. We didn't start the hatred, they did. Stick to your medical books and stay out of it."

Later on, I took a cup of tea and two pieces of challah toast up to Simmy.

"How's the shoulder?"

"It hurts and is very stiff," he replied putting the book down on the nightstand. "But I will live."

I placed the tray on Simmy's lap. "Nourishment for the patient."

"When are Mama and Papa coming?" Simmy took a bite of toast. Butter smeared his cheek.

"Soon. We'll tell them that you fell off the fence. You've done that before." Simmy slurped his tea. It was sweet, just the way he liked it.

"They might believe you," he said, not entirely convinced. "But what will you tell them about your hand?" he asked.

I grinned. "Smart guy, huh? Maybe I should punch you in the nose."

"Then Katya would have to bandage your other hand too."

I laughed, then shrugged. "I'll think of something. There are plenty of things around here for skinning knuckles." I rose. "Eat. Drink up. Stay in bed today. I think we can miss school. The rabbi will understand." As a young boy, Simmy believed what he was told about a higher power. The idea of God comforted him. I never liked the notion of something else being in control. Something above us, something that didn't have to answer to anyone. I wanted to control things myself but as I found out, that can never be no matter how much you want it. The world I knew slipped out of control and spiraled away from me.

"That's easy for you, you don't get smacked with a ruler for being late or not doing your work. And what about Papa? You know he doesn't like us to miss school."

I didn't know how to answer him. "Finish up little brother."

I left the room and descended the stairs heavily. Simmy was right. I didn't have an answer for my father.

Shortly after eleven o'clock, I watched from the upstairs window as Pyotr pulled the Skoda saloon up to the front door. My parents, Chaim and Sadie Goldman emerged. Pyotr stepped out and opened the boot, lifting the luggage. I crept to the top of the stairs to listen. Amalija came out from the kitchen where she had been preparing lunch, a weak smile plastered on her face.

"You are home," she said.

"And the children?" Papa asked.

"At home," Amalija replied, nervously. "They wanted to be here...The little one...he...he...hurt his shoulder and is in bed. But...but... he is all right. Miss Katya has been taking care of him."

Mama's face clouded. Papa's brows shot up but he tried to contain his concern. He went to Mama and patted her plump hand. "Don't worry. If Katya is looking after him, then he is in the very best hands. You know how clever she is."

"I must go up to him," she said and moved briskly to the stairwell. Halfway up, she turned to Papa.

"Chaim, what are you waiting for?"

"Yes," he said. "I want to speak with Mordecai...get an explanation for this..." I heard the anger in my father's voice and skedaddled back to Simmy's room.

Simmy sat up in bed reading his science book. Katya stood nervously by the window looking out at the courtyard. I slouched in a chair with my feet up, glancing at the newspaper, bracing myself for what was to come.

"And what is this?" Mama cried. Katya turned quickly. Simmy smiled shyly over his book and I simply folded down the top half of the paper. "Why are all my children home from school? What has happened?"

Katya went to her obediently and gave her a kiss, then embraced Papa.

"Hello my little darling," he said to her. "You are tending the flock?" But he glowered at me.

"Yes, Papa."

"Simmy fell off the fence and hurt his shoulder a little, that's all, nothing serious," I said.

"I feel fine," Simmy piped in. "Just a little sore."

"And this?" asked Sadie, holding up my bandaged hand.

Simmy laughed. "I told you she would notice right away."

"Have you been in a fight? Again?" she asked.

"Yes," said Papa. "Explain please. And it better be good."

I didn't look at my father but pulled my mother to me. "Of course not, Mama. A stupid accident. The gate swung shut on my hand, that's all. We've given Katya the opportunity to play doctor for real."

"I did my best," Katya said.

"What will the rabbi say?" asked Chaim Goldman sternly. I knew he didn't believe a word of this.

"Only three days left, Papa. Then I'll be working in the mill," I said. "I don't think the rabbi will be too upset once he knows the circumstances, do you?"

"Perhaps," conceded Papa, his brow furrowed. "I am glad to see you are all in one piece, for now... especially you Simmy. As for you, Mordecai..." He waggled his forefinger, "We'll talk later. Amalija should be ready for us. I need a cup of tea. The road was very dry." That put an end to the matter.

School ended that week. I'd be finished with yeshiva finally. Religion didn't interest me. The scholars droned on and on endlessly. Simmy liked engaging in the dialectic, in the arguing back and forth but I found it boring.

I also hated working alongside the men in my father's mill. I received seven zloty a week, less than half of what the Polish workers made. I complained but it did no good. Seven zloty it was and no discussion permitted. I hauled sacks of grain from the farmers' carts and unloaded the trucks.

Simmy worked in Papa's bottling plant, counting cases of soda pop as they were shipped to the distributors' warehouses in Warsaw, Cracow, Gdansk and Lodz.

Katya spent her time dissecting animals, concocting a makeshift laboratory in the garden shed. Katya coerced us, bribing us with lemonade and cookies to help her. We'd find her the specimens and hand her the tools she needed. Simmy and I watched her work with wide-eyed, gut wrenching revulsion.

"Yech," Simmy exclaimed as Katya slit open the abdomen of a squirrel we found in the forest. No species was spared.

"Katya," I said as I watched the small animal's body shudder and gasp. "Are you sure you want to be a doctor and not a taxidermist?"

"You're an idiot. How else will I understand how the body works?"

"It's disgusting," Simmy spat.

"I think Simmy is right. There's something creepy about all of this."

"Be quiet, the two of you. I need to concentrate. Go work on an engine," she said. "I don't need you here, after all."

"Suits me fine," I replied.

I preferred engines and motors anyway. I liked spending time with the mechanics who worked on my father's trucks. If I had a choice, that's how I'd spend the summer, not schlepping grain back and forth like a pack mule.

Chapter 2

On a blistering Saturday in July of that year, a tall, broad-shouldered, golden-haired man came out of the sun. He knocked on our door. My father went to greet this stranger as we children crowded around.

"Come in, my friend," Chaim Goldman cried.

"Thank you," said the stranger, and set his gleaming leather suitcase on the floor in the limestone foyer. My mother came out of the kitchen wiping her hands on an apron. When she saw this blond deity, her hands flew up to fix her disheveled hair.

"Darling. Children, I want you to meet Frederick Valens of Warsaw. I know his father very well. We are in business together … and did you know," he asked, making sure to look straight at me, "that Frederick is still the finest boxer in all of Eastern Europe and Russia?"

"Stop," said Frederick obviously enjoying the compliments. "You flatter me too much. I haven't boxed for over a year." His teeth were brilliant. Katya's jaw hung open while Simmy simply stared. Papa introduced each of us. I muttered a terse hello under my breath, recoiling from the open smile, the glowing good looks.

Frederick bowed low over my mother's hand and she blushed like a schoolgirl. I snorted in derision. Frederick turned to me.

"Your father tells me you have a bad temper and fight a lot, is this true?"

I shrugged. "Now and then. It's nothing really." And what business was it of his?

Frederick nodded in agreement. The shine on his golden hair blazed in the light. "I can see by the marks on your knuckles and the scratches on your face that you have been busy. But while I'm here, maybe you can show me what you can do."

"Maybe," I said. "Anything is possible."

Frederick laughed. "A good fighter enjoys the spirit of combat, wouldn't you say?"

I found myself irritated by this guy. "School's over. I'm working in the mill now."

My father stepped forward, humiliation burning his face, but Frederick held up his hand. "It's all right, Chaim. I don't mind."

Papa beckoned to our guest. "Come Frederick, I'll show you your room. There will be plenty of time for boxing later. Mordecai, take the case."

"Why can't Pyotr do it?"

Papa stopped in his tracks. He balled his fists and as he did so, his lips trembled, his eyes infused with outrage. I knew that look well, so I squashed my resentment and solemnly picked up the case. Papa forced himself to turn back to Frederick, his body rigid with fury.

Reluctantly, I followed the tall, laughing man up the staircase and wondered why he was so happy. Katya stood at the bottom of the stairs and continued to stare after him, open-mouthed. I glanced back while manhandling the valise.

Frederick Valens chatted away effortlessly during lunch telling us about his travels around Europe, his boxing exploits and after, when he entered the family business. He had traveled widely and visited many places, many cities. I took it in sullenly, barely listening.

"Are you a Jew?" I blurted. My parents looked at me in horror. Katya gasped. Only Simmy stifled a smile.

"No, I'm not," he replied then cleared his throat.

"Then you're a Polack?"

"Mordecai," Papa thundered.

Frederick's long face froze, his blue eyes clear and bright.

"No, it's all right. My mother is Polish and my father, a German."

"And why do you do business with a Jew?" I asked.

Papa shot up from the table, but Frederick held his hand up.

"It's because we have a good business together. It makes perfect sense. We all make money and that's why we're in business, isn't it?"

"Mordecai," said Mama sharply. "Enough questions. What is the matter with you?" She stood up to clear the table and by her brusque gestures, I could see she too was annoyed. Katya went to help Mama, turning her back on me. We males sat, as was the custom. There was an awkward silence.

"A wonderful lunch, Mrs. Goldman. But altogether, far too much food. It has made me sleepy."

Mama smiled timidly, unused to compliments. "But I like to see everyone eat well. It is a blessing."

"Then I can see you have many blessings and often," he replied. Then he turned to me, his blue eyes glittering. "Mordecai, what do you say to a little workout. Get rid of this lunch?"

I shrugged. "As you wish."

"Good. Put on short pants and an undershirt. I don't suppose you have any athletic shoes?" I shook my head. "All right. Regular shoes then but no boots. Off you go." I turned to my father who'd been silent.

"Yes, fine... go... go... " He waved his hand, then turned to Frederick. "There is a good spot around the back. It is shaded."

"I like the heat," Frederick replied and stared purposefully at me.

"You were asking for it, huh, Mr. G?"

"Maybe I was. It was the arrogance of youth. From the beginning, I didn't like this fellow. He was too perfect it seemed to me, too pretty if you know what I mean. Frederick had this idea that he was superior, better than others, or so I thought at the time."

"He give you a whuppin?"

I laughed. "Wait and see."

Chapter 3

"Pa-pah…Pa-pah…Pa-pah," Frederick exhaled, dancing in front of me, his fists flashing mere millimeters from the tip of my nose. I felt like a fool with legs splayed wide and hips and shoulders twisted.

"Keep your hands up," Frederick barked. "Higher…higher still. Like this…"

He slapped my hands in an upward motion. Frederick walked around me in a tight circle, nodding and pursing his lips, then came to a full halt right in front of me, put his hands on his hips and stared down. Wearing a benign smile, Frederick kicked his leg out and I went down in a heap. Frederick laughed uproariously. He reached down to help but I batted his hands away.

"What'd you do that for?" I demanded.

Frederick waggled his forefinger. "Balance, Mordecai, balance, if you don't have balance as a boxer, you have nothing. Always remember that." He clapped his hands sharply. "Back in position, let's go," he barked.

I pushed myself to a standing position and assumed the stance; left foot forward, right back, elbows tight, fists high. I barely kept my anger in check.

"That's right," Frederick said. "You need to protect your flank," and he lashed out with a punch that grazed my side. "but more importantly, here," pointing to my abdomen. "How can I find my way in? Right? You are covered. Now, I want you to push against me, as hard as you can. Come on, do it, do it now," he urged.

I punched both hands forward. The impact jarred me up to the elbows. Frederick hadn't budged a millimeter. I tried again, harder this time, elbows back and pushed. No effect. Frederick just looked at me with that infuriating smile. I stepped back, went into a crouch and ran forward, head down, filled my lungs with air , blasted a roar…and found nothing but air. I hit the ground face first and bounced hard.

"Balance," Frederick said, stepping to the side then hopped to and fro. "Balance is the key," he trilled.

"You crazy bastard," I gasped. "You tricked me." And to my shame, I felt hot tears streaking my cheeks.

My lungs burned. I felt a furnace inside me. Far in the distance, Frederick loped ahead, his long legs barely touching the ground as I struggled to keep up. I wanted to lie down under a shady tree, press my face into the cool grass and die. Up ahead, Frederick danced lightly on his toes and gestured impatiently.

"Come on," he bawled. "Faster. Keep up." He waited for me, that mocking grin etched into his sleek face.

We ran down to the banks of the Vistula, turned around and ran back to the villa. I tottered, barely able to put one foot ahead of the other. When I reached the back garden of the property, I sank to my knees and gagged.

Frederick took off his shirt, then wiped his face with it. "Marvelous. What about you? What'd you think?" he asked me.

I continued to pant but remained determined not to show any weakness. "It was wonderful," I croaked.

Frederick laughed. The braying sound hurt my ears.

Some moments later, I came back to consciousness and realized that Frederick was talking. "The best boxers, and naturally I include myself in this category, use their heads, not just their bodies. You must think about what you are doing, look at the man opposite and see his weaknesses. Does he drop his hand a little? Does he fall for the feint? Does he leave his body exposed? Does he fight with spirit? All of these things go through your mind and then you know whether you can win or not. But you can only do these things after you have all of the tools, right? Strength, conditioning, training and practice. It never ends."

From my prone position on the grass, I was forced to listen, but only if I wanted some lemonade. I grudgingly admitted to myself that some of what Frederick said seemed to make sense.

I lay on my bed with a cold cloth pressed to my forehead. Katya knocked then slipped in and sat beside me.

"He's very handsome, isn't he?"

I looked at my sister, who'd never played with dolls and only talked of things relating to medicine, therapies and operations. "What?"

"So very tall," she murmured.

"Katya," I said sternly, sitting up. I grabbed her by the wrists. "What is the matter with you?"

She frowned at me. "Nothing. I'm allowed to say whatever I want."

"But such foolish things. You're only a girl and he's a grown man."

"It's none of your business really, Mordecai, but I was hoping you might understand. I can't talk about this to Mama and Papa."

"Just stay away from him, he's a pig, I tell you."

"Don't tell me what to do. I am older than you," my sister said and yanked her wrists free.

"You warned me before and now I'm warning you. You'll look like a fool."

"You don't understand much then, do you?" she asked, but never gave me a chance to answer. I couldn't tell her I wanted to protect her from this man. I still thought of her as a girl but I knew she had grown up on me. In those days, in Poland, we grew up quickly. We had to.

Chapter 4

"He had your number, Mr. G, didn't he? That Frederick."
   "I suppose he did."
   "Why didn't you like him?"
   I shrugged. "I don't know. Maybe it was just his blond good looks. Too Aryan. That air of superiority."
   "You were jealous maybe?"
   "Maybe," I conceded. "Just maybe."

I suffered through the longest two weeks of my life. During the day, I toiled at the mill. After the evening meal, I submitted to whatever torture Frederick dreamed up – and he had a vivid imagination. We'd run to the river facing forward hands above our shoulders, then return to the villa running backward. Frederick taught me to spar, blow after blow after blow. My arms turned to lead, so heavy, I couldn't lift them above my waist. Then came the drills; up on my toes dancing, side-to-side, forward and back until my calves and arches screamed with pain. Frederick launched bombs at my head and I learned to dodge and weave. More than once, Frederick knocked me flat on my ass, forced me to get up, then did it again. After ten days of this treatment, my anger exploded. I surged forward, wildly raining blows on Frederick's unblemished arms and chest, bellowing at him like a frenzied animal. He didn't lift a hand to protect himself, not once. Calmly, that smile twisted on his lips, Frederick pushed me away.

"Are you finished?" he asked.

I stood there, wild-eyed, staring at him, panting and sweating, drool running from my mouth.

"Are you finished?" he asked again.

"Like hell I am," I replied.

Frederick smiled, for real this time.

"Good. Then, let's box." From that moment, I understood. I hated him but I understood.

The morning he left for Warsaw, Frederick stopped by my room.

"I know you haven't enjoyed our time together," he said. "But at least I feel I have given you some tools that will help you."

"You expect me to thank you?" I asked.

Frederick smiled. "Remember," he said. "Balance is the key. I'll be back at the end of the summer. Keep practicing. We'll see then what you can do." Then he left.

I heard his light steps on the stairs falling away and went to the window. I saw Katya reach up, stand on her tiptoes and give Frederick a kiss on the cheek. Frederick smiled at her, then got into the waiting car and drove off.

I slammed my fist into an open palm with a vicious smack.

That Sunday I answered the door as Papa's two brothers, Herman and Mendel, brought their wives and children to dinner. Six cousins in all. Katya toiled with Mama cutting flowers for the table, polishing the good silverware, helping in the kitchen. Simmy and I didn't have to do anything and couldn't have been happier.

I didn't enjoy these occasions. My cousin Sonya who, inevitably, sat beside me at dinner, had a large wart right in the middle of her nose. She looked like a witch.

"Sonya has the evil eye. You have to spit behind her back," Simmy said. "Then kiss the mezzuzah for luck or she'll cast a spell on you."

"Whatever you say, Simmy," I said. We stood together on the verandah observing the domestic activity inside. Katya glared at us. "I think Katya is giving us the evil eye right now."

"It's not our fault girls have to do all the housework," Simmy said. "It's better being a boy."

Sonya, the witch, sat between me and Simmy at dinner. Simmy kept looking at me and giggling. Papa and his brothers sat at the opposite end of the table while the aunts, Ruth and Sara, sat beside them. The children were sandwiched between the adults. I didn't care for my cousins, parochial schoolboys all of them.

"So, Mordecai," said Uncle Herman, "how do you like working in the mill?" A dribble of borscht ran down his chin.

"I don't care for it much. You can tell the boss from me, the pay is lousy." My two uncles chuckled awkwardly while the aunts looked horrified. The conversation at the table ceased. Papa pricked up his ears and wrinkled his eyebrows.

"So, my son. You think you're not paid enough?" he asked in a querulous tone.

"I do a man's work, Papa. I should be paid a man's wages, don't you think?"

"But you're not a man. Not yet."

"He has a point," said Mendel.

"But a man earns a man's wages, not a boy," insisted Papa. "This is only natural. It's how the system works."

"Then we must change the system," I replied.

"What are you, a communist?" my father asked, anger flashing in his dark eyes.

"No Papa. I'm asking only a question. I don't think it's fair, that's all."

Papa stroked his beard. "I see." He reached for the decanter and poured a glass of wine. "Since you consider yourself a man, then take a drink of wine."

"But a whole glass?" asked Mama. "It will make him sick."

"We'll see." Reb Goldman stood up from the table, strode purpose-fully to where I sat and plunked the glass in front of me. I picked it up and took a gulp.

"Not bad," I said.

"Don't drink too quickly," said Herman. "You'll get a sore head."

"And more than that," added Mendel.

"I'll be okay." I took another mouthful. I'd downed half of it. Papa came around behind and clapped me on the shoulders, digging his fingers through muscle into the sinew. I wanted to shrug him off but kept very still. He could be hard when he wanted to.

"You want to grow up all at once, eh Mordecai? Don't be in such a hurry. The world will wait for you."

I tried to pull away but he held me fast.

"Maybe I won't wait for it," I declared feeling grown up in my defiance. "So, do I earn a man's wages or not?"

My father pondered the question then released his grip. He pulled at his beard then returned to his chair. He spoke deliberately. "No, my son, you do not."

I stared at him for a long while without saying anything. He met my gaze calmly. I picked up the wine glass and drank down the remainder.

"All right," I said. "But I'll take another glass of wine." The room froze into silence; all eyes turned to Papa.

Then Uncle Herman snorted and pretended to cough, finally erupting into wheezing, hacking laughter. The others stared at him in surprise as his laughter burbled around the silent dining room. Without warning, his wife began to titter, burying her face in her hands while her sister-in-law grinned. My cousins brayed like a pack of frenzied mules. Even Papa couldn't hold his composure af-ter that and when Simmy broke out into hysterical giggles, he too opened his mouth to laugh aloud, then guffawed, his cheeks turning red, his chest heaving. I relaxed finally and looked around the table, smiling. Laughter seemed better than tears, I thought.

Chapter 5

The summer ended and the moment I dreaded, occurred. After two months, Frederick Valens returned. He set down his valise and placed his large hands on his slim hips, puffing out his chest. I stood on the verandah saying nothing as he examined me with a critical look.

"You have grown, Mordecai and put on weight too. You look fit and still angry. Why am I not surprised? Have you been practicing what I taught you?"

"Every day," I replied, jaw clenched.

"Good, good. You know, Mordecai, anger alone won't do you much good on its own. In a fight, a match, a cooler head is a better way to go."

I bristled but smiled grimly. "I'll try to remember."

Frederick went round greeting everyone. Katya threw her arms around his neck and Frederick lifted her off the floor and swung her around while she squealed in delight. I watched through the screen door, my blood seething. Frederick set Katya down then shook Simmy's hand so vigorously, his body twitched and his glasses slid down his face. Frederick said hello to my father.

"Chaim, I hope you are well?"

"We'll talk after lunch," Papa replied. I smiled as Frederick bowed deferentially. He'd been stung by my father's brusqueness. Katya disappeared into the kitchen to help Mama with lunch but gave Frederick one last, lingering look. I pushed through the screen door and let it bang behind me. Frederick smiled grimly.

"We'll go for a run after lunch, see how you're progressing."

I didn't want to make a scene in front of my father.

"Sure. I'll look forward to it." Papa nodded, and I was pleased that my father thought we might be getting along a little better.

We ran side-by-side. Frederick's easy lope had tightened, his gait stiff. I breathed deeply, staying relaxed, keeping my limbs loose.

Now, we'll see, I thought and pushed the pace a little more. I heard Frederick's breath echo shallowly in his chest but I kept my eyes straight ahead, focusing on the road. We ran past Solnicki's farm, following the banks of the river leading us to the mill. Frederick lengthened his stride but his breathing came out labored. I smiled to myself and ran even faster. I saw the mill in the distance and went for it, pushing all else out of my mind.

I felt a sublime pleasure even as my arms and legs strained and my body heated up from within. I could hear Frederick falter, listened to the missteps as he tried pushing himself through the stiffness and pain. I surged ahead as Frederick lost ground.

I vaulted forward and as I moved ahead something hooked my right ankle. I fell, going down in a heap of arms and legs, skinning the palms of my hands and kneecaps on the broken road. Frederick loped past and as I went down I saw the bottom of his shoes churning up dust. My chin smacked hard and I felt a wetness fill my mouth. I'd bitten my tongue. The pain nauseated me and my sight went dark for a moment but I pushed myself to my feet, spat blood down my shirtfront and staggered on, chasing the lean figure disappearing ahead of me.

Frederick waited for me in the foreyard of the mill bouncing on his toes, that glib smile twisting his lips. My dirt-stained face hardened into a mask of hatred.

"You dirty bastard," I cried. "You dirty thieving prick."

"You can tell your father if you like," Frederick said quietly.

I shook my head, then spat more blood. "I fight my own battles."

"I thought you might," Frederick replied quietly. "If you believe that your opponents always fight clean, then think again and be prepared. It's a dirty world, my young friend."

"I'm not your friend," I cried. "I will never be your friend." In my fury, I picked up a clod of earth and threw it at him. It thunked off his chest leaving a dirty smear on his clean, white shirt.

Frederick merely shrugged.

"He got to you, huh?" Beulah smirked weakly. "You let him get under your skin..."

"I was only a boy and reacted impulsively. I was filled with anger and outrage. I didn't think he'd do such a thing. It never occurred to me that he'd act that way."

"Surprised you, didn't he? Maybe that was a good thing, taught you a lesson, toughened you up. I've seen things..." She wiped at her lips and I fed her some water. She appeared weak, more than sickly, sweating through her clothes, shivering uncontrollably even though I'd wrapped her in a warm comforter. I got up to get her a cloth for her forehead. She grabbed my wrist, showing surprising strength. "Don't go, keep talking. Tell me more of the story. Please."

I nodded and sat down again, leaning in closer.

"I made it my business to keep track of Frederick. I didn't trust him and my sister was infatuated with him. Just a young girl and he was a full-grown man."

"Knight in shining armor," Beulah said bitterly. "Where was my hero? Never had one and never will."

I didn't have an answer for her.

Chapter 6

After dinner that evening, Frederick sat on the verandah smoking a cigarette. Simmy and I hid around the corner of the house, listening in. I had to shush him several times or he'd have given us away.

"You'll ruin your lungs." Frederick turned to see Katya standing in the shadows. He smiled at her.

"Come," he said. "Sit." Despite her bold pronouncement, she sat beside him demurely. "You're probably right. I don't have the wind I once had. Your brother outran me today. I guess I'm getting old."

"Nonsense," she said then hesitated. "I mean, it is proven that the chemical properties in tobacco cause lung damage. Maybe you shouldn't inhale."

Frederick dropped the glowing butt on the verandah floor and ground it out under the heel of his summer loafers. "I heed your command."

"Don't be silly. I can't command you," and she smiled at the thought of ordering him about.

"You may command me anywhere and anytime," Frederick replied. "Give me an order and I'll obey it."

"Now you really are being silly," she said.

Frederick gathered her hands in his. They were fine-boned and supple. Katya tensed. "Don't be afraid, dear Katya. I mean you no harm." And he pressed his lips fervently to her palm.

Katya stared at him, astonished but didn't pull her hand away. "Frederick, what are you doing?"

"I don't know," and he smiled at her then became serious. "You're too beautiful, Katya. It's painful for me to see you. It's why I came back."

"I thought you were helping Mordecai and working with my father?"

"Just excuses really. I wanted to see you again."

"Frederick, I..."

"Katya. I may be a grown man and you are much younger but your beauty makes you seem older. I'm sure all the boys are in love with you."

"I don't have time for boys. I'm too busy studying and doing meaningless housework."

"No time for love?"

"No, well, not yet," and she watched him for a long moment.

"There is always time for love, dear little Katya." He lapsed into silence and looked at her in the growing darkness. But then Mama's voice crashed through the quiet.

"Katya. Katya darling, where are you? I need your help for a moment."

She stood up. "I'd better go."

Frederick grabbed her arm. "Meet me tomorrow night? I'll wait for you by the fence in the back. I'll wait all night if I have to." She stepped back gathering her skirts holding his gaze as she went inside, reluctant to take her eyes off him. After she left, Frederick turned to stare out into the darkness.

Simmy squeezed my hand and I knew we were both determined to be there, to protect our sister from this man.

All the next day, I waited as the farmers brought in their sacks of wheat. The men, gruffly bearded with piercing blue eyes and peasant caps pulled low on their ruddy faces. Their clothes ragged and dirty, their expressions haggard and suspicious. They brought their wheat and in return, received flour for baking breads and cakes that fed them over the winter. On this day, Pyotr helped out. The farmers were a hard lot and could be quarrelsome, even violent at times. A farmer came in. I'd seen him before and the man nodded without saying anything. Without waiting for me, he dumped his wheat directly into the wooden box to be measured.

"You see? It's all wheat, nothing else," he said. Then muttered something unintelligible and spat.

"Thank you sir," I replied politely. Pyotr stood by silently, arms crossed, watching the farmer. I checked the gauge.

"Thirty-five kilos," I said.

"Eh?" The farmer jerked his head up in surprise. "No," he said. "Forty kilos there."

I checked the gauge again. "No. Thirty-five. Take a look," I said and stepped to the side. The farmer bent over and squinted at the gauge.

"No," he said again. "You cheat."

I could sense the man's anger. This was his livelihood. The bread to feed his family. "Forty," he repeated. "You make a mistake."

"No," I said firmly. "No mistake."

"Fucking Jew. I know how much I put in. Forty kilos."

Pyotr stepped in. "No need to get upset, friend. The measurement is accurate. I'm certain of it."

The farmer spat. "You work for them," he said. "The Jews."

"Do you want the flour or not?" Pyotr asked.

"Of course."

"Then don't cause trouble."

"I cause whatever I want. They steal from us, these Jews. They take our money and they take our souls. Even the priest says so." His voice thundered in the small weighing shed.

I listened and outwardly tried to appear calm. Inside, my blood boiled, my anger raged. I reached behind the counter. The farmer had turned his back to me as he spoke to Pyotr.

"Hey," I said.

The farmer turned. I lashed out. The two by four I held in my hands caught the farmer across the forehead and he fell back in a heap, knocked cold. Pyotr stood stunned and speechless.

"Take him outside. Give him his flour when it's ready and tell him never to come back here again."

Pyotr looked at me with a flummoxed expression, then down at the farmer where a dark welt had swollen up in the middle of his forehead.

"What if you have killed him?" he whispered.

"I don't think so," I replied. "He has a hard head. But if you like, fetch Katya to take a look at him. But get him out of here. Others are waiting." Pyotr gulped, but nodded.

He picked the farmer up under the armpits and dragged him outside. The other farmers looked at them curiously. One came up to Pyotr. I watched from inside then stepped closer to the window to hear better.

"What happened?" Pyotr told him. The other man nodded. "That Slava is a hot head. I would not have called him a fucking Jew to his face. Not here. There are other times and places, eh?" Pyotr said nothing, torn in his loyalty. He backed away and went to fetch Katya. The next man went in to have his wheat put on the scale. The hothead, Slava, now cooled off, began to moan as he slowly regained consciousness.

That evening, I stood out in the yard shadow boxing. Simmy sat in the grass watching me. My father had bought a pair of gloves for me and a helmet. I danced back and forth, punching, jabbing, weaving, keeping up on my toes.

"Mordecai!" came a roar from around the front of the house.

"Papa," I said, and felt the bile rise in my chest.

"He sounds angry," Simmy said.

Papa barreled around the corner. Frederick sauntered after him, a smug grin on his face. "How dare you," Papa bellowed, the color rising into his full cheeks.

"Yes, Papa?"

"What's happened?" Frederick asked with feigned innocence, his hands shoved casually into the pockets of his white trousers.

"Tell him," Papa commanded. I didn't want to say anything to Frederick but he seethed with anger.

"You better say something," Simmy said.

I struggled to speak, but my father's angry glare coaxed the words out of me.

As soon as I finished, Papa interjected.

"This will never happen again. Next week your work at the mill is finished. You will never go back there."

"I'm sorry, Papa. I let myself get angry at what that foul-mouthed bastard farmer said about us. They all try to cheat."

"You were wrong to do this. It will only incite them."

"It will teach them respect."

Simmy wisely elected to stay quiet.

"And what if you had started a riot? What then? What if you didn't knock the fellow out and he attacked you? You might have been badly hurt."

"I can take care of myself."

"Enough!" Papa roared. "This will not happen again. Violence begets violence. I will not hear of it, do you understand? We are a peaceful people. We live side by side with our neighbors. No more."

I felt my heart race and anger flushed into my veins but I loved my father and wouldn't speak against him. "Yes, Papa."

"From now on, if you must fight, then box, like this. You must get this anger out of you. It will hurt you in the end, Mordecai. It will destroy you." I stared at my toes. And then Papa's anger was spent. He just looked sad. "Now go inside and clean yourself up. I want to speak with Frederick."

The following week, the farmers came again to have their grain weighed. The troublemaker, Slava, was not among them. He sent his son instead, a boy a few years older than me. The other men averted their eyes and shuffled their feet but there was no trouble.

Slava's son, a hulking young man, was physically developed beyond his years with thick wrists and broad shoulders. His lank blond hair looked as if it had been hacked at with a machete and fell across his broad face in an uneven thatch. He flicked the hair from sharp eyes that never left me as the boy waited for the grain to be ground into flour. Occasionally, he whistled a tuneless song or bit down on his fingernails, all without taking his eyes away. I ignored the hulking boy's looks and carried on with the work. When the flour was brought out from the back, the boy hefted it easily on to his shoulder. Just as he was about to leave, he turned back.

"You there, Jew," he said. I glanced up at him. "I shall see you soon at school. I won't turn my back." The boy spat on the floor, then turned and walked out the door, ducking as he made the entranceway, his heavy boots clomping on the wooden floor of the shed. I stared after him. The term hadn't even started yet.

"He's mean, that one," Pyotr said. "I know him. He takes after his father. You must avoid him. Cruelty runs in that family."

"I can take care of myself," I replied with a confidence I didn't really feel. I signaled to the next man in line who hefted his sack of wheat and stepped forward.

I was reading at the dining room table when I heard a pounding on the door. Papa went to see who it was. A police officer stood on the threshold.

"Are you Goldman?" the officer demanded.

I went to my father's side.

Reb Goldman smoothed his hair. He glanced at me. "Yes," he replied.

"I have instructions to bring you down to the station. Get your hat and coat and come with me," he said brusquely.

"What for?" I asked. "What is it he's supposed to have done?"

The officer stood tall and wore a waxed moustache. He looked at me with contempt. "It's none of your business."

"But of course it is my business. This is my father."

I felt my father's hand on my chest. "Sshh," he said. 'I'll deal with this. Now, Officer, am I charged with something?"

"Not yet. We are investigating a complaint."

"What sort of complaint?"

"A number of farmers claim you have cheated them out of flour."

"Those bastards," I screeched. "They're the ones who cheated. They've been cheating for years."

"Be quiet," Papa said and turned to me. By his look, I could tell that my father blamed me for this. That this had been my doing.

Papa removed his hat from the stand in the hall. I glanced up the stairs and saw Mama descending rapidly.

"Chaim, what's going on?" she asked. Behind her Frederick followed.

"Nothing, it's nothing. I'm simply helping the police resolve a simple misunderstanding, that's all, my dear. Don't upset yourself."

I saw my mother's complexion pale.

Frederick broke in. "Chaim, let me come with you. I'm sure we can sort this out together, don't you, Officer?" And I saw the even lips part and the white teeth gleam.

"Well, er…"

Frederick rubbed his large hands together. "There, you see? We'll clear this up in no time, don't you agree, Officer?"

I grudgingly admired Frederick's approach. How easy it seemed for him. That confident manner put the policeman off balance.

Frederick removed his linen jacket from the closet and slipped it on.

"We're ready now, Officer. Shall we go?"

"Don't go with him," I pleaded to my father. I didn't know if I meant the policeman or Frederick.

"I must," Papa replied. "We'll be home soon." The officer stood away from the door allowing Frederick and Papa to step out first.

Mama looked on the verge of tears. Katya stood at the top of the stairs staring down at me. Beside her stood Simmy, lips trembling.

Even he seemed to understand what had happened. I burned with shame.

Chapter 7

*I helped Beulah to the toilet where she retched but nothing came up. I
sat her on the wooden seat where she hunched over, barely able to hold
her head above her shoulders.*

"You belong in a hospital," I said.

She shook her head pressing her lips together. "No way," she gasped.

"What if something happens? I won't be able to help you."

*She looked around then up at me. "It's not a bad toilet to die in," she
said. "I've been in far worse. I've seen people die in filthier places." She
held her hands up. "Help me back...please."*

*I carried her back to the cot, laying her down gently then went and
made a cup of tea with lemon and a liberal dose of honey. She had
three blankets and a duvet and still she shivered, teeth chattering like
ice cubes jangling in a tall glass.*

*"Was your father arrested?" she asked me, barely able to get the
words out. I made her take a little more tea before answering.*

*I shook my head. "No, he wasn't arrested that time. Frederick con-
vinced the commandant to let Papa go. That the charge had no merit
and the farmers were grumbling as they always had. My father and
Frederick returned early the next morning close to dawn. The police
had kept them all night. Papa was shaken...he came back a hollow
man. You must remember that he was a businessman. He employed
many people, most of them Poles. His factories brought prosperity to*

villages and towns and yet he could be treated like a common criminal any time the authorities pleased. I don't think he realized it until that time. He was pale, ashen-faced when he came through the door. My mother and sister threw themselves at him. Little Simmy was frightened and he too could see the change. After that, my father never looked at me the same way again."

"What do you mean? How would he look at you?"

"If he'd been a Christian, I would have been his cross to bear, I suppose. Some evil had touched his life and that of the family and he blamed me for it. I was the catalyst, the spark that ignited the flame of hatred. Yet everything I did, I did out of love...for him...for all of them..." I sat back in my chair and hung my head. The memories were still powerful. It was a kind of exquisite torture and this young girl had opened it all up again.

On the Saturday before fall term began, Frederick prepared to take his leave slipping out early in the morning before the others got up. He had his reasons for avoiding company. As he carried his valise treading quietly on the stairs, I blocked his way.

"Blast you boy. You are a complete nuisance. If it wasn't for your father..."

"What would you do? Thrash me?"

I watched him take control of himself. "Out of my way, please, Mordecai. The car is waiting and I shall be late. I have a train to catch."

"What did you do to her?" I hissed.

Frederick hesitated. "What do you mean? To who?" He moved to shoulder his way past but I blocked him again.

"To my sister. To Katya."

"I'm sure I don't know what you're talking about," he replied through gritted teeth.

"She was in her room crying all night. I heard her. I know she met you in the back garden last night. What did you do?"

"It's none of your business what happened. Now move."

"Not until you tell me." I grabbed a fistful of Frederick's sleeve.

"Let go of me, you idiot." He glanced behind him, up the stairs. "You'll wake the others."

"Then you'd better tell me or I'll make enough noise to raise the dead. Either that, or you'll have to fight me to get to the door."

Frederick jerked his arm free. He made to push me out of the way and make a run for it but he sighed, then smiled grimly.

"It's not dignified running from a mere boy, is it?"

Frederick placed his strong hands on his hips and looked down. "Whatever you think of me, Mordecai, I am a gentleman and would never take advantage of a young lady, especially one who is as beautiful and kind as Katya. I would never stain her honor."

I stared at him. "What happened then? Tell me or I won't let you go."

Frederick almost laughed out loud. But he could see I wasn't fooling, even if it was a ridiculous threat.

"I kissed her once, that's all."

"And?"

"I may have told her she was beautiful, which is true."

"And?"

"That's the lot. I swear it." Frederick hesitated. "I'm forcing myself to go away now even though I don't want to because I know the situation is impossible. I'm more than ten years older and your father's business partner."

Frederick indicated the door.

"Now, if you don't mind, I have a train to catch and I'm asking you to step aside. I don't want to have to knock you down but I will."

I hesitated. "Knocking me down wouldn't be easy," I replied.

Frederick smiled ironically. "You may be right. Now, please."

"What happened at the police station? You and my father came home very late. He won't speak of it."

Frederick shrugged. "Mordecai, police stations are places of business just like anywhere else."

"I don't know what you mean."

"Look, everyone has something for sale, all right? At the bakery, it's bread and cakes. At the butcher's, it's meat and poultry. At a police station, it is freedom. And in this case the price was one thousand zlotys. Now do you understand? It was business, that's all. We came to an understanding and everyone left satisfied."

"You paid them?"

"Yes."

"And what about the charges, the accusations?"

"Ridiculous. They had no evidence, just the angry mutterings of some drunken peasants, that's all. They were no match for me, I can tell you."

"But something happened. My father was very upset."

Frederick reddened under his tan, then looked away. "You'll have to ask him about it."

"But he won't say anything. He wouldn't tell me, anyway."

"Perhaps," Frederick replied.

"And now you're leaving."

"Yes, it's for the best, don't you think? In every way. But I'm certain we'll meet again someday, Mordecai. Now, again, please."

I nodded and took two steps backward. Frederick slid past me and strode to the door. Just as he reached for the knob, he turned.

"Remember, Mordecai. Balance, above all else."

Then with a twist of the lips, he turned back and went quickly through the doorway out to the waiting car.

I glanced up and saw Simmy's pale face framed between the banisters.

"You heard?" I asked. Simmy nodded. "Did you believe him?"

"Yes, I did."

"I don't suppose Katya will tell us anything."

"Probably not."

"I warned her. I told her she'd been acting like a fool."

"We all act that way, sometimes, don't we?" Simmy asked.

I glanced up at him again, then shook my head. "Perhaps little brother. I'm just glad I didn't have to try to stop him." I realized my fists were still clenched. "And as for Papa, I..." but I couldn't finish what I was about to say. Our world had begun to crack apart.

We saw Frederick one more time just before the war. He came to visit with his family, a sturdy blond wife and two cherubic children; a girl and a boy. He told us he intended to move to Switzerland where it was safe.

"I'm telling you, Chaim," he said at dinner one evening. "War is coming and Poland will end up in the thick of it. Come with us to Switzerland. Bring everything and everyone with you. After the war is over, we can start again. It is the prudent thing to do."

My father refused to listen.

Frederick insisted. "I have seen the build up of the Nazi war machine and it is impressive, let me tell you. Things are not good for the Jews in Germany. Many have 'disappeared'. Businesses have been ransacked. Families murdered in the streets. Hitler will send his dogs of war through Poland, I guarantee it. I shudder to think of the consequences. Of what will happen to this country."

My father reassured him we would be fine. Although resentment against Frederic lingered within me, I felt he spoke the truth that night.

Frederick and his wife, Mathilde, had brought a governess with them to look after the children. She was buxom and pretty. I noticed she and Simmy, who had turned 18, grown his hair long and looked like a young revolutionary, making eyes at each other across the table.

After dinner, I walked the grounds restlessly, thinking about Frederick's words and my father's curt rejection of them. I heard muffled sounds. Peering around the corner of the house, I saw Simmy and the governess together, her white legs locked about his slim hips. Make love while you can, I thought.

The next morning, Frederick and his family left. We never saw them again.

Chapter 8

September, 1939

I chafed against the thin blanket when something cold and wet touched my face jolting me awake. I surged up. "Tabernac." I clawed at my cheek then spat into the dust swatting wildly at the nag nuzzling me. The horse reminded me of my officer trainer after graduating from high school years ago. We didn't get along very well, me and the horses, even though we were compelled to learn how to ride. I'd been more interested in motors and artillery. A stubborn tank hadn't been a problem but a stubborn horse, that was a different matter. I'd kept my commission after the two compulsory years I served. When war broke out, I answered the call to arms. I graduated as a raw lieutenant, inexperienced and judgmental.

I hadn't slept in fifty-six hours. Fatigue seeped into my pores, melted my bones. I had taken command of an armoured unit that consisted of three motorized vehicles with small anti-tank guns, a lorry and two-dozen horses. I didn't like having the horses. The men were too concerned about them, worried for their safety rather than that of the troops or themselves. The horses, like the men, had to be fed and food was a problem. We had no supply lines. The men had to forage what they could and take or beg from the farms and peasants we met along the way. I had started with a command consisting of one hundred and forty-four men. The numbers dwindled down to less than half. Most had been killed, some got lost and still others had deserted. Peasants mostly, seeing the uselessness of it all. They disappeared during the night, melted away to their homes and farms. It was harvest time and the crops still had to be brought in. Or how would they survive the winter? Who would help their mothers and sisters and elderly fathers if not they? Viewed in that light, they had little choice.

I sat up and rubbed at my eyes. My hands were filthy, the nails ripped. I couldn't remember when I'd last had a bath or a decent meal. I felt around for the packet of French cigarettes I'd taken from the dead Nazi officer. The one I'd bayoneted. I cupped the flame of the match carefully in my hands until the cigarette sparked and did the same to shield the light. No point setting myself and the others as a target.

"Pan Captain."

I glanced up. "Yes, Sergeant?"

"What are your orders, sir?" The Sergeant had been a veteran from the First World War, a career soldier nearing the end of his active days. He knew the routines, knew how to marshal the men, most of whom came raw and straight off the farm.

"Have a seat, Sergeant." I indicated the log behind me.

"Thank you, sir." The Sergeant eased his bulk down carefully. He'd been grazed by a bullet and his right thigh remained tender. He stretched the leg out, then folded his thick-fingered hands together.

"We'll rest here until nightfall. Rotate the watch every two hours. Make sure the men get as much sleep as possible, they'll need it. In the evening, we'll form up and head southwest. Vitaly's troops should be holding in the valley. If not, we keep going until we encounter the enemy or can meet up with our own. That's it. Not much of a plan, is it, Sergeant?"

The Sergeant grinned. His broad moustaches seemed to stretch his face. "No sir. But I suppose it's as good as any."

"We're here to kill Nazis."

"Yes sir." Then he hesitated. "We won't win, will we?"

I turned to look at this man who could have been my father, at least twenty years older than me. "No, we will not win. We weren't meant to win. We kill as many as we can, then we go home."

The Sergeant grunted. Likely, he'd never really known any Jews before. He had only seen them in the towns and villages where he'd been stationed or simply marched through. But I was his commanding officer and I had to show him and the men that I meant business and that they couldn't question my leadership in any way.

Earlier, I'd set up an ambush. A German motorcade. Eight motorcycles and two staff cars. I'd stepped into the road, threw the first grenade and with my machine pistol, cut down the first three motorcyclists as they roared down on me. What's more, I'd enjoyed it and I wanted them all to see it. All of the Germans had been killed, including a high-ranking officer, a general. We kept the motorcycles and removed the staff cars from the road. It would be dangerous to travel the main roads, they'd be full of Germans.

I'd stood over the bodies, holding the machine pistol rigidly, smoke leaking out of the heated barrel. "They don't look so invincible now, do they?"

"No sir," the Sergeant had replied, sweat pouring down his face. "They don't."

I'd looked at the older man then, this veteran of previous battles and a lifetime of military service and the Sergeant shrank back from me. "Strip them of anything useful, then dispose of the bodies."

"It shall be done," and the Sergeant saluted crisply, then turned to beckon to his men. We heard field artillery in the distance. Large shells pounding our comrades-in-arms some twenty or thirty kilometres to the east. The Sergeant organized the men in teams. They picked up the bodies and carried them into the woods where they were dumped in a heap.

"Somehow doesn't seem right," said one soldier, a slim blond fellow.

"What do you think they would do for you? Hold a mass and give you a proper burial? No," said his companion, a thick-chested peasant. "I hear they put all the bodies in a pit, pour petrol on them and set them off. You can smell the stench for miles."

"It still doesn't seem right," repeated the blond one.

"And what are you, a priest?" asked the peasant contemptuously. He dropped his half of the body as he spoke, leaving his partner to hold it by the knees only, now grotesquely bent.

"No. I just want to do the decent thing, that's all."

The peasant hissed at him. "This is war, you fool. Decent doesn't enter into it."

The Sergeant strode up. "Quiet, imbeciles. Get those bodies off the road before we have Germans swarming all over us."

The conversationalists looked at each other, then quickly moved off, back to their grisly task. The Sergeant could hear them arguing still. He shook his head.

I stood on my feet now, shaking off the few hours' sleep I'd taken. "Have the men eaten?"

The Sergeant shrugged, then smiled. "Yes sir. There's a little bit of tea there for you and a biscuit. It was the best we could do."

"Thank you, Sergeant, Popov, isn't it?"

"Yes sir."

"Good to have you with me, Sergeant Popov."

I took my leave of the Sergeant and strode down to the stream near the camp. I waded into the cool water up to my ankles, then bent over and doused my face and hair. It refreshed me. I longed to strip down and bathe but I knew there was no time and it was too dangerous. I shouldn't be in the open as it was. I thought about my family and what they must be feeling, what they have heard. With the Soviet peace pact in place, new borders had been created and the hospital where Katya and her husband Alexis worked now sat on the Russian side. My home lay just five kilometers to the east. I could walk it in sixty minutes or less. I put on my tunic and turned to go up the short hill. I beckoned to the Sergeant.

"Did you secure all the weapons and ammunition?"

"Yes sir."

"Good. They'll be useful, I'm sure."

I unfolded the map and lay it flat on the ground. We were situated in the Janow Woods just west of Lwow in the Eastern Malopolska region. The Carpathian Mountains rose perhaps one hundred kilometres to the south. We had been ordered to push west, cross the San to Jaroslaw and then forge on to the Vistula and follow it southwest to Cracow. God knows what we'd find along the way. This stupid war marked its fifth day. I felt as if each day had taken a full year's toll on the forces and the countryside. I could only hope that we would meet up again with Kutzreba's main force. One prong of the German attack had come up through Silesia skirting to the west of the Tatra Mountains. Perhaps they had captured Cracow by now? And hopefully, Vitaly was not too far away, either. Vitaly's men had been split in two as the Nazis deployed an armoured division that drove a wedge up the middle. Many men had scattered then. Some had found themselves on their own and tried to find their way back. Likely, they had been killed or captured. And if captured, who knew what would happen to them? These German supermen were not merciful. To be captured meant a death sentence. This would be my fate undoubtedly as a Polish army officer and a Jew.

"Sergeant."

"Yes sir."

"Watch out for planes. Keep the horses back in the woods. We don't want to give ourselves away. They'll blast us to pieces otherwise."

"Sir." And snapped off a salute, then marched off briskly to get the men organized.

I held the men back during the day and we moved out at night. I didn't want to be caught out in the open with horses after we left the cover of the woods. I kept the men busy during the day. They took turns on guard, foraging for food and resting. The peasants we encountered were of little help.

Two days after leaving the Janow, we entered a small village. The men were weary, the horses drooped, they were hungry. A small cluster of hardscrabble homes, the ground seemingly barren and dusty and of course, a primitive church. I nodded to the Sergeant who knocked on the first door. After a moment, the door opened and an elderly woman in a nightdress stood with an oil lamp on the threshold.

"Sir."

I roused myself, adjusted my tunic and strode over. "Yes?"

The woman bowed her head. Her hair was grey and wound in tight knots behind her ears. I saw the crucifix hanging between her pendulous breasts. She curtseyed briefly, acknowledging my authority. I gazed at her dispassionately before turning my attention to Sergeant Popov.

"She says they have nothing. The Germans came through and took everything."

"When?"

"Yesterday morning?"

"How many did she say?"

"Several hundred with tanks and artillery."

"I see. Very well then." I turned away.

The Sergeant took my arm and began to whisper ferociously in my ear. "Pan Captain. I know these people. They've buried the food, I'm convinced of it. Let me get it out of them. We can shoot them if they object."

I laughed. "Shoot them, Sergeant? These are the people we are supposed to protect."

"The men are hungry, sir."

"I am well aware of that, Sergeant."

Sergeant Popov stiffened. "Yes sir. Sorry sir."

"Go talk to the priest," I said wearily. "See what he has to say. They should be able to spare some water at least."

"Very well, but..."

"It's all right. I know what you think." As the Sergeant marched to the Church and banged on the door, I wondered if the old veteran knew what I was thinking. That these people probably were hoarding food but they were trying to survive in their own way. When the country fell, life would become even harder. The priest opened the door. He was dressed, ready for business. The Sergeant spoke to him in low, gruff tones but the priest was not intimidated and rejoined irritably. After a moment, the priest waved the Sergeant off, then banged the door shut.

"Are we to shoot him too?" I asked.

"I'd like to snap his scrawny neck."

"Then you'd rot in hell."

The Sergeant grinned. "Yes sir."

"Well?"

"Same as the old woman. No food to be had. Germans through yesterday morning. I told him if we found anyone hiding food, they'd be shot. He banged the door in my face."

"What do you expect him to do? He must eat. The Lord's work is taxing."

"Yes sir, that it is."

"Tell the men we'll rest in that field over there for a few hours, then we'll move on. Send a detail around to knock on a few more doors."

"Yes, Captain."

A group of six men, split into pairs, slung their ancient rifles over their backs and rapped on unwelcoming doors. I watched them for a moment until my attention became distracted by a young girl of six or seven who skipped her way along between the twisted houses with the sublime unconsciousness of a spirit lost in a fairy tale. I rubbed my grizzled face and smelt my own stink rising through my uniform. We must look like medieval marauders, who would blame anyone for being frightened? As she skipped by the church, the door opened and a younger man dressed in a cassock stepped out. He was bareheaded and tanned. He had a muscular walk and carried a book, a bible probably, in his left hand. A handsome man, for a priest. Sergeant Popov drew abreast. He too looked at the priest, who looked over at us and nodded, then began to walk through the village, away from the direction in which our ragtag band had come.

"Have you ever seen a priest look like that?" I asked. The Sergeant shrugged. I leaned over and whispered to him. The Sergeant went off and motioned to half a dozen soldiers lounging in the field, enjoying the warm weather, feeling the heat of the sun. They stood up and dusted themselves off, pulling their mismatched uniforms into place as the Sergeant spoke quietly. The men nodded, then moved off lazily in the direction of the church.

"Just a minute, Father," I called. The priest stiffened, then turned with a smile. His eyes were pale, almost white.

"Yes? How can I help you?" He spoke in a precise, clipped way.

I approached casually, thumbs hooked into my belt in front of my abdomen. The priest waited patiently, the beatific smile, the shining eyes turned on me expectantly. "I was just wondering...?"

"Yes? Wondering what?" His hands lay at his sides.

"May I see your book?"

"But of course." And he lifted his hand to offer it. I glanced at the priest's palms before taking the offering. The cover was shiny with wear as the sweat of many hands had touched it over the years.

"Thank you." I leafed through it idly. The sun beat down on us.

"Was there a particular passage you were seeking?" asked the young priest.

"No."

"May I go? I am late. I must see to an elderly parishioner who is unwell."

"This is a small village," I said. "I would have thought it too small for more than one priest."

"Yes, I see," replied the young priest. "It was not so long ago that I took my vows. I am here to assist Father Walenska until he retires, which will be very soon."

"And where did you study?"

"St. Ignatius in Warsaw, then the Swetlinski Institute where I took my degree in theology and finally, the Bogda Seminary near Cracow.

What is the point of these questions? I am late for my rounds." His tone was strained, increasingly clipped.

"Where did you learn to speak Polish?" I hadn't moved. I'd remained perfectly still and fixed the young priest with an unwavering gaze matching his crumbling beatitude.

"What do you mean?" the priest asked, colour rising to his cheeks. "I was born here."

I pursed my lips, then slowly shook my head. "I don't think so," I replied in German.

"Are you asking me if I speak German? Then the answer is yes. And I speak Latin, French and Italian also. I studied languages at the Institute."

I didn't answer but leaned in uncomfortably close. I placed a hand on the priest's shoulder. "Take a good look. What do you see?"

The priest grimaced and went to take a step back but I tightened my grip.

"I don't know what you mean. I'm beginning to think you are a little mad. War does that to men, you know."

"I agree with you. But if you mean anger that's one thing. If you're talking about loss of sanity, that's another. But I don't look familiar to you? The swarthy skin, the dark eyes and hair, long nose?" The priest shook his head. Sweat ran from under his scalp streaking reddened cheeks.

"Please. I wish to continue my duties."

"You mean I don't look like a Jew? I thought you could sniff us out of a crowd. Juden, isn't that right? How does it feel to have a Jew hold on to you, look you in the face like this?" I seized the young man's face with my grimy hand. "Have you in his power? Would a Jew be allowed to do this in Germany? I don't think so. He'd be beaten or shot on the spot, isn't that right?"

The priest struggled. "Let go of me. You…"

My gaze narrowed, heightening in intensity. "What? Do you have a message for me?" I released my grip, then seized the priest's wrists, turning his hands palms up. "Do priests chop wood? Climb ropes?

Carry weapons? Your hands are very callused for a priest. Remove your robe please."

The priest looked around him. A group of Polish soldiers and villagers had gathered around.

"You are mad."

Two soldiers took up position behind him. One of them prodded him in the back with his carbine. The faces of the villagers remained curiously blank, as if they too, wondered what the priest wore. He removed his robe, pulling it over his head in a smooth motion. He wore cotton slacks and a white cotton shirt buttoned at the neck. All clean and new.

"I'm interested in your shoes." The priest glanced downward. The shoes were made of quality leather and highly polished. "Good walking shoes," I said approvingly. "I used to own a pair. They were made in Berlin."

"That doesn't prove anything."

"No, it doesn't." I took hold of the young man's left arm. I tore back the cuff of his shirt. "But this does."

Two lightning bolts tattooed into the pale skin. The soldiers held him fast then.

"This is the symbol of an elite paratroop squad of the SS."

The young man struggled against his captors. "It won't do you any good. We'll crush you and this entire country in days."

"Too bad you won't be around to see it."

The young man's eyes widened.

"Sergeant," I bellowed. The Sergeant emerged from the rectory, pushing the older priest ahead of him. In his right hand, he held a military tunic, which he threw at my feet.

"I found this, Pan Captain, under some floorboards."

I looked at the older man as he straightened up, then as the Sergeant released him he pulled at the creases in his shirt and pants.

"What happened to the priest?" I asked in a loud voice.

An old woman stepped forward.

"The priest died," she said. "We have been without one for two months now. He got the fever. We don't miss him but the village needs a priest. The church must be occupied."

"He did a decent job on baptisms," another voice called out. "He wasn't all bad."

"The sermons were too long," said another.

I exchanged looks with the young German officer.

"You see?" said the German. "It won't take us long." And he smirked while the older man kept a stony look about him.

"What is your rank?" I asked the older one.

"Piss off," he replied.

I struck him with the back of my hand. A small rivulet of blood trickled out of his nose.

"You won't get away with this. You are dead all of you."

"May I light a cigarette?" the young German asked. I nodded. He reached into his trousers pocket and pulled out a packet of cigarettes, offered one to me. I shook my head. He placed it between his thin lips, then lit it with a gold lighter. He blew out smoke as if seated in a cafe enjoying his coffee and the paper rather than surrounded by sweating enemy soldiers. "I am a captain and he is a major."

"Quiet," hissed the Major.

"It doesn't matter. There is no hope for them." And then he indicated with the tip of the cigarette. "For any of them."

"Why do you say that?"

"I say it because it is true. You are surrounded. There are two armoured divisions on their way here. You can't escape. I suggest you surrender to us now and we will be lenient with you."

I glanced over at the Sergeant whose broad red face burned with indignation. "That is a very generous offer but unfortunately..." And then I shrugged. "You are out of uniform which means that you and your Major are spies. And you know what happens to spies."

The young Captain exchanged a quick worried glance with the Major. "You can't be serious."

The Major stepped forward carefully. He was a stocky man whose grey hair had been shaved very close to the scalp. Part of his right nostril was missing.

"We respect the Geneva Convention, Captain. You and your men will be given all the rights accorded to prisoners of war."

"Thank you for the offer." I turned to the Sergeant. "Take them. It's time to move out. Let's go."

"Where are we going?" asked the young Captain.

I ignored him, said something to Sergeant Popov, leaned over and cupped a hand over the older man's ear. The Sergeant pulled away, looked at me, then nodded curtly. The two Germans had their hands bound behind them with coarse rope. Two soldiers marched in front and two behind. They marched quickly. The older man stumbled but the soldiers didn't help him up. He climbed back to his feet awkwardly, trousers caked with dust on the knees and shins.

"*Scheiss*," he spat as he regained his feet, struggling without the use of his arms. The soldiers kept a tight formation. Motorcyclists went on ahead and the riders walked their horses until they were given the order to mount. We advanced about two kilometres to the east of the village. The men, horses and vehicles kicked up spumes of dust. They drank liberally from their canteens but offered nothing to the prisoners. At a bend in the road stood a tall oak tree with sturdy branches.

Suddenly I felt the way I did when I had been in the ring. My mind contained itself. I focused on logistics only. How to advance to the next point. Where to find water and supplies. What to do with the horses that looked as caved in and drawn as the men. I knew I couldn't keep the Germans with us. And couldn't let them go. That left one alternative. I didn't think about them. Whether there was a wife or a girlfriend, that they had children, parents, brothers and sisters. That perhaps two months ago, they might have been frolicking on a beach or making love. I knew what they were and what they represented.

I pointed to the tree.

"Here," I said.

The Sergeant waved his arm and the prisoners were pushed forward. They had tired from the quick walk. And dusty, their faces streaked with dirt and sweat.

"A drink please," said the young one.

Sergeant Popov spun the cap from his canteen and held it to his lips. The German drank greedily, water spilling down his chin and on to his shirt. Popov held the canteen up to the Major, who shook his head solemnly.

"Get two horses," I said. Two horses were quickly brought. They whinnied anxiously. "Ropes," I called. Popov instructed the cavalrymen to form the nooses. They set to work.

"What are you doing?" asked the young Captain.

"They are going to hang us," replied the Major almost laconically.

"But we are prisoners of war."

"You are spies," I said matter-of-factly.

"This is an outrage," the young one bellowed.

"Calm yourself," said the Major. "Show some dignity."

"Dignity? How can you speak of dignity at a time like this?"

"It is all we have left."

"But I don't want to die. Not here. Not like this."

"You are a soldier..."

"I don't give a fuck old man. Not like this I tell you." He turned toward me. "You fucking Jew. You've poisoned all of us. We'll wipe you out. Every last one of you. You will see..." I struck him and the German crumpled to the ground.

"Let's get on with it," I said. The older German eyed me, smiling sardonically.

"I don't blame you," he said. "I would do the same."

"I know," I replied, then nodded. The noose was slipped over the Major's head and tightened. The cavalryman spurred his horse and the Major rose straight up, his leather shoes kicking wildly in the air. "Tie it off," I said. The Polish soldiers stood and stared at the hanging figure now gone limp.

"Move," bellowed the Sergeant. Two soldiers jumped to it.

"Now the other one," I said. The second cavalryman spurred his horse and the unconscious Captain rose like a ghost into the air and dangled beside his companion. The Sergeant gestured and another man tied off the rope.

"Form up," bellowed the Sergeant. The men began to fall into place still craning upward to look at the hanging men, the white cotton shirts gleaming in the sun.

"God help the village when the Germans come through," said the Sergeant.

"We'll need his help too," I replied.

The Sergeant and I exchanged quick looks. We understood each other. Better the men didn't know. As they marched, some of the men grumbled. They were hungry and thirsty. They'd had nothing to eat for over a day. How were they supposed to fight if their bellies were empty? One talked of slaughtering a horse.

"Don't let those cavalrymen hear you," growled Popov. "They'll slit your throat if you even mention it." The warning silenced their tongues but not their thoughts. When a man is hungry, all he thinks about is food, how to get it and then to eat until the next time. It's as basic as that. I knew all this and was worried. We needed to find something soon. We trudged along the road in silence, each man alone with his thoughts. Thinking perhaps of home, of a loved one, a full table and a bottle of the best they could offer. My actions had proved to the men that the Nazis were not supermen but mere fellows like themselves. That they could be defeated. I had seen the looks on their faces, some seemed smug and satisfied, others fearful. A few averted their eyes.

According to the map, we'd be crossing a stream shortly. At least there'd be water and who knows, perhaps fish too? I looked behind me. The men had strung out in loose formation.

"Tighten them up, Sergeant,"

"Yes sir." Sergeant Popov went down the ranks pushing and prodding, speaking to the clumps until the lines straightened and the distances between them narrowed.

"You are soldiers," bellowed the Sergeant. "Look like it. Straighten up, shoulders back, chin up." And Popov demonstrated for them looking like a soldier in the recruitment posters. Most of those present had been rounded up in the enlistment drive. There were no real heroes among them but by God I'd see they did their duty, that we all did. War made you think the unthinkable and act like a barbarian. I respected the older Nazi in a grudging way but he would have done the same to me. I kept that thought close for the next encounter when it came.

Chapter 9

We marched through the day, kicking up clouds as we trudged along. I felt the dust clogging my throat. As I sweated heavily into my uniform, I felt the grit underneath and bared my teeth. A bath would do nicely. The road curved to the left and before I heard it, I could smell it. As the map indicated, we'd arrived at a small stream. Here we would rest.

"Let's get off the road," I said to the Sergeant, who turned around and waved them off. "Set up a guard and let the men drink and wash in shifts."

Popov saluted crisply. "Yes sir."

Half a dozen men positioned themselves behind the trees, carbines at the ready. They licked their dry lips. Popov brought a canteen full of fresh water to each one in turn. Each man drank deeply, allowing water to pour down his chin and onto his tunic. After a moment, Popov yanked the canteen away and went on to the next man, until they each had their ration.

I filled my canteen, squatting by the bank. Cupping my hands, I splashed water on my face and neck. The water was muddied, stirred up. The stream flowed quickly. Normally, streams with a fast current remained clear. I stood up.

"Sergeant."

Popov came down to him. "Sir."

"Let's walk upstream a bit."

"Yes sir." We followed the bank along, stepping over logs and rocks, sometimes wading into the water where the bank crested until we came upon a flat sandy area.

I pointed. "They crossed here."

"I see it. Artillery and tanks by the look of it."

I grunted. "And not too long ago. We are behind them, whoever they are."

"Don't think they're ours, Captain."

"Nor do I." I paused, hands on hips staring at the murky current. "Well, it's better to be behind them than in front. We'd better keep a sharp eye out. Don't want to run into them, do we?"

"No sir."

We started back. We'd traveled some one thousand metres or more. When we drew near the temporary bivouac, a soldier stopped us, put a finger to his lips and signaled us to crouch down. And then we heard it, the roar of powerful diesel engines and clouds of dust kicked up by pneumatic tires and the clanking metal of tanks. Sergeant Popov and I crawled up the bank and peeked over carefully. The German war machine at close hand, powerful and thrilling, Tiger tanks, howitzers, heavy 88s, pulled along in their harnesses, men on motorcycles and sidecars hurrying the larger vehicles along, infantrymen bouncing in open trucks singing their death song, their *Todt lieder,* as if the earth belonged to them and no one else. It was an awe-inspiring sight. My Polish troops sat mesmerized, watching in silence as the massive column rumbled along, breaking the air with shouts, clanks and mechanical roars.

I rested the men that day. I wanted to give the German column time to move ahead. I didn't know if we were behind German lines or in front of them. In fact, I didn't even know where the line was. We had no radio. It had been blown up along with our radio operator by a mortar round three days earlier, so I could only surmise where the others might be. And yet, I knew in my heart it didn't really matter. Perhaps, I thought, the goal was to come together for one glorious battle and that would be the end of it? I didn't share these thoughts with anyone else. By process of elimination and destination, I remained the only officer. There had been a major, a cavalryman, who'd lost his leg, then died of the infection. By the time I found him, he'd become delirious. We'd used whatever sulfa we had left to clean him up, then some of the men rigged a sled out of saplings and brambles and hitched the Major up to a horse. We dragged him along for two days until he died. The man leading the horse didn't discover this for some hours. Finally, he'd whispered to his companion that he thought the Major looked dead. I was told and formally assumed command. We buried the Major in a shallow grave and one of the enlisted men who'd been to the seminary recited a passage in a mumbling tone. I'd stood at the gravesite, cap in hand, head slightly bowed, as the Major's tortured corpse was quickly covered up. It seemed a nice enough spot, I thought, looking about quickly; in front of a tall maple tree, its leaves glistening in the sun. I looked at the Major's watch and identification papers in my hand, saw the men looking back at me expectantly as if suddenly, I had become their saviour. I laughed inwardly at the notion but showed no sign of it, lest the men take it as a gesture of disrespect to the Major. Instead, I nodded slightly to Sergeant Popov, who got the men moving. I riffled through the Major's saddlebags and found a copy of the regiment's orders. I quickly burned them with a match and kept the map that I had come to rely on diligently. And so I'd been the commander for a full four days now. It felt like four years.

Next to the stream, the men lolled about on their bedrolls, some sleeping, others smoking quietly or whispering hoarsely among themselves. Sergeant Popov posted a watch at either end of the clearing where they settled. I sat up smoking, my back against a gnarled tree. I took a pull from my canteen and longed for a drink, vodka or schnapps, something that would fire me up. I needed the fortification to continue to lead these men in a hopeless cause, one that I had no doubt would see us all killed. I didn't look forward or back, however. I brought my mind and narrowed my thoughts only to the middle. My task was to kill Germans and by God that was what I would do. The greater conflict had no overt interest for me insofar as knowing how many Nazis had been decimated. The more the better. Sergeant Popov stood over me.

"Sir."

"A drink would be good now, eh, Popov? What do you say?"

"Yes sir. And a girl would be nice too."

"You are not married, Sergeant?"

"No sir."

"Nor me. We are two bachelors you and I."

"Yes Captain. When...?"

"At dusk. I think it will be safer then."

"Pan Captain," Popov hesitated. He tried to get my measure. Figure out what sort of a commander I might be. "What are our orders sir?"

I thought about my answer when I suddenly stood up. I held out my hand. "Did you hear it?"

Popov reared back. "What?" He looked about.

I stared up into the sun, shading my eyes. I stood very still, straining my eyes and ears. The faint whine of an engine.

"Do you hear it?" I asked again.

Popov shook his head nervously.

"Get the men under cover. Quickly man, move."

Popov lurched off, shouting now, kicking prone bodies, pulling caps off reclining faces. The men grumbled and shook themselves awake. I ran around the perimeter of the camp, yelling, gesturing wildly. The drone had become louder now and the men could hear it. They began to scramble into their pants and jackets, pulling their weapons to them. I picked up a machine pistol and set myself behind a tree trunk as the first wave came in. Three, no four Messerschmitts dove low and began to strafe the camp. The ground burped up dirt where the bullets hit. I focused and fired, hearing the screams and yells of the men around me, the terrified whinnies of the horses lost in the roar of machine guns and plane engines. I used an entire clip, then watched as the planes arced around for their second pass. There would be bombs this time, I thought. I rammed another clip home and tensed. They came in a sure line one after the other. The clearing erupted as the bombs hit. I fell over backwards from the concussion, then scrambled to my knees, picked up the machine pistol and fired. Like pissing in the wind, I thought as the third plane, then fourth dropped its load. The German pilots enjoyed themselves. They came around again. I looked to my left. Popov kneeled beside me. He too, clutched a machine pistol. Blood ran out of a wound in his scalp.

"Concentrate your fire there, on the second one," I growled.

Together, we fired our machine pistols. I felt the metal grow hot in my hands. A slash of bullets hit the fuselage and the plane dipped one way then the other, then burst into flames and crashed in a fiery ball.

"Run," I screamed, and raced for the next stand of trees, some twenty metres beyond. We ran, crouched low to the ground as the trees behind us splintered into shreds. We dove behind some logs and waited as the murderous drones receded in the distance. We remained completely still for what seemed a long time. I glanced at my watch. The whole thing had taken less than five minutes. I stood up and signaled the all-clear but heard the screams and cries of agony. I looked over at Popov, who nodded to me, then dabbed at his scalp with a neckerchief.

"A flesh wound only."

I turned and saw the craters made by the bombs. Body parts and limbs lay scattered about like refuse.

"See who's left, Sergeant."

Popov nodded. He tied his neckerchief about his forehead, then pulled on his cap, wincing slightly. He picked up the machine pistol and strode off. I licked my lips, wanting that drink more than ever.

Half of the company had been killed or wounded. That left sixty-one men, seven horses, and two motorcycles that were still serviceable. Popov collected all of the identification papers and valuables of the dead soldiers, dropping them into a canvas sack.

"Collect the weapons," I said, "and tie them onto the horses." I looked about. So much for the armoured division. It had just been blown to smithereens. Popov organized the healthy men. They dug a wide and shallow trench, meant to be a mass grave for their fallen comrades.

"Did you know any of them?" I asked.

Popov shook his head. Blood had dried in a streak across his forehead.

"No, not really. None of them were career soldiers." He spat. "Draftees. Young fellows who hadn't started to live yet. I bet some of them were virgins."

I fished a Gauloise out of my pocket, broke it in half and offered the other to Popov, who took it gratefully. I lit them up using a fine gold lighter. It bore the initials G.N. engraved in the side. I held it out to him in the palm of my hand.

"I liberated it from the German officer," I said. Popov said nothing, just inhaled smoke, then he shook his head.

"No sir, I'm trying to quit."

I stared at him incredulously, then threw my head back and guffawed until the tears ran out of my eyes. "Funny fellow. You'll probably be dead by tomorrow."

Popov's red face burned brighter until the colour rose up into his forehead, then he showed some yellowed teeth.

"Of course, sir. You are right. Now what do we do?"

"Finish the burial. Then we better move out. They may come back."

"Which direction?"

"We head west until we meet up with someone, Vistla or Witold perhaps. They are supposed to be in the area. We join up with them until the end, Sergeant."

Popov looked over. The men laid the bodies in neat rows in the earthen tomb they had just furrowed.

"Captain?"

"Yes?" Popov hesitated. "Go on. There isn't much time for anything now," I continued.

"Do you consider yourself a patriot?"

I would have laughed at the suggestion but I could see it had been asked seriously. "Not really. What about you?"

Popov shrugged. "I am a soldier. It is the only thing I do well. I fought with the French in the first one, not the Germans. I wanted you to know."

I clapped the larger man on the shoulder. I examined the round, sweat-stained face. "I don't fight for Poland but myself. In the end, maybe it's the same thing."

"Yes sir."

I looked over where the men stood idly by, leaning against their shovels. Those who could stand gathered around the gravesite.

"Perhaps you'd say a few words, Sergeant, before we get on our way."

After bowing their heads, the Sergeant mumbled some phrases and as the wind kicked up the loose earth and dust swirled angrily, I, Captain Mordecai Goldman, led my sixty-one men, seven horses and two motorcycles toward redder pastures. We turned west toward the San river and Jaroslaw. As we moved along, I turned my head to the left and imagined I could see the Carpathian Mountains cresting the horizon, rising out of the flat lands like angry gods admonishing them to go home. I thought of the two German officers swinging from the branches of the great maple tree. I wondered if the bodies had been discovered and whether they'd been cut down. Not that it mattered to me but I asked myself if the village would still be standing. I guessed not. Destruction of that kind was one of the few predictable things about war. Not much else except the bland moments that fell between euphoria and mortal terror.

Chapter 10

General Witold stood tall, thin and tubercular. He coughed blood into a soiled handkerchief he pulled out of his tunic. Light blue eyes glowed out of deep sockets in a skeletal face. He shook my hand.

Between gasps and wheezes he spoke.

"Captain Goldman, welcome to the San. I have seven hundred men with me out of a force of five thousand just three days ago. Across the river," and he thrust his bony chin out in that direction, "there are ten thousand Germans. They have artillery, tanks and mortars. We have three Howitzers that we stripped from a regiment we had pushed back and as they ran, these blond supermen, we collected their weapons, then disappeared into the forest." Whereupon, Witold, having exhausted himself, bent over double and heaved, splattering yellow and green mucus tinged with red into the dirt. After several moments, he recovered his breath and straightened up. His complexion resembled chalk.

"As you can see, Captain, I am a marked man in every way." He smiled, spreading his thin lips ever so slightly. It transformed his face into a laughing skull. I said nothing.

"You look tired, Captain. Why don't you rest for now? We engage in the morning, perhaps our last here on earth. I should tell you too that the Germans have bombed Warsaw. The city will likely fall in a matter of hours."

"General, would you have anything to drink?"

"What did you have in mind?"

"Vodka would do nicely."

Witold nodded. "I think I might. Colonel," he called. A dark-haired man looked up. His face was mud-streaked. He wore a shredded tunic and his left arm had been bound in a sling.

"Have you a drink for the Captain, here?"

The Colonel looked momentarily annoyed. He'd been discussing tactics with his subordinates but realizing the absurdity of it all, nodded.

"I'm sure I can find something, General."

General Witold raised his eyebrows, held out a gloved hand. "Good luck to you, Captain. God knows, you'll need it."

"No hope of reinforcements, I suppose."

"None."

"What about the French and the English?"

The General spat in response. I saluted and stumbled off toward the Colonel, who looked up at me expectantly, forgetting momentarily who I was and what I wanted. The Colonel had been pointing to a map, muttering more to himself than anyone around him. His name was Lepinksi and he had been a lawyer just three weeks earlier. Now he plotted maneuvers and tactics that couldn't hope to delay the inevitable. Lepinski's eyes cleared and settled on me. "Come with me to my quarters," he mumbled. Whereupon he turned, sat down on a tree stump, reached into his jacket pocket and pulled out a silver flask that he handed over. I unscrewed the cap, wet my lips and took a long pull.

I felt the liquid burn into my gullet. "Aaahh."

The Colonel looked at me blandly with a faint sneer on his face.

"I have some more. Finish it if you like. It might help you sleep tonight. I haven't slept since the war started," he added. I nodded, tipped the flask and drained it in one go. I felt the heat of the liquid but nothing else. There came no numbing effect, no insulation against the oppression I felt. Carefully, I replaced the top and handed the flask back to Colonel Lepinski who assumed an amused look.

"Thank you."

"There's some food if you want it. There isn't much but it's something."

"I'm not really hungry. Just tired now. It's been a long day." I sat down in the dirt and eased my back against a fallen log, splaying my legs and booted feet out in front of me.

"You are a Jew…"

"Yes."

"And an officer…"

"Yes." I waited for the rest. I wondered if the Polish army might throw me out for hitting a fellow officer.

"Well," Lepinski remarked mildly, "that's something."

"If you say so."

"Have you experienced any difficulties?"

"No."

"The men? Your fellow officers?"

"Most of the officers were killed almost immediately. I demonstrated to the men they should show respect."

"And how did you accomplish this?"

"By killing Nazis. We hung two as spies three days ago outside a little village."

"I've been with the General since the beginning. We began as a full division and now look at us. Half the men are either wounded or starving, the rest are just sick. We have no medicine, no doctors, little food. We have nothing. Sometimes, when the wind is right, we can smell the food cooking on their fires. They don't lack for much."

"I'm not complaining."

Colour rose in the Colonel's ruddy cheeks. "And you think I am?"

I might have reassured him but merely shrugged instead. "Whatever you say, sir."

For a scant moment, the Colonel obviously thought about rebuking me but changed his mind. It didn't matter anyway. After tomorrow we'd probably be dead. The Colonel said nothing, just poked a stick into the ground. Then he slowly pushed himself to his feet.

"Goodnight Captain. Tomorrow will be a long day. Best to get some rest." Lepinski ambled off into the darkness. I sat and watched the fire.

I had a dream. I hunched in a tunnel running in the darkness. Water sloshed over my boots. I smelled the dank and bitter odours of rancid garbage. A light shone ahead of me. It blinded me. I shielded my eyes against the glare and stumbled forward, careful to bend low to keep from bumping my head. It wasn't a tunnel I realized but a drainpipe, large enough for a man of average height to stand up fully. But I took no chances. I wanted to move quickly without hitting anything. And yet the light came no closer. I had intended to keep my footing but, desperate to reach the light, I became sloppy. My foot slipped, rolled over my ankle and I fell to my knees. I braced myself for the oily wetness, waited for it to envelope me. Instead, I landed on hard-packed earth, kicking up red dust that swirled into my face and eyes, lined my throat, the inside of my nostrils. I saw the two Germans. They spoke to each other. The older officer handed the other a cigarette and lit it with the gold lighter. I couldn't understand how they could be so calm, converse so casually as they swung from the branches of the tree. The older German waved to me, then tossed the lighter. I couldn't make out what they said but the younger one laughed, then turned to look at me. I was desperate for a drink, my throat parched. A hand clutching a silver flask appeared. I took it and drank but it was only water. I swallowed gratefully, then handed it back. It disappeared into the gloom. The swinging Germans applauded me and I bowed ironically in response. I sat back, then lay down in the dirt as a cloud of dust enveloped me like a blanket.

I awoke as the ground imploded and a shower of debris landed on my face. I felt my body leave the earth and then return. A hand grabbed me by the shoulder and pulled. Shells hurtled through the diminishing darkness. Popov kneeled at my side. My ears rang. I stared at the crater some fifteen metres from where I lay.

"Where are the men?" I yelled hoarsely. Popov pointed behind him. He helped me gain my feet. I grabbed my cap and machine pistol and steadily as I could, followed behind. The barrage fractured the atmosphere, the ground shifted and heaved as if it were alive, tree roots burst through the surface as the trunks splintered, boulders pulverized. I couldn't hear my own footsteps or the screams of the men around me. I could barely hear the blood pounding in my ears. In my youth once, I'd crossed a suspension bridge. It felt like walking on coiled springs with no sure footing, held only by the narrow handrails that stopped me from toppling over into the rugged gorge far below. The earth heaved and surged beneath my feet bucking like that flimsy bridge. Like panicked ants, the Polish troops rushed about, desperately trying to find a path deeper into the woods. I knew the artillery blasts would continue for a few minutes, perhaps a half hour at most before the main assault.

We picked our way through the forest, stepping over branches of fallen trees and in some cases, the limbs of wounded or dead soldiers. We covered five hundred metres until we were out of range of the artillery fire and the noise of the bombardment receded. At least we could hear our own voices.

General Witold stood in a clearing with the men gathered around him. About six hundred were left. Witold looked calm. He was impeccably dressed. His uniform remained pristine and his leather boots shone. He held a linen handkerchief in his left hand that he brought delicately to his thin lips. I noticed the dried pinkish stains on the white fabric. I and the rest of the officers stood behind the General while the men kneeled or sat, panting with fear, sweating it out of their bodies.

"Men," said the General, "eighteen days ago our homeland was invaded. We put up a brave and valiant fight. Twenty German divisions were held back by only five divisions of the Polish army. I have received word that Warsaw has fallen." A circuit of murmurs and moans swept through the assembly. Witold held up his hand.

"The Germans and the Russians have signed a pact of peace. From our rear," and here he pointed an immaculately gloved hand with finger outstretched, "the Russians are sweeping the forests clear. Any man found in a Polish uniform will be shot or at best captured and sent to a slave gulag never to be seen or heard from again." Witold unfolded a map and pointed to it so all could see. "The new border is here, two hundred kilometres due east near Podole and Kolomiya to the southwest. Our land is now occupied. We are heavily outnumbered. Before us is a German division." And here he hesitated as a spasm seized him. He covered his mouth with the stained cloth.

"As you can see, I have little left to lose. That may not be the case with all of you. I propose to make a stand here." Witold hesitated then, as his eyes swept the faces of the men before him, many of whom looked down in shame or fear. "You have all fought well, with courage and bravery. I will understand if you do not wish to follow me. I give you permission to leave but you must turn over your weapons. There is no shame in wanting to go home, to see your families again. I, God and Poland will understand that you will be there another day when the time is right to rise again. God keep Poland." And just then, a mortar shell screamed into the clearing. Everyone dove to the ground and when we looked up, Witold had disappeared. I found shreds of the white linen cloth. Lepinski looked as if he were in shock, a dazed expression on his face, his eyes registering no awareness of what had happened. I found one of the General's boots with part of the leg still in it. Lepinski picked it up and wandered stiffly off into the woods. I could hear the Germans advancing through the forest. There was little time. I waved Popov over.

"Sir?"

"Gather the men. Quickly." Popov nodded, then moved off. Without the General, the rest of the men panicked. There was no control, no order. I waited while Popov organized those that were left. Barely thirty men. They huddled around, looked at me expectantly.

"It's over," I said bluntly. "I suggest we disperse now. Try and make your way to your homes. Get rid of your uniforms as quickly as you can. Travel by night. It's safer. If you can kill some Nazis without endangering yourselves, then do it. Otherwise, take no chances. I too, am returning to my home, to see my family. Good luck to you all." And one by one, I shook each by the hand and gave each a firm clasp on the shoulder, until finally it was only me and Popov.

"Time to go Sergeant. They are advancing quickly. Take care of yourself. Perhaps we'll meet again."

Popov saluted smartly. "Thank you, Captain. And may I say, it was an honour serving with you, brief as it was."

I smiled. "For me too."

Popov hefted his machine pistol and with a final salute, moved smartly off into the forest. I watched him until he had disappeared, then turned east and started off at a run.

Chapter 11

I walked for five days, sleeping during the day and moving by night. I stripped off my uniform and buried my machine pistol behind an oak tree but kept the revolver tucked into the trousers I'd stolen from a peasant's hut while the fellow had been working in the fields. I'd taken a shirt and a tunic and a little bit of food and left a few zlotys on the table. During my journey I ate what I could, sometimes buying food from peasants when I felt it safe to show myself, drank from the cold, fast-moving streams I forded and picked gooseberries from the vine. This, and the emotional hunger to get home, to see my family, moved me along.

On the morning of the fifth day, I washed my face in a stream thinking that home felt close by. I knew the nearest village, Pauk. The farmers had come to my father's mill to buy flour. I knew many of them and they knew me and were not to be trusted. My belly growled angrily. I picked some berries and, finding a good spot that afforded cover, lay down to rest after a hard night's walking. I slept for hours, and when I awoke the sun was high, although it was cool and shaded in the forest. I stood up stiffly and stretched, forcing some of the dampness out of my bones that seeped in after sleeping on the ground. I made my way carefully back to the stream to get a drink, looking about so I wouldn't be spotted, then drank gratefully. In several hours, I would be home. It was remarkably peaceful. No signs of the war. I could almost pretend it had never happened and life went on just as it had before, but then I smelled the stink rising from me, felt the bristles on my face and stared at my callused hands, nails broken and dirty, the seams of my skin infused with grime and the sweat of fear. What had happened? Again, I heard the scream of the shell, saw the proud, erect figure of General Witold framed in the morning sun and then, nothing—a thundering concussion, scorched earth and a smoking hole where he'd been standing. Everything had changed in an instant.

Finally, darkness came and I set out determinedly, certain now of the direction. As I strode ahead, I let myself think about what I might find. Would they be there? I knew that Katya and Alexis, her new husband, worked in a small hospital over the border on the Russian side. It meant they stayed safe for the time being. I felt the weight of the pistol in my waistband, the itch of the barrel against my skin. I longed for a cigarette and a drink, the desire burning inside me. Instead, I took a quick swallow from the canteen I carried. Traveling at night I missed the sights of the day, didn't take in the destruction of the brief war between Poland and Germany. Skirting towns and villages, I passed burned-out huts, didn't see the bodies caught in cross-fire or shot cold-bloodedly in line-ups, didn't notice the animals taken to feed the new overseers, didn't hear the screams of the women and young girls violated by men drunk on their newfound power. I smelled the burning embers in the fields where crops had been set alight, spotted abandoned troop carriers and the hollowed-out shell of a tank that had taken a direct hit - now sitting like a decomposing house in the middle of the lea, shelter for forest creatures. I didn't see the survivors who crept out at night to quietly bury their dead. I didn't see these things, but absorbed them in my skin as I strode forward through the blanket of darkness, uncertain in my purpose, anxious at what I might find. I walked parallel to the roadside but down in the gully where I wouldn't be seen. It was harder going but safer. I reached Pilsudski Street, the main thoroughfare that led directly into Krasnowicz. Another five kilometres and I would be there. I took another pull from the canteen and thought about the men briefly and Popov. Had he made it home? I hoped so, he seemed a good man. I capped the canteen and moved on. A light suddenly shone above my head and in the distance I heard the full-throated growl of a motorcycle. I threw myself to the ground then crept forward, dazzled by the yellow oval of the lantern, hearing the snarl of the engine as the driver throttled up into high gear. Mere seconds later the machine and its driver, a man in uniform with a machine pistol slung over his back, roared by. I rolled back into the gully mopping my face and forehead, then stayed in a crouch for a few minutes, listening intently. No more engines penetrated the stillness.

I climbed the wooden fence that marked the perimeter of our property just as I'd climbed it hundreds of times as a child. My pulse quickened and the saliva in my mouth dried as I crept from tree to tree. I knew every stump, every mound, every rabbit hole. As I moved forward, I made out the front of the house. All seemed quiet and dark, settled in for the night. No vehicles parked in the yard. I made my way carefully around the back. I kept close to the wall and stopped at each corner, the pistol firmly in hand. The back door had a trick latch and quietly as possible, I jimmied it and the door swung open. I stepped inside and closed it behind me, stopped and listened, straining for the normal house sounds, anything out of the ordinary. I made my way to the dining room and the liquor cabinet. I felt for the handle and the bottle. On the sideboard I found glasses. I set the pistol down. My hands trembled and I fumbled to remove the cap. As I poured the vodka into the glass, the bottle clinked against the rim. Just as I was about to put the glass to my lips, the light snapped on. I swiveled, hand outstretched, grabbing for the pistol and pointing. The barrel wavered until I lowered it to my side. Mama. It seemed like an eternity before she spoke.

"Mordecai?" She put her hands to her cheeks. "Is that you?" I knew she saw a gaunt peasant, dirt and grime-streaked, dressed in ragged clothes, pointing a weapon. Not a person but some sort of feral beast.

I slid the pistol into my waistband, set the glass down and stepped forward, arms outstretched.

"Mama." Her arms came around me and I inhaled the mingling of lemon and flour. Comfort and warmth. She gripped me tightly and the tears flowed. "It's so good to see you," I said into the folds of her dressing gown.

"My God," she exclaimed. "When did you eat last? Come into the kitchen and I'll get something for you," she said before I could even shrug. She took my hand. I picked up the glass and followed her. "And you are filthy too."

"Yes." I could barely speak. The words came out as a croak. She sat me in a chair and I could barely believe that I sat again in my own kitchen. I drank some vodka and felt it melt into my innards. Mama bustled about.

"We haven't got much. Supplies have been scarce but still we have a little bit put by. We are luckier than most."

I watched her for a few moments. Then, fatigue flooded into me. I'd been fighting it for three days. I drifted off, then started awake.

"Poor darling. You look exhausted."

"I'm fine."

"What happened to your uniform?"

"I threw it away. The Germans are shooting anyone who fought against them."

"Sssh. Not too loud, darling. We don't want to wake anyone." I hadn't noticed I'd been speaking in a loud voice but I supposed that any sound might carry early in the morning. I just didn't realize. If I'd been more alert, maybe it all would've been different.

"I shall make you an egg. It's our last one but no matter, it's a special occasion, isn't it?" She took a long look at me again, then put her arms around me and sobbed into my chest.

"Mama, please. It's all right. I'm fine." Then it occurred to me that perhaps she wasn't crying for me. "Papa? Is he all right?"

"Yes." She kept her head pressed to my filthy shoulder.

"And Simmy?"

"He is fine." I lifted my mother's head and looked at her, the tear-streaked cheeks, once rosy and full, now had begun to hollow. I saw dark circles under her eyes.

"What's going on here? What is this? Some stranger is touching my wife?"

I turned. "Papa."

I rose swiftly and embraced him, feeling his bones through his nightclothes.

"My son," he breathed. "My son," was all he could choke out. "Please," he said and examined me at arm's length. "You are well, but filthy I see."

Mama tended to the egg.

"Mama. Papa. Listen to me. I have plans..."

"Shush," Mama said. "Eat first." She put the plate down in front of me with the fried egg and some bread and jam. The smell of the food was overwhelming and I almost swooned but I ate. It seemed as if it all disappeared in mere seconds. Mama poured out a cup of tea. "We have no sugar but there is milk."

I sipped the hot liquid. "That's all right. It's fine, better than fine. It's so good to be here. To see you." An arm snaked around my neck and squeezed, and I reached up. My brother's face appeared.

"Simmy." I jumped up and we hugged like bears waddling across the floor and laughing. "You've grown since I last saw you."

"You look like a scarecrow," Simmy said, pushing his glasses up his nose. "I smelled the egg. It woke me up."

"It was the last one," his mother said.

"Ah."

"We shall get more," she promised. "Amalija and Pyotr keep chickens. They will give us."

"So listen," I began.

Simmy interrupted. "Does he know?" Silence descended. Simmy looked to each of my parents, then my father shook his head.

"Know what?" I asked.

Simmy started. "That..."

"That this house is under occupation," said a new voice. I lurched, grabbing the pistol I'd left sitting on the table. I saw a rotund figure with close-cropped dark hair swathed in my father's best robe, wearing his slippers. He held a gleaming Luger in his right hand. "Welcome home Mr. Goldman."

I relaxed my hands. "Herr Roediger." I smiled uneasily.

"It's Colonel Roediger now, Goldman."

I bowed. "Colonel. You've come a long way from teaching high school."

"But of course."

"Mordecai please." Mama reached for my arm but I stepped away and faced my former physics professor, the one I hated the most in school.

"Don't do anything foolish, Goldman. I am well-trained and there are guards about."

"I didn't see any."

"Perhaps you didn't expect to." Roediger smiled. He barked a command and two guards appeared behind him. Three more came in through the back door in the kitchen. "Now I think you can see them? The question is, what are you going to do, Goldman?"

As he said it, the three guards behind me each grabbed Mama, Papa and Simmy.

"I could shoot you," I said. "It would give me great pleasure."

Roediger shrugged. "You might - but then you know what we would do to them, don't you? And of course, we'd make you watch, which wouldn't be pleasant but rather amusing, nonetheless."

I considered my options. I might be able to shoot Roediger but not the guards, and I couldn't risk causing any harm to my parents and Simmy. Ultimately, fatigue won over. The fight had gone out of me. Slowly, I raised my hands with the pistol aloft.

"Wise decision," Roediger hissed. "You were one of my brighter pupils, if not a little arrogant."

"You've left physics far behind you I see."

The rotund Colonel shrugged. "The world changes and we must adapt to it, Goldman. Even a physicist understands this. Take him."

The guards seized me and twisted my arms behind my back.

Then, a new voice echoed across the room. "What is going on here, Colonel?" I looked up to see a bullet-headed man with cold, blue eyes, and despite the late hour, dressed in the immaculate black uniform of the SS.

Roediger stiffened.

"I was just about to inform you, Major. We have had a slight disturbance but nothing to worry about."

I heard the creak of his boots and smelled the essence of polished leather. He stood of medium height and appeared very trim. He held himself stiffly, as if he'd been starched into his uniform.

"Who is he?" the Major spat.

"The son, the older one," Roediger replied.

"I see," replied the Major.

The Major took two steps. The guards stepped quickly aside holding themselves at the ready. He stopped in front of me and sniffed, wrinkling his nostrils in disgust. "And where has he been?" the Major inquired.

"I'm not certain, Major," Roediger replied.

The Major smiled thinly. "Come now, Colonel. The man is dressed like a peasant and he is filthy. He looks like he hasn't slept in some time nor eaten I should think. Doesn't this suggest anything to you?"

"Just that he was on the run, perhaps?"

The Major spun around, smashing his riding crop on the table.

"You take me for a fool, Colonel? Do you?"

Roediger paled and swallowed. "No Major, of course I don't."

"This man is an enemy; a partisan perhaps or even a Polish soldier."

"I wouldn't know," Roediger replied. "We just caught him sneaking in, that's all. We haven't had time to interrogate him."

"Interrogate him?" And the Major laughed, showing flashes of silver inside his mouth. "Now why would you want to do that?"

"To find out what he knows, of course."

"Waste of time, Colonel." The Major put his arms behind his back. "Shoot him. And if the others protest, shoot them too."

"But Major, we need them."

Papa went pale. I thought he would pass out. Mama began to cry and I thought Simmy would be ill but he didn't utter a sound.

"Yes, yes," the Major replied. "For the war effort, I understand. Feeding the men and so on - but be careful, Colonel. I know you are from this area but make absolutely certain you don't develop a sympathy with these vermin, do you understand?"

Roediger nodded, even managed a smile. "Completely, Major."

"Then make sure it is done, immediately."

"Of course."

The Major then spun on his heel and strode out of the room. I heard the click of his heels echoing down the hall.

Then the room erupted.

My mother sobbed. "Please, please don't, please."

"There must be something we can do," my father said. "I'm a businessman, we find solutions, there must be another way. Please consider. We'll pay you. We'll give you anything you want."

"Be quiet," Roediger roared. "There is no other way. It is out of my hands. I'm sorry, Goldman. This is not the way I would have chosen but the SS have tremendous power and I cannot contradict the order."

"Promise me you will make certain my family is kept safe," I said.

"I will do whatever I can," Roediger replied.

"Promise me," I said.

"How dare you ask me such a thing. Such arrogance. That's what I didn't like about you Goldman and I can see nothing has changed."

"It's my only request and my last one," I said.

Roediger twisted his small head around until I thought it might drop off his shoulders, his complexion went a deep red but finally he effected a curt nod. That was all I was going to get out of him. He waved his arms and the guards forced me outside the house into the back garden. My mother collapsed on the floor.

"No. No. Please no," she cried.

My father tried to go to her but the guard held him back. I couldn't say anything to them. I didn't know how to say goodbye. Simmy and I exchanged looks.

Outside, one of the guards handed me a shovel. I dug as slowly as I could. The guards took turns hitting me with their rifle butts.

"Dig faster."

At the insistence of the SS Major, the guards dragged my parents and Simmy outside to watch.

"Halt," Roediger ordered. I stopped digging, panting over the shovel. "Give the shovel to your brother. He will bury you."

I looked down at the grave. It was shallow, almost too shallow I thought, but who was I to complain? Wearily, I handed the shovel to Simmy as Roediger slowly drew his pistol from its holster. He motioned Simmy closer then leaned in to speak to him. I couldn't hear what they said but Simmy glanced up suddenly, although his face betrayed no emotion.

"Move back," Roediger said to the guards. They withdrew. "Now Goldman, it's time. You may say your prayers if you wish."

I laughed hoarsely. "Just get on with it, Roediger."

The rotund Colonel came up behind me, pressing the barrel of the pistol into my back. Again, the thought occurred to me fleetingly that I could escape but he read my thoughts. "Don't try anything, Goldman. Remember, we have your family."

He marched me toward the open pit of the grave. "I promise," he said in a loud voice. "This will be as quick and painless as possible."

I felt the cold steel pressed against the back of my neck. Then Roediger hissed in my ear. "Remember Goldman, I did what I could."

Before I could reply, thunder exploded in my head, my vision went dark. I thought I heard a soul-piercing wail emanate from the earth and for a split second I felt myself fall forward into eternity.

Chapter 12

Beulah stared at me, her breath ragged. Her thin chest heaved.

"Holy shit, Mr. G. That guy shot you?"

I nodded.

"Yes, he did."

"But you're alive. You ain't no ghost."

I chuckled.

"Not yet, anyway."

"What happened? Please tell me."

I gave her some more water.

"In good time. If you want to hear the story, then you have to let me tell it the way I want to."

She pouted.

"Okay."

Krasnowicz 1925

On the first day of high school, I rose early, the image of the hulking farmer's son floating in front of me. My appetite had fled. Mama sat with me holding my hand.

"Mama, please. I can't eat anything," I said and yanked it out of her grasp.

"I'm sorry, my darling." She took my slight in stride. "I just can't believe how grown up you are now. First day of high school."

"It won't be long and Simmy will be going too."

Mama looked sad and gathered her robe around her throat and shivered. "It's damp now in the mornings. Soon winter will come."

"Summer isn't over yet."

"But it goes so quickly. It saddens me to see all these beautiful things turn drab and ugly."

I took a single bite of the toast, then set it down. I managed to slurp some tea.

"Well that's nature for you, it gives you the good and the bad, doesn't it?"

"Mmm, very profound. You're turning into a philosopher all of a sudden." Simmy slipped down the stairs in his night shirt. "I've heard smarter things from a peasant," Simmy declared. "But I came to wish you good luck on your first day. And I'd like some tea."

Simmy poured himself a cup while Mama slathered some jam on a thick slice of bread. He sat down to eat it happily, smearing jam on his chin.

A short time later, I stood before the front entrance in blazer, tie and slacks. Mama handed me a packed lunch and gave me a warm hug and kiss. Papa came up behind her.

"Try to stay out of trouble, Mordecai. Get to know your teachers well and work hard."

"Yes, Papa." Simmy merely stuck his tongue out and gave me a mischievous grin. "We'll see you this evening," his father said.

"Of course," I replied with a conviction I didn't feel and pushed the door open. I glanced back, and saw them holding hands. That was the image of them that I always remembered, even after seventy years.

Four kilometers to school and four back. I'd have to move briskly.

I looked up at the imposing stone building. I'd seen factories with more appeal. Chiseled limestone steps swept upwards to forbidding oak doors. I saw prisoners instead of students. The grounds consisted of packed earth and scrub grass. Beyond the swath of tarmac lay the patchy soccer field. Most of the teachers and students rode bicycles. Some were dropped off by horse-drawn carts or rode horses they kept tethered to a convenient tree. The headmaster's assistant hadn't yet come out to ring the hand bell heralding the start of classes, and students gathered in small clumps enjoying the sunshine. I made my way to the main doors. Three Polacks blocked my way. The middle one looked to be a giant. His frayed jacket barely covered his wrists and the pair of slacks he wore showed his ankles. One good sneeze and the shirt and jacket would split at the seams.

"Remember me, Jew?" he said. It was the farmer's son.

"I remember."

Other students edged away. A thick finger poked me in the chest, hard enough to force me backward. Balance, Frederick had said.

"I am Jerzy and you will have to answer to me here. Do you understand?"

I looked up at him straight into his eyes. The boy seemed huge, like a wall. I balled my fists and tensed. "Maybe you'd better explain it to me."

Another poke with the blunt finger "Your father cannot protect you here, Jew. He can't buy your way out of this."

"I don't need his protection or his money."

Jerzy turned to his companions and sneered. "Do you hear the Jew? He says he can protect himself." He turned back. "That's a good laugh." Others had stopped to stare at the group for a moment and then hurried on without stopping.

"You there. Boys."

Heads snapped toward the voice. One of Jerzy's cohorts, a stocky youth, hissed.

"Headmaster."

We separated as the ramrod-straight headmaster bristled up and looked at each of us in turn.

"What's going on here?"

Everyone shifted uncomfortably. There was an awkward silence.

"Nothing sir," I said. "We're getting ready for class."

"I see," the headmaster replied. He removed his pince-nez and turned to Jerzy. "I know you - and you are a troublemaker. I shall have my eye on you, yes?" Jerzy didn't reply but nodded silently. "Very well then. On your way."

We trudged up the steps as the headmaster's assistant emerged ringing the hand bell vigorously, ensuring that anyone within a radius of five kilometres would know that the school day had officially begun. Just before we separated at the other side of the entrance, Jerzy leaned his shaggy head in and whispered, "Remember, Jew."

I said nothing, but forced myself to look Jerzy in the eye again.

As we entered the hallway, the echo of footfalls became almost deafening. One of the professors stood to the side scanning the lines and directing traffic. "New boy?" he said to me.

"Yes, sir."

"What level?"

"First, sir."

"The end of the hall and turn right, second door, room eight," the professor said crisply.

"Thank you, sir." I moved off into the current of students.

The first class of the day was algebra. The professor droned on and on. All I could think about was Jerzy waiting for me in the schoolyard. Forty, bored boys hunched over scarred wooden desks scratching out math exercises. When they shifted their weight, the elderly chairs creaked in protest. I couldn't wait for the period to end and when it did, I flew out of the room, knocking into boys as I went, agitated cries ringing around me.

I went outside and waited, clenching and unclenching my fists. Students sat in circles or strolled the grounds. I stood at the bottom of the steps, looking up. I didn't have to wait long. Jerzy and two of his goons swept down toward me. I thought briefly about calling it off but I knew my life would be misery from that moment on. I had to go through with it. Part of me enjoyed the feeling of fear radiating in my gut.

"Come on, Jew, let's go. This way," Jerzy said and smiled maliciously. "So the monitor won't see." I followed him around behind the school. We picked up a small pack that sensed danger and excitement. These gawkers formed a small circle. I placed my books on the ground and carefully removed my jacket. I hoped my knees wouldn't give way or my hands shake. I was surprised to see some girls in the crowd. They too came out for blood. I faced Jerzy, who indicated with his hands that I should come for him. I waited and took some deep breaths, forcing myself to relax, to stay loose.

"Well, come on. What are you waiting for?" Jerzy growled. I took up the stance I had practiced with Frederick, keeping my eyes on Jerzy, focusing on him.

"What are you looking at?" the hulking lad asked and sneered before trundling in.

He looked powerful but moved awkwardly. I went to move but my knees locked. Jerzy took a wide swing at my head with his right hand. At the last second, I shifted my weight slightly and the intended punch missed wildly. Jerzy moved in again and took another wild swing. Panic screamed at me to move again. I ducked Jerzy's fist, but barely.

"What's the matter, afraid? You a coward, Jew boy?"

I breathed deeply and bounced up on my toes. Jerzy threw out his left. By instinct, I blocked it and hit the large Pole in the solar plexus once, twice. Sounds of dismay circled me. Jerzy gasped, bending over, then after a moment, straightened up.

"Lucky that," he hissed and feinted then lunged sharply at me, throwing himself forward. He knocked me to the ground. Jerzy pressed with his weight, trying to pin my arms with his knees and pummel me with his ham-sized fists. I struggled desperately to work my arms free. I was helpless, a sitting duck.

I heard someone speaking harshly.

"That's enough of that. Get up, the pair of you."

I heard mutterings from the group. "Professor Laszlo," they whispered.

Laszlo pulled Jerzy off me easily, using his broad shoulders and thick arms. I got to my feet, slowly dusting off my shirt and trousers.

Jerzy stood swaying, his face bloated with anger, his eyes creased with hatred. Laszlo looked from me to him.

"Gentleman. I see you are both interested in the pugilistic arts." Laszlo made a fist and waggled it. I shrugged, while Jerzy stood with his long arms hanging at his sides, glaring angrily.

"Good. Tomorrow at one o'clock we shall have a formal bout. In the ring. And then we shall see how well you match up. No scrapping outside the school, eh? That is for peasants and you are both gentlemen, aren't you? Then you may settle your differences the way men do, with honor, according to the rules. I, of course, shall have the pleasure of being the judge and referee. Agreed?"

Jerzy and me continued our staring game. Jerzy nodded.

"Yes sir," I replied.

"What's your name?" asked Laszlo.

"Mordecai Goldman."

"Welcome to the school, Mr. Goldman. This brute I know already. He has been in the same level for two years at least." Laszlo flashed a smile. None of the students dared to laugh as Jerzy glared at the group gathered around, remembering every smirk, every lopsided grin.

"Perhaps he's taking his time sir," I said. Everyone turned to look at me.

"What?"

"He helps his father on the farm when he could be doing schoolwork is what I meant."

Laszlo gave me a thoughtful look. "Perhaps." He looked about him. "The period is almost over. Tomorrow at one, gentlemen."

Laszlo parted the crowd and disappeared. Slowly, the group broke up. I unfolded the jacket and put it on, picked up the satchel and books. I pulled out the sandwich Mama had made and began to munch as I walked back around the school. Jerzy said nothing. We eyed each other suspiciously.

"That was very brave of you," a voice piped up. I turned to see a slim, blonde girl following. I took another bite of the sandwich.

"Maybe it was just foolish."

"Aren't you afraid?"

"Yes, I was but I couldn't let that stop me."

"Why not?"

"Because my life would be a nightmare if I didn't stand up to him, so I didn't have a choice really. Better to get it over with."

"It's too bad you feel that way. I'm Maria," said the girl. "Maria Slobodan."

"I'm..."

"I know who you are. Everyone does."

"I see. A Jew is such an unusual creature, is that it?"

The girl smiled. "Something like that." She walked off, hugging her books, glancing over her shoulder once before joining a group of giggling friends. I watched them for a moment, then went back to eating lunch.

Chapter 13

The next day at one o'clock, a large group had assembled in the gymnasium. Laszlo cleared a space in the centre, marking out the approximate dimensions of a boxing ring.

"Welcome gentlemen," Laszlo said. "You have an audience. Come." We stepped forward. "Go into the changing area and strip down to your undershirts. I have proper shoes and gloves here for you."

In the change room, I stripped off my shirt, then kicked off my shoes. I glanced over at Jerzy, who had done the same. The Pole was heavily muscled and stood a head higher at least. Jerzy flexed, then pounded his fist into his palm and smiled.

"I shall enjoy this, Jew. Better pray now."

I returned the smile calmly and looked him again straight in the eye. I didn't say anything but held Jerzy's gaze until the young Pole flinched. Then I walked out of the changing area. Jerzy followed.

Laszlo told us to put on the boxing shoes he had. He helped lace up my gloves.

"You know what you are doing?" Laszlo asked in a subdued tone, focusing on the lacing.

"I sure hope so." Laszlo finished tying off the gloves. "Put your hands together." I did so. "Good." Then he fitted the loose helmet over my head. Laszlo's assistant laced up Jerzy's gloves.

Laszlo strode to the centre of the makeshift ring.

"Come gentlemen."

We stepped toward him, and stopped one on either side. Laszlo turned to Jerzy. "Show me your hands." Jerzy held out the gloves and Laszlo examined them quickly.

"Good. Now. We'll begin with three rounds of three minutes each. Blows must be above the waist and no hitting from behind. No butting of the head and no tripping. If I say stop, you stop. If I say the match is over, it is over and no protest will be tolerated. Understood?"

We nodded.

"Now each of you go to your own corner and wait for my signal."

I bounced up and down and waved my arms to loosen up. My heart pounded. I prayed I would remember everything Frederick taught me. It was strange to think of Frederick as being on my side. I imagined the twisted smile and my blood rose. I looked at Jerzy, who seemed like some kind of monster.

Laszlo put a whistle to his lips and gave a shrill blast then waved at us to come to the centre. We moved warily, shuffling forward, then touched our gloves together.

"Begin!"

I tucked my elbows in, fists bunched under my chin. Jerzy took a wild swing with his right and I ducked it easily. Then came another wild swing came from the left, then the right again. Jerzy's left fist caught me flush in the side of the head and I staggered, my knees buckling. I felt a tingling and a numbing down my left side. I shook my head clear as Jerzy smiled and waded forward. A yell ripped from the crowd as Jerzy's supporters urged him on. Frederick's instructions came to me and I moved to my right as Jerzy swung high, exposing his middle. I stepped in with a combination to the midriff as my opponent grunted and stopped, his mouth hanging open. Jerzy swatted me away slapping my face with an open glove. I stumbled but regained balance and got back on my toes, looking for an opening. Jerzy lashed out and caught my ankle with the toe of his shoe. It stung like blazes and I hopped quickly out of reach.

Laszlo stepped in. "None of that, do you hear? This is boxing, not football."

Jerzy grinned but nodded. I tried to shake the sting out.

I kept moving side to side. Jerzy swung again, his long arms over-reaching. I ducked and hit him hard with a right in the ribs. The bigger boy winced. I put a left into his abdomen and another right to the ribs. Jerzy stepped back, trying to move out of range. I moved in, jabbing with my left, flicking punches off his face. Jerzy bellowed in rage and rushed forward, grasping me in a bear hug.

Laszlo moved swiftly and forced himself between us. I staggered back feeling my sides throb where Jerzy had crushed me. Jerzy wasn't moving now but standing still, wavering, breathing heavily. We circled each other warily. I found an opening and stepped in, raining sharp, stinging blows to Jerzy's face and jaw. Sweat flew off Jerzy's head and hair as each jab snapped his head back. He blinked but stayed upright. I felt exhausted and bent over protecting my side, but pivoted around as Jerzy followed my movements.

"Fucking Jew," he hissed.

I tried to swallow the rage welling within me. Jerzy sneered at me, egging me on, daring me to step toward him. Frederick's taunting voice rang in my head…balance…balance…balance…

I took a good look at Jerzy, saw his hands hanging low, elbows wide apart. There was the target.

I got up on my toes even though my calves screamed. Jerzy had long arms. They wouldn't do him much good in close quarters. I took a deep breath and waded in. I managed to put together a combination of rights and lefts, working him hard in the ribs. Jerzy grunted and swung his arms. He hissed, sending air through his lips and brought both hands together, using them as a cudgel. I threw myself backward, rolling on the floor, then scrambled up. Jerzy veered around forcefully just as I managed to gain my feet. His elbow caught me in the hip and I yelped but saw his exposed cheek. I set my feet and threw an overhand right that caught Jerzy on the left cheekbone, snapping his head to the right. He was hurt and touched his face gingerly, leaving his side open. I stepped in with a vicious left hook. Jerzy winced and groaned, dropping his arm. Just as his arm dropped, I pushed solidly off my back foot and brought an overhand right to Jerzy's face. His nostrils exploded and a spume of blood splattered his face. Jerzy's big body sagged. I watched as the young Pole's knees buckled and he crumpled, like a decrepit barn folding in on itself, to the floor. Laszlo signaled to his assistant, who bustled over with a bucket. No one moved or spoke. The assistant lifted Jerzy's head and waved something in front of his face. The boy started, then fluttered his eyes, groaning as he came to. I bent over, holding my side.

"Well done," said Laszlo. "Are you all right, Goldman?"

"Yes sir, at least I think so," I wheezed. "Will he be all right?"

Laszlo glanced at Jerzy, who lay on the ground sputtering and moaning.

"I expect he'll recover," Laszlo said.

My lungs felt like they had burst but I held out my hands. Laszlo began to unlace the gloves.

"I coach a boxing club. Perhaps you'd care to try out?"

"I don't know. I'd have to think about it."

Laszlo smiled grimly. "What I just saw wasn't a match, it was a war." He looked at me critically. "You've had some instruction I think."

"A little."

"Do you mind if I ask who?"

"A family friend," I replied, trying to keep the bitterness out of my voice.

"Yes?" Laszlo looked puzzled as he pulled each glove off in turn and tossed each to the ground. "Who might that be?"

A small group had now gathered around Jerzy who was sitting up. Through darkened eyes, he glanced my way. The rest of the spectators dispersed, too embarrassed to say anything to Jerzy and too proud to approach me in public.

"Frederick Valens."

"Indeed?" Laszlo looked both impressed. "A fine boxer. One of the best in Europe. I saw him fight the British champion, Montague, in 1922. My god, what a battle."

"Well, I understand he was pretty good," I muttered.

"Indeed," Laszlo responded. "More than pretty good, I'd say but it seems he has taught you well. Valens was strong and very, very smart."

"Yes, he is very smart," I replied. I looked over at Jerzy and told myself I hated that boy. That he was everything I despised about Poland and my life here. Jerzy sat up now, pressing a blood-spattered towel to his face. Laszlo's assistant helped him unsteadily to his feet. I wanted to gloat, to go over and spit in his face.

"Excuse me," I said to Laszlo. Jerzy was up and walking slowly about, an unfocused expression on his face. Jerzy stopped. I stood in front of him and we exchanged looks for a long moment. Neither of us spoke. Then in a move that surprised me as much as anyone, I stuck my hand out. The larger boy hesitated. He blinked into the blood-stained towel then looked up and took my hand and shook it, even managing a slight grin. I nodded, dropped the grip, then went into the changing area to clean off and get dressed. I noticed the girl from the other day in the corner watching. When I emerged, she was gone.

Score one for the Jews. Make your enemy your friend, I thought.

Chapter 14

Every male high school student received military training. I received a uniform. The trousers sagged and the sleeves of the tunic almost covered my hands. The cap came down around my ears.

This made me think back to my military service after high school. In 1931, I was billeted in Cracow. I still remember it like it was yesterday.

"Pan Lieutenant. Pan Lieutenant?"

"Yes. What is it?" A hand shook my shoulder vigorously. I had been dozing in a comfortable wingback chair in the officer's mess. I blinked myself awake, ran a hand through my hair and tried to focus on the young cadet before me.

"Pan Captain Vishna wishes to see you right away."

I stood up and straightened my uniform. "Thank you Corporal. I shall attend to the Captain presently."

"Yes sir."

The boy was barely sixteen with blond hair neatly parted down the middle of his scalp and an expression of expectation on his smooth, young face. The boy saluted and I saluted back, smiling to myself at the silliness of it all. A year earlier, I had been like this boy although my rank had been second lieutenant at the time. I had been placed in the tank division, a laughable commission as we had five armoured cars powered by Fiat engines that broke down constantly. Instead of cannon, we carried unreliable machine guns that jammed more than they fired. The mountings were so old and rusted that in rough terrain, the guns fell off and had to be retrieved and re-attached. This happened time and again. I was constantly fixing the tanks and other vehicles in the compound that broke down. In a short time, I had made myself useful to the military command.

I strode across the compound. The heels of my boots kicked up dust that whipped in swirls by the wind. I put my head down and leaned forward to keep the blowing grit out of my eyes, went into the Captain's office and waited while the corporal seated behind the desk acknowledged me, a bare gesture by the slim, prissy young man with dark hair slicked to his scalp. The corporal glanced up. I grinned. I bent forward at the waist and put my hand over the fellow's, who was in the midst of scribbling something on an important-looking document. I squeezed.

"When I salute you, Corporal, you must return my salute, do you understand?"

The Corporal's eyes widened with pain but he nodded. I removed my hand. "Let's see it, then. And stand up while you're at it." The man stood and snapped a salute. "That's better."

"My apologies Lieutenant. I forget sometimes."

"The Captain requested my presence."

The Corporal smiled. "Please go in." I felt his reptilian eyes on my back, as I knocked once, opened the door, then stepped inside. The Captain stared out the window. He was an ebullient man, short and broad with thick wavy hair. The skin of his face was ruddy, darkened further by the wind. His eyes showed a kind of madness.

"Goldman. Come in. Come in. Have a seat." Captain Vishna seated himself, then jumped up and began to pace the room in front of me. "What do you think of us, this army of ours, eh?"

I hesitated. "I'm not sure what you are asking, sir."

The Captain jerked to a halt and peered at me. The rims of his eyelids shone bright red. "I am saying, do you think we are ready to wage a war? Give me your honest opinion."

"Sir, I don't think so. The equipment is inadequate, constantly breaking down. We don't have enough in the way of armaments, no tanks to speak of and we operate a horse cavalry against mechanized forces. The men are willing enough and there are some good ones that I can see."

"I will take that as a no. These are my thoughts exactly, Goldman. I ask myself what are we doing here? Can we help in any way? But I do believe in the spirit of the fighting man, don't you? That Polish fighting forces will acquit themselves well in battle as we go down to inevitable defeat. It has always been thus. History proves it and our time is no different, yes? We too, shall go down in defeat. The question remains, will it be a glorious defeat or merely mediocre or worse, embarrassing?"

"This I cannot say, sir."

"Of course not. I wouldn't ask anyway. Who can predict the future?" The stocky captain fingered a deep scar at the corner of his mouth absently. "Do you think I got this scar in battle?"

I nodded. "I had thought so, sir."

"That would make a good story wouldn't it? Yes, it happened in the War but during my leave. I got drunk in a bar and got into an argument with a fellow who grabbed a bottle of slivovitz off the counter and smashed it into my face. There was a time when I thought I would lose the sight in my eye. I was taken to a military hospital. He was arrested by the police. It turned out the fellow was a deserter. I had surgery several times. By the time I recovered, the war was all but over. I was lucky in a way. I should have thanked the fellow instead of cursing him, eh? But two years in the trenches was enough for any man, I can tell you."

"Yes sir."

"One of the armoured cars has broken down again. They are on maneuvers in the Braga woods 15 kilometres up from here. I've given you a driver and a car. Do you think you can fix it?"

"I'll do my best sir."

"Will you stay in the military after your service is up?"

"I wish to study engineering at university, sir. In Paris, I hope."

The captain nodded sadly. "I don't blame you."

"But I will keep my commission in the reserve."

The captain smiled wistfully. "Good fellow. See what you can do with that damned armoured car, will you?"

"Yes sir."

"And God help us if we ever go to war."

The next day in school, I found myself marching in the field adjacent to the school. Proper military training would help me I thought, but this is a joke. The entire class had buttoned their ill-fitting tunics and pulled on their sagging caps. None of the boys had boots and wore their regular shoes. The field was muddy and sucked at our heels. Laszlo barked out drills while his assistant demonstrated proper marching technique and rhythm. He looked like a wind-up toy. Laszlo explained the commands.

"Poland is like your mother," he said in a loud voice. "You must obey her and be loyal. You must serve her and protect her. To do that properly, you must be trained. Training involves practice. Practice involves repetition. You will practice the drills until you can march properly in a straight line, turn and march the other way and so on. Every day at two o'clock, you will march properly. And in time, your mothers will be proud of you. When we practice these drills, you will speak only if I speak to you first. If you must ask a question, raise your hand and I will recognize you." Just as he finished, I raised my hand. Laszlo tightened his face in annoyance. "Yes?"

"When do we learn to shoot?"

"Shooting is second term. First term is marching. And remember," he said, raising his voice so all might hear, "you must do this well or it will appear on your academic record. As long as I have been instructing, no one has ever failed. And no one ever will. Is that understood?" The boys remained silent. I felt an urge to burst out laughing.

"All right then," bawled Laszlo, "let's begin."

I looked to my left and there stood Jerzy, practically shoulder-to-shoulder. He gave me a slight nod. The line shuddered forward. Boys stepped on the heels of the boys in front, who, out of instinct or rage, lashed back with the heels of their shoes to kick them in the shins. Some hopped out of alignment, holding their bruised shins while others grabbed at their injured heels.

"Halt!" Laszlo cried. He shook his head and pursed his thin lips. "Get back into line. You there, stop hopping and stand still. Form up now, you lazy idiots." Laszlo sent his assistant to physically place boys back in the proper row. Jerzy and I stood and watched the goings-on with grim amusement.

"My pigs can do a better job," Jerzy hissed.

"What was that?" cried Laszlo, who stalked over and glared at us.

"It was nothing sir," I said. "I was just saying that marching isn't as easy as it looks."

Laszlo gave me a stern look.

"Very well, then. Get ready to march, you devils," he yelled. And turned away. I caught Jerzy's eye, who unexpectedly winked. And then it was time to march. The uneven, ragged lines of boys, all shapes and sizes, half-dressed in moth-eaten, unkempt tunics and caps. The pride of Poland stumbled with them.

Later that day, I was sitting on the grass eating lunch when a shadow passed over the pages of my Physics text. I glanced up, shielding my eyes against the sun.

"Why do you come here?" Jerzy asked. His tone seemed reasonable enough.

"Because it's the only public high school."

"What's wrong with your own school?" The larger boy crouched down so we were on the same level.

"I didn't want to go there. All they talk about is religion. I'm interested in science and mathematics. I want to do mechanical engineering in university and I need the courses offered here to qualify."

Jerzy nodded. He pulled a shoot of grass and stuck it between his teeth. "You understand this? This Physics."

"Yes."

Jerzy hesitated, for a moment, mulling his thoughts. "This is my second time in Level Two," he said. "If I don't pass this time, I must leave to work on the farm." He spat out the grass, then wiped his face. "I hate working on the farm. So, I can't fail. Can you help me with this?" And he poked at the book.

"You're asking me for a favor?"

Jerzy nodded, then felt around his nose gingerly. It remained swollen and his eyes were black. "I understand you. It was because of my father. He wanted me to beat you up. Fortunately, he has a very hard head. I'm surprised you didn't break that piece of wood into a thousand pieces."

"Surprised me too."

"I don't like my father much," Jerzy said matter-of-factly and looked away. "He's a bastard to my mother and two sisters. I was happy when you hit him. I am only sorry that he got up." I looked at him in surprise. "You don't feel that way about your father?" I shook my head. "Then you are lucky. Most of my friends feel the same way about their fathers."

"I'd never talk about my father like that."

Jerzy rolled his eyes. "If my father caught me, he'd beat me with an ax handle. Better that he hits me and not the others."

"I'm sorry to hear it," I said and meant it.

Jerzy shrugged. "Well, maybe you'll think about the Physics." He stood up and flicked some of the grass off his pants. He nodded curtly, then strolled off. I watched him go, then slowly shook my head.

After school ended that day, Jerzy stood waiting at the bottom of the limestone steps. Students streamed around him. I spotted him then slowly descended.

"Come on then," I said. As we began walking, three others came up. I stopped. "What's this?"

Jerzy grinned. "They need help too."

"And I suppose they also get the ax handle?"

"Something like that."

I looked at each one in turn, letting all of them know I wasn't afraid.

"Let's go then."

The four young Poles exchanged deadpan looks, then followed along.

"It is far?" Jerzy asked.

"About four kilometres."

"That's not bad. I walk at least six each way. And I help my father before I go. When I come home at night, it's the same routine. Doesn't leave much time for studying. My father doesn't think school is important, only his pigs and cows."

"My father thinks that school is the most important thing."

"You don't have to work?"

"Only in the summer time." I jerked my head at the others following behind. "Their names?"

"The skinny one is Vasily. The one with the freckles is Ivano and the other fellow is Perchik. They're good lads, farmers too, like me. I don't want to work on the farm after I'm finished. I'm sick of it." He spat on the side of the road then wiped his lips on the back of his sleeve.

"And what will you do?"

"I don't know, maybe join the army, anything that gets me out of here," he muttered.

"I want to be a mechanic," I said.

Jerzy looked at him. "You? A mechanic?"

"Why not?"

Jerzy shrugged. "No reason, I suppose. If you like the work."

"It's motors I'm interested in."

We trudged along for another forty minutes before turning down the long drive to the house. "This is it?" asked Vasily.

"Yes."

"How many families live here?" Perchik asked.

"Just one."

Jerzy let out an appreciative whistle. "And you have your own room?"

"Yes."

"Not bad," replied the larger boy.

"Come on," I said. I opened the door and gestured for the others to follow. I took them into the kitchen where they settled down to do their work. I offered them tea and biscuits, which they readily accepted, slurping and chomping noisily. We went over the Physics lesson for an hour and a half. Simmy had bounded in but when he saw the Polish boys at the table, he went silent, then backed his way out. As the boys packed up their things, Papa arrived home in his car. The boys stood on the doorstep, readying to take their leave. I introduced them and they all shook hands curtly.

"Thank you," Jerzy said. The others mumbled their thanks. They started off down the drive back to the road. Papa and I stood and watched them go.

"These boys. They're friends of yours?"

"No Papa. They're not my friends."

Papa raised his shoulders. "Then what are you doing with them?"

"I'm just helping them with their school work, that's all."

"But if they are not friends to you...?" Clearly, he seemed puzzled and wrinkled his brow. He reached under his Homburg to scratch at his scalp.

"Because I can. And because they know I'm not afraid of them."

"Don't trifle with these boys, my son," Papa said. "Better to stay out of it."

I looked at my father.

"We shall see. I'm not a Christian who turns the other cheek. If someone hits me, I hit him back and hit him harder if I have to."

Papa groaned. "Ach, this is not what I want to hear from you. Yes, take care of yourself by all means. But don't go looking for trouble. If there is trouble, it has a way of finding you on its own. Believe me, we don't need anything extra. We're full up. Got it?"

"Of course, Papa. Full up. Like you said."

Chapter 15

There came a bright day in late September and the wind stirred. I sat under an oak tree eating lunch and flipping through the Mathematics text.

"May I join you?" Maria.

"Sure. Why not?"

The girl sat down, tucking her legs underneath her but making certain her skirt was spread around, covering her knees like a blanket. "You always sit here by yourself," she said.

"Uh-huh." I looked at her. I thought her very pretty; shining blonde hair, a splash of freckles across her nose and liquid blue eyes, as blue as the sea. "It doesn't bother me."

"People are friendly if you give them a chance."

"I'm giving you a chance."

She blushed. "Do you remember my name?"

"Maria."

She nodded. "That's right. Maria Slobodan. I live in town. My father is a baker."

"Ah," I said. "And he buys flour from my father's mill."

"Yes."

"And that's how you know us?"

"Yes."

"And what does your father say? Does he say that he's charged too much? That the Jews try to cheat him?"

The girl paled. "Is that why you hate us?"

I shrugged. "I only hate those who threaten my family. You can't understand unless you've been chased in the street or had rocks thrown at you for no reason. Have you ever been beaten up because you're a Catholic?" The girl shook her head. "Then you don't know what it's like. A few months ago, my little brother was stabbed in the back with a knife. By boys who were his friends. He ran home with the knife sticking out of him. We were lucky it wasn't more serious."

Maria looked shocked. "This can't be true."

"I'm not making it up. You can believe me or not."

"You seem full of hatred."

"No. Only anger." I looked at her. "But it goes away too."

"I just wanted to tell you that I thought you were very brave the other day."

"Thank you. I just had to do the best I could. I didn't know what was going to happen."

"I was glad," said the girl.

"Really? Why?"

"I don't like that boy. He is mean and cruel."

"Believe it or not, he's not as bad as you think."

At that moment, the headmaster's assistant came out and rang his bell, signaling the end of the lunch period. "I must go. Perhaps we'll chat again?"

"Yes, why not?"

I looked at her and thought I saw something in her expression. "If you need help with any of your schoolwork, then..?" I left the question hanging.

"Maybe I will help you," she said, standing up and flicking bits of leaves from her long skirt. She began to walk away but glanced at me over her shoulder and smiled, then went off to join a group of her girlfriends. The girls in the group quickly surrounded her and began asking questions, their heads bobbing up and down excitedly. I slowly made my way back to class, not sure what to make of this girl.

That Saturday afternoon, I went into town to pick up some bread. It was early, not yet ten o'clock and the streets and shops remained quiet. I traveled to the Polish side. All the Jewish bakeries and shops had closed for shabbos. My father's true religion was business, so he kept working on Shabbos but remained respectful of those in our community who were observant of the laws. He contributed handsomely to the synagogue and gave generously to the community. The bell above the door jangled. It startled me for a moment. There were two customers in the store, the baker's wife and shop assistant behind the counter. The customers had been served and whispered together.

"Yes?" said the baker's wife. She was a large woman with doughy arms and red spots on her cheeks.

"I'd like a pumpernickel and two rye breads, please."

I spoke politely but firmly to the woman behind the counter. I noticed that her hair had once been blonde naturally but now she'd given it a platinum rinse and the darker roots showed. Her face had the pasty look of the fluffy white bread they sold in the shop. Her elbows were dimpled and her hands were thick like a man's. She picked the breads off the shelf and bagged them quickly.

"Anything else?" she asked.

"Yes," I said slowly. "Some of these rolls. A dozen."

The baker's wife nodded, then quickly counted out the rolls. The shop remained silent. All interactions had stopped. It was as if I had entered a foreign world.

"How much?"

"Seven zlotys," she replied impassively.

"That much?"

"You think I cheat you?" Her plucked eyebrows went up.

I smiled woodenly and tossed the money on the counter, then picked up the paper bags, turned and walked out. I felt their eyes on my back. I wondered if it would always be this way.

As I closed the door I didn't notice the young girl standing there.

"Hello," she said and I jumped. She laughed pleasantly. "I didn't mean to scare you."

"I didn't see you there, Maria."

"Was Mama mean to you?"

"No more than most. It doesn't bother me," I lied.

"Then you're more tolerant than I am."

I took a good look at her.

"I hate this," she said with unexpected vehemence.

"Hate what?"

"This dislike. This prejudice."

"Why should it bother you? You're not involved."

"It's not what a good Christian should do."

"Does a good Christian stop and talk to a Jew in the street?"

"Why shouldn't she? We're supposed to be charitable to everyone." And she squeezed her thin lips together.

I laughed. "I didn't mean to make fun of you. Let's get some tea. What do you think? There's a cafe not far from here and it's open."

She hesitated. She bit her lip, then decided.

"Of course. Let's go."

She took my arm. Together we walked down the block and around the corner. I glanced back and saw the curtains rustle in the shop window.

The cafe sat nearly deserted at that hour. Out of consideration for her, I selected a table away from the window. We seated ourselves. A waiter pulled himself away from his morning coffee and paper and came to take our order.

"Yes?" he asked, listlessly.

"Two teas with lemon and a roll with butter," I said.

The waiter wrote down the order on his worn pad. "Right away sir," he said laconically and sauntered off.

Maria giggled. "He's very funny, don't you think?"

"He's a lazy sod and doesn't want to work."

"You're always so serious, Mordecai."

Her observation surprised me. "Am I?" And then I thought about it. "Yes, I suppose I am. Is there anything wrong with that?"

"No, of course not." She smiled prettily. "But don't you like to have fun?"

"Yeah, sure."

She burst out laughing. After a moment, I joined her.

"There, that's better," she said.

"You're very handsome when you laugh."

"Then I'll do it more often."

She took a sip of her tea. "And how are you liking school?"

I held the teacup. "It's all right, I suppose."

"You've made friends?"

"Not really. But I didn't expect to."

"Why not?"

"I think you know why."

"And what about me? Do you consider me your friend?"

She asked the question seriously. She held the cup just below her bottom lip, practically resting it on the rim, her eyes fixed, a fearful hope on her face.

"If you like," I said softly. "Perhaps my only friend."

She smiled then, warmly, welcoming me to her. I didn't expect it but something moved me to put out my hand. She placed the cup in its saucer and put her hand in mine. I closed my fingers around hers.

"Here you are!" roared the baker's wife, all quivering outrage. The sagging flesh of her arms lay caked with white powder. Her eyes looked inflamed. She hauled Maria to her feet and brought her hand across her cheek in a vicious smack that made me flinch. I jumped up.

"You have no right..."

The baker's wife shook her fist under my nose. "Shut up you."

"Mama, no, please. We were just drinking tea." Maria cried, sobbing into her hands. Her mother yanked at her arm.

"You're coming home now." She dragged her daughter out of the cafe. I froze, watching the furious figure of the baker's wife and her frail daughter pulled along with her like a broken doll. Anger seethed in me. All eyes were on me and saw me for what I was, a mere boy outmatched by the vengeance of a mother. Even the waiter looked at me sympathetically as he came to clean up. Maria's cup had tipped over, the roll knocked to the floor.

"I wish…"

I reached into my pocket but the waiter shook me off.

"No, no. It's all right," he said putting the dishes quickly on his tray. "I pity her with a mother like that."

"Yes. Me too."

I picked up the bread and quickly left the cafe, walking briskly up the street without looking back. This was something I couldn't defeat, couldn't pummel into submission.

Chapter 16

Beulah lay curled up in a ball rocking and moaning. She held the blankets tightly, pulling them around her. They looked like a shroud.

"Oh Mama," she groaned. "Mama, mama."

I sat by her side holding her hand.

"Keep talking, Mr. G. Keep talking."

"Maybe you should get some rest?"

"Can't rest, I'm on fire. Talk to me. Take my mind away, okay?"

"Okay." So I continued.

Krasnowicz, 1929

The summer I turned sixteen, I began my last year of high school.

As I rode my bicycle to school that first morning, I thought about Maria and in fact, could think of nothing else. I had only seen her once all summer and that was by chance. She worked in her parents' bakery, kept as a prisoner locked away. Each time I passed by I looked for her. Then one day, she stepped out of the shop. She wore an apron just like her mother and I wondered if that was to be her life. I waited until she walked down the street and turned the corner. I grabbed her elbow.

"You frightened me."

"I didn't mean to."

Maria looked around her. I saw her fearful look and it saddened me.

"Come, let's keep walking. I have errands to do. They expect me back soon."

I fell into step beside her. Now she seemed quite small, petite. She had to turn her head upward to look at me fully.

"When can we see each other?"

She shook her head, her hair swinging. It caught the early morning light, strands becoming translucent. "We can't. It's too dangerous. Just talking to you on the street is dangerous enough."

"Am I such a monster?"

She bit her lip. "No, of course not. It's just the way they are."

"And you?"

"You know I don't feel that way. I'm rarely out of their sight. If we go out it's as a family. We'll have to wait until school."

"But that's another five weeks."

"That's not long," she replied.

"It is to me."

"Don't be childish."

"Don't call me that. Am I an idiot because I miss you?"

Maria turned her back on me, her posture stiff and unyielding. I saw her shoulders shake. She didn't make a sound but I realized she was crying. I grasped her gently by the shoulders and turned her toward me.

"I wish you hadn't said that. I was doing so well." Tears streaked her face. She used my shirt to dry her eyes. "We'll just have to wait. There's nothing else to do. I'm praying for school to start."

"Me too..." I didn't know what else to say.

Maria roused herself and pushed away from me.

"Do you tell your family everything, Mordecai?"

"Not everything."

"And...?"

"They know I've been seeing someone."

"Someone who is not Jewish?"

"I don't know. Perhaps."

"But you haven't said anything?"

"No, I haven't."

"There you see. It's both of us. We are guilty, the two of us."

"Partners in crime," I said. "Romeo and Juliet."

"Don't say that," she cried. "It had a horrid ending. You think we're star-crossed lovers?"

"I don't know, Maria."

"I must go in here," she said and indicated the milliner's. "Don't come with me. I'll see you at school." She caressed my cheek, then turned and strode into the shop. I stood on Sandusky Street, suddenly alone, fingering my damp shirt.

And now as I rode my bicycle to school, I thought of nothing but her. Everything had the feeling of familiarity; the road, school, the woods, the mill, even Frederick had returned. Thank god Katya had left for school.

I had come to terms with my feelings for Frederick. I still didn't like him but realized that Frederick had done me a favor.

The first day of his return, we had sparred for an hour. It was devilishly hot but I wasn't bothered. Frederick showed me some new moves. That meant I was knocked flat on my back again and again. This irritated and frustrated me, but I didn't feel like taking Frederick's head off. Not this time.

I knew Jerzy and his cronies would be waiting for me. I had seen them over the summer. They came to get their flour from the mill. Jerzy's father never came, not after the last time.

I was known at the school, but not popular. Students would nod or say hello to me but only Jerzy and Maria actually said anything. I parked my bike. Students gathered in groups, chatting, waiting for the morning bell. I strode along, looking for Maria. Each time I thought I saw her, my heart began to pound. As I approached a group of young girls, one of them turned toward me, breaking away from the others. It was Katrina, a slim, dark-haired girl.

"Have you seen Maria?" I asked her.

She looked about her, then took me by the elbow.

"Come with me," she said.

"What is it?"

When we moved out of earshot, Katrina stopped.

"Look," she said. "I'm not sure how to tell you this but Maria isn't coming back to school."

"What?"

"Her parents have sent her away."

"But why? Where?"

Katrina looped a strand of hair behind her left ear. She peered at me intently. "You don't know?"

I shook my head.

"Boys are such fools," she muttered. "They didn't want her to see you so they dumped her in a convent school."

"Do you know where?"

Katrina shook her head. "No."

"Can you find out?"

Her dark eyes narrowed. "You care for her that much?" Katrina looked puzzled.

I didn't answer. I felt embarrassed to be talking about feelings in front of this girl.

The girl shrugged. "I'll see what I can do. She's bound to write me sometime. Don't get your hopes up, okay? I might be able to find out something. But no promises."

"I understand."

The girl smiled then.

"It must be something to care that much," she said, then turned away, back to her girlfriends.

The first bell of the new school year rang out across the courtyard. As I drew near the limestone steps, I kicked out, striking the nearest bike. It toppled into the next and the entire line of bikes fell over in a screeching metallic wave. I stalked into the school, my mind turned inward in a stony silence.

I came out of myself when I got to the gym and changed into my shorts. Professor Laszlo greeted me and began to lace on my gloves.

"You had a good summer, Goldman?" I nodded. "You look fit. That's good. Did you work in the mill again?"

"Yes. Not that I wanted to."

"I saw your friend, Frederick Valens, in town. We took a drink together."

"He's my father's friend, not mine."

Laszlo's swarthy face tightened. "I see. Valens and I boxed together on the national team. Different weight classes, of course. He was a light heavy-weight then. And I am a natural middle-weight. More like you, eh?"

"I guess."

"What do you weigh now?"

"Ninety kilos."

"And your height?"

"One point eight two meters."

"Good. You haven't quite filled out yet but you will. We were discussing you, Goldman." Laszlo finished tying the right glove and began with the left. "Valens mentioned the army boxing team to me and I think it is a good idea. It will give you something to do during your service. But afterward, what about that? Do you know what you want to do?"

"I'd like to study mechanical engineering in Paris."

Laszlo tied off the left glove, then stepped back and surveyed his handiwork. He grunted with satisfaction. "Engineering is useful. A good profession. We were thinking that you may wish to try out for the national boxing team. You'd travel to matches in various cities and even other countries too. Wouldn't you like to see Europe?"

I tested the gloves, smacking them together explosively. I shook my head. "I don't want to box for Poland, do you hear? I hate this fucking country."

I clammed up, realizing maybe I had gone too far, then shrugged and stared at my feet.

Laszlo's eyes blazed. "You are lucky I am a tolerant man," he said through gritted teeth. "I will let this childish outburst go by this time - but only this time."

"Yes Professor. I'm sorry, I..."

"What's the matter with you, Goldman? You're like an enraged bull..." And then Laszlo stopped.

"So that's how it is, is it? Difficulties with a young lady?"

I continued to stare sullenly at my toes.

"Work it out in the gym. You'll feel better."

I looked at him, then nodded. I spent the next ninety minutes going through the routine; ten minutes of warm-ups, fifteen minutes of footwork, fifteen minutes on the punching bag, five minutes of skipping, twenty minutes of calisthenics and the rest sparring with teammates.

Laszlo pulled the windows open but heat radiated in the gymnasium. I felt better. I punched myself into exhaustion. I ran into the shower before heading off to Physics class, taught by a German-born Pole named Roediger. He insisted that students call him Herr Professor Roediger and wore a monocle in his right eye.

"Have fun with Herr Professor Roediger," Laszlo called, enunciating his colleague's name with precision. I considered what Laszlo had said. The national team. Even Frederick thought I might make it. I knew I'd never try out but given that Frederick and Laszlo had boxed at that level, I felt pleased at their confidence in me but of course, I'd never admit it.

Chapter 17

I watched Professor Roediger's back as he wrote complex formulas on the board. His fingers were smeared with chalk and the dust clung to his tweed jacket. After some ten minutes, he put down the chalk, slapped his hands together sending up a small cloud, and surveyed the class. A neatly trimmed Van Dyke offset his round face. Dark beetle brows furrowed as he surveyed the room intensely, the green eyes strangely vacant and somewhat chilling. I felt warm in the airless room but the Professor appeared at ease, enjoying our discomfort. I thought of Maria and what she might be doing.

"Young gentlemen," Herr Professor Roediger began in a low voice. "This is the most difficult class you will likely have. I do not suffer fools and idiots. If you are an idiot then I have no time for you. I hope this is clearly understood. Physics is for superior minds and if you have any desire to leave this institution successfully then you must pay attention and be prepared to work very hard." I glanced over at Jerzy who caught my eye and shook his head once, his face sinking at the words. I knew that this was Jerzy's do or die class. If he failed, it was the farm forever.

The remainder of the class consisted of drills. The rotund professor went over each equation he had written on the board and stated it would be the only time it was to be explained. We had better copy them down quickly and learn them immediately. Everyone bent their heads to the task. Roediger surveyed the quiet intensity in the classroom.

It was the last class of the day. When it was dismissed, I and my fellow penitents filed out slowly under the watchful, squinting eye of Herr Professor Roediger. I walked behind Jerzy up the aisle to the door.

"Mr. Goldman."

I turned to face the rotund man.

"Yes?"

"A moment, if you please."

I hesitated while the others walked around me. Finally, the room had emptied.

"Herr Professor?"

"You enjoy Physics, do you?" the little man asked, bouncing on the balls of his feet.

"I do." There was a point to this, I thought.

Roediger took a step closer. "You captain the boxing team I hear."

"Yes sir."

"Professor Laszlo says very good things about you."

"Thank you."

"You see, Mr. Goldman, in my day," and he hesitated slightly, "Jews were only allowed to stand in the classroom, not to sit. But I want to assure you that in my classroom you are welcome." I wasn't sure if the man was mocking me or being sincere and so I kept quiet but watched the Professor intensely.

"I can see that you are insulted by the suggestion of that. You have pride. I would be careful about letting this pride control you. Some of my most gifted students were Jews. They were true Physicists, some of whom went on to distinguish themselves in the field. I don't know if that is your intention but I would like to suggest that you concentrate on your studies first. Sport is all right such as it is but it is the mind, Mr. Goldman, that is the finest muscle humans possess. I won't tolerate any lapses in my class or make any allowances because you are the captain of the boxing team or any other team. You must be prepared to work and work hard to achieve. I just wanted to make that clear to you."

"I understand. I must be grateful to you for being allowed to sit in your classroom and I must work harder than anyone else because I am a Jew," I said.

Roediger's round face reddened with anger. "Don't be insolent, boy."

"I wasn't sir. Merely clarifying the situation."

Roediger swallowed his anger though his fists were balled at his sides. "I will make an exception this time, Mr. Goldman. Yes, you are very proud. Work hard. That is all I ask."

"I always work hard, sir. At everything."

Roediger nodded curtly. "Good. Then we understand each other."

"Yes sir. I believe we do." I turned quickly and precisely, then strode out of the room. I rode home furiously. Pompous little bastard. I slammed the front door so hard the windows rattled in the parlor. Mama looked up from her sewing as I stalked in and threw myself down on the sofa opposite her.

Her glasses had slipped to the end of her nose. "What is it? You seem upset."

I blurted out what happened.

"Mordecai," his mother said sternly. "You must feel sorry for such a small-minded individual. But is he a good Physics teacher, do you think?"

"I suppose so. I've heard that he is."

"Then leave it at that. Learn what you can and ignore the rest. Rise above."

Mama was not an ignorant shtetl woman. She had gone to the university at Crakow where she had studied science and mathematics.

"Show him by doing well. That is the greatest victory. Triumph of the intellect."

I knew she was right but my anger ran too deep. "I'll think about it," I muttered. I shook my head and sighed.

"You seem to know the right things to say."

"Of course. What good would I be otherwise?" She turned her attention back to her sewing.

"Is Simmy home?"

"Upstairs in his room."

I climbed the steps. Simmy's door was open. He lay on his bed reading.

"Hey bucher boy."

Simmy glanced up. "Fists of iron. Did you beat anyone today?"

I grinned and faked an attempt to slap his cheek. Simmy didn't flinch. I sat on the end of his bed. "What are you reading?"

Simmy sighed and put the book down. "If you must know, I'm reading Hegel."

"Oh and is this on the approved list at the yeshiva? This German philosopher?"

Simmy smiled indulgently. "Of course it isn't."

"So why are you reading it?"

"For pleasure."

"This is what you read for pleasure?" I shook my head sadly. "Only thirteen and an old man. How can you get pleasure from such things?"

"It is the ideas I like. The things he says make me think. I like the religious texts too but this is different." I stood up and yawned, absently unbuttoning my shirt.

"Where are you going?" Simmy asked.

"Nowhere. I'm just getting changed out of my school uniform. Dinner will be ready soon."

Chapter 18

I descended the staircase to the dining room where the family awaited.

I watched Mama as she read aloud from a letter she'd received from Katya.

"...I have seen where Kafka is buried, such a forlorn, isolated place. When the days are gloomy, Prague can be the most forbidding city but on the whole it radiates elegance and beauty. I spend my days at the university buried in my studies. There is so much detail, so much to learn. After classes, I return to my room and study more in the evenings, often until midnight or later. Classes begin again at eight o'clock. It doesn't leave much time for anything else. Since I arrived, I've been to one Mahler concert and to the cinema, once only. Last Saturday, I spent a few hours at the art gallery but that's all. There are a few Polish students here and I've gotten to know them a little. The Czechs are friendlier and more outgoing. They don't seem to care who you are or where you're from. This is a refreshing attitude, don't you think? I have been introduced to the local beer and although I don't care for beer as a rule, it isn't bad. The locals are very proud of it and indeed proud of everything that is Czech...their institutions, government, culture...it's invigorating in a way to feel this free, this liberated. My dear parents, I miss you so and our home. I long to return but know there is much yet ahead of me. I will return as a physician and will treat the sick and injured as I always intended. I believe in dreams and that they can come true. Give my love to Mordecai and Simmy. I hope they are staying out of trouble, especially Mordecai; I'm not there to stitch him up when he needs it. I'll write again soon. All my love. Katya."

A tear rolled down Mama's plump cheek and plopped on to the tablecloth.

"There, there, my dear," Papa said and patted her on the shoulder. "It won't be so long. You'll see, the time will pass quickly and she'll return to us."

"Yes, of course you're right, Chaim. But still..." and she left her thoughts hanging in the air.

"Are we eating tonight?" Simmy asked.

The next day, I worked out with Laszlo in the gymnasium. Most of the students had left for the day. Jerzy and his buddies lounged in a corner, waiting. After physics class, Roediger had heaped on the work. Jerzy, bewildered and confused, sought me out once again. "Okay," I had told him. "After I do some work with Laszlo."

Laszlo talked, telling me to counter right, then left. He moved me back and forth, up and down non-stop, as if it were a strange little dance we followed in unison.

"Move your head," Laszlo ordered. "You'll get hit, easily. Step in. That's it. Put your weight into it. Now counter. One. Two. And again. One. Two. Go to the body. Hard. Hit the ribs. Harder. Harder. Again." My arms sagged. "Arms up. Up I say. I can take you out with an overhand right. Child's play. All right. Rest." I dropped my arms and staggered over to the bench.

Laszlo came over to me. "It's hot, I know. But don't you think others feel it too? Your opponents will be in top condition. Some of them will be bigger than you and faster. If you let yourself give in to it, you'll be knocked down in the first round. There's a great deal more to boxing than just skill and physicality. It's the supreme test of character, Goldman. To see what you are made of, right? You haven't been tested yet. But you will be and then you'll come to know yourself. Let's hope you like what you see, hmm?"

I didn't say anything, just buried my face in the towel up to the bottoms of my eyes where I could look at Laszlo, the dank gymnasium and the four Polish youths in the corner watching me with either contempt or amusement. Jerzy lifted his hand in acknowledgement. I didn't respond.

"You should have worked harder over the summer," Laszlo said.

"I trained for the month of August," I said.

"Not good enough." Laszlo paused, thinking he had gone far enough. "Go and get changed. You've done enough for today," he said gently. "Your friends are waiting."

"My friends...," I repeated in a bitter tone, then stood up awkwardly. My legs felt tired, even a bit rubbery. I walked over to Jerzy. "I'll be out in a minute." And headed off to shower and change

I walked my bicycle while Jerzy took long strides beside me. Since that first week of school four years earlier, Jerzy had been to the Goldman household many times. I had never seen where Jerzy lived. It was never discussed. Jerzy told me that his mother and father had asked if he'd witnessed the blood sacrifice of Christian babies.

"I told them that good Christians worked in the household and they appeared not to be corrupted in any way. Still, my parents were unbelieving, not willing to accept what I said and remained suspicious. They believed that God was with them on this and consulted the local priest, Father Kulik, to confirm it. In truth, he did that and more, calling the Jews God's cursed children who must mend their ways or be punished in the kingdom of heaven." Jerzy barked laughter. "Such foolish people. I don't know where they get this nonsense."

"It's hammered into their heads down through generations. It's always been that way and I don't see it changing much," I said.

"If we Poles are to survive, we can't be that ignorant. We must change our society from the ground up."

"Still preaching revolution, I see. You have been making the wrong kind of friends. There are revolutionaries behind every tree, it seems. You'd better be careful. That's dangerous talk."

"I don't give a shit," Jerzy replied brushing his hair to the side away from his eyes. It had grown long and shaggy over the summer. "The priests can hear me, I don't care. We'll crush them."

"And how will you do that?"

"By abolishing all religion."

"That will make them happy."

"It's not about pleasing anyone. If they're upset, who cares? It's for the good of the people. All the people." And he smacked his large hand into his fist.

"People won't give up religion without a fight."

"We'll make them."

"And how will you do that?"

"We'll destroy all the houses of worship everywhere across the country and make it illegal to pray in public."

"So, they'll pray in private."

Jerzy shrugged. "Maybe so. But their spirit will be crushed. A few public hangings wouldn't hurt, either. Set a strong example."

"So you instill terror and that will be better?"

Jerzy smiled wryly. "Sometimes, people need a little convincing. But after, it will be better because they'll realize it's for their own good and then we can pull everyone together as a people. There'll be no distractions. Everything that happens will benefit the people and only the people. We all will share. There'll be no differences between us. We all shall be brothers."

"Until you need to hang someone to prove a point?" I was unable to take this drivel seriously.

"I know it sounds harsh but most will be better off, believe me. And the same will be true of you too. For the Jews I mean. You'll have nothing to fear from us."

I stopped. "That's a laugh."

"You make fun now. But you will see. In time," the larger boy said. "It will come to pass."

"Speaking of passing, you won't pass Physics if we don't hurry up."

Chapter 19

That evening, Mama handed me a letter. I stared at the envelope, not certain of the handwriting. I noticed the postmark; Cracow. A plain envelope made of coarse paper. I looked at the elegant hand, the delicate loops and suddenly knew. I ran up to my room.

"Mordecai?"

Eagerly, I tore the envelope open feeling the thick pages between my fingers.

"…My Dearest Mordecai. Have you forgotten me? I pray you haven't. I hope you aren't too upset about my leaving but it happened very quickly. My parents didn't give me a chance to say goodbye to you. I'm attending a girl's school that's run by the nuns. They're very strict here. No visitors are allowed and we may write letters only twice a month. We say prayers three times a day. I don't mind that so much except that I pray to leave this place. I should like to see you, to look at your face, just talk a little. You can't write me here. I have my own room because I'm a senior girl but it's very small and very bare. I do feel as if I'm in a prison. The days are long and tedious. How I long to touch your hand, my dear Mordecai, hold your face and look into your eyes. At night in bed, I feel like my soul is burning. I'm so unhappy but I must obey the wishes of my parents. Why must it be this way? We get very little news here only what the nuns tell us. Is all well with you? Are you enjoying school? Say you aren't enjoying it too much, will you? And the boxing? I hope you haven't been hurt. I worry so much. I'd hate to see your beautiful face battered about. I'm writing to stay alive. Please forgive me if this seems so incoherent. I trust we shall meet and talk soon. I pray for it every day. Just to see you again. Love, Maria."

I clutched the letter, pressed it to my face and inhaled. To find a trace of her, just the littlest bit. I wanted to smile and frown together. I was thrilled that she wrote but desperate to find her. The postmark said Cracow and had been mailed three days prior. How many convent schools were in the Cracow area? There could be dozens. I lay back on my bed feeling feverish and soon fell asleep.

I opened my eyes and focused properly. Mama sat in the chair opposite. She had a distracted expression on her face. "Mama. What are you doing?" In her hand, she held the letter. "You had no right."

I sat up and moved off the bed quickly snatching the letter from her. "You shouldn't have read this. It's private."

"How long has this been going on?" she asked in a low voice.

"What?"

"This...this love affair."

"It is not what you think. We're only friends. She's the only one who talks to me."

"Nothing more has happened?" She placed her hands to her breast, a saint in supplication.

"Nothing. I swear it."

"Tell me, Mordecai. What are your feelings for this girl?"

"I care for her. I like her a lot. What's wrong with that?"

"But you both go against her parents' wishes."

"They don't care. They just hate me because I'm a Jew."

"Naturally. What other reason would they have?"

"I could be a poor peasant, boorish and uneducated. That may be reason enough."

"Still, they would prefer a lout, Mordecai. Unfortunately, it's the way things are. What are you going to do?"

"To see her, of course. She needs my help."

"What kind of help can you offer her?"

"I don't know, exactly...my support. She's all alone in that hell hole."

"Maybe she is just a young girl given to flights of fancy. Perhaps she over-dramatizes her situation? Has this occurred to you?"

"No. She wouldn't lie."

Mama moved to the edge of the bed. She took my hands in her own. I could feel their warmth and the roughened palms callused from housework.

"I don't want to see you do anything you may regret. I don't want you to get hurt. We have a certain place in this society. And it can be a dangerous place, one where we must be alert at all times to see what will be thrown at us. It has always been this way and will always be. In some way, this could happen to you with this girl. I can't stop you. You're almost grown. Next year, you go into the military. I can't protect you either. But we have faith in your practical nature and good sense. When it comes to love, things change. There is no such thing as good sense. What you are doing could hurt all of us."

"You sound like Katya."

"Katya is sensible."

I wanted to blurt out that she wasn't so sensible when it came to her feelings for Frederick. But I bit my tongue.

"You're playing with fire."

I pulled away. "You don't understand..."

"You think you're the only one to ever fall in love?"

"Of course not."

"Then don't act like you are. Otherwise, this will end badly."

"I don't care...besides, I don't even know where she is...so..."

Mama sighed. "You will find her."

"How do you know?"

"Just because I do," she replied.

Her certainty was unnerving because I knew she was right.

Chapter 20

"So, it was true love, Mr. G?"
  I swallowed hard. "Something like that," I croaked.
  "What happened to her?"
  "Get some rest, now. You need to save your strength."
  "Keep talking, Mr. G. You're doing fine."

A gloved fist arced upward and caught me in the forehead, snapping my head back. I staggered, shook it off then waded in again. A right jab caught me on the chin and then another, followed by a solid blow to the ribs. Jerzy stepped back, looked over at Laszlo, then shrugged. Laszlo motioned him in. I wasn't paying attention. I felt relaxed, kept my stance in perfect balance. I just wasn't moving, wasn't countering any blows or punching back. Jerzy stepped in with a few tentative blows to the midriff. I looked up at him, then raised my gloves. This time when Jerzy stepped in, I countered but held back, just tapping Jerzy lightly. I thought of Maria, picturing her in a white cotton gown getting ready for sleep, kneeling at the foot of her bed, her fine hair brushed out, saying her prayers before slipping beneath the cool, clean sheets. I believed then that when she closed her eyes, she saw me and we were together, hand in hand. I stepped back and blocked an uppercut, then stepped forward with two blows to the middle, a quick combination to the head ending with a sharp punch that caught Jerzy square on the jaw and forced him to fall on his rump. Jerzy shook his head. Laszlo waved his arms, his face dark with anger.

"What was that?" he demanded, and helped Jerzy to his feet.

"What do you mean?" I asked.

"That wasn't sparring, it was dancing. You must have thought you were at the ballet. I can see you're not really here. In a tournament, you would have been knocked out in ten seconds. Perhaps you should be. It might be good for you. Get dressed. You're finished for today."

"I'm sorry, Professor." I glanced at Jerzy, then turned and headed for the change area.

Laszlo waved his hand dismissively. Jerzy curtsied, then ran on his tiptoes in a lumbering way, to strip off his clothes and get showered.

I stood under the water feeling the water purify me.

"You've got it bad," Jerzy said over the hissing of the water on the cement floor. I watched it flow into the drain.

"What?"

"I think you know," said the Polish youth. "You're in love. You look like a sick dog who whines for its bitch."

I glanced at him but said nothing. I didn't want to break the sanctity of my thoughts and feelings.

"They're nothing but trouble you know. Before you can blink, you'll be married and have babies. I don't believe in that. I believe in free love."

"What is that? Not paying for it?"

"Of course not," Jerzy replied with contempt, soaping his arms and chest. "It means that men and women are free to choose their partners and be with as many as they like. There is no single bond to one man or one woman but to the group. They are one."

"And if one of the men or women happens to be ugly and repulses you?"

"Then you have the right to say no and no one gets upset. They just move on to the next person. In this way, it's all understood. There are no games, no guessing. It's straightforward and simple."

"What about children?"

"Children belong to the group. They don't have individual parents but each adult is a parent to all of them at different times."

"And you think this will work?"

"Absolutely. I'm convinced of it."

"And you don't think there will be jealousy or possessiveness? Or that children will go to their natural parents by instinct?"

"Not if it's done right. Believe me, I would rather have had other parents to choose from than my own. They understand nothing. I can't discuss any of my ideas with them. They would call a priest and have me exorcised. How can you talk to people like that? How can you expect them to understand?"

"And they're wondering how they got a son like you. They're wondering where you came from."

"Is it wrong to want to improve society?" he asked.

"But still," I said. "These are radical ideas. I have the feeling they're not your own."

Jerzy shrugged. "I have an older cousin. I went to a few meetings with him and then I began to read on my own. What they're talking about makes sense to me. More sense than slaving on a farm for the rest of my life."

Jerzy turned the shower taps off. We each grabbed a threadbare towel and began to dry off.

"At least," I said. "They pay for your education."

Jerzy shrugged. "My father sold a piece of his land to pay for it."

"Why?"

"My mother convinced him that a good education is the way to a better life."

"She's right. Without a good education, you'll be a peasant forever."

"And what will my education make of me?" Jerzy asked. "I'll probably still end up a farmer. Farming is a noble profession even if I do hate it. Or I'll be a soldier and die in the next war."

"How do you know there will be another war?"

"There is always another war. History tells us that, doesn't it? Do you ever listen in the Polish history class?"

"Of course I listen," I replied.

"What is it but a series of wars, conflicts, invasions and the like? Poland isn't a country that controls its own destiny. It's in the grip of others. We weren't involved in the last war but the next one will be right here. And perhaps then I will find my calling."

"You're a Marxist. Marxists don't believe in war."

"Perhaps it's just another name for revolution."

I finished buttoning my trousers, then hooked my suspenders over the white shirt. I went to the grimy, cracked mirror to adjust my tie. "You think revolution is the answer? Overthrow the established order and begin again?"

"The world needs a cataclysm to shake it up," Jerzy replied with a tight smile. He sat on the bench with the damp towel around his shoulders. "Don't you think it would be good for you?"

I looked at him. "For me?"

"The Jews."

"Why?"

"After the revolution there'll be no discrimination. All will be equal."

"And some are more equal than others," I said wryly.

"I'm serious."

"Of course, of course," I murmured and turned back to the mirror to comb my hair.

"I should have decked you when I had the chance. Daydreaming about some girl." Jerzy snorted.

"Why didn't you?"

"I didn't want to hit you when you weren't looking. It wouldn't be right. If I am to beat you, then it should be square, full on."

"You can't beat me."

"Is that so?" Jerzy stood up, letting the towel drop. "Who is she? Is she that important?"

"Never mind. I won't make that mistake again."

"You were distracted. That's dangerous in a boxing ring."

"I didn't mean that. I meant admitting to it."

"You need to keep your guard up."

"I will."

"Come," Jerzy said. "The revolution awaits."

In spite of myself, I laughed.

At lunch I lay on my back staring up at the clouds.

"Hello," I said, squinting up into the sun.

"I know where they've taken her," she said. It was the dark-haired girl, the friend of Maria's.

"Where?" I asked, sitting up alertly

"To a convent school on the outskirts of Cracow."

"Which school?"

The girl seemed to be ignoring me. She looked off into the distance. "I shouldn't even be seen talking to you. My parents might find out."

"I won't eat you," I said.

"That's not what they say," she replied but smiled down at me.

"It's like that, is it?"

The girl nodded. "I saw her the day before she left. She was very upset. She wanted to finish here. She wanted to say goodbye."

I stood up and brushed myself off. The girl moved back a pace.

"Don't be nervous."

"I'm not," she replied airily. "I can contact her for you."

"How will you do that?"

"Her parents are going for a visit in two days' time. I'm sending a letter with them for her. You can include a message with it."

"What sort of message?"

"Whatever you like. I won't read it."

"What about Maria's parents?"

The girl sniffed. "I shouldn't think so. It'll be sealed when I give it to them. They have every reason to trust me." She smiled conspiratorially, small lines like hooks appearing at the corners of her delicate mouth.

"And why should I trust you?"

The girl kept smiling. "Maria is my friend. She's unhappy. I just want to help her. Those convents must be terrible places, like being kept in a prison." She shuddered.

I looked at this girl with her dark curls and green eyes. She was very pretty, tall with slim legs and a nicely developed chest beneath her school sweater.

"All right. I'll write a letter and give it to you."

"I must have it tomorrow."

"I'll write it tonight."

The girl smiled again. "Good. It's settled then. I'll see you tomorrow." She backed away, keeping an eye on me while I remained motionless. I spent the rest of the day thinking about what I would write and how we could meet.

As I cycled home, I had an idea. The following week, the boxing team was in Cracow for a tournament. There had to be some spare time in the schedule. If I could get Laszlo to arrange two matches in one day, then I'd have a whole day to spend on my own. I'd speak to him about it and see if it could be done.

Chapter 21

When I awoke the next morning, the small clock on the mantle read 7:10 am. Classes started at eight. Throwing back the covers, I leapt out of bed, rinsed my face with cold water, then toweled off vigorously. I heard my mother's and brother's voices downstairs, echoing faintly up from the kitchen. I burst in, wild-eyed.

"Why didn't you wake me?"

"You were sleeping so soundly, I didn't have the heart," Mama replied. "I have toast and tea ready for you. Perhaps you'd like an egg? It would be no trouble."

"Thanks. No time." I stood at the table and slurped the tea. The toast disappeared in three bites.

"Slow down. You'll get indigestion."

"I'm running late." And glared at Simmy as if he had some part in his dilemma. Simmy took this as his cue to stand up and stretch.

"I'll be late too. Can't keep the rabbi waiting, now can I?"

"No darling, you can't. Run along now. Mordecai, more toast?"

"I'll eat on the way," I said grabbing another slice, taking a last gulp of hot tea and bolted for the door.

"Bye," I called, and grabbing my books and lunch from the hall table, flung on my jacket, and charged through the front door. The books thunked into the bike carrier as I pedaled furiously down the road. I wanted to catch Katrina before classes. I reached into the pocket for the note. To my relief, it was there. I pedaled faster. I might make it in thirty minutes if the road stayed clear.

I flew down the road, eyes smarting from the wind. Mud flew off the front tire and splattered my pants below the knee. I'd forgotten the pair of old socks I normally pulled over my pant cuffs for protection. The uniform would be a mess. Laszlo wouldn't care but Professor Roediger might. I'd have to see about getting cleaned up before class. About a kilometre from the school, a military lorry rumbled around the bend. I swerved in front of it, but lost control of the bicycle as the back tire skittered back and forth. The lorry driver pulled on his horn and stepped on the brakes but it moved too fast, and I flew head over heels across the road into the brush. A moment passed. I lay face up staring at the sky. The lorry had disappeared.

I forced myself to my feet. My head throbbed and my right pant leg had been ripped up to the knee. The bicycle was a mess. The front wheel was bent. It would be impossible to ride. I began to run, pushing the bicycle in front of me. Sweat ran into the corners of my eyes as I focused on the road. Finally, the school appeared. Would she have waited? I swiped at my face with the sleeve of my splattered jacket. Yes. It was Katrina waiting under the boughs of the big oak tree. She looked up. I saw the look on her face.

"I'm sorry...I was run off the road. That's why I'm late but I have the letter here," I gasped and handed it to her.

She nodded and took it from me, tucking it away in her schoolbag. "You must be careful. It won't do Maria any good if you are flattened by a lorry."

"I was late and in a hurry."

"Even still," she said in an irritated tone "The bell has rung. It's time to go in. I don't want to be late." She marched off. I didn't know what upset her. Was it my appearance or something else? I shook my head and started to wheel the bicycle toward the school.

Herr Professor Roediger took one look at me and motioned me aside.

"And what is this, Mr. Goldman? What have you to say?"

"I had an accident on my bicycle. A lorry. It ran me off the road."

"Then you are lucky to be alive," said the rotund professor, tugging at his goatee and adjusting his pince-nez. "But this is no condition to be in. It does not reflect well on the school or your classmates."

"Yes sir."

"I would go home and change."

"Yes sir."

"And be quick about it. You will miss too much work otherwise. Hurry now." And the professor dismissed me with a curt wave of his pudgy hand.

"Yes sir. I will." I wheeled about and walked back down the long hallway. As I walked back along the road, I felt light-hearted, knowing that Maria would receive the letter and with luck we would meet in Cracow.

Chapter 22

I started the engine of the ancient ambulance. It turned over in the cold air but failed to catch. I stepped out, lifted the hood and, removing a screwdriver from my coat pocket, adjusted the carburetor. I closed the hood carefully, then slid back in behind the wheel. I turned the key and the cranky engine sputtered, then caught, roaring to life. I drove forward slowly, then stopped and put the ambulance in neutral while I closed the barn doors. The hospital had forty-five beds and just the two ambulances, one of which had broken down. It was all I could do to keep the other running given the lack of spare parts. I had become a cunning scavenger, however. Whenever I saw a derelict vehicle or a tractor, I'd strip down the engine then re-tool the parts in the small workshop I'd put together at the back of the barn. Demand for petrol had soared. Bartering was common; a piston for a carburetor, a spare tire for a repaired gas tank and so on.

For the past eighteen months the border had held. Sometimes, when I drove over that way, I could see the movement of German troops and armaments, machines chewing up dust, clanking mechanically, engines screaming, men on parade singing their blood songs. It gave me a cold feeling. There had been no word from the family. All the letters Katya sent came back unopened. Unspeakable fear bonded us and we tried to carry on our daily tasks while feebly pushing away the dread that ate through the veneer of routine.

"Whoa, Mr. G. You're jumping the gun here, aren't you?" Beulah's eyes bugged out of her emaciated face.

"What do you mean?" I asked her.

"You know exactly what I mean. You can't just start the story again and skip the part where that dude shot you. I got to know what happened there. I mean, he did shoot you, right?"

She licked her lips and I fed her some water.

"Right?" she repeated.

"Right," I replied. "So you want to hear that part of the story?"

"I just said so, didn't I? It's kind of important, don't you think?"

"I suppose not."

"Well then?"

I held up my hand. "Okay."

"And what about Maria?"

"I'll get to that. It is a long story, you know."

Herr Roediger, now Major Roediger had indeed shot me in the head. He placed the barrel of his Luger against my skull. I felt an explosion of pain in the back of my head, like my brain had blown apart, which I thought had happened. Then I blacked out and must have pitched forward into the shallow grave that I had dug for myself. Sometime later, I came to. And panicked. Earth clogged my nose and eyes and ears. I felt like I couldn't breathe. So I clawed my way up and broke through the surface, then sat up and tried to get my bearings. The back of my head throbbed. When I put my hand to it, it came away covered in blood. So, Herr Roediger had made a convincing job of it but he must have aimed the Luger away just at the last second. A risky move, perhaps but the man was a scientist and put his faith in precision. He saved my life. In my fuzzy state, I concluded he wasn't a monster, after all. That my school days counted for something in his eyes. An arrogant snob perhaps, but not a vicious murderer.

Night had fallen. The house lay shrouded in darkness. I groped to my feet and stumbled off, walking like a drunkard. The severe pain caused me to retch but little came up. I must have been delirious because my journey to the Russian border some five kilometers away, seemed like a frantic dream.

The peasant soldiers saw me stumbling along, and heard me mumbling and cursing in Russian. Seeing the look on my face, the madness, the blood, they just waved me through. A few days later the border shut permanently. I found a convenient mound of hay in a nearby field, and fell asleep. When I awoke several hours later, the sun shone high on my face. I hitched a ride with a farmer going into Pripeta to pick up feed for his animals. He looked at me curiously but said nothing. In Pripeta, I would find the Comrade Lenin Hospital run by my sister, the chief administrator. By her side was her husband, Alexis, the chief surgeon. In addition to the villagers and the peasants, they treated the soldiers stationed in the area.

My reunion with Katya and Alex had been joyful, though perforated with sadness. Seeing my sister who was so capable and efficient, so caring and attentive, buoyed my spirits.

Katya looked at me as if she saw someone she thought never to see again. I walked like a drunkard, looked bloody and unkempt and smelled of the fields. The nurse hadn't wanted to let me in, thinking I was a tramp.

"Katya Goldman is my sister," I snapped. "Get her at once." Then I hit the floor.

I opened my eyes and saw her. She'd been bathing my face. I realized I was in a hospital bed. It smelled of disinfectant. I felt the back of my head. A plaster had been put on it.

"Hello, little sister."

"Once again, I am taking care of your wounds, Mordecai." Large tears rolled down her cheeks. Katya leaned over me and kissed my cheek.

"What's this?" I asked and held her back from me. She smiled through her tears then and nodded happily. "And when is the child due?"

"About two months."

"Good. We'll celebrate when the time comes." I felt a sudden thirst. "I could use a drink."

She took my hands caressing the calluses. "We'll have tea. Would you like to clean up, put on new clothes?"

"Yes, little sister. I must look deranged."

She stared at him. "I can't believe you're here. I never thought..."

"I don't die easily, Katya."

"I'll fetch Alex. I don't think he's operating this morning. He'll be so pleased to see you."

My brother-in-law greeted me warmly, clasping me with both hands and kissing me on each cheek then stepped back with a quizzical eye. "You look like you've been through it."

"I haven't really slept in some time."

"Or eaten I think."

Alex turned to Katya.

"Darling, we must get him something to eat."

"Yes, of course. I'll see what we have left in the pantry. We have some local women who cook and do the laundry for the hospital."

I bathed and changed, managed a rudimentary shave and felt something approximately human. We sat in Alex's cramped little office. His files spread across the desk. I touched Katya's hand.

"Little sister," I said and couldn't finish the sentence as my thoughts turned to my parents and Simmy.

"Yes?" But she knew my mind. "We must have hope," she said. "What else can we do?"

Alex looked as if he worked himself to death. "And you? You look as if you can barely stand."

Alex smiled wanly. "There's so much to do. We are a little hospital but very busy. There are babies to be delivered, farmers have accidents, soldiers get shot or fall off the back of lorries when they are drunk. Motor vehicles overturn on the roads. It's unbelievable. There's something new every day, even in this little place."

"And then there's the war."

Alexis nodded. "Yes, the war. It's coming."

"We won't avoid it. I think about my family and what's happened to them."

"When you left, were they...?"

"Yes. For now. My father is needed to produce flour and bake bread for the Germans. That may keep him alive, I hope. But the house is under occupation. An SS Major and an army Colonel had taken it over for their private billet." My stomach lurched when I said it.

"How was it for you?" Alex asked.

I kept my lips tight. I didn't want to talk about seeing the General blown to pieces before my eyes or the hanging of the two Germans or the men who died around me. Alex waited for a moment.

"I understand," he said grimly.

You don't, I thought but in time you will, God help us all. Alex patted me on the back.

Katya found me a room where I could rest. There were always one or two spare rooms in the hospital.

"Sleep here," she had said. "You look like you need it."

"So do you." And I smiled at her.

"I'll wake you in a few hours." She embraced me again. "It's so good to have you here, Mordecai. I only wish..."

I shushed her. "We must pray they'll be all right."

I stretched out on the cot. There was only a dresser and a wash-stand in the bare little room. One small window let the light stream in. I fell asleep with the sun on my face dreaming of days long be-fore when I'd lie down in the meadow behind the house and look at the clouds, feel the sun through the layered branches of the trees, smell the moistness of the air as it blew in from the river. Almost instantly, I fell asleep.

Three months later, the snow ebbed. Katya had given birth to a baby girl they called Nathalie. Nathalie was cared for by one of the nurses during the day so that Katya could spend time with her, have her close by. She and Alex and the baby could find some time together, a quick lunch or a few minutes for a cuddle. I often carried the baby around with me. When I wasn't driving the ambulance or fixing one of the motors, I made time for the child, feeling her connection to the future. I didn't know whether I would ever marry and have children, or even whether I would survive the coming war.

The Soviet authorities knew of my presence. I had to be reported. It was Katya and Alex's duty to do so. The Soviets knew I had been a commissioned officer in the Polish army, that I spoke Russian fluently and that I had been attached to an armoured division.

"They will take you," Katya said tearfully.

"There is no war with Germany."

"Not yet," she replied. "I've heard some of the officers talking. It might happen any time. Stalin has been building up the army, stocking tanks and guns, converting factories to manufacture munitions and artillery. Any fool can see it."

"Maybe he uses these things to keep the Germans at bay?"

"You think Hitler doesn't want to conquer Russia as he has conquered the rest of Europe, Poland, Austria, Czechoslovakia, Hungary and France? He's a madman. That's what madmen do."

"Then there's nothing we can do about it, little sister. You think about Nathalie and Alex. That's all you should care about."

"I'm frightened, Mordecai. I have this terrible feeling. Mama and Papa and Simmy. What's happened to them?" She began to sob.

"Hush. Remember what I said? We must believe."

She looked wrung out and rested her forehead against my shoulder.

"When will this madness end? We live a nightmare and pretend it's a dream." She stood up, dabbed at her eyes. "I must do my rounds now." I watched her go, her slim figure in the white lab coat disappearing into the white walls of the hospital corridor.

Winter melted into spring. Thank god. It had been one of the fiercest winters I could remember. Bone-cracking cold; walls of snow tumbled from the sky ten centimeters at a time. Fighting the snow with an old ambulance was difficult. Early in February, I just gave up and began to use a horse and sled until the snow had been trampled down on the main roads. Finally, the weather began to break. Tufts of grass poked holes through the frosty surface. Shrubs began to bud. The hospital was kept very busy as the Soviet army's ranks swelled in the area – with them came more injuries, sicknesses, accidental shootings, farmers slipping in front of ploughs, falling off the backs of wagons or being trampled by horses. Then there were the drunks who got into trouble and came in with split brows, cracked knuckles and broken noses. Alex might perform five or six operations a day and often there weren't enough beds, medicines or experienced nurses to handle the load. I drove around the area at all hours and spent little time with Alex and Katya, they were always so busy. On occasion, we had a quick meal together. Otherwise, work.

On the other side of Pripeta ran the Vilna Road. Just beyond that lay a guard tower and a sentry post with a gate. The road ran through the Kozak woods, a small but dense stand of trees that began on the Soviet side and spread into Poland. I had walked through the woods to cross over. I often stopped the ambulance near the guard tower and stared across as if I could see through the trees and the rolling hills directly to my parents' house, as if I could see them and Simmy, imagine them gathered in the kitchen sitting around the sturdy wooden table drinking tea and chatting as they used to.

No more.

When my thoughts turned to them, I saw a deep hole with no bottom. I would sit in the ambulance for a few moments and stare into the past. I never speculated on the future.

Alone in my room, I drank vodka and smoked while sitting up in bed. I'd read what I could find like the copy of Tolstoy's *War and Peace.* It amused me, his depiction of the lives of the Russian aristocracy under the Tsars and how privileged they were.

I wasn't without company. A young Russian nurse named Raisa came to me often in the evenings when she finished working. She came from Petrograd originally but moved west when she was young. Her father managed a collective farm. Raisa was a petite girl with dark hair that curved down from her scalp like the halves of a chestnut. High cheekbones and almond eyes made her look slightly Oriental. Her legs and thighs were slim and her hips rounded.

"You've been drinking again."

"Yes."

"You drink too much."

"I don't drink enough."

She unbuttoned her uniform from the back and slipped out of it. She sat down beside me in her underthings. There were no garters and stockings for the nurses. They wore wool socks if they could get them or went bare. Raisa preferred to go bare. Her underclothes were made of coarse cotton and badly stitched.

"One day I shall buy you silk underwear. What do you think of that?" I asked.

She smiled and shifted her position.

"I think it is the vodka talking." She hugged herself. "I'm cold."

I shifted over and flipped back the covers. "Then you'd better get in." Gratefully, she climbed under. She felt like a young girl except for her full breasts. They filled my hands. Afterwards, we'd lie quietly together in the dark. Or I would smoke silently.

"Do the soldiers pinch you and try to squeeze your breasts?"

She giggled. "All the time, but I just slap their hands away. Most of them are too weak or tired to do anything."

"But they want to."

"Wouldn't you?"

Her question surprised me. "Yes, of course."

"You see? You're no different. You'd take advantage of a girl if you could."

"And you think I take advantage of you?"

"No. You never ask me to come here. I come because I want to. I forget about things when I'm with you. The pain I see here. The pain I feel when I think about my family and what will happen to us. It's not good to think too much about these things but I can't help it."

"It's a natural thing to do." She began to stroke me. "Be careful or I will drop my cigarette and start a fire."

"I'll take my chances," she whispered.

I sighed, then stubbed the end into the ashtray I kept by the bed. "It's too harsh anyway, this Russian tobacco."

Raisa said nothing but I felt her pulse quicken and heard the rapid intake of breath as we came together. Her body yielded to me and I let myself go with her.

The moderate nature of spring gave way to the oppressive heat of summer. A heavy, clinging heat. The air dripped with moisture. I put on my shirt and trousers and they felt damp. I kept the sleeves of my shirt rolled up, then did the same with the jacket. Mornings were beautiful as sunshine broke through the mist rising from the ground sending shafts of light from above low hanging clouds. Often, a rumble of thunder rolled through the sky during the day, and occasionally we saw lightning. It seemed to crackle and boom just over our heads, then the heat descended like a blanket. This went on for weeks. Everyone was exhausted. Raisa came to my room and stripped immediately to her underclothes, dropping her damp uniform on the floor. I lay on the bed clad only in an undershirt and boxer shorts smoking calmly and quietly. Raisa snuggled up to me. I felt the heat of her on my skin. Her hot breath on my face.

One early morning in June as the sun peeked over the horizon, I awoke from a troubled sleep. My heart raced, yet all remained quiet and still. Then I heard it. The whistle of heavy shells cutting through the thick air. I braced myself. From several hundred metres away I felt the reverberation. I leapt out of bed and pulled on my clothes. I raced to Katya's office. I could see that she too had just gotten out of bed. As I burst in, she put down the phone.

"We're evacuating the hospital," she said. "The Germans have just crossed the border."

"What about you?"

"We'll see the patients safely out, then leave."

"And those that can't walk or be moved?"

"We've been ordered to leave them."

I understood the implications. There was little time to think or feel remorse.

"I'll ready the ambulance. Get Alex and the baby and meet me there."

She looked ill, her skin had turned green. "All right."

"Hurry," I said. "They'll move fast. I am going to pack a few things."

She got up unsteadily from her chair. I grabbed hold of her. "Are you all right?"

She gasped, then nodded.

"Yes. Don't worry. We'll meet you outside."

I gave my sister a quick hug, then left the room. The pounding had steadied now and the explosions encircled us. In the corridors, nurses and orderlies ran, patients screamed. I heard children crying. That feeling, the beginning of the end, engulfed me. I felt powerless.

"Mordecai." I turned. Raisa. She cried hysterically. I grabbed her wrist and pulled her along with me, pushing through the congested thoroughfare. In my room, I pulled my duffel bag out of the closet and quickly tossed some things into it. Raisa sat on the bed, mute, her hands pressed to her ears.

"Come," I said. She didn't answer. I slapped her once, then again. Slowly, her eyes focused and she looked at me, then nodded slowly. I put out my hand and she took it. We made our way to the barn where I parked the ambulances. As we approached, I saw smoke billowing from the back.

"Wait here," I said. I lifted the crossbeam that held the doors and hurled it away. I kicked the doors open and smoke poured out. Covering my face I went in, groping for the side of the ambulance. The smoke burned my eyes and throat. I coughed as tears flooded down my face. I found the door handle and climbed inside. Debris fell from the roof. A beam crashed just to the side of me. I put the key in the ignition and turned. The motor groaned but didn't catch. I smacked the steering wheel, then waited a few seconds and tried again easing the throttle, pulling on the choke slightly. The engine turned over, then caught. As I pressed the accelerator, a section of the roof crashed in front of me sending up a wall of flame. I hit the pedal and barreled through, dragging splinters of the burning boards. I wheeled around to where Raisa stood, braked then thrust open the door. "Get in."

A shell thudded less than one hundred metres away. She ducked her head, then scrabbled in to the cab. I tore away and drove to the front of the hospital.

"I'll just be a moment."

I ran inside looking for my sister. Her office was empty, papers scattered. People ran up and down the corridors. I grabbed a nurse.

"Have you seen Dr. Goldman?" She shook her head vigorously, then pulled away. I drove around to the side entrance. A soldier holding a machine pistol stood in the middle of the road. He came around the driver's side. I leaned out the window.

"Yes? What is it?"

"This vehicle is confiscated. It's required for transport."

"I must look for someone."

The soldier lowered the machine pistol.

"I'm getting in and don't try anything."

He came around the passenger side and stepped up, pulling himself on to the seat. Raisa scrambled to the back. The soldier gave her a cursory look.

"Comrade." He pointed with the barrel of the machine pistol. "This way." The soldier was young, practically a boy. The uniform and hat seemed absurdly large, plumping out when he sat. The hat came down almost to the bridge of his nose. He had been trying to grow a pale moustache. But I could see he took himself and his responsibilities very seriously.

"Where are we going, comrade?"

"You'll see," the boy answered. We passed the hospital. The road forked again. "To the right."

I made the turn when I glanced left. The wind and the tires of the ambulance kicked up dust and grit but something, some instinct made me stop suddenly.

"Why are you stopping?" demanded the boy.

"My sister, her husband and child. I see them. They're just a few hundred metres up the road. I must pick them up."

"No."

"But they're in danger."

The boy lowered the machine pistol, aiming it at my chest.

"Drive on or I'll shoot you. This vehicle has been commandeered by the army. Your family will be all right. They're heading toward our lines. Our comrades will save them."

I made out Katya's white smock. She held the baby. Alex carried two bags. "Shoot me then, you little pipsqueak."

The boy pulled the machine pistol up to his shoulder. A high-pitched scream filled the cab. Raisa threw herself in front of the boy, winding her arms around me. She sobbed into my chest. I stroked her hair.

"All right, little one. All right."

The boy lowered the machine pistol. "Drive on, I say."

I nodded then put the ambulance in gear and drove on slowly staring off to my left, watching the figures of my sister and her family grow smaller then disappear as they passed a wooded clump. I moved my eyes forward and glanced at the absurd young boy in his ridiculous uniform who eyed me warily, his hands gripping the weapon tightly. I cursed myself. As the ambulance drove deeper into Russia and away from the advancing German army, I swore I would find them.

Chapter 23

Beulah looked at me. Tears rolled down her drawn cheeks.

"What happened? Did you find them? Please tell me you found them."

I couldn't answer her. All I could do was shake my head.

Cracow, 1929

The shrill whistle pierced my consciousness. I sat up on the wooden seat, shaken and alert. Laszlo glanced at me.

"What's the matter? Are you nervous?"

I shook my head. It wasn't the tournament that had been on my mind. Would Maria receive my message? Would she be able to get away?

"No, I'm fine."

The metal wheels ground down on the tracks and the train lurched, throwing the five of us in the compartment off balance. Laszlo put out a hand to steady himself. From Krasnowicz, the trip to Cracow took roughly five hours. The train began to gain momentum as the motion of the wheels came faster and smoother, steel gripping steel.

I peered out the grimy window. We sat in a second-class compartment with our daypacks stowed under the hard, wooden benches. I watched the flattened ground move swiftly by. The barren trees shook off their leaves, leaving a bed of fading colour. I leaned back and closed my eyes. Laszlo appeared to be sleeping. The other two students on the boxing team remained silent. Jerzy stared out the window at something, thinking perhaps, that he would finally experience life away from the farm. Jerzy glanced back at me but I kept my eyes closed.

"I know you're faking it."

"Not now."

"I hear this fellow Poplowski is good."

I shrugged. "I'm not worried." I didn't want to show it.

"His father is Russian."

"So?"

"You know Russians. They can be very stubborn. You can hit them with a hammer and still they won't fall."

"There's a point system – or have you forgotten?"

Jerzy grinned, spreading his thin lips like a wolf.

"No, I didn't forget. But with Russians you must hit hard and damn the points. That's what I would do."

"We'll see." I'd heard of Poplowski. That he was one of the finest boxers in the region in the ninety-kilo class. My weight class. At seventeen, he'd built himself a reputation.

"There are two pools. I'll see him fight first."

"Yes," Jerzy agreed. "It should be interesting." The air in the compartment smelled of damp clothes and boots, of hardened sausages, onion and garlic.

"Someone must have kept a chicken in here recently," I said. Jerzy lifted his eyebrows and went to open the window.

"Just a crack, then, to let in some fresh air," Jerzy said.

"Winter will come soon."

"I like the winter."

"Why?"

"Because all of the work on the farm is mostly done. Just feeding the animals, that's all. The ground is readied for next year. We wait until the warmth returns. I'm free for a little while. That's why."

"Maybe you'll like the city," I suggested.

Jerzy nodded. "I expect so."

"Bye bye farm?"

Jerzy sighed. "I'm not sure. One of my sisters would have to marry a farmer. Someone approved by my father. I don't think he would give it over to an outsider," he said glumly.

"You can farm for the collective good. Give all of your produce away so all people may eat freely."

Jerzy snorted. "Over my father's corpse, you mean. No, he needs to be paid for his labor."

I stepped into the aisle. I needed to get up and move about; the seats were too cramped, the air too stale. Jerzy stuck his big boot up and I tripped, falling toward the benches opposite. Laszlo caught me from behind.

"What'd you do that for?" I growled. Jerzy smirked.

I shook my head angry at myself for getting annoyed. It'd been just a joke. I turned away and started up the narrow passage. I'd gotten halfway to the end of the car when I saw her and stopped. She blocked my path. A large, pale-faced woman with blonde hair, now streaked with grey, tucked up under a cloth hat. She wore a simple wool coat that covered her ample knees and plump ankles. The small mouth pressed tight, thin lips quivering, her eyes narrowed and cold. Maria's mother. What was she doing on the train?

I hesitated, then moved toward her. The baker's wife remained where she was, watching as I drew closer. Finally, we were inches apart.

"Mrs..."

Maria's mother coughed deep in her throat and spat in my face.

"Don't ever touch her," she hissed.

Her spittle burned my skin. Acid eating me away. As I drew my sleeve across my cheeks, she backed up slowly, never taking her eyes off me. I didn't move. Finally, she felt for the handle of the compartment, opened the connecting door, then disappeared.

I returned to my seat.

"I'd rather have the devil than a mother like that," Jerzy said.

The train station at Cracow resembled a place of lost souls, blackened by coal dust, peopled by bleak, hard-mouthed faces. There seemed a collective sadness in the looks, the stance, the way the haggard passengers huddled on the platform, checking the large tower clock against pocket watches, to verify how much longer they'd wait.

We stood in a clump waiting for Laszlo to return. People flowed about us like a steady current. Some cursed at us for stopping their progress.

"There's a lot of noise," Jerzy said, practically shouting to be heard.

"Of course," I shouted back. "What did you expect?"

I noticed that the other two, Sarin and Vladimir, remained tight-lipped. Perhaps they missed the silence of the countryside.

"And the smells." Jerzy shook his head and spat. "Like the stockyard when the wind has come up."

"What's that?" asked Laszlo who had appeared out of the crowd.

"It stinks," Jerzy shouted.

"Welcome to the city," said Laszlo and smiled, showing his even, yellowed teeth. "Come, we have to take a bus to the dormitory where we are billeted. We're staying at the University. Perhaps some of you will attend one day. It's this way." He made a gesture and we hefted our bags and joined the flow of people moving along the platform. We merged into a great doorway that, in turn, opened to a vast expanse of soaring height, bright tile floors, tall windows with leaded glass. Although the light shone weakly, the patterns of the glass formed shapes on the scurrying passengers that reminded me of rats caught out in the open. Laszlo went to talk to a man in a shabby uniform who spoke something in reply and pointed to a doorway where the current of people flowed in and out. Laszlo touched the brim of his cap, smiled and backed away, then returned to the group.

"There's a motor coach we need to catch. Through this exit over here." He pushed off into the crowd. I watched the others scramble behind him, taking care not to bump into anyone and that seemed impossible... everyone in the vast building headed for the same doorway. Jerzy followed Laszlo and the others fell into line behind him, moving in the wake he created.

The conductor of the motor coach gave each of us a disapproving grimace as we hauled our baggage into the narrow, crowded aisle. He told me to move as far to the back as possible. All the seats had been taken. Laszlo informed the conductor where we were going and paid the fares.

"I can't breathe in here," Sarin muttered and Vladimir coughed, choking on the close air filled with sour smells. "Is it far?"

Laszlo shrugged but reached across an elderly woman and yanked open the window.

"Is that better?" he asked and pushed Sarin ahead of him so he might catch the draught of air. The elderly woman glared at him angrily.

"The boy isn't well, mother," Laszlo explained softly. "You don't want him to be ill, do you?" The woman turned away, face pinched tightly.

The aged bus belched and we stepped on to the sidewalk burdened with our luggage, ignored by the passersby. Laszlo pointed a finger.

"This way." And we followed him, wending our way through pedestrians, vendors, cyclists and the odd policeman on horseback.

The student dormitory looked new, having been built not more than twenty years earlier. There had been no attempt to maintain the facade of the university. It stood out as a utilitarian, postmodernist stone block, out of which were carved doors and windows. Otherwise, it remained entirely featureless.

"This is what prison should look like," Jerzy remarked.

"No bars," I replied. "Yet."

The warder assigned us rooms on the fourth floor. He also dispensed the keys. I looked at the man's worn burgundy jacket along with the tarnished gold crest over the left breast pocket – the Polish eagle, seen on uniforms throughout the land.

Jerzy and I shared a room – if you could call it that, with its bare, grey walls, a wash stand, two single beds, two desks and a straight-backed chair each.

"Be in the dining room within half an hour," Laszlo said. "Meals are served promptly at six in the evening. There are no second servings and if you're late, you go hungry, all right?" We nodded.

"Can you imagine spending four years in this little cell while studying for a degree?" Jerzy asked.

"It's not so bad," I replied. "You've got the library and the whole city to take in. You don't have to stay here all the time."

"Even my room back home has more warmth than this."

"There's no reason it can't be fixed up a little bit."

"And these beds. Built for midgets. Bah." He yawned throwing his head back.

"But it would be nice to get away, wouldn't it? Isn't that worth it to you?"

Jerzy blinked at him, then smiled mirthlessly. "You're a clever fellow. Yes. Anything would be worth it to get away. Even this dungeon, this relic from the Middle Ages. But I doubt I would come."

"Why not?"

"My father wouldn't let me. He sees no sense in continuing school. He's afraid it will pull me away from the land. He needs me to keep it going in the family. I know enough to take over the farm. Why should I go to university? No one in my family ever has before. Most didn't go as far as high school. I'm the first to finish."

"And aren't they proud?"

Jerzy shrugged. "They don't say anything."

"Maybe you'll get a scholarship?"

Jerzy shook his head. "Not if Herr Professor Roediger has anything to do with it."

"Physics isn't that hard."

Jerzy snorted. "For you."

"For you too."

"It's a dream that won't come true, Goldman. Better to leave it than be disappointed in the end."

"That's defeatist."

"I don't care."

"Do you take the same approach to boxing?"

"Yes."

"Then you'll never win."

"Who said I wanted to win?"

"Then why bother?"

"I am here, that's why." And he spread his wide arms out practically spanning the room.

"That's not good enough," I said. "That's the attitude of a loser."

Jerzy bristled. "If you think I'm a loser, then what's your reason?"

"To win. When I look at the guy I'm fighting, I don't think of him as a person but an obstacle, an object. I'll do anything to put him down. Whatever it takes, I'll do it."

"You enjoy it?"

"It's a good feeling to win. Better than being the loser, that's for sure."

"Like when you beat me four years ago?"

"You better believe it. You thought your size would scare me off but it didn't work. I took a look at you and I saw your weaknesses right away. You haven't changed much but you are a better boxer now than you were then."

Jerzy cocked his head and bowed mockingly. "Thank you, Herr Professor. When you kicked my ass, it made me see things a little differently."

"Oh yeah?" I tensed in case he tried something.

"I could always get what I wanted. If I couldn't get it by asking I just took it, because I was bigger than everyone else. I didn't know any Jews. We would throw stones at them in the street, sometimes we put bricks through their windows. My father hates the Jews. He blames them for everything bad that happens. If there is a frost, the Jews have called down a curse. If there is no rain, it is the fault of the

Jews. Growing up, I believed this bullshit because I had no reason to think it wasn't true. Does it make any sense? Of course not. My father is an ignorant man and a peasant. He is superstitious and crosses himself and spits thirty times a day. He is like most stupid peasants. Face it, the Jews will never be accepted here."

"My family has been here for over two hundred years," I said.

Jerzy shrugged. "And my family for at least a thousand. It makes no difference. You're an outsider. Your people will never become a central part of the life of Poland."

"We're misunderstood."

"Maybe. But that's only if the other side wants to understand. And we don't. Many see you as a nuisance, some as a threat and many more as simply vermin, something to be eradicated, do you see?"

"You don't have to tell me. I see it every day."

"We can never be friends, you and I," Jerzy said quietly, without remorse or regret. He was simply stating a fact.

"I know."

"We can be friendly, for now, while we're at school, I mean."

"If you say so."

Jerzy looked at me intently. "But there may come a time when something will happen. If that time ever comes, I'll warn you first. I owe you that."

"But the hate never leaves."

"No, it doesn't. It's bred into us."

I tapped my forehead. "You can use your mind to change. You're smart."

"I'm not strong enough to resist it. It's too powerful."

"You're just lazy."

Jerzy laughed and shook his head, slowly, almost sadly. "No, I'm not lazy you crazy bastard, just weak." He stood up to his full height. He towered over me. "Maybe you can use this when you fight the Russian."

"Believe me, I will." I stood up.

"And the girl?"

"What about her?"

"You're meeting her somewhere?"

"I'm not sure."

"You're taking some chance, especially with that mother of hers." And he shook his head.

I took a deep breath and held it. "I don't care."

"And of course your family approves."

"That's none of your damn business."

Jerzy was silent for a long moment. "Whatever you say... friend."

"Let's go for a stroll," Jerzy suggested after dinner. I agreed. Jerzy wore a frayed coat that still had the smell of sheep on it. Over many years, oil and dirt had discoloured the cloth. I wore an old wool overcoat of my father's that was tattered at the elbows and shoulders but had a quilted lining to keep me warm. Outside, the air was brisk and visible when we breathed. The streets remained quiet. Most had scurried off to the warmth of their homes. We walked the few blocks around the university as curious onlookers, watching the noisy, creaking buses that belched dark fumes into the air.

Near the entranceway of the dormitory stood a young girl, bundled up. She had her dark hair tucked into a beret. She must be meeting her sweetheart, I thought. As we passed by, I caught the girl looking at me intently. Then she screamed.

Five shapes appeared out of the darkness surrounding her. She struggled as they grabbed at her. We launched ourselves at her attackers. It was five against two but Jerzy's size and my quickness caught them by surprise. The intruders wore woolen hats pulled down over their faces. Two of them dragged the girl away. I pounded one in the kidneys until he doubled over. He turned and Jerzy kicked him in the jaw, sending him sprawling. Jerzy turned round, facing the other three, who began to advance on him. Meanwhile, the injured attacker lay on the ground moaning. His companion had released the girl and drew a long-bladed knife from within the folds of his coat.

"That one is yours," Jerzy said and turned to the others. Bellowing like a bull, he charged, throwing himself at them.

I removed my coat and wrapped it around my left forearm. The girl had shrunk back toward a stairwell. I watched the one with the knife, noticed how he stood, how he held the knife and gambled that he'd come in high and stab downwards. I watched the blade carefully. I heard grunts and shouts behind me.

"Mordecai...watch out..." I jumped to the side as one of them came from behind. Bringing my knee and fist up I grabbed the fellow and, using his momentum, propelled him forward toward the knife man, who quickly pivoted but kept his poise. We stood of equal height and build. I watched the knife as it shifted from hand to hand, back and forth until the grip went into the palm of the right hand, and the intruder brought his arm forward and leapt, slicing downward. I blocked the knife with my coat and spun my back into the attacker, jamming my elbow into a hard abdomen and was rewarded with a breathy "Ooofff". I slammed the knife hand down on my knee and the weapon clattered into the gutter. I spun again to face the attacker, threw off the coat and raised my fists lashing out. I grabbed for the fellow's hat, catching only a glimpse of a beveled cheekbone. The man stepped back crisply, grabbed at his companion who'd managed to stand. The attackers took off.

"They've done a runner," Jerzy panted, straightening up.

"Are you all right?" Jerzy nodded then turned to the girl. "And you, Miss? Have you been hurt?" he asked.

The girl shook her head, her eyes still wide, lips trembling. I swept up my coat and placed it over her shoulders. "Come in where it's warm," I said.

We brought her into the cafeteria. We found a table in the far corner and I brought them each a pot of tea and a stale biscuit. The girl couldn't stop shaking.

"Take a deep breath," I said. "Try to relax. It's over. They won't be bothering you again."

Jerzy had a cut in the corner of his mouth that he dabbed at with a paper napkin.

"I almost enjoyed that," he said.

"Are you Goldman? Mordecai Goldman?"

I turned to her. "I'm Mordecai Goldman."

"I'm a friend of Maria," she said. "I have a message for you."

I seized her arms. "Maria? Tell me, is she okay? Will I see her?"

The girl shifted uneasily. "Please."

I released her. "Sorry. I didn't mean...I was excited."

The girl smiled. "I understand." She glanced up at Jerzy who stared at her.

"This is my team mate. His name is Jerzy..."

Jerzy snatched off his cap. "Jerzy Malinski." He stuck out a large paw that engulfed the girl's hand. She withdrew it quickly.

"Very nice," she said. "I have a note for you." And she drew a folded piece of paper from her coat pocket and handed it to me.

"How did you get this?"

"We go to the same school. A number of girls attend during the day as I do. I'm not a resident because my family lives in town. I'm glad. It would be a horrible place to live."

"Is she very unhappy?"

"Well, I think she'll be happier now, for a short time, anyway. I have to go now. I can't stay out too late."

Jerzy stood up. "Do you need an escort, Miss? I'll walk you home. You'll be safe with me."

She tittered into her hand. "No, thank you. It's not far but thank you for your kindness, Mr. Malinski. Goodbye."

"Goodbye and thank you," I said.

The girl moved briskly without glancing back. Jerzy watched after her. I glanced at the piece of paper in my hand, scarcely believing it was from her.

"She's not bad, not bad at all."

"A snobby town girl."

"Maybe she is, but still..."

"You think she'd be interested in a proletariat like you?"

Jerzy shrugged. "Love isn't about class. It's about the heart."

"Who said anything about love?" I asked.

We climbed the staircase and went to our room where Jerzy could dream about the girl he'd just met and I, with trembling fingers, opened the piece of paper I'd been given. Before getting into bed, I did one hundred and fifty sit-ups and one hundred push-ups, more to force the tension out of my body so I might sleep better.

"You think that will help?" Jerzy huddled under his blankets. The room was cold. No matter how he tried, his feet stuck out the end of the mattress.

"Wear your socks. At least your feet will be warm." I lay on the cold floor panting, catching my breath. "Or do some exercise. That will keep you warm too."

"Thoughts of Maria will keep you warm tonight," Jerzy said and snickered.

I stood up. "That's why I don't need socks." I got under the covers. "Good night. Let's do well tomorrow." Jerzy grunted. I reached out and switched off the lamp. The room sputtered into darkness. I saw her face. She smiled. I drifted off to sleep with thoughts of seeing her very soon.

A hand shook me roughly. "Uunnhh." The hand persisted, squeezing my shoulder. I rolled over to shake it off but the fingers of this hand had an iron grip. I opened my eyes. The room was still dark. I blinked and saw Laszlo's sharp profile. I switched on the lamp and blinked against the pain of the light. Jerzy snored lightly but began to stir.

"What time is it?" I asked.

Laszlo grinned darkly. "Five-thirty. We need to prepare. You're on at ten. First, get washed and then come downstairs for breakfast. Hurry now." He shook Jerzy, who groaned.

"Go away darling," he mumbled.

Laszlo laughed. "He's having a good dream. It's a shame to spoil it." He tapped Jerzy's face. Jerzy slapped at his fingers. Laszlo persisted until finally, Jerzy popped one eye open, then groaned again.

"Ach. This is just like the farm. I thought I was getting away from all that."

"Then you know how to get ready quickly," Laszlo said. "Be downstairs in fifteen minutes." He left the room. I sat up in bed.

"I can't remember a time when I didn't get up in the dark," Jerzy said, his voice raspy. "I wonder what it would be like to get up after the sun rises."

"Forget about it, comrade. A proletariat's work always begins in the darkness of the early hours and ends after the sun has set. You'd better get used to it." I stepped on to the cold floor gingerly and crept over to the sink to wash my face. My skin puckered from the chill in the air. I turned the taps and waited. "Just as I thought. No hot water. Welcome to the revolution, comrade," I said. I splashed myself with cold water and winced.

"We have long memories," Jerzy replied. He slipped out of bed and began to dress, hopping from one foot to the other. "At home, my mother would have the fire going and hot biscuits and tea ready before we went out to the fields."

"I'm sure the kitchen is open downstairs. Students, like armies, need food in their bellies."

We found Laszlo sitting at a table by himself, spooning steaming hot oatmeal and sipping tea. There were thick, crusty rolls, honey and butter. "Come. Eat," he said, beckoning to us. "The others are coming." We sat down and began to help ourselves. Laszlo had the settings organized already, with cups, bowls and cutlery. Jerzy dug in right away. I selected a roll carefully, split it open precisely then began to spread a thin layer of butter on the soft, spongy surface. "Your matches are at ten and then again at two." I had anticipated such news. I looked around. The cafeteria stood mostly empty at this early hour but students began to drift in. Four of the tables were now occupied by bleary-eyed patrons hanging their heads over their mugs of tea. I bit into the roll. It was stale but I forced some of it down. My stomach felt tight. "We'll have a light workout, get you warm and ready, help you stay loose."

"Who are we fighting?" Jerzy asked.

"You've got Kaminsky," Laszlo said. "You've got four or five inches on him in height and at least that much in reach. He may be heavier but he is slow. Kaminsky always moves forward and he tries to cut off the ring. You have to force him backward. He has a habit of dropping his left and is open to the body. You should have no trouble. And you," he began, turning to me, "it will be interesting. Emil Spruch. You will be well-matched. He is very quick and well-balanced but has no real power. He's very light on his feet and moves well. You'll find him an elusive target but hit him once with a strong uppercut and he'll go down like a sack of potatoes. With him, you must be careful not to get cut. He'll sting you with very fast jabs around the eyes and nose. If he cuts you, it won't go well with the Russian because he'll take advantage. Protect your head and look for an opening. You should be able to take him in the first round."

I listened carefully. I was anxious to get going.

After breakfast, we got dressed, carefully lacing up the shoes that came high above the ankle, strapped on the leather protector between our legs and adjusted the shorts. Through generous donations by some of the parents at the school, Laszlo had provided us with thick cotton robes to keep us warm between matches. He taped our hands, wrapping carefully before sliding on the boxing gloves and tying them tightly at the wrist. The others would keep their hands taped while waiting. Jerzy was the first up and as he tied the gloves on, Laszlo gave him some last-minute words.

"Watch the overhand right. He's slow but very strong. Look for the opening to the body and hit him there hard, then you can back him up. If he gets you into the corner, grab hold and get out of there or he'll finish you. Keep moving and he'll tire. Okay?" Jerzy nodded grimly, his mouth tight and anxious.

I patted him on the back. "Just in case, we'll be there to carry you out."

Jerzy bared his teeth. "Thanks. And I'll do the same for you."

"Come on," said Laszlo. "It's time." I followed them out and took a seat at ringside. I had an hour before my match with Emil Spruch. I'd need ten or fifteen minutes to warm up and get loose. The matches ran a maximum of twelve minutes; three-minute rounds and a minute between each round. Some five minutes between matches for the judges to tabulate their scores and declare a victor, then get ready for the next match. Judges rotated every third match. There was a lot of hubbub in the gymnasium, especially as a number of university students had wandered in, taking a break from their studies to watch the tournament. I sat on a bench and looked about. Most of the spectators were young men. As I scanned the seats, I caught sight of the girl who had given me the letter. She sat by herself, looking about nervously. Just as Jerzy entered the ring, I went over to her.

"Hello again."

She started. "I didn't recognize you."

I grinned. "My dress, I suppose." Some yells sounded as the match began. I glanced up to see the two boxers come together.

"Isn't that your friend?" she asked.

"My teammate, yes."

She caught the inference. "I thought you seemed friendly enough that first evening I waited for you."

"We get along," I answered simply. There was a roar. I glanced over and saw Jerzy take a strong right to the head that pushed him back. Kaminsky had a large, square body with slabs of muscle down his chest and arms. Remembering Laszlo's admonitions, Jerzy pushed off from his back foot and found an opening in the blonde giant's ribs that halted his forward motion. He slipped an overhand right and found the body again. The blonde muscle man winced and hesitated only slightly before moving forward again.

"How is he doing?" she asked.

"He's doing pretty well actually. We'll see in the next round."

"The other one looks so strong. Such big muscles. Your teammate seems almost skinny beside him."

"Don't worry, he's strong and accurate. That's what counts. As many blows as you can get in. That's what the judges look for." I turned back to her and just as I did, a roar went up. I turned back. The girl gasped. I saw Jerzy's head snap back and he staggered, his knees buckling. Kaminsky had landed a powerful blow to the head.

"Oh no," she cried. "He's hurt."

"He'll come out of it. He must. The round's almost over." The bell rang and Jerzy staggered back to his corner. I saw Laszlo talking to him urgently. Jerzy nodded his head. Laszlo sponged him off and gave him a drink. He swilled it, then spat into a bucket.

"Will he be all right?"

I shrugged. "It's up to him now," I said. "You have a message for me?"

The girl had been mesmerized by the action in the ring. She pulled her attention back to me.

"Yes, of course. I'm being silly. It's just that... I've never seen this before." She reached into her pocket and handed me another note. "This is my address. Tomorrow at one o'clock, she'll be there waiting for you."

"She'll be there for sure?"

"Yes. Didn't I just say so?" The bell rang again. Jerzy stood up and did a few deep knee bends against the ropes, shook his head and ventured out into the ring. His opponent rushed in quickly, hoping to capitalize on the damage done earlier. Jerzy snapped his head back with a jab, snapped another one, then put together a one-two combination that forced the larger youth backward. As Kaminsky raised his arms to protect his face, Jerzy worked the body viciously and suddenly, it seemed as if the air had gone out of him. Kaminsky didn't know where to hold his arms, up or down. His coach yelled at him to grab hold. Jerzy stepped back out of reach and hit him flush on the jaw. He punched him again. Suddenly, like a bull with its legs shot out, the young boxer went down and stayed down. As the referee counted out, Jerzy raised his hands in the air.

"He won?" the girl asked.

"Yes. He won."

"How exciting. It happened so quickly."

I scrutinized the girl's address, then slipped the paper into the pocket of my robe. The girl stared at Jerzy. He caught her eye and grinned, then made a gesture of triumph.

"It's only the first round of the tournament. There are many fights left yet."

The girl turned to me. "You're jealous."

"Me? No, I'm not jealous. It's just that it's a long tournament. Jerzy did very well. It was a good win for him."

"You're better?" she asked, interested.

"Yes. I'm better."

"We shall see."

"You plan to stay and watch? Mustn't you go to school?"

"I'm ill today."

I nodded and smiled pleasantly.

"Thank you for all your help. Enjoy the tournament today. I must go and warm up. Will I see you tomorrow?"

The girl shook her head. "No. Maria will be by herself."

"I hope this won't cause you any trouble."

She touched my arm then. "She really cares for you. You must be kind to her. Do you understand? That's the most important thing. She's an exceptional person."

"You needn't worry. I won't hurt her."

"It's probably too late for that," the girl muttered.

"What do you mean?" I demanded.

"I think you know," she muttered again. "I'm doing this for her, not for you."

"Thank you again," I said stiffly and moved off. Jerzy came through the ropes and I offered my congratulations.

"He caught me," Jerzy said. "I didn't expect it."

"Laszlo chewed your ass."

Jerzy laughed. "I thought I'd roast in hell. A good Catholic concept. Good thing he was as slow as molasses, otherwise..."

"It can happen to anyone."

"I saw you talking to her," Jerzy said and indicated the young girl in the stands.

"She thinks you're a god. Now you can conquer her if you like."

"You're mocking me."

"No, I'm serious. She was very impressed with your victory. Here's your chance now to step out of your proletarian shoes and romance a member of the intelligentsia." Jerzy's opponent jostled us. His coach walked him unsteadily back to the dressing room. "That was a good combination. Very solid."

"It felt good."

"Go and talk to her. Make her swoon. I have to get ready for my match." I patted him on the back and made my way through the crowd. The girl's words had angered me. That was good. I'd use it against Emil Spruch. Too bad for him, I thought.

Laszlo rubbed my neck and shoulders. The first round had gone well. We had felt each other out. It was fast-paced, a lot of footwork, feints and quick hands. I had landed a number of punches including some good combinations. But nothing had connected solidly. I was certain I was ahead on points. Most of Spruch's punches had been blocked. Yet, Spruch remained elusive and I found that frustrating. Laszlo handed me a bottle. I took a swig and spat into the bucket. I glanced around the arena. Not many paid attention. People walked about. Most talked to their companions. Only a few watched what went on in the ring.

"Slow the pace down," Laszlo ordered. "Measure him with your punches. You control the rhythm."

"He's fast."

"His feet are fast but he hasn't landed a punch yet. He wants to tire you out first."

The bell rang and I got to my feet. I took a long look at Spruch who stood about my height, perhaps half an inch shorter. His torso was well-tapered and his shoulders square. His black hair had been cut very short, like a prisoner. He held himself in perfect balance, I noted. He had been well-trained.

Spruch came up on the balls of his feet, but I held my ground and merely pivoted, keeping pace without moving too much. Spruch flicked out his left to keep me back but I moved in and countered with a solid hook to the abdomen. Spruch grunted and jabbed again. I kept my elbows in tight and the jab glanced off my right shoulder. As I stepped up, we stood almost toe-to-toe. I began working inside to the abdomen, looking for an opening, for Spruch's arms to spread. I got in another solid punch to the abdomen and Spruch grunted harder, then grabbed for me. Before the referee could move in, I broke his grip and Spruch staggered back a pace. I moved in swiftly and caught him a hard shot to the ribs. Spruch winced and brought his arm down to cover. I hit him flush with a left, then a right and again with a left and Spruch went down to the canvas in a heap. The referee immediately began the count. I could see that Spruch wouldn't get up in time. The strength had gone out of his legs and his arms flailed uselessly. I glanced at Laszlo who nodded and smiled. The referee came and lifted my hand up. As he did so, I caught someone looking at me from the gallery. Pale eyes the colour of ice and straw-coloured hair. Below, a face of classic Slavic proportions, all angles and planes with thin lips that smiled at me mirthlessly. I met his look. The Russian craned his head to hear something someone said, a man leaning in. The Russian nodded, then turned back to look at me with a self-satisfied expression. I knew that between us, it would be a good contest. Two days to go. I slipped between the ropes. Laszlo tossed me my robe. I put it on and headed toward the change area.

I towelled off in the change room when the Russian strolled up. Jerzy had sprawled on a bench, his long legs stuck out in front of him. I watched the Russian laconically from under hooded eyes. I paid him no mind, didn't look up as the Russian appeared.

"You fight well, Jew." I kept toweling, then wrapped the towel around my waist. "We'll see how you do when you have to fight a real opponent."

I smiled and flicked my hand catching the Russian on the cheek with a light slap. The Russian flushed and brought his hands up. I didn't move. Jerzy shot up in a flash and forced himself between us.

"Save it for the ring, eh?" The Russian looked up at him, then back at me. He pointed his finger just millimetres from my face.

"I will pulverize you."

I held his look until the Russian stepped back and turned away.

"Dos vidaniya," I muttered. Jerzy watched the Russian push his way through the other young fighters without looking back.

"Nasty, that one. You'd better watch it."

"He doesn't frighten me," I replied.

"He's supposed to be very good."

I picked up my clothes. "We shall see this afternoon. I look forward to it."

Spruch came into the change area. He walked slowly but otherwise seemed to have recovered. "That was a good combination," he said wryly, rubbing his jaw.

"I hope you're all right," I said.

"I'll recover," Spruch said, then paused. "I hear you will fight the Russian."

"Yes."

"Watch him, he's very strong, very powerful and very tricky."

"So am I," I said.

Spruch merely rubbed his jaw without saying anything.

The rest of the day went slowly. Both Jerzy and I breezed through our afternoon matches. I fought a slow, lumbering boy with a thick neck and swollen arms. I didn't try to knock him out, just won on points by dancing around and flicking out jabs and combinations whenever I saw an opening. The thick boy plodded, chasing me around the ring for the entire three rounds. Jerzy scored a technical knock within two minutes of the first round. Laszlo was very pleased, almost ecstatic. Our two teammates were not so fortunate. Both got through the first-round matches well enough but suffered losses in the next. They were out of the standings for medals but would continue to box for the consolation prizes. Still, Laszlo seemed satisfied. For a regional competition, we had made a good showing.

Chapter 24

I awoke early and lay in bed thinking. Jerzy snored away. He muttered and moaned in his sleep as if talking to somebody, making conversation within the dream he was having. The time would click by slowly until I met Maria at one o'clock. I hoped I could concentrate on the match this morning. I tried to see her face, hear her voice. Each had faded over time. Was she still the same girl I had known? Or had she changed since we'd last met? I threw back the covers and put my feet on the cold floor.

"What are you doing?" Jerzy mumbled.

"Getting up."

"It's too early."

"Then stay in bed."

Jerzy's reply was to turn over with his back to me. "You'll get no argument from me."

I slipped out into the hall and padded quickly down to the lavatory. I washed my face and hands, then after getting dressed, found my way to the eating area. I had no appetite yet and drew a small pot of tea. I was surprised to see Laszlo seated by himself at a corner table.

"You can't sleep?"

I shook my head, then sat down and poured out the tea.

"And you?" I asked him.

"I haven't slept well since before the Great War. I still hear and see things, you know."

I settled myself, then took a sip of the boiling liquid. "Why did you fight on the German side?"

Laszlo smiled, then shrugged. "We had so many choices, you see. The Tsar on one hand and the Kaiser on the other. One type of imperialism or the other. Did it matter? In my town, we joined with Germany. In other towns, it was different. I knew that whatever side I chose would lose."

"Why?"

"Poland is always the loser, Mordecai, no matter what side it fights on. In some ways, it was more convenient to join the German army. It was closer. Because they were united, I thought the British and the French had a better chance. If I'd gone with the Russians, I might have ended up as a Bolshevik or in Siberia," he said dryly. "And you? You're all right?"

"Yes."

"And that's why you're up in the so early on the day of a tournament."

"Yes."

Laszlo sighed. "So be it. You can go far in this, Mordecai. But it can be a dangerous place for a Jew."

"Why?"

"You'll call attention to yourself outside of the world of the Jews."

"I don't care."

Laszlo sighed, then smiled sadly. "You're young and fearless. You haven't learned to be afraid yet. And that's all right for now. But sometimes, fear can be a prudent thing."

"This is something you learned in battle?"

"The fearless ones died first, Mordecai. Each day you lived was a triumph. Each moment was to be cherished. So many died in foolish ways. I had a friend who liked to tell jokes. His name was Tomas. One day he was telling a story and got very caught up in it. For a moment, he forgot that he was in a muddy trench in France. We, his comrades, also forgot for a moment. We wanted to obliterate the despair around us, even for a short time. Tomas reached the climax of the story and in his excitement, he stood up. His head was just above the line of the trench. A sniper got him. Just a second before we were laughing and joking, and the next second we were covered in the blood and brains of Tomas. I saw his eyes turn up to the sky and for an instant, a quick flicker of understanding and then, the slightest of smiles. He knew he had escaped. The rest of us were left behind. Doomed to wallow in the misery and shit. In that brief moment, Tomas had lost his fear, Mordecai. A little fear can be a healthy thing because then you learn to fight the thing that frightens you. You learn to overcome it. If not, you must live your life scurrying like a crab moving sideways. This is one of life's great choices. How will you live?" Laszlo took a sip of his tea but it had gone cold and he spat the liquid back in his cup.

"If I'm afraid, I'll fight it."

"We fight our battles in the ring for now. I pray they are the only battles you will fight, Mordecai."

"You think not?"

Laszlo looked reflexively at his hands. They were thick and powerful and heavily callused like those of a workman. "The way the world is going, conflict is never far away. The history of Poland is one of conquest. In these times, it will be Russia or Germany – if not both."

"When?"

Laszlo shrugged. "Who knows? There's so much turmoil everywhere. And we attempt to bring order in the world between the ropes. I heard that you and the Russian were involved in a disagreement."

"Not a disagreement. Not really."

"But something happened?"

"Yes. He challenged me. And before he could do anything, I slapped him. He said some things."

Laszlo nodded, then clasped his hands together. Suddenly, he appeared small, almost shrunken to me. "He's very good but you can beat him. He may be stronger physically but there's nothing here." He touched his chest. "No heart or emotion. That's a deep flaw in a boxer. You can't be like a machine. Once you're down – and it happens to everyone – you must know how to come back. To do this, you must have both will and the spirit. The heart," he repeated and touched his chest again. Laszlo looked at me, then looked away as if he was embarrassed. "Think about your friend Frederick Valens and what a great champion he was. An extraordinary athlete. Grace and power are a rare combination, you know. I suggest," he said, pausing, "that you go and get some rest. There's time before the first match. There are two more fights before the Russian. Go and leave me to my memories. Some days, I feel it's all I have." Wordlessly, I rose and left Laszlo, who sat silently, deep in his thoughts. I went back to the room and stretched out on the bed.

I was awoken by a vigorous shaking and opened my eyes to find Jerzy looming above me. "He's asleep yet in his clothes. This is strange," Jerzy said to no one in particular.

I yawned. "I went for a walk. I couldn't sleep."

"Ah, does your conscience bother you? For punishing that boy in the ring yesterday?" I shook my head. Jerzy had a deep bruise under his right eye where he took that hard shot.

"You never told me about the girl," I said.

"What girl?" Jerzy had put on his gym clothes, the baggy old cotton tracksuit that had seen much better days. He wore a wool cap pulled down low on his head, almost covering his eyes.

"Don't box with me. You know."

Jerzy sat down opposite and smiled. "She's a boxing fan, it seems. Finds it very exciting."

"Uh-huh?"

"She's coming back this afternoon, she said. I think she likes me. I told her I'd win for her."

"And what's her name, this little convent girl who's so excited by the big strong boxers?"

"Sonya Padwa." The name meant nothing to me. She only represented my hopes and desires for Maria. And for that I was grateful.

"Be good to her. Don't do anything foolish."

Jerzy frowned. "What do you mean?"

"I mean, don't take advantage of her. She's young and knows nothing."

"And what do I know?"

"You live on a farm. You know how animals breed and humans too. That's what I mean. Just be careful with her, that's all."

Jerzy stood up, his brow creased. His blue eyes flashed. "I should've let the Russian go at you. You dare tell me how to behave? After what you plan to do?"

"What are you talking about?"

"Sonya told me."

"I'm meeting with her to talk, that's all. Sonya had no right to say anything."

"But she's helping you. There's some risk for her."

I nodded. "And I'm grateful. That's why I want you to treat her well."

"Who says I won't?"

"No one."

Jerzy wagged his finger. "Sometimes you go too damn far, you bloody..." And he held himself back, his face flushed deep red. He sputtered.

Jerzy exhaled noisily. "Nothing." He turned away. "I've said enough. You wouldn't understand anyway. You come from a rich home."

"And?"

The tall youth shrugged. "I'd like my life to be different. Is it wrong to want these things? This girl isn't like the ones I know. That's all."

"She has a family who may not agree with you. I know what it's like. At least you're a Polack and of the same faith."

Jerzy sat back on the cot opposite. "It may not be enough. I'm not from the right class."

"And perhaps you'll change this with your revolution."

Jerzy lifted his head. "Perhaps," he agreed but his tone wasn't convincing.

As I walked along the street, I fingered my jaw tentatively, then moved it around like a horse chewing oats. Speaking of chewing, Laszlo chewed me out angrily for the way I boxed that morning. It seemed as if I hadn't been there and it wasn't until I took an uppercut to the jaw in the second round that I woke up. I'd been thinking of Maria. I won the match on points but only just. Laszlo said the judges gave me the benefit of the doubt but the scores were very close. The other fighter, a red-headed boy, looked deeply disappointed having thought he had won. Laszlo harangued me for a good twenty minutes after the bout. I could only think of how to slip away. Barely having time to shower and dress, I hurried out of the gymnasium thinking only of Maria wondering how she would be, how she would look and how we would be together. I yearned for her and soon my feelings, I hoped, would be fulfilled.

Chapter 25

I boarded the number twenty-three motor coach and rode it for five or six minutes. I disembarked at Krechma Street, walked north a block to Spietszka and began to look for number ninety-eight, second floor. The houses sat neatly, looking well-tended with the remnants of cultivated gardens. Unlike the inner part of towns I was used to seeing, there was no laundry hung outside or animals kept in the yard. Quiet stateliness permeated the neighbourhood. The exterior of the three-story home had been painted recently. I glanced up at the second floor windows and thought I saw some movement, the jostling of a curtain perhaps. My mouth had gone dry and my heart felt like I'd been skipping rope for ten minutes. I trod up the steps to the front door, turned the heavy glass knob and stepped inside. To my left a staircase went up. I took the steps slowly, the sound of my footfalls muffled by the thick carpet. Weak light shone through a leaded-glass window on to the staircase. Otherwise, the interior of the house appeared dark and gloomy. At the next landing stood a door. I rapped once and the sound echoed throughout the house like a hollow gong. Before I could lift my hand again, the door was flung open and Maria stood before me.

Her hair had been pulled back severely and deep circles ringed her eyes, yet her skin was flushed. She seemed paler than I remembered. We stared at each other for a long moment.

"Maria," I croaked and reached out for her. She came to me swiftly, burying her face in my shoulder and began to cry. Her slim body wracked with powerful sobs and shudders. After a moment, we separated and I realized we still stood in the doorway. Maria half-laughed and half cried as I stepped inside.

"I never thought I would see you again," she murmured. Then she pulled back to take a closer look at me. "You've changed. You're taller and stronger. I can feel your muscles." I laughed, embarrassed. She laughed with me. "I'm sorry, I've lost my manners. Please, give me your coat. I shall make some tea." I removed my overcoat and handed it to her.

"How are you?" I asked her softly. She tried to smile, then shook her head as if afraid of what might come out of her mouth. As she did, heavy tears squeezed out of her eyes and rolled down her pale cheeks. She wrapped her arms around my coat and buried her face in it. After a moment, she emerged from its folds.

"It smells of you. And the outside," she said. She stepped back without taking her eyes off me, draped the overcoat on the arm of the divan and looked toward the kitchen. "I'll be just a moment," she said.

"I'll be here, Maria," I replied.

She nodded, then with quick, furtive steps went off to make the tea. As she went, I noticed she wore a simple white blouse and a dark skirt, black stockings and plain shoes with buckles. I sat on the divan and looked around the room, thinking it was what Mama would call well-appointed. The dining room table gleamed from frequent polishing, its deep burnished brown glowing in the pale afternoon light. I couldn't remember if I had wiped my shoes. As Maria appeared with a tray full of the tea things, I took the tray, easing it gently out of her hands and carried it over to the low-slung table in front of the divan. I set it down gently, then took her hands and kissed them. She put her hand to my cheek. We came together then and kissed, our first real kiss. Her lips trembled but she didn't pull away. After a long moment, we parted, her bosom heaving.

"You had better pour the tea," she said breathlessly. "Before it gets too strong. Is it hot in here?" And she waved her hands about her face.

"No." I poured out the tea and handed her a cup. "How did you get away?"

Maria took a sip of tea. "It wasn't easy. My parents took me out of school. I made an excuse to come and visit Sonya for a few hours. I don't have much time before they come back."

"And I must return to the gymnasium."

"But not yet," she cried. "You've just arrived."

"No, not yet," I said. "What are we to do, Maria? It all seems so hopeless. Your family doesn't want us to speak. You are locked away in school..."

She set down her cup again. "But that's only for this year. Then I am finished..."

"But I do my military service next year. That's two years."

"Where will you be?"

"Here. In Cracow."

"My parents want me to work with them in the bakery."

"But why can't you go to university? And then I can see you. I'll be living with my aunt, not in the barracks."

"University?" she asked herself, as if it were a brand new thought. "Why not?"

"I, I, just didn't think..."

"But you're a good student. Why shouldn't you go to university? You can do anything you want."

She shook her head. "My parents, they wouldn't allow it. It's all right if you're a boy but I am supposed to stay home until I marry someone acceptable."

"And that is not me, is it?"

She moved closer to me and took my hands. "That's not what I think or feel."

"My family," I began. "My family too would have concerns."

"Is everyone against us?" she asked.

174

"It would seem so."

She snuggled in close to me and I put my arm around her. We stayed like that, each not daring to let the other go. I could feel her warmth and the gentle heave of her chest. I wanted to hold and protect her. She seemed so fragile. Then she turned her face up to me and we kissed for a very long time. This was a different sort of a kiss. I felt a stirring between my legs and I know she felt something too. I pulled her closer.

"I love you," she murmured.

I didn't know what to do next. I touched her breast. To my surprise, she placed her hand over mine and pressed it to her. I could feel its firm ripeness and the swell each time she took a breath.

"Make love to me."

She ran her hands through my hair. I eased her back on the divan and moved my weight on to her. Her kisses were deeper now, more passionate. She pulled her skirt up and I touched the smooth skin of her thigh and she shuddered and moaned slightly. She pulled me to her and kissed me harder, hot fierce kisses. Her breath was like fire and infused me with heat. She unbuttoned her blouse and pushed down the top of her camisole. I put my mouth on her and she moaned. She reached down and unsnapped her garters.

"Quickly, my love. Quickly."

I began to fumble with my fly. Damn buttons were so awkward. Finally I got them free, almost ripping them out of the seam, when a terrible pounding sounded at the door. We froze. Who could that be? I sat up. Panic flooded Maria's face as we scrambled to put ourselves back together. The pounding increased in ferocity. The door crashed open. Two burly men charged in. An older man came in behind. I leapt up.

"Papa," Maria shrieked. The older man strode over to her and struck her brutally across the face. I leapt to her but was blocked by the two men. One of them grabbed me from behind and the other hit me in the belly. I went over.

"Hold him up," said Maria's father.

"No!" she screamed.

I was yanked to my feet. Maria's father stood short and wide, with ham fists spent kneading dough for many years. I looked him in the eye and saw nothing but rage.

He bellowed. "Yaaahhhh!" The fist cracked against my jaw. My knees buckled but the two oafs held me up.

"Papa. Stop. Stop." But her words drove him on. Each time he hit me I looked back at him with contempt. It drove him mad. Finally, one of the others stepped in front.

"Enough," he said.

I dropped to my knees. I managed to lift my head and smile through the blood and the bruises.

"Never again," he hissed. "Do you hear?"

Maria's father took hold of her and began to drag her out of the flat.

"Maria," I croaked but was cut off by a hand on my throat. A knife flashed before my eyes.

"Shut up, Jew. Or I'll cut your balls off. Understand?"

I nodded.

The husky voice continued.

"We'll wait here a moment until they're gone. Then we'll leave. You will never see her again. If you try to find her, we will kill you."

I heard Maria screaming and sobbing as she was dragged down the stairs, screaming, calling out my name. A door slammed and it went quiet. The man in front of me wore a long dark coat and a hat pulled down low on his forehead. He was unshaven.

"You stay here or you'll get this in your guts."

He brandished the knife. The blade gleamed in the pale light. The first man nodded to the other and I felt myself released. I fell over on to my back, panting. The two burly men backed away, with the first still pointing the knife in my direction. I heard them charging heavily down the stairs as I crawled to the window. There was no sign of Maria. I scrabbled for my overcoat, then stumbled out of the apartment barely keeping my balance down the stairs, half sliding down the wall. By the time I got out to the street, they'd gone. I looked one way, then the other. She'd disappeared.

I slumped down against a low wall and cried, head in hands. Tears of frustration, of anger and hate. Pedestrians looked at me curiously. I paid them no mind. After some minutes, I calmed down, wiped my eyes on my sleeve and blew my nose. Took my handkerchief and daubed the blood. I felt cut off and lost. After a while I felt strong enough to stand. I began to drift, having no idea where I was going or why. To look for her. When I returned home, I would go to the bakery and demand an explanation, demand to see her. They would tell me. I would force them. Let them call the constable, it didn't matter. I would see Maria again no matter what.

Chapter 26

It was late when I returned to the room. Jerzy lay deeply asleep, snoring heavily. I fell across the bed, fully clothed. I wanted to sleep like the dead. I didn't want to dream, to see or think about anything. I had worked myself into exhaustion and fell instantly into a dreamless sleep. I would need all my resources. The next day I was to fight the Russian. As I drifted off, I saw the smirk on the Russian's face, the cruel twisting of his thin lips. Maria, suddenly, seemed far, far away.

A hand shook me roughly awake. I groaned and rolled over, pulling the pillow over my head.

"Time to get your gloves on."

"Go away."

"He's being coy," Jerzy said.

"What time did he get in?" Laszlo asked.

"I don't know. I was asleep. It must have been late."

"After twelve," I replied. My thoughts turned to Maria. Yesterday had been both a dream and a nightmare. I recalled the soft feel of her skin, the scent of her hair, the taste of her lips and body.

Laszlo leaned in close. "How do you feel? You've got an important match today."

"Fine." I rolled over and looked up.

"You don't look fine. What the hell happened to your face?"

During the night, my left eye closed up. I could barely see out of it. My nose felt okay, not broken.

"I'll be all right," I said. "What time is the match?"

"It's been moved back a bit to twelve. You're now the main event. The two of you have attracted a great deal of interest. Apparently, one or two members of the Olympic committee have come from Warsaw."

"I don't care."

"What? Are you insane? You wouldn't want to make the Olympic team and represent your country in international competition?"

"This isn't my country," I replied. "I only live here."

"You were born here," Jerzy said.

"So what."

Jerzy turned to Laszlo. "He's in a foul mood. Something must have happened."

It was then that something occurred to me. I threw back the covers and leapt out of bed, seizing Jerzy fiercely by the arm. "The girl. Have you seen her? Did she come around yesterday?"

"What girl?"

"Sonya. Her name is Sonya."

"Ah yes, her." He paused, then shook his head. "No, I didn't see her."

I released him. "Damn."

"What is it?" Laszlo asked.

"I need to speak to her urgently."

"Perhaps she'll show up today."

"What time is it?"

Laszlo looked at his pocket watch. "Eight-thirty."

"What time must I be at the gymnasium?"

"Ten-thirty."

"That gives me two hours."

"Where are you going?" Laszlo demanded.

"I must go to this girl's house and speak with her."

Jerzy shook his head. "He's mad."

Laszlo seized me by the shoulders. "You can't go. You must prepare for the match. I'm not even sure you're in any condition to box at all."

"I'll be back in time."

"You need to get some ice on that eye to bring the swelling down."

"I'll be fine."

"You can't see and the Russian will pulverize you."

Laszlo glared at me. Jerzy looked away, not wanting to get involved.

"The Russian will be waiting for you. He'll be loose and you'll be tight. Do you want to be humiliated? We've come so far. Don't you want to beat him?"

I flung on my coat. "Of course I do. But I must do something else first." I pulled open the door and ran down the hall.

I caught the motor coach on the fly and swung inside. I paid the fare and took a seat, panting from the effort. I put my head back and prayed for the vehicle to move along faster but at the same time, I felt tired and wanted to rest. The stop by Sonya's street loomed up and I leapt out. I marched up to the house, went up to the second floor and rang the bell. There was no answer but I heard some stirring within. I rang again. Tentative footsteps came toward the door. It parted only a crack and an eye peered through.

"Sonya."

"Go away."

"Please tell me where she is. Where have they taken her?"

"I don't know."

"Sonya, please. I beg you to tell me." I slid to the floor, down on my knees and peered up at her. She saw my pain, felt it in my voice. She opened the door and looked down on me.

"I'm truly sorry but I don't know. They've taken her far away. I shouldn't have helped her. Maybe this wouldn't have happened. My parents are very upset with me. I'm not to go out. I can't go to school. I'm to be tutored at home. It's bad for me but for Maria, I just don't know. I just don't know." The girl glanced quickly over her shoulder.

"Sonya, who is that?" A voice called from behind her.

"No one, Mama. Just a tradesman."

"You'd better go," she hissed. "I can't help you." She slammed the door while I stayed on my knees.

"I will never kneel to anyone again," I said defiantly to the stolid wood door. "Never," I hissed.

As I descended the stairs, a dark, malevolent anger boiled up in me. I brushed by a man and almost knocked him over. The man protested but I kept going. I was deaf to his cries of outrage, blind to his indignation.

I caught the electric car back to the gymnasium, sitting on the bench seat jostled by other travellers as they moved up and down the narrow aisle. I felt the vibration of the car as it scraped along the steel rails. Pain welled up in me surging through my chest. I wanted to double over and hug myself to make it go away. But I didn't. Instead, I became a piece of steel inside, tempered and molten.

I arrived back at the gymnasium twenty minutes before the match. Laszlo was frantic. He shouted. He waved his arms but I kept quiet and ignored him. Laszlo looked at me curiously. Clearly, something had happened. He stopped shouting.

As I slipped into my trunks and held my hands out to be taped, I felt like a slab of finished metal, polished and indestructible. Laszlo taped my hands in silence but looked at me intently. I don't know what he saw, maybe rage, maybe determination. After he was done, I smacked my right fist into my left palm, then nodded. I did the same with the left. Then I held my hands out and in turn, Laszlo slipped on each worn boxing glove, then laced them up tightly.

"Let's go over to the mirror," he said. "Do some light moves. You need to warm up. How's your vision? Can you see?"

"Well enough," I replied.

"He'll work you there."

"I know."

Laszlo watched as I stretched, bent at the waist and touched the floor with my elbows, then did some lunges. I danced lightly on my toes and began to throw punches at the mirror. Laszlo moved around and forced me to move with him, throwing punches all the while. After a few minutes, I sweated freely. I felt warm and loose. Laszlo brought out a robe and draped it over my shoulders.

"Are you ready?" I nodded. "All right then. Let's go."

Jerzy appeared and patted me on the back. "Good luck. May God go with you."

"I thought you didn't believe in God."

Jerzy shrugged. "It's deep within me. There are times it doesn't hurt to believe."

Chapter 27

Laszlo pushed me forward. We left the change room area with its littered towels and the smell of sweat. We moved down the aisle. The seats were full. A good crowd had turned out. I saw the Russian approaching from the other side. He looked over and gave me a cruel smile. I neither shirked nor shrugged away but kept looking back until finally the Russian turned to his coach and whispered something.

We stepped into the ring and removed our robes. We took some stretches against the ropes. The referee, a heavy-set Pole with a shaved head and thick moustaches brought us to the centre. As the referee talked, I stared at the Russian until I thought I saw a flicker in his eyes, a flash of puzzlement. As we put our gloves together, the Russian spoke, "Feel the pain, Jew."

I didn't respond but in place of the Russian, I saw Maria's father, the sneer and outrage on his face. I saw again as he slapped her and dragged her out of Sonya's apartment. I saw his fist come at me.

"Are you all right?" Laszlo asked as I came back to the corner.

"Yes. Fine."

Laszlo didn't look convinced but he didn't have time to think about it. I had a few moments for his last instructions. "Don't rush into anything. Feel him out. Watch the overhand right. It is his best punch. He likes to use it but when he does, he's vulnerable inside."

"He won't use it."

"Stay alert," Laszlo admonished.

The bell rang and we jumped to our feet and moved into the centre of the ring. At first, we moved around each other warily, feinting and testing. I knew what I had to do. I had seen the Russian fight but I also knew it meant I would get hit hard. Points didn't matter to me, I was determined to go for the knockout. I swung wide with my left and the Russian blocked it with his shoulder. I swung wide again and caught the Russian above the right bicep but was repaid with a jab to the face. I kept my balance and bounced on my toes, moving back and forth. I swung with my right, a hard blow that caught the Russian on his left arm just below the shoulder. The Russian looked surprised and stepped back but flicked out another jab that caught me on the chin but it was a glancing blow. And so it went for the entire first round. I landed twenty-five or thirty blows up and down the Russian's arms but paid for it with jabs and uppercuts. There was some more bruising along the ridge of my nose and under the right eye.

"What are you doing?" Laszlo said, while sponging me off and giving me water. I took the bottle, drank, then spat into the bucket. "He's loading up on points. I don't think you scored once."

"You'll see."

"You're leaving yourself exposed. One good punch and he'll knock you down."

"I don't think so."

The bell rang for round two. Laszlo looked at me in exasperation. We moved out to the centre of the ring. The Russian had a confident, almost cocky expression on his square face.

I continued the pattern I'd started earlier, swinging wide and landing blows on the Russian's arms, all the while taking shots back, but the Russian couldn't get the solid punch he wanted, as I continued to slide step and bounce on my toes moving about. The second round continued much in the same manner as the first. I kept swinging wide and the Russian piled up points with crisp jabs to the face. I kept myself in motion. I sensed the Russian's frustration. At one point the Russian stopped and gestured as if to say, come to me and fight. I simply waited. Red welts appeared up and down the Russian's arms, bruising coming up under his pale skin. When the bell ended for round two, the Russian dropped his arms at his sides. He had thrown a lot of punches that scored but none had hurt. Laszlo had been watching. At first, he began to panic and then he saw what I was doing. He understood. He handed me the water bottle and toweled off my face.

"You're sure about this?" he asked.

I spat into the bucket. "Yes. He hasn't hurt me at all, just little stings. Now we shall see what will happen." We looked over at the other corner. The Russian's manager talked to him earnestly.

"He's saying they're far ahead on points and to stay away from you. Your only hope now is a knock-out," Laszlo said as if reading the other man's lips.

I smiled. "Exactly. That's what I want."

"You may have to chase him."

"I have plenty left."

"You take big risks, boy."

"For big rewards." I slipped the mouthpiece back in and waited for the bell.

At the beginning of the third round, we came into the centre of the ring and touched gloves. I could see the bruising on the Russian's arms and shoulders clearly now. He winced slightly as he brought his arms up. Despite his coach's advice, I counted on the Russian's arrogance to ignore it. It was a matter of his pride. Why should he run away from a miserable Jew?

Again, we felt each other out, measuring from a distance. The crowd had grown restless. Some had begun to clap, others even booed. They had come for fireworks, not a polite dance. They didn't have to wait long. I dropped my right arm and feinted left. The Russian saw the opening and brought out the overhand right. I stepped back and it grazed my chin, then stepped in with a right to the body that brought the Russian to his toes, followed by a left to the abdomen and another right to the ribs. The Russian grabbed for me but I danced out of range. The Russian's nostrils flared. He began to breathe hard. I looked at the broad face, the thin lips and flat nose. Once again, I saw the face of Maria's father and a tide of anger and hatred surged through my body in an electric pulse. Tempered steel. I stepped inside, moving my hands, quickly working over my opponent's body, and got in a hard right that forced the Russian back. Out of the corner of my eye, I saw the Russian's head come forward. I turned my face as the blow caught me on the cheekbone. A cry rose up from the crowd. The right side of my face went numb.

If it hadn't been for the headgear, the Russian might have knocked me out with the head butt or broken my nose. I glanced at the referee who watched impassively. Laszlo jumped up and down, screaming and gesturing from the corner. The Russian's eyes narrowed and his lips twisted into a leer but he held his arms low. I shook my head, stepped in and landed a vicious left to the Russian's face that snapped his head back. I followed with another left and then a right that caught the Russian square on the nose. Blood spurted. Drops ran down my chest but I didn't back off. Now the Russian shook his head and came toward me swinging.

"Jew bastard."

The blood ran in rivulets down the Russian's face. I got in a right uppercut that extended the Russian's neck and exposed his chin. I stepped back then forward and came in hard with a right anchored by my back foot. The punch connected solidly and I felt the jolt down to my elbow. The Russian's knees sagged just a little and his arms hung. All of the pounding in the first two rounds had taken its toll. I followed with another right and then a left. Another right caught him flush in the chin. I saw the Russian's eyes glaze over and begin to roll when I hit him again. I stood and measured the Russian carefully and landed a punch to the head. Sweat sprayed backward out of the Russian's hair.

Before I could raise my gloves to continue, the referee blocked me. We turned to see the Russian swaying on his feet like an ancient tree in a high wind and then it was as if his bones disintegrated and he crumpled to the canvas in a heap. The referee stood over the Russian and began the count. After ten, the Russian hadn't moved. The referee waved his hands, came over to me and lifted my right arm to the ceiling. The gymnasium echoed with yells and screams. Some sounded outraged. Some seemed delighted. All the rest just screamed because it was the thing to do. I went to my corner. Laszlo embraced me. I spat out the mouthpiece.

"I think he broke my cheekbone."

"We'll take a look in the change room," Laszlo replied.

"He should have been disqualified. Anyone could see what he did."

"You won," Laszlo said. "It doesn't matter."

I looked back at the Russian who had begun to come to and lay groaning on the canvas, his coach and a doctor leaned over him, talking him around. "I think he'll remember me."

Laszlo laughed. "I doubt that he will forget."

"I could have killed him," I said quietly.

Laszlo placed the robe around my shoulders and helped me through the ropes. I felt tired but it was a good feeling, although my cheek throbbed. The pain I felt and the pain I had inflicted didn't quell the same within me as I thought again about Maria, how she was forced down the stairs and out of my life forever.

Laszlo threw me a bound cloth filled with ice. "Hold it there. It'll help with the swelling." I placed the ice to my cheek. In the shower, I washed the Russian's blood off my body.

I examined my face in the mirror. The cheek had been badly bruised, mottled with purple and yellow clouds tinged with green. To grimace was painful, even to smile. The tournament hadn't been completed but I was done. No more fights on the agenda, anyway. Jerzy too, had won all of his bouts. We were each to receive a handsome medallion, Laszlo had told us. "What have they done with the Russian?"

"He's been taken to hospital. Broken nose and two cracked ribs is what I heard. Did you hate him that much?" Jerzy asked.

"I don't hate him at all."

Jerzy gaped. "You don't?"

I shook my head. "No. He isn't worth it."

"Then I'd hate to see how you treat someone you truly didn't like," he retorted.

"Let's hope you never find out, comrade."

Chapter 28

On the train ride home, I slumped back in my seat and tried to sleep but the throbbing of my cheek kept me awake. My hands were sore. I had hit the Russian hard. Harder than anyone else in my life – and it had felt good. Mama would not be pleased, of course. Confronting my mother was not something I considered lightly. I looked over at Jerzy who seemed glum.

"What are you moping about?"

He sighed.

"I enjoyed the excitement of the big city, the size and noise of it. Returning to the farm and its dull life with my parents and two sisters will be boring. With winter about to settle in, my life will be quiet and monotonous. My father will spend his days drinking vodka and criticizing me. In the afternoons, he goes to meet his cronies for games of cards and drinks in the local tavern, but he's never invited me. I know he goes there to get away during the day. To escape the sharp tongues of my mother and sisters who disapprove and cluck their feelings loudly, like hens with distemper. So you ask why I am not happy and that is the reason."

It was early Friday afternoon when we arrived at the train station. School for the day had finished. Jerzy trudged back to his weary existence at the family farm. The other two had melted away after saying their goodbyes. I looked about, then spotted Pyotr with the car, its engine idling.

I turned to Laszlo. "Can I offer you a lift into town?"

Laszlo picked up his own duffel bag. "Why not?"

Pyotr's eyes flicked to my bruised cheek but otherwise he said nothing other than a good day and welcome home. He stored the duffel bags in the motorcar's boot. Laszlo rode up front while I stretched my legs along the back. It had been an exhausting four days. As we drove along the road leading into town, I thought of Maria. When we came abreast of her family's bakery, I ordered Pyotr to stop.

"Wait, please."

I jumped out of the car and ran up to the window. The door had been boarded up and the windows papered over. I pulled on the handle. Locked. I trudged back to the car, shoulders slumped, head bowed.

"Drive on," I ordered tersely.

Laszlo lived in a walk-up flat in a no-man's land between the Polish and Jewish sections of the town. "So this is where you live," I said.

"Yes."

"Well..."

"You have talent, Mordecai. This is but the first of many contests you'll face."

"Thank you." We shook hands, then Laszlo hefted his duffel bag on to his shoulder and began to climb the metal steps to his flat.

I'd never thought about him outside of school. Was he married? Did he have children?

"See you on Monday."

Laszlo waved without turning about but continued the slow climb upward.

Mama shrieked when she saw me. She rushed to take me in her arms.

"Oh Ma."

"You're hurt. I shall call the doctor."

"I'm fine. It doesn't hurt at all."

"What did they do to you?" she asked, as tears slipped down her face.

"Please. Don't."

Simmy came running down the stairs, then pulled up abruptly when he saw me. "God in heaven," he said. "What did that?"

"Somebody's head."

"Mordecai!" I looked up to see my sister emerging from the kitchen. She threw her arms about me and I swung her into the air.

"Katya. It is so good to see you."

"Put me down," she ordered. She examined my face. "Getting into trouble again I see. Don't worry, I'll take care of it. I have my bag upstairs."

I looked up and a tall, slim man appeared behind her. He had wavy brown hair and liquid eyes. He smiled pleasantly. Katya stepped back. "Mordecai. I want you to meet someone special." She held out her hand and the young man took it and blushed. "This is Alexis. We met at school. He's a year ahead of me."

I straightened up and put a hand out. "It's nice to meet you, Alexis." The young man's hand was warm, the grip firm.

"Thank you," he said. "Thank you very much." I nodded, aware that I looked severe especially with the deep bruise on my face.

"I shall prepare the tea," Mama said. "Papa will be home tomorrow. Isn't that wonderful?"

Simmy came up to me. "Did you win?"

"What do you think, yeshiva bucher?"

"From your face, it's hard to tell."

I reached into the pocket of my coat and took out the medal. "What do you think of that, eh?" The others crowded around. I hung up my coat. Katya went upstairs to fetch her bag.

"Come into the kitchen," she said. She took me by the elbow and squeezed. "I've missed home very much."

I looked at her and saw the changes, the womanliness in her. Only twenty, yet she had the air of someone older and wiser. Her young man seemed boyish to me.

"And we've missed you too. Who'll patch me up if not you?"

"You must learn to stay out of trouble."

"I'm a slow learner."

"Come," she said and pushed me down on to a chair. Mama sliced up a honey cake and hummed, content that her family was altogether again. The samovar heated up. Katya probed my face. I winced. "What did this?"

"I told you. Someone's head."

"I thought you were boxing, not bullfighting."

I shrugged. "Sometimes, it's hard to tell the difference."

"I think the bone is fractured but we would need an x-ray to be certain. What do you think?" she asked, turning to Alexis. The young man stepped closer. His fingers probed around the cheek expertly without causing me any pain. The touch was sensitive but sure.

"I think you're right about it being broken."

"And so, what would you do about it?"

Alexis shrugged and smiled. "There isn't much to do when a bone is broken in the face. If it's severe, it might be repaired through surgery but here I think it's a crack which should heal on its own."

Katya cleaned the area around the cheekbone carefully, then applied some salve. "I can give you a bandage."

"No. I don't want it."

She closed up the bag, then stroked my jaw. "You've grown very handsome. Are you breaking any hearts yet?"

I coloured, then shook my head without speaking. Katya laughed. "Mama, I do think Mordecai is hiding something from us."

"What?" asked Mama, carrying tea things to the table. Alexis took the tray from her. "What things?"

"Things of the heart."

"Ah," but then she said nothing further.

"There's nothing to tell." And I gave my sister a pointed look, willing her to shut her mouth as I felt a terrible flood of pain.

Alexis interrupted. "I think the tea is ready."

"Come. Come. Sit down everyone." Mama handed out slices of cake while Alexis filled the cups from the samovar. There was talk and the clatter of cups and spoons drawing on the warmth of the kitchen. Katya held Alexis' hand under the table. It was plain to see they were very much in love.

"Welcome to our family," I said.

Alexis blushed. "Thank you. This means a great deal to me." He looked around the table at each one of us. "I'm an orphan you see, raised by my uncle and aunt with no brothers or sisters. Being welcomed by you means a lot. It's a special feeling. I. . . " He stammered, fighting his emotions. "Just thank you," he said softly. Katya smiled and squeezed his hand.

"I'll have another piece of cake," Simmy said.

"Please," said Mama.

"Yes. Please," Simmy acknowledged.

"They're pushy in that yeshiva." I asked. "Everything is grab, grab."

Simmy smiled. "Of course. How else will you be heard? Everyone's shouting all the time. There's no order, no politeness."

"As long as you don't forget here." I tapped the table with my forefinger.

"You sound just like Papa," Katya said.

"What's wrong with that?" I replied.

"No. It's just funny. I'm noticing things since I've been away, that's all."

I leaned toward her and thrust out my cup. "Then you will notice that my cup needs refilling. Please."

Katya shook her head and laughed softly. "Who'll stitch you up when I go back to school, troublemaker?"

"I'm not a troublemaker. I never look for trouble."

"Children, please," Mama said. "I want to hear about Katya and her life in Prague, her schooling. But first, when did the two of you meet?"

After the tea was finished, we boys took a walk in the garden. The day was brisk but clear and sunny. "How did this happen really?" Alexis asked indicating the cheek.

I fingered it gingerly. "My opponent butted me with his head. The referee did nothing."

"Shouldn't he have been disqualified?"

I shrugged. "You're not a Jew."

"I've told Katya I will convert."

I stopped and looked at him. He stood slightly taller but had the physique of a reed.

"Then you're a fool."

Alexis gaped at him. "Why would you say such a thing?"

"Because we're hated throughout Europe."

"But aren't you proud of your heritage?"

I stepped up to him and looked him fiercely in the eye.

"Of course I am. And I'll use my hands and my brains in every way to prove it. But that doesn't take away the fact that life is always harder for us, especially here in Poland. Did you know that Katya couldn't get into medical school here not only because she was a woman but also a Jewess?"

Alexis swallowed hard. "No, I didn't know."

"That's why she had to go to Prague and be away from the family. It was difficult, but it's what she's wanted all her life."

"She told me."

I put my hand on the young Czech's arm. "I don't want to alarm you but I think it's important you know how I feel."

"And do your parents feel the same way?"

"You need to ask them. They know how I feel."

"Mordecai's a fighter," Simmy said. "He's always getting into scrapes. That's his nature." He adjusted his spectacles, then squinted up to the sun. He shivered. "It's getting colder."

"Let's go in," I said. "We'll see what Mama has prepared for dinner."

The next morning I was sitting at the kitchen table drinking tea and munching on toast when Katya came in. "You're up early," I remarked.

"I am used to it," she said. "My classes begin at seven-thirty. Some days it would be good to be able to lie in but I just can't imagine it anymore." She looked at me. "How's your cheek?"

"Sore, but I'll live."

"You're such a man now, so big and strong but you don't look happy. What has happened? You can tell me. I won't say anything to Mama and Papa if you don't want me to."

My face flushed. I clenched my teeth, then shook my head. "I'm not ready to talk about it."

Katya sat beside me and stroked my hair. "I can see that you're in pain."

"You'll make a good doctor, Katya, but some things you can't heal with medicines and bandages."

"Is it someone I know?" I shook my head. "What happened? Did she reject you?"

I shook my head again. "She was sent away. I'll never see her again."

Katya looked shocked. "Can this be true? In this day and age?" She was, after all, a scientist and thought in absolutes as if everyone and everything was enlightened.

"They are Polacks who hate Jews."

Katya bit her lip. "I'm sorry."

"There's nothing you can do for me, Katya." I patted her hand. "I hope you'll be happy. He seems nice."

"Yes he is, isn't he? He's made the time go very quickly. Most of the time, we study. There's so much work to do. So much to learn but it's wonderful. And I love Prague. Such a beautiful city. The people are warm and friendly."

"That's good. I'm happy for you," I said.

"Then say it like you mean it." And she gave me a playful slap on the wrist, probed my arms with her fingers, squeezed my biceps. "How strong you are. When did you get so strong?"

"When you weren't looking, little sister." I downed the rest of the tea. "Now I'm going to school. You go back to bed. Enjoy it." I rose and put on the school jacket with its gold crest.

"I want to wait for Papa."

"He could be all day."

"That's all right. I don't mind. It's been such a long time."

I kissed the top of her head. "You always were stubborn. It must run in the family."

Chapter 29

I strode out the kitchen door to the shed where I kept my bicycle. I buttoned up my wool coat and pulled my cap down low to keep the wind off my face. Frost layered the ground. Winter was coming.

I cycled vigorously to keep the chill out and warm up my legs. In the aftermath of the shock of losing Maria, my mind had cleared a little. I couldn't help but wonder how her father had found us. How did he know where we were and what day and time we were to meet? Did they simply become suspicious? It was possible. Or did something else happen? As my feet went round and round on the pedals, so did my thoughts. Apart from the shock and pain of losing her, something else nagged at me. Some small thought swimming up from the murk.

I placed my bicycle in the rack and slowly trudged up the stone steps. A group of girls stood huddled at the top, talking and giggling. When she saw me, she broke away immediately and as I climbed up, her dark, pretty face came into focus. The elegant brows arched and I could smell her cologne even in the open air. Her grey-blue eyes opened wide with curiosity. I climbed the last step and we stared at each other wordlessly. Her eyes narrowed, then widened and an expectant look formed on her face; one of knowledgeable self-satisfaction. In that instant, something passed between us. Suddenly I knew. I stepped back, almost losing my balance on the stairs, but quickly righted myself. I stepped closer to her so I could speak quietly. Now the girl looked afraid. Her friends looked at us curiously.

"It was you, wasn't it?"

"What?"

"You told them, didn't you?"

She stepped back now, shaking her head haughtily. "I don't know what you are talking about."

"You were her friend. You betrayed us. Betrayed her confidence. Why? Why?"

"You must be mad."

I grabbed her wrist. "I know it was you. I know it."

Something settled in her and she steeled herself. "So what? What if it was?"

I held her shoulders now. "You ruined everything. Why?"

Katrina's face turned into an ugly mask. "I was jealous of her. Why should she, a silly convent girl have all the fun? It wasn't fair." She shrugged herself out of my grip. "Besides, I never liked her. Miss Goody-Goody."

"What kind of person are you? What sort of person does such a thing?"

She snarled in contempt. "You're such a boy. Perhaps one day you'll be a man. But for now, such a disappointment." She laughed and backed away to her friends, continuing to laugh and point at me. Her friends, not even knowing what she laughed about, joined in. I stood there helplessly. I wanted to destroy them but stood powerless. I couldn't fight a woman's scorn. I didn't know how. I swore to myself that I would keep looking for Maria, that I would never give up even if it took all my days. Yet, I didn't know how events would conspire against me, that I'd be forced to make dark choices even against my better judgment. In the arena of war, two people became insignificant and at times, had to let each other go forever.

Chapter 30

I thought Beulah had died. She lay in the cot with her eyes closed, a secret smile curving her lips. She looked at peace. I gave her shoulder a shake.

"Thought I'd gone off, did you?" she asked.

"It crossed my mind."

"Nah. I'm feeling better. I was thinking about what happened to you, Mr. G. All that trauma, real soap opera stuff, huh? Snatched out of the arms of your girlfriend, getting beat up, fighting that other Russian guy, then finding out her best friend betrayed you because she was jealous? Man, not even TV is that good. But I'm sorry for what happened to you. It musta been painful."

"Yes, it was," I said. "All of it."

"Seems like you live in the house of pain, Mr. G."

"I've been there and it's not a pretty place."

"I hear you on that one. I know that place too well."

Stalingrad, 1942

The Krechma tank manufacturing facility equaled the size of ten airplane hangars placed side by side. Twenty-five thousand men and women toiled there. Since the peace pact in 1939, operations had been converted from building tractors to tanks for the war effort. Stalin had spent one hundred million rubles on the conversion while proclaiming a metal drive that saw every spare piece of scrap transported by lorry, wagon or donkey melted down and beaten into a tank shell.

The Germans had moved quickly, eating up hundreds of kilometres of Russian soil in mere weeks. Towns and villages fell, some disappeared forever. The roadways had been lined with the horror of the occupation; men, women and children strung up in the trees. The Nazis didn't discriminate, they gloried in the blood sacrifices, sending a message – that Russia would scream along this pathway of pain. Stalin proclaimed a scorched earth policy. I thought bitterly about the two years prior when trainloads of food and supplies had been shipped to the Germans across the border. These supply trains stretched for kilometres, sometimes taking days to get through the lines. Stalin fed and clothed them and now this. This time when the Germans came, they found burning fields and cottages, the stink of soot in their nostrils. Animals were slaughtered and set ablaze as the peasants fled east toward Moscow. Advancing quickly, the German supply lines had to feed, clothe and service a million men and their machines. Stalin feared them. But he knew the Russian spirit and the deep attachment to the land. He knew history and that invading hordes had been confronted and pushed back. Russia could break the back and sear the soul of anyone. But I also knew that the Soviet Union was not for me. To live under the yoke of communism would be like living death. I vowed to get out as soon as the war was done and search for my family.

I travelled by train from Moscow, sitting upright for two days. The trains were crowded with hollow-eyed men and peasant women wearing shell-shocked expressions. The Germans had captured Rostov and controlled all of the Crimea. The front lay just one hundred kilometres to the west and closed rapidly. Field Marshall Paulus and the German 6th Army, soon to be bolstered by the 4th Panzer division, went on the move. Afraid that Moscow would be vulnerable, Stalin kept most of his troops stationed around the capital. Only the 62nd and 64th armies had been dispatched to the aid of Stalingrad under the command of Marshall Vasily Zhukov and General Vasilevsky. I thought back to what seemed another lifetime when I rode the train to Cracow. I thought of my teammates and wondered what had become of them. For an agonizing moment, my soul ached as I recalled the image of Katya and Alex, clutching the baby as they fled on foot that horrific day. And for my parents and Simmy, I kept my hopes alive, burning within. The movement of the train and the heat in the compartment rocked me to sleep.

A hand shook me roughly. "Wake up, Captain."

I looked up into the creased, slanted eyes of an army Sergeant, a veteran old beyond his years. Leathery face and flaps of skin over his eyelids suggested he had spent a great deal of time outdoors, squinting into the sun. He wore long, thin moustaches in the Chinese style.

"Stalingrad?"

The other nodded. The fellow had been seated opposite me the entire trip. We hadn't spoken but I was aware the man had been watching.

"What are you doing in Stalingrad?" he asked.

Anger flashed through me.

"None of your business, Sergeant."

I stood up and stretched, then gathered my kit bag and duffel from the overhead compartment. I waited a moment. The Sergeant brought an amused expression to his face, then shrugged and joined the flow of bodies leaving the train.

Will I die here? I asked myself. I knew the situation. Outnumbered and lacking in artillery, the Soviet troops were outmanned and outgunned by the Nazis. It was here we had been sent to make a stand. The General had been very clear and to the point at the briefing three days earlier. We were in for it. The Panzer divisions were tough, maneuverable and fast.

I joined a group of officers who, like me, found ourselves transported directly to the Krechma factory. The officers stood around talking quietly, leaning in to make themselves heard above the noise of the trains entering and leaving the station, and the pounding of boots on pavement. All non-essential civilian personnel had been evacuated, especially women and children. Across the tracks, the station teemed as peasants and city folk lined up with whatever they could carry and waited for the next train; anxious, strained expressions etched on their faces.

I lit a cigarette standing apart from the others. There were no Jews in the group that I could see. I had come across a handful of Jewish officers but none in the tank corps, not in my division anyway. It didn't matter. I had no desire to get close to them. I thought of the Polish action and how dark it all seemed. This, to me, seemed even bleaker. I knew we acted the role of human barricade thrown against the advancing marauders. Kill or be killed, that's all that mattered. I had no ties or other responsibilities, I remained shackle-free. I didn't think about dying, I just thought about killing. I felt little loyalty to the Soviet state. To me it was no worse or better than Poland. It gave me the opportunity to kill Nazis but I wasn't a communist, either. I didn't believe in the state as my master unlike my old friend, Jerzy, who seemed destined to become a cog in the Russian machine. The stationmaster appeared and beckoned to the thirty or so officers standing around. The group threw down their cigarettes, then shouldered their bags and walked off behind him. I trailed.

"Well Captain Goldman, what do you think?"

I stood, legs splayed and stared up. I took in the metallic sheen, the breadth of the rivets, the jutting power of the cannon, the width of the treads. The sheer size of it.

"Impressive."

"The T-34 weighs 220,000 kilos. It can attain speeds of close to one hundred kilometres per hour on flat terrain. It can knock over an oak tree or smash a brick wall as if it was made of eggs. It can climb mountains and dig its way out of valleys. It is equipped with internal communications that uses radio frequencies. You can speak to the other commanders within a five kilometre radius. The cannon shells weigh twenty-five kilos and the gun has a range of between two and three kilometres depending on the terrain and wind conditions. It is the most powerful tank ever built. No one else has anything like it. It is a supreme fighting machine. This tank will stop the Germans in their tracks."

I looked over at the plant manager. "I beg your pardon, but it is men who will stop the Germans, not tanks."

The plant manager hesitated, then smiled. His teeth were full of metal.

"Of course. But our tanks will be of some use I think?" I nodded. "Care to go in?" He indicated the ladder at the side. I clambered up, unwound the hatch, then nimbly dropped inside. I stared intently, taking in every detail. This would be my home for god knows how long. It had to accommodate four men. Tank life was not for everyone. I would have two days to get prepared. Two days of training and familiarizing myself with all of the controls of the mechanical beast. Two days to get to know my crew and work with them before we went out into the field. Already, operations at the huge plant were being dismantled and shipped by truck and train to Moscow. After two days, this would be the largest abandoned tank factory in the world. Smaller plants had been established around Moscow and worked at churning out munitions and artillery for Stalin.

Inside the tank was dark and airless like a tomb. I switched on the auxiliary lights, touched the surprisingly small steering mechanism, looked out the viewing slot to assess the range of vision. It was limited. I fiddled with the hydraulics, swiveling the cannon left, then right, up and down. Its fluidity surprised me. Some of the older tanks had to be hand-cranked into position. To my left and right were the machine gun placements and in the rear, the tube for loading cannon shells.

I strapped on the headset and flicked the switch for the radio. Static burst into my ears and I ripped it off. At least it worked. Holding the headset close to my ear, I fiddled with the dials to see if I could find a workable frequency, but there was too much echo and metal about to pick anything up. The strong smell of oil and diesel caused my nostrils to flare. Another innovation, I discovered – night lamps for navigating in the dark. I could imagine what it would be like driving this beast in the dead of a winter's night, the heat burning us up within while outside the ground froze solid. But for now, the weather remained clear and hot. And there wasn't much time. I switched everything off, clambered up the hatch, then shinnied down the side, dropping the last several feet to the ground nimbly.

"Satisfactory?" asked the plant manager.

"Very."

"Come then. There's no time to waste." I took note of the number, 330. The bureaucrat marked it on a sheet attached to his clipboard.

The noise in the plant deafened with the roar of tank motors, trucks barreling in and out of the loading area, men shouting amid the clanging of metal as the machinery was being dismantled. A team of engineers strung wires and rigged explosives. When all looked clear, the massive factory would be dynamited. Nothing left for the Germans but rubble. I looked back at the massive machine. The linked tread that powered the tank stood more than six feet high. Two hundred and twenty thousand kilos of metal. Would it be enough?

I had been assigned a room in the workers' barracks that had been emptied out. Over the evening meal, it was announced that the Germans had swept through Estonia and Lithuania. The Ukrainians had welcomed them with open arms. The Nazis now occupied Minsk. Rumours of the mass executions of Jews passed from ear to ear. I met my crew, two Russians and a Pole.

The men sat at a small round table, smoking and drinking vodka. Training exercises started the next day. Each had been studying the manuals they had been given. Mischa – the right gunner – was a tall excitable fellow with close-cropped blond hair and blue eyes set close together as if his head had been squeezed when a young child. Yuri was a small man, neat and compact, who wore a short bristled moustache. His shoulders were enormously broad, his torso dwarfing his short legs. He had been an amateur wrestler and weightlifter.

Rolf came from a Russian father and a part-German mother. He seemed sensitive about the German blood in him. Rolf was shorter and slimmer than me but extremely lithe. He could balance himself on one hand. He demonstrated his prowess in the mess. The soldiers erupted into cheers; someone brought out a balalaika and the dancing began. I sat back and watched amused. Mischa, the other Pole, sat with me.

"You think this is strange, Captain?"

I looked at him, trying to focus on the too-narrow eyes.

"No, it's fine. There'll be little time for dancing later. Dancing won't help defeat the Nazis."

"Perhaps not. But it's the spirit of the people that makes a difference, don't you think?"

"You fought in '39?"

Mischa nodded. "Yes. I was with Tadiz. We met them at the base of the Carpathians, then got pushed back all the way to Warsaw and farther. Most of my comrades were killed. I fled east toward the end of September. I have relatives who lived over the border. They got me across." He lowered his voice. "It was touch and go with the Russians too. Several times, I was almost killed. But now I suppose, they need us and we have a common enemy. Besides, they'll need loyal Poles once this is over."

"What do you mean?"

"I mean that Stalin will expand his borders also should he win. If he doesn't, then it won't matter to any of us. We'll either be dead or prisoners in these famous camps we hear about."

"You're cynical."

Mischa shook his head. "No, just realistic. I'm not a communist but I will swear allegiance to them if it will save my life, wouldn't you?"

"I'm not a communist…yet," I replied. Was I being tested? We heard of spies who reported back to the commissars. Loose talk could be a dangerous thing. Perhaps this fellow wanted to probe my loyalty. "I'm interested in killing Nazis, that's all."

"Very noble."

"You mock me? Don't forget that I'm an officer and you are a Sergeant."

Mischa's eyes narrowed even further until they looked cross-eyed. "Of course...sir."

"What did you do before the war?" I asked.

"I taught literature at the university."

"Which one?"

"Cracow."

"I've been there."

"I know."

"Ah..."

"Yes, I'm a boxing enthusiast. I recognized you although it must be about ten years ago. I was a young student then."

"Eleven."

"I thought there was going to be a riot that day. It was quite exciting, wasn't it?"

I laughed at the man's perversity. "Yes, it was. I had a great deal on my mind then."

"If it wasn't boxing, then it must have been a woman."

"There is always a woman. But I fought in Cracow twice. Once in high school and once when I was doing my military service."

"And your family?"

"Still in Poland. My sister and her husband disappeared when the Germans invaded. We were separated."

"I have only my mother and I haven't heard from her in almost two years."

I poured each of us a shot of vodka. We clinked glasses, then tipped our heads back. Mischa pulled a pair of spectacles from his pocket and put them on. The effect served to narrow his eyes even more. The irises radiated cobalt blue.

"How well do you see?" I poured another glass for each of us.

"Well enough."

"Can you use a machine gun?"

"Of course. Every professor of literature knows this."

"Good. Rolf will take the other gun. Yuri will load the cannon shells. He seems strong enough and there's little room in the back of the compartment. It's a good fit for a smaller man."

"Don't worry, Captain. I'm a good shot."

I stood up and patted him on the shoulder. "You had better be. And now I have some manuals to study if I want to figure out how the damn tank operates. Good night." Mischa gave me a short salute. Rolf and Yuri sat at a nearby table and nodded to me as I went by. They sat with some of the other tank crews getting drunk. I didn't mind. There wouldn't be much time for leisure after the next few days. I settled into my makeshift quarters and pulled out the manual. Half an hour later, I fell asleep.

A horn blared through the barracks at five-thirty the next morning. It had been hot during the night. I went to the sink to shave and prayed for hot water. A stream of ice erupted from the tap. I wondered if there was any chance of a shower. After shaving, I walked down the hall only to find a long line-up. I decided to get in the tank straightaway and gathered up the other three men to accompany me. I turned the key, pressed the starter button and the massive diesel engine roared to life. The interior shook. I felt the vibration running up my arms and legs. I adjusted the headset and switched the microphone on.

"Can you hear me? Am I clear?"

"Yes."

"Yes."

Mischa waved and grinned from his low seat.

"Good. We're ready."

Two signalmen down in front directed the line of tanks to the factory exit. We proceeded to adjacent grounds for maneuvers. One of our first tasks would be to test the cannons by firing into the factory.

"Have you got everything?" I asked. "There's no going back now." I took in nods all around. The men seemed nervous. The interior sweltered. I turned on the internal fans and ordered the hatch open. Yuri went up and stayed there, enjoying the respite from the heat below.

"Yuri, how long is the line?"

"About thirty ahead of us, Captain. They're being waved on."

"Good. "

In a moment, I saw the tank in front of us jolt forward. I waited a moment, then released the throttle and the T-34, number 330 shuddered forward.

It seemed slow going, stopping and starting as each tank trundled forward. After each line had cleared, the building was evacuated. Engineers on motorcycles swept through to make certain no one had been left behind. The roll calls had been checked scrupulously and all men had to be accounted for. If anyone had gone missing, it meant a court martial and possibly, a firing squad.

The tanks rumbled out one by one, spewing dust and dirt behind them. They assembled in rows on elevated ground about a kilometre from the factory buildings. From there, the front row would fire their cannons, descend the hill, then from the middle turn right or left and come around behind the other lines which would then move up. I drove to our designated spot while Yuri shouted directions. Signalmen wearing white armbands pointed us forward. I got a feel for the tank, how it responded to the controls, whether they were tight or loose, especially the braking mechanism. It took some time for the behemoth to get moving and similarly, demanded time and distance when coming to a full stop.

I followed the tank in front slowly, ten kilometres per hour. We crested the hill, then drove parallel to the crest for one hundred metres.

Yuri came over the radio. "We're to stop here, Captain."

"Very well, come inside."

I waited for the tank in front to finish its maneuvers, then I turned, changed gears to reverse and backed in just as if I were docking a small ship in its berth. A voice came over the radio requesting all officers attend a briefing in the clearing several hundred metres to the southeast. I left the tank's engine idling.

"You can relax outside. Have a smoke. Don't do anything without me." The others exchanged looks.

"Yes, Captain." Mischa responded for the crew.

I went up first, then the rest followed. I could see it would take some time to build a rapport, for them to trust me. The day glowed brightly with a light breeze. I felt a thirst and yearned for a drink, the thought of vodka burning back in my throat. I adjusted my cap and pulled my tunic into place. Most of the time, I would be wearing coveralls but for the maneuvers I kept my light uniform on. Everything else had been stowed on board the tank, now our portable home.

Over one hundred officers attended the briefing. We stood about in a large circle as we received our orders. The training exercise would begin, then we'd form up in the eastern part of the city near the west bank of the Volga and make camp there for the night.

A signalman waved a flag, then sprinted quickly away. The tanks lined up some twenty wide and thirty deep. Our position was now in the third row back and close to the centre. After I fired two cannon shells, we would descend the hill and veer to the right, then form up at the end of the line. It would take hours for the entire line to fire. We had been ordered to keep all hatches down. I had the fans blowing at maximum yet it remained suffocating. The men, me included, stripped out of our uniforms and into the light coveralls we'd been issued. I had my coveralls unbuttoned to the waist so I'd be free to work in my undershirt. The others followed suit. For the first time, the men saw the small blue tattoo on my right bicep.

"What's that?" Yuri pointed.

"It's the insignia of my old regiment."

"But why...?"

"Because when you're together as a unit, solidarity is important, no matter your personal feelings. Do you understand?"

"Yes sir." I looked around at the others, who nodded in turn.

"We're here to stop the Nazis. Nothing should interfere with that. And it won't be easy, believe me." A voice crackled in the headset.

"Let's get ready. Yuri, load the first shell." The small man leapt to the task, sliding the cumbersome shell into the breech as if it were a light caliber bullet. I checked the sight lines, called out a reading. Yuri adjusted the controls.

"Fire."

The cannon recoiled and the entire skin of the tank shook from the reverberation. I followed its trajectory and watched the shell burst into the building, bringing down an entire corner in a plume of dust and rubble.

"Again. Two degrees higher this time."

Yuri moved smoothly, not hurrying, relaxed yet efficient. Again, the cannon recoiled and the men held on to their positions as the massive vibration swept over us.

"Good."

The crew had done well. I set the tank in motion and we descended the hill. To the left, other tanks had commenced firing and the whistle of shells filled the air. We heard the echo of multiple explosions and witnessed the gigantic factory begin to crumble. After assuming the new position, we were put on stand-by, and the men climbed out. Two hours later, the exercise had finished. Whole sections of the factory had collapsed in heaps of concrete and steel but the basic infrastructure remained standing. The sappers quickly and efficiently went to work, running spools of wire to a series of detonators. It took some minutes but soon all of the detonators had been set and the men holding the plungers awaited the signal. A colonel strode to the top of the hill with his arm raised high. All eyes fell on him. The colonel brought his arm down, sword-like, cutting through the thick air, and almost as one, the plungers went in. There was a few seconds delay, then there came a rumble followed by a series of booms that rolled out over the plain in waves. I watched through my field glasses and saw the foundation of the mighty factory disintegrate as the remaining walls slid downward into a newly ruptured crevice. The men felt the rumble inside themselves as the mighty factory collapsed into a great cloud of dust that spread up then outward like a blanket. Everyone watched. No one moved. There was complete silence as this symbol of Soviet power disintegrated. After a long moment, a man broke ranks, then another, then finally the men slowly turned and went about their business.

In groups of twenty, the tank commanders made their way to the west bank of the Volga. And there, we bivouacked for the night. I sat up smoking a cigarette and drinking from a bottle of vodka that I passed around. It was a clear night and cooler. In the distance, we heard what sounded like thunder. We knew it was mortar and artillery fire not far off, perhaps fifteen or twenty kilometres to the west, no further. The men looked tense and no one spoke much. Mischa crouched beside me. I held out the bottle and he took a swig.

"What do you think, Captain?" He jerked his head toward the sounds coming to us out of the night.

"We'll see action soon."

"You don't think about dying?"

"Not too much. I think about killing. The other will happen and no one can stop it." The others stopped their quiet conversation to listen in.

"That doesn't give me much confidence."

I took a drag on the cigarette. "I can't help you. You need to decide for yourself. I'm here to fight. No one wants to die but that's always a possibility. You saw that in Poland two years ago, didn't you? I saw General Witold blown to pieces in front of my eyes. The men scattered. Who knows what happened to them? I went home to see my family then I came here. Nothing has changed, has it Sergeant? We face the same enemy, the same dangers as we did two years ago."

"Perhaps it's worse this time."

Mischa crouched beside a large rock, removed a tobacco pouch from his tunic pocket and began to roll a cigarette. "There's talk the Germans are sending a very big force and we don't have enough artillery and men to stop them."

"There's always talk."

"But what do you think?" Rolf asked quietly. "What have you heard?"

I looked at him and wondered if his loyalties were torn because of his mixed blood. "I haven't heard anything. I know what you know."

"But..."

"I think we should get some sleep. We may not have another chance anytime soon." We bedded down beside the monstrous T-34, number 330. Quiet conversations drifted over the air all around us. The glow of cigarette ends arced in the night air. As I lay in the dark, I thought they looked like fireflies, the ones I'd seen as a boy in back of our property. I stared up at the sky. The moon shone brightly, not quite full and barely shrouded by scant, ghostly clouds gliding by. I drifted into sleep.

A droning woke me up, the pervasive hum of powerful engines infusing the night sky. The moon had clouded over. The sound formed all around us.

Mischa sat up. "What's that?" The others had awoken too.

"Planes," I said. "Bombers. Listen to the heavy throb of the engines. Get dressed quickly."

A few moments later, they were clothed and ready, gathered by the side of the tank. They gazed toward the city some fifteen kilometres away. They heard the high-pitched whistles, then the muffled gasps of explosions. Shards of light split the sky. "They're bombing the city." Mischa's voice was toneless, almost devoid of life.

"Who's left?" Rolf asked.

I shrugged. "The city hasn't been fully evacuated yet. It's difficult to know how many are left. They'll be captured and shot by the Nazis."

Fires had broken out. The flashes continued as wave after wave flew in, released their deadly cargo and flew off. "There must be hundreds," said Yuri. The flickering light of destruction illuminated their faces in a ghastly pallor.

We stood for what seemed like hours as the planes swept in and systematically razed the city of Stalingrad. We remained motionless, paralyzed by the power and the horror before us, explosions reverberating in our ears. There we stayed until a runner came by with orders for me. He whispered urgently in my ear, then moved off in the semi-darkness to alert the others.

The crew turned to me expectantly.

"Gather your things. We must cross the Volga before they bomb out the bridge. We'll make our stand there. Quickly now." The camp cleared in a matter of moments. The crew clambered up the side and dropped down the hatch one by one. Inside, we took our positions, strapped on helmets and headsets. The tank's engine roared to life. I tuned into the command frequency and awaited instructions. I knew now that the fight to the finish would begin. I looked forward to it but still, the pit of my stomach heaved, my mouth went dry. I hoped it would all go our way.

Chapter 31

Over the next two days the German airforce blanketed the city, bombing Stalingrad to rubble. The Soviets knew that behind the air-borne destruction, Field Marshal Paulus and his 6th army awaited, primed and ready to mop up. The Soviet 62nd and 64th hunkered down on the other side of the Volga. No one slept. The bombing raids jarred everyone's nerves. We existed on cigarettes and tea and sips of vodka, the only supply that appeared to be plentiful. We joked that the commissars brewed it up in the forest from discarded potato peelings.

I thought about the future. We'd heard rumours that the Germans had amassed more than a million men with the arms and artillery to support them. Meanwhile, the warmth of the summer began to give way to the sharp air of the autumn. The nights grew colder and when we awoke frost permeated the ground. It melted by mid-morning but the men knew it was time to pack away the summer gear in anticipation of the worsening weather. The summer had been unusually hot and dry. Hotter than many could remember. It would make the winter seem even colder.

After the last tank and the rear guard had crossed the bridge, the sappers finished wiring it up and waited. The bridge, built in 1927, had been a marvel of Soviet engineering. Almost two kilometres long and constructed out of new materials, steel and concrete, the structure had collapsed twice before the designers figured out how to keep it standing. The outer walls constructed of stone, the base poured concrete and the interior, a new type of tempered steel imported from Germany. The consulting engineers were German too. But it had stood as an example of Soviet modernism, spanning its brave new world. Looking at it, you might think it would have stood forever.

On a clear, cool morning, three days after the bombing of Stalingrad had ceased, I squatted behind the T-34 to relieve myself. I lit my first cigarette of the day. A faint cry went up and spread along the banks of the river from group to group. I hitched up my pants, threw away my cigarette and retrieved the field glasses from the branch where I'd hung them. I climbed on top of the tank and scanned the horizon. Mischa's head popped up out of the hatch.

"What do you see?"

I handed him the glasses. "Take a look."

Mischa peered through the lenses. A low mist drifted above the water. Through the haze, however, he saw men and machinery emerge out of rolling clouds of dust. A massive force lined the banks opposite. I observed our camouflage netting and wondered if they were fooled. The Germans halted along the banks.

"My God," Mischa exclaimed. "I've never seen an army so large. There's no end to it."

"What's happening?"

"They're stopped before the bridge. I can see a group of officers. It looks like they're having a discussion. One of the officers is waving. Two Nazis on motorcycles are coming. They're being waved on to the bridge."

"Let me see." I took the field glasses. I focused on the two riders moving cautiously. They rode back and forth on an angle examining the pillars carefully as they zigzagged by. "Arrogant bastards," I muttered, noting the shine on their helmets and the polish on their boots. I then saw one of them throw up his arm and stop. The other stopped behind him. The first rider dismounted while the other watched. He stooped, then knelt by a pillar. He'd found something and called the second one over. The second rider dismounted and examined something the other held up.

"They found the wires."

The Germans straightened up, ran frantically back to their motorcycles and gunned the engines for all they were worth – but they'd left it too late. The bridge detonated. Section after section collapsed into the river in an elongated wave. Chunks of concrete and scraps of metal shot into the sky. The first rider was blown out of his seat. The second disappeared amongst the collapsing buttresses, his motorcycle careened over the edge and arced into the water. Within moments, the entire bridge had broken apart, sending arched waves outward from the concussion.

Our line of troops stood and watched in silence. Once the dust and debris had thinned and settled into the water, a much clearer view of the enemy came into focus. I trained my glasses on the far bank. I saw a mass of grey and black uniforms, lorries, tanks, and artillery; in short, a vast fighting force fresh from victory and the taste of blood. On our side, I couldn't testify to what experience we'd tasted. The energy ran from my limbs leaving me feeling lifeless, inert.

I shook myself. "Let's get ready."

"What are we to do?" Yuri looked at me anxiously.

"We await orders," I replied. "It won't be long."

I felt the weight of history, two great armies facing each other across a divide. This could have been the Napoleonic Wars all over again. The fate of the world depended on the outcome.

Steering a steel monolith demanded skill and strength. The gears were managed by a large lever I worked with my right hand. Forward, neutral and reverse. There was no steering wheel but two pedals by my feet. If I stepped on the left pedal, the traction on the left stopped and we turned in the same direction. To turn the tank right, I did the opposite. To stop the tank fully, I jumped on both pedals at once but the momentum of the T-34 kept it moving for some 10-20 metres before it halted. Then I yanked the lever into neutral and the tank sat idling until I wished to start up again. Inside the cockpit, the ride was jerky, full of vibration and noise. The crew spoke to each other through the radio headsets or yelled back and forth. The men had to remain alert at all times. I might crash through a wall or drive over a peasant's abandoned hut without realizing it. The T-34 was a mechanical monster without feeling.

For some hours after the Volga Bridge had been destroyed, the two great armies faced each other in silence. Some movement stirred on the German side. I could see light glinting off the dull metal finish of their vehicles as they scurried about making preparations. Everyone's nerves were stretched taut awaiting the first move. The men ate their rations quickly in shifts. No fires were lit. I passed around a flask of vodka and the crew took nervous sips.

Shortly after midday, a puff of black smoke wafted up. I had my glasses trained on the other side. I thought I'd seen the recoil of a cannon just below the smoke.

"Get down," I yelled.

All the crews within earshot took cover. The high-pitched whine of an incoming shell filled our ears. We heard the full thud, felt the trembling of the earth, looked up to see the dust billow some thirty metres behind us.

"Let's go." We scrambled back into the tank and Rolf pulled the hatch shut. Within seconds, each was in position with headsets on. I listened attentively.

"They want us to respond, then shift position." I was relieved. If we'd been ordered to stay put, the Germans would get a fix on us. Then we'd be a fat target. The coordinates barked out through the headset.

"Load the cannon."

Yuri jumped to, lifting a shell and then sliding it into the breech. He capped it off.

"Ready."

I called out the coordinates. Rolf made the adjustments and gave me a signal. "Fire."

The force of the recoil washed through the body of the vehicle.

"Again."

Yuri heaved a shell into position. His actions went a little smoother this time, more certain. He signaled that he was ready.

"Fire."

As the second shell hurtled into space, I tried to follow the trajectory of the first. With such a limited field of vision, it was difficult. We felt the pounding from the artillery on the other side. Shells poured in fast and furious. The ground heaved all around us. I felt the sweat pour down my face. A message came over the headset. I put the motor in gear and slowly, the tank swung around to the right.

"What's happening?" Mischa asked.

"We're falling back. The Germans are sending in their planes. We're easy victims here."

"What about our planes?" Rolf asked.

I looked at him and shrugged. "Take my glasses and get up top. Keep a look out. You direct the other two on the machine guns when the planes come."

"But they'll be too high."

"No. They'll come in low, believe me."

"Yes sir."

Rolf clapped a helmet on his head and climbed up to the hatch. He braced himself on the ladder. Many tanks, men and trucks had gone on the move, scrambling to the wooded area some two kilometres to the east. It was rugged terrain ideally suited for tank travel as the treads bit into the small hills and passed over gulleys, broke through downed trees and scattered hedgerows. Over the roar of the engines and the distant voices, Rolf looked up.

"Here they come," he yelled. The machine guns swiveled into position. The guns opened up, pouring molten bullets into the sky. The aircraft answered, spraying the ground in front of us, shards of metal pinging off the tank's outer skin. Rolf dropped down inside, pulling the hatch after him. The gunners followed the path of the plane through their scopes. After a death tomb silence, the ground rumbled and the tank shuddered. I felt the left side of the tank lift from the force of the explosion but forced myself to keep my focus on the pedals and the lever, holding course. The gunners followed the tail of the plane pouring fire until it went out of range, then swung back to look for the next one.

The German aircraft came in waves, one after the other. I wove in and around burning trucks and charred tanks. We passed one tank that was on fire. I pulled up beside it.

"Quickly, check for survivors." Yuri and Rolf scrambled out. "Mischa. Keep looking." Mischa nodded, then licked his dry lips. I could hear shouts from outside. Yuri poked his head inside the hatch upside down.

"Three dead, Captain. One injured."

"We'll bring him with us."

Yuri nodded, then his head disappeared. A moment later, a shout came from up top. Mischa sprang to the hatch. A pair of scorched legs appeared. I set the brake and grabbed hold. We lowered the poor fellow gently inside. The others followed down carefully until the injured soldier was handed down and his weight fully supported.

"Prop him up."

We positioned him behind the left machine gun. I could see his left arm was useless, the bone exposed at the elbow. A wound in his abdomen oozed, blood soaking through his tunic.

"Give him some vodka if he can stand it."

I set myself back behind the controls.

"Mischa, man the gun, Rolf take yours. Yuri help the poor devil as best you can." The wounded man looked young, with close-cropped blond hair and bold cheekbones. He passed in and out of consciousness.

I radioed for instructions. I was told a hospital tent had been set up and we were to proceed a kilometre further to a clearing in the woods. Planes continued to scream overhead but the trees gave us cover now. German aircraft came under counter-attack from the shore guns and Soviet fighter planes arrived to intercept them. A vicious dogfight danced in the skies overhead. I concentrated on reaching the clearing, checking my coordinates against the map I had. The young soldier moaned, barely conscious. The tank slammed over a low ridge and pitched forward over the rise and into the trough. The wounded man groaned aloud.

"Do we have any morphine?" Mischa shook his head. "Where is that damned hospital?" We broke through a small stand of trees. I brought the tank to a halt. "Let's go."

The others scrambled out. I knelt by the barely conscious soldier. "You'll be all right now, Comrade." I examined the boy's blackened face streaked with oil and blood. His short hair stood up stiff with dried perspiration. I peeked at his belly. The opening was to the side and didn't look too deep. The blood had begun to congeal and harden. Yuri poked his head down.

"We've got a stretcher boss."

"Give me a hand."

I knelt and got my arms under the boy's body and lifted him up. I managed the first two rungs, when two sets of hands lifted the boy clear. He was handed down to Mischa and an orderly who placed him on a stretcher. They carried him into the tent some forty metres on ahead. I climbed out and sat in the grass. What had started out as a sunny day had now gone cloudy. I felt a chill. The drones of the planes seemed farther away but the pounding of the guns and the explosion of shells still drifted through the trees. I lit a cigarette. The others came and sat by me. We all lit up. Mischa emerged from the tent and came over.

"I think he'll be okay. He was the tank commander."

"Didn't look more than eighteen," Rolf said.

I inhaled deeply.

"We'll see plenty more like him before this is over. We'd better get used to it." The others didn't speak, just sat smoking quietly, thinking. I stood up and ground the cigarette under my heel. "We'd better get back. They'll be wondering where we are." In all the chaos,

I didn't know how the commanders kept track. Like soldiers everywhere, the tank crew moved reflexively, got rid of our cigarettes, straightened ourselves and got back to the business of war.

Chapter 32

"This sounds like a movie I saw on TV once," Beulah said. "I can't re-member the name of it."

"Maybe looking back it seems that way but believe me, it was real enough."

"Were you scared?"

"Yes, some of the time. Often, we were too busy to be scared. You act by instinct and it is only afterward when you have time to think that the fear comes."

"That must have been hard."

"We didn't have much choice," I said.

The Germans and the Russians faced each other across the Volga in stalemate. Every day, artillery bombarded each side with equal devastation. The ground erupted. Men were blown into the air. Many died. Overhead, planes flew. It became a lethal guessing game. When would the bombers come? When would the fighters strafe the camp? How many times would we change locations in an attempt to fool the airborne enemy? How many air battles would the tank crews watch like spectators at a soccer match? During those few months, we stayed on alert. The Germans might attempt a crossing farther up or down the river. The Russians had troops at each cross-ing point. Where the bridges hadn't been blown already, the faithful, dogged, engineering corps had them wired up and ready. I thought I sensed their impatience, the Nazi war machine, the wolfhound with its blitzkrieg pulling at its leash and snarling. This made me smile, grimly.

Meanwhile, it grew steadily colder. The troops no longer slept outside but in the cramped confines of the tank. Some mornings we'd wake up, the blankets stiff with frost. Supplies trickled in. This meant boiled potatoes and thin soup, saving tea leaves to be used again and rock hard bread. No matter. I managed to scrounge a bottle of vodka when stores ran low. I shared the bounty with my crew. To make matters worse, all of the crews were stricken with lice and constantly scratched. I never got them. My solution came from a homespun remedy. I dipped my undershirt and shorts in diesel fuel and hung them out to dry, then put them on.

"The fumes drive them away," I told my skeptical crew.

"They'll drive us away too," Mischa grumbled.

"Try it."

The others tried it and soon got used to the smell.

"One match and we'll all go up like a bonfire," Yuri said.

I smiled at him. "At least we won't have lice, not like these other poor bastards."

I knew something the others didn't. As the weeks, then months, ground on, briefings were held amongst all the commanders. A bold plan was being concocted. Every day brought colder weather, and thicker patches of ice forming along the banks of the river. By the middle of December only the centre of the river remained free and flowing. Within a month, that too would be frozen solid. How long would it take to hold the weight of a monstrous tank?

Once again, the engineers went to work. As the tank crews and the army behind them idled the days away trying to keep warm, watching out for enemy planes and generally observing the bombardments from across the river, the engineers kept busy with their calculations. They drilled holes in the ice each morning and evening. They calculated tonnage and displacement. The T-34s were the heaviest pieces of equipment. The engineers decided that the ice must be at least fifteen centimetres thick to take the weight of a T-34. Twenty centimeters would be better but fifteen would do, just. Naturally, this theory required testing as soon as possible.

General Vasilevsky was a tall man with a face cut so sharply by angles it looked as if it had caved in on itself. He wore his iron-grey hair cropped short. His complexion was sallow. He sported remarkably large and shiny false teeth. When he smiled, he looked like a horse laughing. The men thought him quite mad, and they were probably right. Some nights, after the evening briefing, he and I would share a drink and talk for a while.

"Are you married, Captain?" I shook my head. "Probably wise, with the way things are going." Vasilevsky smoked continually, lighting one cigarette off the end of another. Yellow stains tattooed his fingers. When he coughed, it came out as a wrenching, hacking spasm that rattled his skinny chest.

"I should give these damn things up," the General laughed, knowing he'd never do it. "Ah, who am I fooling? I'd rather smoke than eat."

I smiled, then accepted a cigarette from him.

"Thank you, sir."

"You've heard the talk I suppose?"

"Sir?"

"The counterattack, man. It all depends on the ice. Is it thick enough? Will it hold?"

"Is it?"

The General shrugged. "Who knows? We have to get some damn fool to try it out." And he looked at me meaningfully, his eyes small, grey, piercing marbles; shrewd yet hopeful.

I dropped my cigarette into the snow, where it fizzled.

"I'll do it. But I'll go on my own. I won't risk my crew."

The General nodded, then patted me on the shoulder.

"I have a daughter you know. She's a doctor here in the field hospital. A surgeon ."

"You must be very proud, General."

"I am Captain. Her name is Olga. Perhaps you'd care to have dinner with us one evening? It won't be much of course. But I might be able to scrounge some herring and beets, some bread that isn't more than a week old?"

"Thank you sir. It would be a pleasure." I hesitated. "When is the test?"

"Soon. I'll let you know. We'll move upstream about ten kilometres, in case the Nazis are watching. We don't want them to get wind of our plans."

I returned to the tank where the crew had bundled up, huddled inside against the cold. We had standing orders to run the engines for two hours only to generate some heat. The high command wanted to preserve fuel.

The test would be run at night. January 22, 1943. An armed contingent had broken off from the main camp and motored ten kilometers to the north following the line of the Volga. We came up the evening before and made camp. I was summoned.

Vasilevsky sat on a narrow folding chair, hugging himself. As usual, he was smoking. A glass of vodka and a bottle sat on the rickety table before him.

"Ah, come in Captain. It is colder than a witch's tit. Have a drink?"

Beside him sat his adjutant who held the rank of Soviet commissar. Vasilevsky shot him a look. "Don't say anything Leonid, the man is about to risk his life for mother Russia." Leonid the commissar swallowed heavily but held his tongue.

"No thank you sir. I need to keep a clear head."

"I think it must be close to forty below zero, eh?"

Vasilevsky took a long pull on the cigarette then exhaled a slim plume of smoke. I couldn't tell whether it was smoke or merely his breath. It was bitter. A vicious wind rattled the tent flaps. "You'll need an observer. One of your men has volunteered, Mischa something or other. You must drive with the hatch open. If the ice begins to crack, you will have about ten seconds to climb out but no more.

Don't be foolish. Abandon the tank immediately. We will have rescue crews on standby."

"But sir…"

"He volunteered, Goldman. And you will need him. Keep your speed low but deliberate. He can spot the cracking before you feel it. He can give you enough time to save yourself. Understood?"

"Yes, General."

"Good. Then may God go with you." Vasilevsky glanced over. "Not a word Leonid or I'll post you to the coal mines in Siberia." Leonid smiled again.

"Yes sir."

I left the tent, angry with Mischa for disobeying me. The wind licked my face. Its tentacles felt like a knife blade probing my skin. "I had given you an order," I said.

Mischa didn't apologise. "Your chances are much better with an observer. You know that."

"I didn't want any lives risked unnecessarily."

"Who said any lives are at risk? If the engineers think the ice is thick enough, that's good enough for me. I won't worry about it." And he licked his dry lips. "I'll jump out ahead of you. It won't be a problem."

I shook my head. "You're mad."

"Who isn't? What are we doing out here anyway?"

The engineers drilled a hole near the shoreline. The report came back. Fifteen centimeters. I waited for the drilling report from the middle of the river. Mischa and I stamped our feet and clapped our hands to keep the circulation moving. Finally, a voice crackled on the radio. It said, "12.5 centimeters." Two lorries and an armoured car had made it across and back safely. Now it was our turn. The General appeared. He clapped me on the back.

"All set?"

"Yes, General."

The General sucked on his cigarette, then exhaled dramatically.

"Good luck then, Captain. And you too, Sergeant."

"Thank you sir."

I climbed into the tank. Mischa assumed his position up top. Once we had our headsets on, we received their orders to go. The General watched through his field glasses. Mischa scanned the ice, but it was difficult to see clearly in the murky light.

"It's freezing up here," Mischa muttered.

"Serves you right. I hope your nuts drop off. I'll go extra slow, no more than five kilometres per hour."

I eased the great tank down the shoreline on to the ice. There came the sensation of shuddering but it might have been the vibration from the engine. Was there the sound of cracking? Everything ground under the noise of the tank's motor. Would the sound carry down river to the enemy encampment? I shrugged it off. At the current speed, it would take some thirty minutes to cross over. I was far more interested in not plunging through the ice and disappearing into the numbing waters of the Volga. I peered out. Not much to see. The ice lay covered in snow. I followed the tire tracks of the lorry that had passed over earlier. Out on the ice, I felt very much alone. Despite the extreme cold, sweat wormed its way from under my fur-lined hat.

"Stop," Mischa called.

I jammed on the pedals and pulled the lever into neutral.

"I want to take a look."

I would learn that Mischa frequently needed to investigate in person. Look until he was satisfied about something. I heard the clang of boots on metal as Mischa went over the side. As he came around into my field of view, I observed. Mischa scanned the ice carefully, sweeping back and forth in front for some twenty-five metres. He motioned to me and I let up on the pedals and slid the lever into forward but kept my feet tight on the brakes. Mischa continued to motion, then, without looking back, held his hand up. I stopped some two metres behind him. It was some moments before he straightened his lithe figure, then came around the side of the tank.

"What did you see?"

"Cracks in the ice. Plenty of them. I suggest we keep moving."

I put the tank in gear and continued crossing. There came a new sound, that of the ice groaning. Low-pitched and steady, I could hear it under the wind, like a bear growling. I felt the sweep of cold air on my neck. My grip on the gear lever was tight. I tried to imagine what it might be like to drown. To let the cold, icy water swallow me up. The winter gear and heavy boots would pull me down, sink me like a solid weight. I imagined a peaceful numbness as the cold took over, took control of your mind and limbs.

"Veer right. Hard." Mischa shouted.

I stepped on the right pedal and the T-34 swung on its axis on a right angle.

"Now straight."

I trod on the left pedal until the tank swung forward, then I lifted both feet and we continued.

"What did you see?" I shouted.

"An open section of ice. We just skimmed it. Another piece broke off. If we'd kept going, we'd be swimming now."

"Mark it on the map."

"Of course."

My hand and fingers went numb from the pressure. I tried easing my grip on the lever but my muscles were too taut. Just as the moon passed out from behind a cloud a sliver of light cut a swath across the dark ice. I saw the shoreline now some fifty metres ahead. By a parked lorry, a huddled group watched us. I heard crackling in the headset. I eased it up over my ears.

"Almost there, Captain."

"I know."

Moments later, the T-34 climbed the embankment and came to a halt on level ground. I left the engine running. I felt the need to urinate. But first I took a long pull from the flask of vodka I kept in my parka. The raw heat of the liquid boiled within me and I passed the flask to Mischa, who put it to his thin lips. He handed it back to me and grinned.

"That might have been close," he said.

I didn't think of what might have been but what was to be. I knew we weren't heading back across the ice. The General had a plan.

Rolf and Yuri drove across in a lorry with a number of other crews. All the next day, the river was busy with traffic, tanks, lorries, armoured cars and artillery. Three lines of traffic formed a crawling line of machinery. They had to move quickly and as quietly as possible involving over 100,000 men, equipment and their supplies. The temperature read minus twenty degrees at least. But the men, for the most part, shrugged it off. They wore their white camouflage uniforms. A makeshift camp took root. Covered fires were lit to prevent the smoke from drifting too high, allowing the men to huddle and smoke. Much vodka passed many lips as flasks moved quietly from hand to hand.

Toward the end of the day as the sun rimmed the horizon, the General summoned me. I found myself driven back across the river. I had tried to clean myself, having changed the diesel-soaked undershirt for one that didn't reek of fuel, over which I wore my dress uniform. I put on the padded white parka and hood, and shined my boots. My comrades saw me off.

"Don't let him talk you into anything, Pan Captain," Mischa advised.

"Don't worry."

I waved and looked back over my shoulder. My crew faded into silhouette, the diminishing light forming an aura around them. As I and the driver proceeded across the river, the details of their faces and bodies dissolved into a solid mass, a single entity. This is the Russian army, I thought. A single entity moving to one rhythm. Where would it take us? The air had stilled but remained bitterly cold. Drawing breath hurt my lungs but the world stood quiet and pristine, exuding an unsullied purity.

"I see you made it in one piece," the General said, cigarette in hand. His tent was quite large, the size of three good-sized rooms. Propane heaters stood in each of the corners and glowed. Without my parka, it felt tolerable, not warm but not cold either. I could barely see my breath. The mess remained simple, a table and a few chairs for conferences and eating. There was a cot in the far corner, but noting the deep circles under his eyes, I doubted whether he got around to sleeping very much. A slim woman with dark hair cut short and green eyes stood behind him. She wore a standard-issue army uniform with the rank of Major. She gazed back at me coolly, the hint of a smile on her lips. The General followed my look and swiveled slightly.

"Ah yes. Captain Goldman, may I present my daughter, Major Olga Vasilevsky."

"My pleasure, Major."

I took her hand and shook it. She had a strong grip, her hand almost rough-hewn. The Major nodded without speaking.

"The Major is a skilled surgeon," her father said proudly.

"Quiet, Papa," she admonished. "Captain, would you care for a drink? We only have vodka, I'm afraid." She poured me a stiff measure, then one for herself. She raised her eyes to the General, who shook his head. We clinked glasses.

"Salut," I said, and tossed it back. She did the same. Before I could blink, she poured another.

"You've been to France?"

"Yes, when I was a student. I studied mechanical engineering there."

"Really? How long?"

"Three years."

"I'd like to go to the West and study surgical procedures and techniques. Find out what advances have been made and share what we know. In this way, all would benefit."

"Hush now," said the General.

"I agree with you, Major. Medicine is for mankind, don't you think General? It should be shared with the world?"

"As long as Russia hears about it first." Then he laughed and lit another cigarette.

"Papa is just being perverse. Think of how many lives we might save with modern drugs and better-equipped operating theatres. I'm talking about your men wounded in the field, Papa. If we had new ways of doing things, fewer would die. They could be rehabilitated and lead useful lives, perhaps continue to serve. Wouldn't it be better to send them back to their families?"

"Of course, my darling." He turned to me. "Her mother was the same way. Headstrong and stubborn. Between the two of them, I had to run away to the army just for the sake of my sanity."

"Come. I'm sure our guest is hungry and isn't interested in our family stories." She gestured to a chair and I took a seat. The General drank, ate and smoked all at the same time. The first course, served by the General's orderly, consisted of a thin cabbage borscht and dark rye bread, only slightly stale. After the borscht, we had blackened sea bass and potatoes. Dessert was a fruit compote that had been baked. I hadn't eaten like this for many months. A samovar was brought in for tea. The General took a bite from a sugar cube, then sipped his tea from the tall glass provided.

"Not bad, eh, Captain? Being a General brings some privileges, precious few as they are," he added sourly.

"Don't pout, Papa. You'll win the battle especially if you have courageous men like the Captain by your side."

"I'm not courageous, Major. We do what we are told. Nothing more."

"Captain, I see death every day. This morning I amputated a man's leg with very little anaesthetic. I'm sure the Nazis could hear his screams on the other side of the Volga."

"But it was necessary?"

"Yes."

"Then we work in the same way. We do what is necessary to defeat the enemy."

Olga looked at her father and smiled wearily. "You see, I told you there are no worries." She glanced back at me. "Perhaps you're wondering, Captain, if I achieved my rank because my father is a general or whether I really earned it?"

"I don't care about such things."

"Why not?"

I looked at her, finding her face very attractive. "It's the person that matters and it doesn't take long to judge."

"And what do you think of me?"

"I hardly know you, Major, so I am not yet in a position to judge."

"And I am the daughter of your commanding officer," she said.

"That wouldn't change my opinion one way or the other, I assure you." I sipped the tea. It was weak but hot.

The General lit another cigarette, then stood up.

"I'm going to walk the perimeter. Maxim," he called. The middle-aged orderly appeared with the General's heavy coat and cap. He helped the General on with his things, then handed him a pair of sheepskin gloves. "Maxim takes very good care of me, don't you Maxim?"

"Yes sir."

"Come then. Captain, thank you for joining us this evening."

"Thank you, General. I enjoyed myself." I stood up awkwardly.

"Don't get up on my account. Stay and keep the Major company. You have a great deal to do over the next few days. Goodnight." The General disappeared through the flap in the tent, bending his long form to clear the doorway.

"Please sit down, Captain. Another drink?"

"It is Mordecai. And please." She stood to retrieve the bottle from across the table and poured each of us another measure of vodka. From her tunic, she took out a packet of cigarettes, put one between her lips then offered them to me. I leaned in to accept a light and as I did so, caught those extraordinary green eyes staring at me through the smoke and the flames. I felt a tingle of excitement. I exhaled slowly, then took a sip of the vodka.

"Then I would be happy if you called me Olga, at least between ourselves. You're not married?" I shook my head. "Why not?"

"No time. And I haven't met the right woman. What about you?"

"Yes, I was once." Her voice quavered, tinged with sadness. "But he died in a plane crash. He was a pilot. This was three years ago."

"Forgive me. It was a stupid question."

"No. You didn't know. I'm beginning to forget him. Sometimes, I can't remember his face. And then other times, I think I hear his voice. It's strange. We had no children."

"You have regrets?"

She drained the vodka, then took a long pull on the cigarette before shaking her head. "No, I don't. What kind of mother would I be when I am up to my elbows in blood every day? This is no place for a child. Not now. Perhaps later, when it's all over."

"And the General? Doesn't he want to be a grandfather?"

She ran her hands through her hair, then stared down at the table-top. "He adored Nikolai. I think he mourned his death more than I did. They were a lot alike. Perhaps that's why I married him. I don't know. Let's talk about something else."

"Like what?"

"Anything. Tell me about your childhood. What was it like growing up in Poland?"

"As a Jew, you mean?"

"Yes, if you like. As a Jew and a man. I want to sit and listen, just hear you talk. I want to go away to somewhere else in my mind, just for one night. Can you understand that?"

"Yes. I can understand that."

And so I told her in small detail. I spoke for hours and finally, when I finished, I saw that she had fallen asleep with her face side-ways on the table. I rose, then lifted her in my arms, placed her gently on the General's cot and covered her with a blanket. Her face looked serene and undisturbed as she breathed lightly through her full lips. She looked like a child. I lingered for a moment, then pulled on my winter coat and stepped outside. The sunrise cast a golden beam on the dark ice bringing light to the world. I caught a lift back to the other side with a lorry filled with mess supplies.

That day, preparations for battle continued. My crew turned melancholy. Mischa thought of his mother back in Poland.

"She has a weak chest," he said. "Supplies are scarce. One elderly Polish woman more or less, what does it matter to them?"

Rolf missed his wife and young son. His wife lived with her parents in Moscow. Yuri had a girlfriend in Petrograd. He carried her picture with him. Frequently, he removed it from his billfold and stared at it. He showed the image to me. I saw a round, dark face with high cheekbones and slanted eyes – a strong Tatar influence there but pretty nonetheless, with long, dark lashes and glossy hair.

We passed the vodka around, huddled up inside the shallow confines of the tank, trying to stay warm, each lost in his own thoughts and dreams. The radio crackled.

"Captain?" said a distant voice.

I picked up the headset. "Yes."

"You're wanted at headquarters. Transport is being sent."

"Now?"

"That's correct. Be ready in ten minutes."

I looked at the others and shrugged. Slowly, I pulled on the winter gear, then climbed up and out of the hatch. I waited outside. The weather was still bitterly cold, the wind howling like an animal, wounded and venting its hurts to the sky. Within a few moments, a staff car drew up. The General's orderly sat behind the wheel. The orderly stepped out and smartly opened the rear door for me. There were no other passengers. I felt puzzled but didn't question anything. The orderly turned the car about and drove slowly across the ice. We didn't speak. Occasionally, the man's dark eyes flicked up at me through the rear view mirror but I contented myself with staring out the window at the swirling snow, watching the patterns in the air.

We pulled up in front of the General's makeshift quarters. The orderly stepped out smartly and opened the door for me. I looked at him curiously but the small man stayed silent, then lifted his arm to indicate that I should go in.

"I was hoping you would join me for a late supper," Olga said. "I've just finished my last operation for the evening." She looked at me, her lips trembling slightly. I went up to her without a word and took her in my arms. I kissed her and felt her body pressing against me. She pulled away.

"We'll need to keep warm."

"I don't think it'll be a problem. And the General?"

"Off inspecting troops. He won't return until tomorrow afternoon."

"What's that smell?" she asked, wrinkling her nose.

"Diesel oil."

"Hmm. I love the smell of diesel."

Now unencumbered by her uniform, her body was fuller and rounder than I imagined. She smelled of antiseptic and starch but it pleased me. We took to each other like lost souls found. At first, I played rough. We moved and fought, two antagonists in a contest, maneuvering to see who would win. She arched her back, shook her head, muttered "No" under her breath, then dug her nails into my shoulders. She held me to her, pushed my face down her body, wrapped her legs around mine, forcing me to her. She felt savage and wanton, thrashing beneath me, panting like a tigress, her breath quick and shallow until a low moan welled up from the underside of her belly, mellifluous at first, then climbing in pitch until it was virtually a shriek. I saw the veins stand out in her long supple neck as she bucked against me violently. She held herself there for a long moment, then slowly the air drained out of her and she softened, melting into me. We became tender then, murmuring in hushed voices, touching, stroking, caressing. She smiled girlishly and decided to take a really good look at me.

"You're quite handsome. Not in a Russian way. But dark and exotic like those who come down from the mountains."

"How did you know I was a mountain man?"

"You're teasing me."

"Only a little."

"I think I'm hungry now."

She scampered over to the table and picked up a platter that held some dumplings and bread and dried fish. She moved quickly; the air and floor were cold. Then she went back and brought a flask of vodka and two glasses.

"The General won't mind crumbs in his bed?"

"Maxim will take care of that."

She shivered, then draped the blanket around her and began to eat. "Mmm. I'm ravenous. Here, strong one, eat." She fed me some dumpling and bread. "It tastes so good, don't you think so?"

I laughed. "Yes." She hugged me and her lightness was a delight.

"I feel so happy. It's wonderful to feel some happiness again, even if it's for a short while."

"Why do you say that? Are you finished with me now? On to the next one?"

She slapped me on the shoulder. "Don't say that. You know what I mean. Life is so uncertain."

"Not for me."

She took a drink, licked her lips and looked at me. "You think so?"

"Yes."

"What do you think?"

"I don't think about living or dying, just doing my job."

She took another drink. "That's wonderful, comrade. You're the perfect proletariat, no?"

I laughed back. "No."

"Let's not worry about anything right now. I'm not a General's daughter and a surgeon in the army. I'm just a girl who wants to be happy with her man. Is that all right?"

I didn't laugh or smile. "Yes, of course, Olga. You are my Olga now, aren't you?"

We lay together, arms around each other in the narrow cot. She whispered in my ear.

"And you are my man, Mordecai. As long as we can have this, it will be something to remember, to see me through the pain of doing my job. Oh, some days I can barely stand it, seeing them brought in the way they are. But I must do my best. It's what is expected. By my father and my country and by me. Many times, there's little I can do for them. I never thought it would be like this. I just want to be safe. I want to be a little girl again playing in the snow at our dascha."

"If that's what you want, so be it. You can go outside and play in the snow. I'll stay here and be warm."

She pinched my arm playfully then harder. "Just hold me for now. It's too warm to go outside and play."

Chapter 33

Counter Attack, 1943

I looked at my chronometer – 4 a.m. I stood outside the tank with my field glasses trained to the east. It would start soon, I thought. From across the frozen expanse of the Volga sounded the cough of an engine, then another and another – a fusillade of motors fired up, building to a steady roar, the hum and rumble of which floated through the frigid night air. Under my parka and ulanka, I could still hear it. I thought of the men and machines we had left some ten kilometres to the west.

The first wave of machines motored toward me. As I looked eastward, I had the thought that at the first light of day, blood would flow. The first tanks rumbled by. The General patrolled the perimeter calling for the count. Signalmen stood on the frozen river directing traffic, waving flags, sending the mechanical beasts along to form up properly. The General wanted to be on the move just as the action began to the east, when the Germans would be engaged. The tanks swarmed forward by the hundreds now. I felt a flash of pride, overwhelmed by the sight of this powerful fighting force. We could defeat the enemy. After all, this was Russian soil.

Mischa tapped me on the shoulder, then handed me a tin of tea. The steam rose eerily, then dispersed as I blew on it. It tasted hot and bitter. I tried not to think of the horror of the past. The nightly bombardments, the buzzing of the Messerschmitts, the whistling of the bombs as they fell through the night sky, the whump-whump of the explosions and finally, the screams of men, their cries finding me in my dreams. Not even the warm body and comforting hands of Olga moved these things out of my mind. Her hands, expert in touching me in a way I'd never been touched before. The General found reasons to be absent, attending staff meetings or walking the frozen fields in the darkness, his loyal orderly, Maxim, trailing behind him.

I thought of our last evening together. We both knew it might be months or longer before we met again. My life had changed. Before, I had been on my own, only concerned about the War and my command. Now, there was nothing but her. I wondered vaguely, if Olga would get along with my mother and sister. I tried to imagine the three of them together, but the image came up blank.

On our last night, we drank vodka and smoked.

"We are silent tonight," she said, her eyes searching my face. We lay squeezed together in the cot.

"It's enough to be here. There isn't much to talk about."

"On the contrary, my love, there is everything to talk about."

I pulled deeply on a cigarette, then blew out smoke in a long stream. "You mustn't think of me while I'm away."

"And how do you suggest I do that?"

"I don't know."

I felt miserable for saying it. "And I'll try not to think of you."

"But you will?" Olga searched my face.

"Yes. In the quiet moments. When it's dark and I'm too tired to sleep, I'll see your face. Feel your touch. I'll want you with a terrible ache I can only begin to describe, to feel. And then I'll try to shut it out so I can do my job. So I won't be distracted."

I dropped the cigarette into the mess tin and pulled her to me. I felt the smoothness of her thighs and the coarse ruff of hair between her legs. She moved on to her back and drew her heels up along the backs of my thighs. We kissed deeply and she arched beneath me, reached between my legs and guided me into her. She thrust her hips upward against my pelvis, feeling the weight of my tensed abdomen on her. She moaned deep in her throat, pulling me in tighter and deeper. We stayed poised as long as we dared, until she couldn't hold herself back any longer, and she bit into my shoulder, her breath coming in quick gasps. I was afraid I'd break her open with the force of my thrusts. After a long moment, I felt myself relax into her. We lay back together, damp and exhausted, but content. Despite the cold, her dark hair lay matted and wet against her scalp. She reached down for me.

"Whatever you do, protect this and bring it back to me."

I laughed. "As you wish. Consider it done." She kissed me then, very tenderly.

Now, outside the tank, I shivered as the wind cut through my parka like a stiletto. I stared again to the east as the tanks and lorries rumbled by, men crunching ice and snow underfoot, barely recognizable as human in their white alpine gear. Now, I thought, was the winter of my life. I would be away now for weeks or months, perhaps forever. A hand clapped me on the shoulder. The General.

"It has begun."

"Yes."

"Come. You and I will lead the way. Bring your tank up forward."

I nodded. The General began to turn away, then paused. "It's how she'd want it too."

I spilled out the remainder of the tea, heard it hiss in the snow. "I will follow."

The General turned, then walked off into the swirling darkness, his footsteps shrouded by the yowling wind.

In the semi-darkness of the tank's interior, I spoke to the crew.

"It will begin soon."

The pronouncement was greeted with silence, then a few mutterings. I thrust the tank in gear and it lurched away behind the General's staff car. I eased up on the brake pedals, following slowly.

"Why are we out of formation?" Mischa asked.

"We're following the General."

"But why?"

"He wants it that way."

"That's a reason?"

I glared at him for a moment. "It is for me."

Mischa shrugged. "All right then. I suppose he knows what he's doing."

I hoped so too. The staff car stopped. The General stepped out. He beckoned.

"I'll be right back."

I left the engine idling and climbed out the hatch. The General dipped his wrist before the car's headlights and peered at his watch.

"Look to the west. It should be any second now."

I turned and waited. Then it was as if a light had been switched on. Bright flashes mushroomed up from the ground. I strained my ears. Between the howls and shrieks of the bitter wind, I heard the steady thrum of engines.

"Planes."

The General put his gloved hand on my shoulder and leaned in closely. He removed the cigarette from the corner of his mouth.

"It will be the mother of all battles, Mordecai. Many will die. Many will be sacrificed. Pray that we do not fail."

Then there were winking lights in the sky. I looked to the north. A fleet of German bombers and fighter planes rolled in like thunder and engaged in a dance of death with the outnumbered Soviet pilots. I imagined the bombs descending, saw the ice splintering, opening craters and almost felt the burning chill of water broiling and funneling upward. I turned away and found myself held by Mischa's mad gaze.

"Can you hear them?"

Behind him stood the others, stock still, locked in silhouette. Mischa nodded. In unison, we listened to the imagined, tortured screams of our compatriots as they disappeared beneath the ice. I could see cracks in the ice running madly along the banks and the awkward groping and grasping of machinery as tanks, trucks and artillery foundered then vanished into the frigid waves.

"It's a massacre," I whispered and stared wild-eyed at the General, who nodded and gave me a fierce look in return.

"It's our turn now," he replied harshly. "Come. It's time to go. The enemy is engaged." He threw his cigarette butt down, turned on his heel and marched back to his staff car. I knew what I had to do. Follow. As simple as that. That gaunt man, that scarecrow with the deep-socket eyes was my commander. I turned away. The others trailed after me.

Inside the T-34, I was happy to have mechanical things to do. Flicking switches. Moving levers. Pressing pedals. The horror of my imagination plagued me. I didn't want to think it or see it. My most conscious thought had been that it had been them and not me. In a way it didn't matter. There would be survivors. There always were, so why shouldn't I be one of them?

"Check your equipment. Keep the breeches open. Yuri, make sure you have unobstructed access to the shells. We'll carry one in the cannon at all times from here on in."

The replies trickled out, muttered. They were focused but nervous. The horizon materialized as the first rays of light appeared reflected in the ice and snow.

"Mischa, as soon as it's light, we'll ride with the hatch open so you can take a good look at our surroundings. Keep your rifle and pistol with you at all times. Remember, keep a shell in the chamber always."

"Right."

A phalanx of T-34s led the way. The General's staff car had fallen behind and would soon be replaced with a halftrack. The terrain was too hilly and the snow too deep for an ordinary automobile. Although surrounded by men and tanks, I felt isolated. We were the 62nd and our numbers had swelled to 400,000 men and machines. It would take several weeks for the plan to unfold. During those days, our comrades back at Stalingrad attempted to cross the Volga while the Germans bombed the ice out from under them. And overhead, the Messerschmitts chewed up the frozen sky. My mind flickered to Olga but even as I thought of her, her warmth drained away. I knew she would be worked off her feet operating on the fractured bodies brought before her. She wouldn't know if it was day or night and wouldn't care. After twenty-four or thirty-six hours, she'd fall into a stupor for some fitful rest, only to begin again. Who was better off, I asked myself?

Chapter 34

Three days later, I lay on my belly in the snow, training field glasses on a Panzer division in the swirling distance. The wind had kicked up again and it drove ice pellets into my exposed cheeks. The German tanks looked like a mirage, hard, grey shapes moving against a white, stormy background.

"How many do you figure?" Mischa asked. He lay beside me and peered into the blank distance.

"Perhaps two hundred."

"And how many do we have?"

"About eighty-five."

Mischa looked at me incredulously.

"The numbers don't balance," he said in a prissy, professorial way.

"No, they don't."

"Do they know we're here?"

"Perhaps. Here, why don't you look?"

I thrust the glasses at him. He pulled back his hood, peeled off his snow goggles and peered through the lenses.

"They're advancing."

"I know."

We lay fifty kilometres to the north of Stalingrad and twenty-five kilometres to the east of the Don River. General Vasilevsky had cast his troops in a wide net that slowly encircled the German 6th army, under the command of Field Marshall Paulus, one of Hitler's favourites. This, in itself, gave the General enormous pleasure, almost a sense of glee in battling such an illustrious opponent. Their supply lines would be cut and the entire perimeter would be held, effectively isolating the Germans. They would have no avenue of escape, nowhere to retreat or move forward. It was a devilishly clever trap if it worked. But the costs so far had been staggering. In the first three days, the Soviets had lost 5,000 troops. Many had died from exposure.

Two days later, we encountered advance forces from the German 6th. We'd crossed a stream, cracking through the ice into shallow, swift moving water. Suddenly, the right tread dipped dangerously. A great roar and an echo vibrated through the tank's interior.

"What's happening?" Rolf screamed.

Mischa swiveled his gun, peering through the sights. "Enemy tank two hundred metres off to the right."

"Give us a bearing."

"I just did. Two hundred metres to the right."

There was another roar and a great shuddering.

"Jesus."

I swung the T-34 to the left while keeping the cannon level by swiveling it to the right.

"Fire."

No sooner had we felt the recoil than Yuri had the next shell loaded. Mischa peered through his gun sight.

"Give it to him again."

"Fire."

Again the cannon loosed its shell. We broached the bank, climbing upward. I hadn't realized the bank was so steep. We'd gone almost vertical.

"Look out."

The Tiger tank loomed directly above. I stared at its underbelly.

"Cannon," I roared.

"We're too close," Mischa screamed.

"I said, fire, goddammit."

Yuri loaded the shell. The recoil from the cannon caused the tank to slip down the bank. I'd lost control. I stood on the brakes with all of my strength. The Tiger Tank blew up and jerked backward, flames erupting from underneath its treads. The T-34 sloughed to a stop at the edge of the riverbank. I looked around. Everyone seemed to be okay, eyes wide, tongues out, staring like hungry dogs.

"Mischa. Yuri. Take a look. We'll climb the bank first."

When I drew level, I saw twisted, blackened metal, thick smoke and flames. Grabbing their automatic rifles, Mischa and Yuri climbed out while Rolf manned the machine gun. I set the tank in neutral and climbed up the hatch behind them so I could take a look. The snow lay deep in this part of the forest and the going heavy, the stepping slow and awkward. The heat from the fire looked intense. The Tiger's hatch burst open. Mischa and Yuri stood tensely, rifles at the ready. What we saw emerge wasn't human, more like a moving torch alive with flames. Somehow, this thing managed to clear itself of the hatch and leapt into the snow writhing in agony, seeking salvation from the fire. They stood and waited another moment. No other figures emerged. The metal of the tank glowed and began to melt.

"We'd better get out of here," said Yuri. "It's going to blow."

"Just a minute." Mischa forged his way over to the inert figure lying prone in the snow. When he drew near enough, I saw him gasp. A uniform clung to a form in charred strips, much of the flesh burned away. Somehow it lifted what was left of its head and looked at him pitifully. One eye was missing from its socket. It seemed to be pleading, skin hanging from where its mouth once was. Yuri gagged, then retched at the odour of burnt flesh. Mischa raised his rifle and squeezed off a shot. The creature sank back into the ground, the snow hissing from the heat. Mischa hurried back to where Yuri had bent over clearing his mouth with snow.

"Poor bastard," he gasped.

"I hope someone would do that for me," Mischa said grimly.

The intensity of the heat and fear of an explosion drove them back to the tank. I gestured for them to hurry. After they had climbed back in, Mischa growled.

"Let's get out of here."

I swung the tank hard to the left and followed the line of the river-bank for several hundred metres before heading back inward. The sensation of that first kill hadn't begun to sink in or the realization that, for want of a bit of luck, the circumstances might have been very different. Behind us, the German tank exploded into shrapnel, sending up a ball of flames and black smoke. Fragments of metal came down pinging against the exterior of the T-34. No one spoke.

"Boss," Yuri said after a moment.

"What?" I focused on the path ahead. We radioed our position and the kill. Mischa noted the Panzer tank's registration number.

"Their uniforms."

"What about them?"

"Something I noticed but wasn't sure. I mean, there wasn't that much left of the guy, you know?"

"What is it?"

"It was a summer uniform."

"Summer?" I repeated. "You sure?"

"Yes."

"I'll report it to the command. Very good work, Yuri. And to you too, Mischa. You've done well."

And now, three days later, I lay on my belly watching the German tanks advance, I glimpsed troops walking behind the tanks. I handed Mischa the glasses.

"What do you see there?" I pointed.

Mischa took the glasses, raised them and peered intently for a long moment. "Troops, lightly armed. And handlers with dogs."

"Why the dogs?"

Mischa shrugged and shook his head. Within the hood, his small face looked tighter and rounder. There was a glint off the rims of his glasses.

"Watch those glasses. They'll give you away." Mischa nodded. "Why dogs?" I muttered to myself. Far to their right, a line of Soviet tanks advanced. The Germans would be in view in just a moment. Then, it would begin.

The wind gusted and blew sheets of snow across our field of vision. It was like watching them in a dream.

"Captain." Mischa touched me on the shoulder. "Take a look."

I adjusted the field glasses and saw two soldiers bent over a dog, a handsome German shepherd. They fastened something to its belly and tightened it with straps, a kind of harness. One of the soldiers gave the dog a biscuit, then shooed it away. The dog loped off into the woods. I followed it, tracking its progress through the bush and scrub, around trees. I was puzzled. Then suddenly, as if pennies had been lifted from my eyes, I saw.

"Oh my God. Get the radio. At once."

Mischa scrambled away, only to return moments later with the portable radio set. I barked into the transmitter while Mischa listened incredulously. A moment later, there was an explosion. I stopped speaking and trained the glasses in the direction of the noise. Like the Panzer before it, a T-34 had burst into flames. I saw the hatch open and the crew leap out, then scramble for cover as a trio of machine guns opened up from deep inside the woods.

"They've armed the dogs," Mischa said. "With bombs."

I nodded grimly then resumed speaking into the transmitter

"We'll need a rifle crew up here. Get the ones who shoot best. The dogs are hard to spot and move quickly over the terrain." I heard the acknowledgement, then rang off. "Bastards. Dirty, rotten bastards. They waste nothing, these fucking Nazis. We can't stay here. We'll move back to the other side."

The T-34 rumbled through the woods and over the ridge. I swung the tank around so the nose faced toward the way we had come.

"Get your rifles," I said.

We took a position lying flat on the ridge. In the distance, the sounds of machines and men came to us. But immediately around us it remained still. The trees creaked in the cold as the wind whistled through the bare branches. The landscape chilled the outside and the inside of a man far from his home. I held the field glasses, then spotted something.

"There," I said, handing the glasses to Mischa. He saw a dog loping through the woods, the bundle of explosives strapped to its back. It was a handsome brute, keen looking and intelligent.

"I had a dog like that once," Mischa said as he followed its path. He hesitated.

"Shoot. What are you waiting for?" I demanded.

"Nothing."

He squeezed off a round. It pinged off a tree. "Shit." He resettled and took aim again, squeezed off another round. This time, he hit the animal in the foreleg and it went down in a heap. I watched. After a moment, the dog got up and began hobbling forward.

"It's up."

Mischa took aim once more. Through the field glasses, I saw the spurt just in front of the ear. The animal crumpled into the snow and lay still. Mischa put down his rifle and looked at me. "I don't know what's worse, shooting a man or a dog." It felt like killing an innocent.

"See if you can hit the explosive. Quick, before they pick it up."

"Right."

He had pulled off the glove from his right hand so he could feel the trigger but in the cold his fingers quickly grew numb. He blew on them before resuming his grip and taking aim. The first round missed, sending up a spray of snow just beyond the dog's body. Mischa wrapped the rifle strap more tightly around his left hand then fired off another round. The dog's body fragmented with an almighty roar, forcing us to cover our ears. When the smoke and disrupted snow cleared a moment later, the earth lay rutted and exposed, trees split and uprooted. Bare ground and rock showed where once it had been a blanket of snow and ice. I saw bits of fur and flesh spotting the ground, scraps caught in the low-growing brambles and scrub.

We stared at the sight without saying a word.

"They're serious about this," Rolf said.

The field radio began to squawk. I put the headset on, listening for a moment. Mischa looked in the direction of the scattered dog. There would be others.

"Come, we must go. Quickly." I grabbed the radio and we moved back in rapid order. I waited for the others to go first, then I handed the radio up to Rolf and climbed up after him. I turned the T-34 around and headed back toward the Soviet lines, crashing through trees, driving over windfalls and rock buried beneath the snow. We lurched in jarring vibrations as the tank moved through the woods, carving its own path. I slowed and studied the map for a moment, then stopped and turned the tank around.

"We had to clear those coordinates. Rolf go up and take a look."

I tossed him the field glasses. Rolf scrambled up and opened the hatch and cold air flooded the close interior. He scanned the horizon, the field and the sky.

"I hear something," he called.

"Good," I said. The others looked at me questioningly. "Air strike. A big one. That's why we had to get out."

From up top we heard Rolf say, "Planes – and plenty of them. They're ours."

The whine of engines became more distinct, growing from a distant hum to a rapidly heated vibration. At first, it was one shadow joined by another and then another and another, until the sky grew leaded and dark. I climbed up the hatch to see where Rolf was. I found him lying down on his back staring up at the sky. I thought of my childhood, when my brother and sister and I would lie in the field and count stars. The noise of the engines had expanded until it became part of our blood, jumped inside our heads, making molecules dance and leap. I too, lay down and looked up. That is how the others found us and despite the cold, they also gazed up at the droning sky. The shrill whistle of bombs being dropped touched us like music. The distant eruptions and explosions filled in the chorus of this mechanical symphony. It looked and sounded like a thing of terrible beauty. For the first time in a long time, I felt hopeful. Maybe we would get through this. Maybe I would find my family.

The first wave of bombers had come and gone. In the distance, the formation of planes appeared as specks in the sky, lazily turning in a wide, wobbly arc heading back in the direction from which they came. The second wave had begun to fill in the blank spaces, black blots on the airy landscape. We perched on the surface of the T-34 and watched the spectacle as it unfolded. Two hours passed. No one stirred or spoke. Behind us came the sound of crashing and an engine. I jumped up, my legs gone stiff from the cold. Mischa grabbed his rifle.

"It's the fuel truck. Good."

I climbed down to wait for it. I saw three men in the cab instead of the usual two. "Oh shit," I muttered.

Commissar Brancovic was the unit's protocol and propaganda officer. He climbed down from the truck cab awkwardly. A stocky fellow, with a very square head and thick drooping moustache, he'd had his hair cut like Stalin's, short on the sides and bristly on top. He trudged over to where I waited.

"Good day to you, Comrade," Brancovic boomed.

"And to you, Comrade."

The squad busied themselves re-fueling the tank.

"May I offer the Comrade a cigarette or a drop of vodka?"

Brancovic's eyes narrowed. "It is too early in the day for drinking, Comrade. We have work to do. But I shall take a cigarette. If you don't mind."

I dug into the pocket of my parka and pulled out a crumpled packet of cigarettes. I lit a match and we bent our heads together to shelter against the wind.

"It's a glorious day for the proletariat," Brancovic said, puffing vigorously. "Don't you agree? We begin to beat back the fascist hordes."

"Of course. We're doing our work well." I put the emphasis on the "we", knowing that Brancovic didn't do much of anything. But still he had to be appeased.

Brancovic's eyes narrowed but he continued to puff away easily. He held up a brown envelope. "I've brought you and your men your pay."

"Thank you, Comrade. It's welcome."

"But I know," Brancovic continued, "that out here you have no need for money and would undoubtedly prefer to make a vital contribution to the state, to enable us to continue the glorious struggle against our enemies."

I inclined my head, thinking I should tell this pompous idiot to go to hell.

"And I'm sure the Comrade sets the best example of all."

Brancovic sputtered, choking on the smoke. "There's no question, Comrade. No question at all."

I wondered how much went back into his own pocket.

"Then, of course. We're soldiers and we give everything to the state, Comrade. Our lives and our money to further the glorious war effort." I could see Mischa and Rolf unloading boxes of food and storing them in the tank. "And now we must go back to work. Thank you, Comrade." I walked away and helped with the loading.

Inside the T-34, the men stripped down to their coveralls. I restarted the engine and let it warm up. Commissar Brancovic and his two lackeys had left. As we waited, I passed around a small bottle of vodka. I'd obtained it from General Vasilevsky's driver, who had an active trade going. No one asked where he got it but it was suspected that he had access to the general stores. I took one swig, then another and a last, long pull on the bottle before handing it to Mischa, who did the same.

"Ah, that's better. Warms things up. Get ready."

I slipped the lever into gear and the tank lurched forward.

"Yuri. Get the coordinates on the map." We'd been ordered to assess the impact of the bombing raid. Yuri made some calculations and brought the map over for me to see.

"About three kilometres?" I asked.

"Roughly." Yuri poked the map. "Here and here. Shouldn't take long to get there."

"Depends who we meet on the way."

We lurched on in silence, each of the men manning his post, watching carefully. We met up with several other tanks and ground troops who followed along. T-34-330 took the lead. The troop commander sent a scout up ahead. Progress remained slow as we encountered massive craters, exploded trees, fragmented rocks. Frozen mud and earth mixed with ice and snow. The word was passed for us to halt.

We sat around a fire in a clearing. We'd dug a pit to keep the firelight low and managed to find enough dry wood to burn. Mischa fried up the remainder of the meat ration and suddenly I remembered it was Friday night. The night my family came to the table and my mother said a blessing over the Sabbath candles. It was a warm memory, full of laughter. Simmy told jokes in a very serious voice. Thinking of him trying to sound so grown up gave me a pang and I sipped my tea, lost in those memories that now seemed so distant. Another place and time.

They came at us out of the trees. Howling like crazed animals, they ran forward, bearded, clothed in rags, their eyes wild and unfocused, mad expressions on their faces. The men froze, then Mischa picked up his rifle and took aim. I drew my pistol.

"Not yet."

I held out my hand. I didn't see them holding anything. "Draw your weapons," I said to the others. "But don't fire, unless I say so."

We waited. There were about ten of them. As they grew closer, the yells turned to whimpers and tears. The group of madmen pulled up in front of us and we stared at each other wordlessly. Finally, one of the men stepped forward.

"Please," he said in a quavering voice. "We're hungry. It's been three days. Please."

I turned to the others. "They want food."

"It could be a trick," Rolf said.

I stepped forward.

"Put your hands up. We need to search you. If you're clean, you'll get something to eat. If you're not, you'll be shot. Agreed?"

The one who had spoken glanced at the others, then nodded. He put his hands up in the air. The others raised their hands too.

"Rolf. Yuri."

The two men stepped forward and began to pat down each of the men. They, in turn, couldn't take their eyes off the fire and the food that sizzled in the pan. They stared at it silently as if it was a thing of wonder. Finally, the search was completed and Yuri nodded.

"Nothing."

I motioned with my pistol.

"Sit here, in a semi-circle and keep your hands in front of you at all times."

Rolf began handing out plates of hot food. The prisoners ate greedily, tasting the food and moaning and groaning with pleasure.

"Thank you sir," said the first man who spoke.

"You're with Paulus?" I asked him.

"Yes."

"What happened?"

"We were cut off during the last bombing raid. We're all that's left of our unit." A few of the others nodded. "Our Captain was killed. It was chaos. Everyone was going in different directions. And then the tanks came." He stared at the massive T-34 before him. "That is quite a machine, eh?" he said with genuine admiration. "Before the war, I was a mechanic. I owned a garage with my brother-in-law in Hamburg. It was a decent business but then…" his voice trailed off. "I want you to know that I am a conscript. All of us are. We're not all monsters like those in the SS. We're very much like you. Nobody wanted to come here, God curse us for our trouble."

"Perhaps," I replied. "You are my prisoner. Yuri, you better let them know what we've got." Yuri nodded and went off to fetch the radio.

The prisoner smiled like a mournful cur. "What will they do with us?"

"I don't know. A labour camp perhaps, if you cooperate and tell the truth."

"I am telling the truth," the man insisted. "We've been forced out here in the middle of nowhere in the freezing damn cold. We don't have adequate supplies. We don't have winter uniforms or enough food. Morale is very bad. We talked among ourselves about giving up."

"What about the rest?"

"There was a rumour," the prisoner said *sotto voce*, as if his superiors might hear him. "...The field marshal wished to surrender. The Fuhrer refused, and ordered him to fight to the death." The man laughed weakly. "To the death. We're half-dead already."

"Are you sure you want to be heard saying this?" And I indicated the others, who listened as they ate. "It could get you shot by the Nazis."

"We all feel the same way. We have families, wives and children. We all want to go home. We all want to live to see them again. Is that a bad thing? Don't you want that too?"

"Eat up. They'll be coming for you soon."

The prisoner wouldn't let go.

"Is it wrong? I sense that you feel the same way. Tell me. Do you agree?" The man stood up holding his plate. "We want to be free just like everybody else."

I struck him. The others tensed. I pointed my pistol at them. They shrank back.

"Just shut up. This isn't like any other time. We're not like anybody else. We're fighting a brutal war. Just thank your God or whoever you pray to at night that you aren't in fifteen pieces or lying in a snowdrift with the life ebbing out of you. You're our prisoners. We'll crush Germany and Hitler."

"Yes, you're right," said the fellow holding his hand to his mouth.

I motioned him down with my pistol. The fellow slumped to the ground. I walked away then and stood against the monstrous tank, staring at the ragged band of starving men. Mischa, Yuri and Rolf had monitored the exchange wordlessly. Only Rolf spoke German and followed it.

"I thought you were going to shoot him."

I shrugged, then took a sip of tea.

"It would've been too easy. This is more fitting. He should live the humiliation and pain of being a prisoner. This is better. Better he should live and see what Germany will be like after the war."

"How do you know we will win?"

"Because we must. Anything else is unthinkable."

"But still..."

I gripped him firmly by the shoulder.

"Don't think of anything else. It must be but the sacrifice will be very great. Stalin understands this."

"Comrade Stalin will be safe in his dacha." Rolf spat on the ground.

"Yes. But he is a leader and it's important for him to be seen leading. And Hitler will be living in his castle well behind the front lines. Roosevelt is in America. Churchill is in London. These are our allies and they know what they're doing."

"But they're not threatened as we are."

"For the moment, but we'll push them back. Look at these men. Starving and in rags. This is what we'll be fighting."

"They won't all be like that," Rolf declared.

I smiled and emptied the dregs of the tea. "True."

A lorry bumped up, its engine grinding and groaning as it made its way through the rough-hewn path. It jerked to a halt, splattering snow. I walked over to the prisoners and indicated with my pistol that they should stand up. Armed guards jumped out of the back of the truck and began herding the Germans along. As he passed by, the talkative one spoke, "Thank you for the food."

I nodded to him but didn't reply. Rather, we exchanged glances. After one of the guards hooked up the back gate, the lorry full of prisoners lurched off. I wondered what would become of them. But as the sound of the lorry eased and it disappeared out of sight, I no longer gave it much thought. It was time for us to turn in.

The General looked even more tired, his face drawn, the droopy eyes yellowed and bloodshot. He poured a glass of vodka and handed it to me, then poured one for himself. "How goes it with you?"

"Well."

"Well?" The General cocked his head.

I poured the vodka down my throat. "Well enough." The vodka burned pleasantly. "This is good."

The General raised the bottle. "Have another." I pushed the glass toward him and he filled it. "You're anxious to hear?"

"Yes."

"She is well. Worked off her feet. Sometimes standing twelve hours at a time until she can't see straight and her hands are so numb they can't hold the instruments she needs. Once or twice, she passed out in the operating theatre from sheer fatigue. I think she is working harder than we are."

I felt pained, imagining Olga like that. Seeing her pale face faded, deep circles under her eyes, the dark hair lank against her scalp. "Isn't there any leave?"

The General shook his head curtly.

"Not yet. There's too much to do. No one is allowed – not even a General's daughter. And certainly not a General. Or a Captain, for that matter."

I snorted. "I wouldn't ask for myself."

"Good."

The General laughed. As he did, the skin stretched so tightly across his high cheeks that I thought I could see the bone beneath.

Yes, Olga resembled her father. They were both tall. Her face was smoother with sculpted bones and full lips. And those amazing green eyes that mesmerized me. The ones the General focused on me now.

"Did she send a message?"

The General nodded. He reached into his pocket and removed a piece of paper that had been folded many times. He passed it over. I slipped it into my tunic.

"I'll read it later."

"Maxim," the General called. The nimble batman appeared bearing two plates of hot soup. The General shrugged. "Cabbage borscht. The best we could do."

"It will be more than enough." I dipped my spoon in. Watery, thin. A few lumps of meat and shreds of cabbage. A single potato. Stale black bread, no butter. And this was how a General ate. I thought back to the first meal we had together and my mouth watered at the memory. Then, supply lines stayed open. In the field, we had to make do and often there was barely enough.

"Tell me how it goes."

"The men are doing their best. They fight and work without too much complaint. There's the odd grumble here and there. Every day, we see more Germans. They have no will to fight. They stumble out of the woods, from behind burnt-out tanks and lorries, even from under the snow. They're poorly dressed and supplied. It's shocking in some ways. Not that I care about them."

The General smacked his fist down on the rickety table.

"We've got them on the run. They're surrounded with nowhere to go and we're closing the net. You and your tanks are the key to forcing them into the centre. Paulus has got three or four hundred thousand men with no supply lines and only summer provisions. This will be a great victory." He held his bony fist up to the lonely glare of the flickering lamp. "There are two choices only. Fight and die or surrender."

"Which will they choose?"

The General shrugged.

"Paulus is a practical leader. He cares for his men. Why sacrifice them needlessly? If he gives up, he'll be considered a traitor by Hitler. He won't be welcomed back by the German high command."

"What are our losses?"

"It has been steep," the General admitted. "A hundred thousand at least, possibly more. Between us, we have more than a million men in the field, Mordecai. History has rarely seen battles of this scale. Nor where the stakes were so high. The right to become the dominant military power in Europe. It's what drives us."

"Yes, General."

I poured myself another shot of vodka. It went down and I didn't feel it.

"Tomorrow is the beginning of the end for the German 6th Army, Mordecai. We close in. We shall be ruthless. We shall pursue our military goals relentlessly. It shall be our triumph over those bastards. Those supermen."

He said the words slowly, drawing them out. The vodka was having its effect. I could see the General existed beyond fatigue, on to some other physical state somewhere between waking and sleeping.

"There are still plenty of fanatics willing to defend the Third Reich to the death. They're not beaten yet."

"You're right. I shouldn't say so. And I shouldn't let a lowly captain tell me. And a Polack at that. But my daughter thinks very highly of you. She says you're brave and fearless."

"It would be foolish to have no fear, General. But we've been very lucky so far. No casualties in my group directly."

The General nodded but didn't speak. I believe he saw himself on a ridge overlooking a snow-covered valley. This valley was called the Valley of Angels. Ringing the valley, the metallic grey and green behemoths clanked their way to the floor below. Behind them, tens of thousands of troops in alpine gear, white snowmen advanced step by step, forcing the Germans to confront their own horror.

I watched the expression on the General's face. I too, could see the coming days' events unfold before me.

I drove through the rutted field. Even the great treads of the T-34 bounced and jounced into craters, up over cracked boulders and fallen trees. New mounds of earth had been created where bombs had landed. The tank skirted the burnt-out shells of lorries charred to a skeleton. And of course, the bodies. I avoided them when I could but it was not always possible to see. The crew stayed quiet; no chatter over the line, the radio blared static. I felt very much on my own. The General said we approached the end of this battle but it seemed to stretch before me as far as the limit of my horizon. It was then that I felt the weightlessness. First the concussion that knocked me backward. Mischa sprawled onto the floor. I glanced behind me and saw Yuri pinned behind a mound of twenty-five kilo shells. Rolf dug at them. Another great concussion boomed, and then another.

"Mortars," I yelled. I switched on the radio frequency. "We're under attack."

I gave the coordinates just as the T-34 lurched to the right. I grabbed hold of the lever and tugged, but there was no response. Mischa picked himself up from the floor. Rolf finished digging Yuri out. He was bruised but otherwise unhurt.

"We're stuck. Get your outdoor gear on. We have to get out." Quickly, wordlessly, they got dressed, slipping on the heavy winter pants and parkas over their coveralls. I climbed the ladder, opened the hatch. Machine gun bullets pinged off the metal ricocheting crazily. I ducked down. I looked at the expectant faces staring at me.

"We'll go to different sides, then circle around him."

The others nodded, licking dry lips and swallowing parched throats. I tensed my muscles, then launched myself upward. As I cleared the hatch I rolled to the left, clear of the tank. Bullets whizzed around me. I felt a tug at my elbow and knee. Just before I hit the ground, I relaxed and tumbled, coming up to my feet, rifle at ready. I waited for the others. Yuri went next, but his foot slipped on the ladder and the gunner was ready for him. Before he could clear the hatch, he took two hits in the shoulder. He dropped his rifle and slumped down. Mischa and Rolf caught him. They propped him up.

Yuri breathed painfully. Blood oozed through his winter uniform.

"Give me the rifle." Rolf handed it to him. "Now go. I'll be all right."

Rolf and Mischa looked at each other, then shrugged.

Rolf went up through the hatch and rolled to his left. Mischa followed closely on. I waited for him when he hit the ground, giving him a hand up.

"How's Yuri?"

Mischa grunted painfully. "Shoulder wound. But I think he'll be all right."

Rolf came around from the rear of the tank.

"Rolf, you circle around that way. Mischa and I will go left. Be careful. Watch your step." Rolf nodded. "Go."

Rolf disappeared through the dense bush. Mischa and I waded off. We stepped carefully through the snow, taking turns scanning to the right and the left, one behind the other. We concentrated on the ground. I looked up as two Germans dropped out of a tree and swung my rifle up to block the impact. One of the Germans grunted. Each carried a bayonet. I couldn't see Mischa but knew the other was on him.

The rifle was gone, submerged in the snow. The German had one hand on my throat and pressed the bayonet toward me. We grappled and rolled. The German's helmet flew off as we rolled and heaved over rocks, twigs, logs, branches and dirt. His face loomed huge, dirty and bloodied; cold, blue eyes intent on murder. The German rolled on top and pressed his weight down, forcing the bayonet closer to my throat, millimetre by millimeter, until the point pricked the skin. It drew blood. And then I remembered my parents and brother and sister. I let out a strangled cry of rage and pushed, forcing the German's hand back. Freeing a shoulder, I twisted and leveraged my weight over on to my side. I forced my hand under his chin and pushed with all my strength. Slowly, like a rusted vise opening bit by bit, the German's neck was exposed. I moved his body upward in a slow surging wave, turning the wrist and hand with the bayonet away in a reverse tide until I rolled on top of the German. The cold blue eyes widened with fear as they watched the tip of the blade twist, then flatten and slowly descend. As I pressed and pressed, the German let out a low gurgling sound. He kicked his legs spasmodically but as I held him, looking deeply into his eyes, I thrust the blade home until the eyes went vacant and the jerking body stilled. I leapt up, bayonet in hand, and saw the other one on top of Mischa. I plunged the bayonet through his body. The German stiffened then toppled to the snow-covered ground. Mischa lay panting, wordless.

"Are you all right?"

My throat had gone raw. Mischa nodded, incapable of speech. I put down a hand and pulled him up.

"Let's go."

Mischa stood up and stared down at the dead German soldier. He shook his head.

"That was close. I believe I saw eternity."

"Don't worry, professor. You're still here in the land of flesh, and blood. Come on."

I led the way cautiously through the trees. We circled around moving some five hundred metres. The cold wind had stilled. I no longer heard the whistling through the bare branches. The snow deadened our footsteps. I focused, then peered intently. As we continued in the wide circle, I caught a glimpse of something metallic. I crouched. Mischa followed suit.

"There." I pointed.

Mischa nodded.

"I see."

We continued on, careful not to make any noise. There came a burst of machine-gun fire. Rolf, I thought. He's drawing their fire. Good. We continued. The makeshift bunker came into view. Rocks, twigs and branches had been piled up, with the machine gun mounted behind. Only two soldiers manned the position. We scanned the surroundings. I tugged at Mischa's sleeve and motioned. Mischa nodded. We split up and began to crawl through the snow on our bellies. Ten metres. Twenty. Thirty-five, then forty metres, until we drew close. We split up. I moved left and Mischa to the right. Neither of us had any grenades. When I was in position, I raised my rifle. The first shot caught the machine gunner in the shoulder. He cried out in pain and cursed mightily in German. As the second swung his rifle around, I saw a figure running toward the machine gun, quickly scale the man-made barrier and fire downward in a long burst. The Germans jerked backward in surprise, then slumped to the ground. Rolf raised his hand and beckoned. We got to our feet quickly and trotted over. I prodded each dead man in turn.

"I was beginning to wonder what happened to you," Rolf said.

"We had a few guests," I replied. "Take the rifles. I'll carry the machine gun. Rolf, you take the ammunition." Only one of the Germans had a great coat. The other had a scarf wrapped around his helmet, an extra sweater on under his tunic and torn gloves with the fingertips cut off. I hefted the machine gun on to my shoulder and stalked off, not giving the dead another glance. The others picked up the gear and followed.

We found that Yuri had passed out.

"He's lost a lot of blood," said Rolf.

"See if you can get anyone on the radio. We may have to carry him out."

The T-34 lay disabled. We transported Yuri through the woods on a stretcher fashioned out of two poles and some canvas. Yuri remained unconscious but moaned in his sleep, his head lolling on the bucking stretcher as we stumbled through the ragged terrain.

After an hour, we came upon a supply truck. The driver obligingly turned around and brought us to base camp.

"Ease him down gently."

I slid the stretcher from inside the truck into the waiting hands of Mischa and Rolf.

"Where's the hospital tent?" I asked the driver. He lifted a finger and pointed. Rolf and Mischa began moving in that direction while I followed behind, checking on Yuri to ensure he was all right. The General, surrounded by a group of officers, came towards us.

"Ah, Captain." The others set the stretcher down and saluted. "Carry on. Your comrade needs medical attention. A word, Captain." And he bent his head toward me.

"General?"

The General looked at Rolf and Mischa sternly, who picked up Yuri and hurried off. I watched them go.

"Spring is not that far away and then we will be moving on. Did you hear that Paulus has officially surrendered?"

"No, I didn't. Congratulations sir."

"We've broken their backs, Mordecai. This is the turning point in the war. Mark me. You and I shall march up to the Reichstag in Berlin."

"I hope so, General."

"You have my word on it, Captain. Now go see to your man."

"Sir."

I saluted. It felt strange yet very appropriate. I wasn't one for the trappings of the military, yet I respected Vasilevsky, a true soldier and patriot.

I met up with Mischa and Rolf in the hospital tent. They sipped tins of hot tea.

"He is being looked at now."

Mischa handed me a tin that had steam rising out of it. "There are some pieces of the bullet still in his shoulder. They need to remove them."

"And...?"

"The shoulder bone is broken. It'll take a few months to heal."

"Goddamn!" I pursed my lips, then took a reluctant sip of tea. "How long is it going to be?"

"An hour or more," Rolf said.

I didn't know what would happen next. "Drink up. We'll get you two settled somewhere."

Mischa set the tin down on the rickety wooden table. A dour matron sat there in a starched uniform and a stern expression, watching the three of us intensely.

"Thank you, comrade."

She inclined her head but that was all. I took two sips then returned the tin. She glared at me but I ignored her. Rolf drank hastily, handed her the tin. I stood by the entrance waiting.

We found the temporary quarters for the enlisted men. I secured them beds that were shared with others. They took turns using the beds in four-hour shifts.

"With luck, we'll be out of here in about four hours," I said. "Get settled and get some rest. I need to speak to the mechanics about the T-34."

Rolf and Mischa looked at each other then nodded. They'd be back looking in on Yuri in a short while anyway.

I went off to find the mechanics' area. I followed a sick-sounding lorry to the far side of the camp where an expansive lean-to had been erected under camouflage netting. Here all sorts of vehicles in varying degrees of wholeness lay scattered about. Men in coveralls danced about pulling bits of engines apart or assembling casings. A madman's workshop. I pulled one of the grease monkeys aside.

"Who's in charge here?"

The fellow pointed.

"He is."

I walked up to a fellow with enormous shoulders and long, powerful arms. He worked a hoist by hand pulling on the chains, hauling a lorry engine out of its moorings. Only a man with significant strength could manage that on his own. I waited for him to secure the engine that swung slowly back and forth. The fellow's grease-stained face broke into a grin.

"I can do something for you, comrade Captain?"

He wiped his hands on a filthy rag blackened with oil.

"My tank is disabled." I could see no rank on the man's coveralls.
"And?"

"It needs to be fixed."

"Where is this tank, comrade?"

"It's out in the woods. A man has to go out with it, uh...?"

"Sergeant. Sergeant Suchov. What's the problem with it, this tank?"

"The left tread took a mortar round. It needs to be replaced or reattached."

Suchov smoothed his long moustaches with the back of his hand.

"Replaced is impossible. Reattached?" And he shrugged. "Give me three hours to do this engine job, then you can show me, yes?"

"Of course, comrade. In three hours then."

Suchov called out to my retreating back.

"And bring some men with you. We shall need them to help with the lifting."

I turned and nodded, then spun on my heels.

The air was wet. I sat by the turret of the tank, a rifle cradled on my knees. I smoked a cigarette and sipped from a tin of tea. Mischa sat to my left and Rolf to his right. They did not smoke or drink. They had their rifles at the ready. Spring was coming. The snow was heavy. It drenched everything. Before us an endless line of German soldiers trudged past. They were men barely holding on to life, sagging and listless. Walking took effort. They stared at their feet. A number were bandaged about the head and face. Occasionally, one might look up with an expression of defiance or anger that flashed in his eyes but it was quickly extinguished. I stared at the men thoughtfully. I didn't grin or gloat but inside I felt satisfied. I remembered what they had done to the Poles when they invaded. I had seen what they did to the Russians after they crossed the false border. To me, they looked like beaten animals robbed of their strength and arrogance. Seeing them humiliated compensated a little. But only a little.

"Where will they go?" asked Mischa.

I shrugged.

"To the labour camps in Siberia, I expect."

"You think so?"

I cleared my throat and spat. "At least they'll be alive."

Rolf adjusted the grip on his rifle. "I wouldn't want to be sent there." And he shivered thinking about it.

I waggled a finger. "Stick to business, comrade, and there'll be no need."

"And what do you see when you look at them?" Mischa asked.

"I see men with all the pride drained out. What was once mighty is now pathetic. And I am glad for it too."

Chapter 35

The General sat in his tent in the dark, the only light coming from the glow of the ever-present cigarette.

"Come, share a drink with me, young Captain."

He turned up the wick on the kerosene lamp so that it cast an oaken, morbid glow inside the tent. I found a stool and the General handed me a mess tin filled with vodka.

"For once, I am a little bit drunk."

The General shook his head, looking almost skeletal, his iron-grey hair close-cropped to his skull. "We've won a victory. We've taken bold steps to ensure the future. So, why do I feel so deflated, hmm? Why am I not happier?"

I sipped the vodka. Rotgut. My stomach clenched.

"Because there's no glory in this, General. It's a tainted victory."

The General raised his craggy eyebrows as if surprised and then nodded. "But men always die. That's the way with war. It wouldn't be otherwise."

"Perhaps it's that there's no meaning. Paulus and the 6th Army had to be stopped. If not...?" I left the question hanging.

The General laughed harshly.

"Yes, of course, you're right. I've sent two hundred thousand men to their death for no reason."

"I didn't mean it that way."

The General waved his hand. "I know." He dropped his chin to his bony chest. "I am not questioning myself you understand, but it plagues my mind. Would it do me any good to write to all the mothers of those men to ease my conscience? I don't know. I see their corpses lying on the frozen ground. Some died as they fell, others suffered intolerably. It's a stark, brutal picture that doesn't go away. I don't question myself. We made the right decisions. But the price, the price."

He shook his head slowly from side to side.

"No one would ever think such a thing," I replied firmly. "You have the respect of all your officers and men. There was never any question of pushing ahead. Otherwise, the Germans would be in Moscow this minute and Russia would be lost. It's kill or be killed. This is what I tell myself. This is what has kept me alive. Kill the enemy first."

The General stilled his head and gave me a piercing look. "Do you love my daughter, my Olga?"

I started. I opened my mouth, closed it, then opened it again.

"I care for her very deeply."

"You didn't answer my question."

The General rose slowly to his feet. In the gloomy cast of the lamp, the lines on his face deepened, the cheeks and nose becoming more prominent. I sensed a note of warning in his tone.

"You must understand, General. I don't know what will happen to me. In a war, who knows the future? For both of us, we share whatever moments we can. We bring whatever joy we can. And for now, that must be enough. I wouldn't make Olga a promise and then break her heart if something happened to me. I go to bed at night thankful to be alive and wake up in the morning hoping to live through the day. That's all I can do. In a war, there's no room for love. I'm sure you've experienced this too, haven't you?"

The General stood over me, sweat dripped down his bony face. Then he collapsed back into his chair.

"You're right. We're soldiers. We don't know the future. I can secure you a job with central command, what do you say to that? Out of the line of fire."

I wasn't sure if the General was being serious. I wanted to grin but dared not.

"Thank you, sir, but my place is with my men. We work together. We trust each other. I need to maintain my position."

The General nodded, took another gulp of vodka and smacked his lips.

"I thought as much. I wasn't terribly serious anyway but I do care about my daughter and her feelings."

"She's a grown woman."

"True. You needn't point that out to me, Captain. But sometimes, perhaps, I need reminding. I still see in her the little girl who was so serious about reading and drawing, who asked such grown-up questions when she was just five. 'Daddy, where do people go after they die?' Paradise, my child, I'd say to her. Then she'd ask, "Then it is a good thing to die?" And I'd answer, sometimes, it is necessary. She would think about what I said and then accept my explanation. She hasn't changed. Still asking serious questions and expecting answers. She wanted me to guarantee your safety and as her father and a General, I couldn't. It's a terrible thing when a father lets down a daughter. I wouldn't give my darling a promise because I couldn't guarantee it wouldn't be broken. Children hold these things close to their heart. I never once broke a promise to her. Not once. And I never will."

"Yes sir."

"A toast then."

The General filled his tumbler and held out the bottle. I lifted the tin cup and held my hand up. The General ignored me and filled it to the rim.

"Now then, Captain." He raised his glass and held himself rigidly upright. I followed suit.

"To Olga Ouspenskaya Vasilevsky."

"To Olga Ouspenskaya Vasilevsky."

"Salut."

The General put the tumbler to his lips and drank, his Adam's apple bobbing as he gulped the harsh liquid down.

I drank deeply, matching the General gulp for gulp until, with a smack of the lips and a wiping of a sleeve, we finished, putting the empty tins down on the rickety table before us, each wavering slightly and grinning in a foolish manner.

"Bravo, Captain. You can hold your liquor, I see."

"I can."

I fought the desire to lie down which suddenly washed over me, as my limbs felt leaden.

"You're a strong man, Mordecai."

"Thank you, General."

"I don't mean physical strength. That too, but we all have that when we're young. And it always goes in time. I mean in character. It's this strength in you that I like and it is what, I believe, attracts Olga to you. Her husband wasn't like that. He was wild and reckless but ultimately a weak character. He couldn't make difficult decisions. He couldn't look terror in the eye without backing away. I sense in you that this isn't the case, eh? Maybe you look forward to it."

"No General, I don't. But I make myself do what's necessary. Right now, we're at war and I do what's necessary to get through it. You want me to attack and I will. You want me to kill and I will. You want me to drive a tank all the way to Berlin and I will. But after all this is over, then I will do what's necessary. And it won't involve the war or killing. That'll be finished for me."

"Before that time comes, you will have your fair share, Captain."

"Yes. And I don't want Olga to know these things. She sees enough dealing with the broken men in the hospital. She cries because she can't fix what's been shattered. I won't add to her burden any more than that. I do care and I can't do that to her. I wish I could do more."

The General stood and stared at me, his face filled with anguish. He reached out his hand. I took it. "I wish this too, Mordecai. May the state watch over us."

Two days later, we said goodbye to Yuri. The company moved out. The battle had turned toward Poland and then came the push through into Germany. It would be a month or more before he'd be able to rejoin us. For now, we'd carry on as three. Yuri's shoulder had been heavily bandaged. We could see that, as he lay in the hospital cot, he was in a great deal of pain, wincing every time he attempted to shift position.

"Before long you'll be pinching the bottoms of the matrons," Mischa said.

Yuri smiled weakly. "Right now I'll settle for a good piss."

"You can let them hold it for you." Mischa made a gesture between his legs. The others laughed. I knelt down beside Yuri.

"Take care of yourself, my friend. We'll be waiting for you. Make sure you're completely healed before you leave this place."

Yuri held up his good hand. I took it. "Thank you, my comrade and brother. Guard yourself and the others."

"We'll be waiting for you."

I squeezed Yuri's hand and he squeezed back, tears welling in the corners of his eyes. Rolf and Mischa then each, in turn, took Yuri's hand. We left the tent and as we did so, Yuri turned away. Outside, I spotted the head matron and called her over.

"Comrade?" growled the matron, a heavy-set woman with a trace of a moustache.

"Look after Yuri Simonovich, Matron. He's to have the best of care. Is that understood?"

The matron swallowed hard.

"All of our patients receive the very best of care, comrade."

I stepped closer to her but the matron held her ground.

"Now you listen to me. If he's not well looked after, I personally will come looking for you and you will answer directly to General Vasilevsky."

The Matron swallowed hard. Her dark upper lip trembled.

"I understand, Comrade. Yuri Simonovich will receive the best possible care. We shall be very attentive, I assure you."

I strode away, Mischa and Rolf following. Mischa glanced back at the matron who had formed a stony expression.

The last of the prisoners had been marched out from the temporary encampment where we had the T-34 repaired and left Yuri to be nursed back to health. There was a surreal air of calm within the landscape. I perched on my helmet and drank some sour-tasting soup out of my mess tin. I added a measure of vodka, for the taste and to warm myself as the temperature still hovered near the freezing mark, even though the weather had started to break finally. The sun had broken through low-lying clouds, casting shadows and igniting crystals of light on the disappearing snow's surface. It was a rare, beautiful day and I closed my eyes to concentrate on the sun's heat, willing it to penetrate my skin.

Mischa clapped me on the shoulder.

"Come, wake up. Don't fall asleep yet."

"I wasn't sleeping."

"No?"

The expression in the narrow-focused blue eyes brimmed full of amusement.

"No. Daydreaming. Pretending I was somewhere else."

"We all want to be somewhere else, comrade."

"Of course, that's why I was indulging myself a little bit."

I glanced at my watch. Time to break camp.

Chapter 36

1944: The Road to Berlin

My joints ached. I sweated like a pig, anaesthetized with vodka and hot tea. At night, the chills came. The others piled blankets on me yet my limbs quaked and trembled. I saw visions. My parents, just as I remembered them. My mother sat in the big overstuffed chair near the window where the light was better. She sewed delicate blouses for Katya and repaired torn socks and shirts for me and Simmy. Papa sat reading, holding the book very close, mumbling some of the words back to himself. I pictured a tranquil scene, a place that brought me peace. The vodka helped dull the ache in my soul.

"He should see a doctor," I heard Rolf say.

"What doctor?" asked Mischa. "There isn't one for hundreds of kilometres."

"There must be a field hospital somewhere," Yuri said. He had returned six months earlier, pleased to be back with the crew. His shoulder had healed finally but he still felt some pain and the bones clicked loudly every time he raised his arm.

"I don't think so", Mischa said.

He had taken over driving the tank since I had fallen sick with typhus but had proved so inept I knew that the others feared for their safety. He drove into trees, banged up against boulders, got them stuck in riverbeds and gulleys. Twice, other tank crews had to tow us out. Finally, the General told us to stay behind until I had recovered. We would catch up. The line advanced and we'd be safe on our own for a while. So, we located a nice mound where Mischa managed to park the T-34 next to a stream. Here we made camp until my fever broke. The General had managed to scrounge some sulfa drugs but only a few days' supply. Some weeks earlier, we had come across a motorbike left behind by one of the German units, abandoned as they retreated. I had been delighted and mounted the bike, riding off into the woods. We strapped it to the tank and took it with us. While I convalesced, the others rode the bike for amusement, to offset the long hours of idleness.

During the month of May 1943, we advanced by inches. The Germans had dug in along the regions of Poland and resistance remained fierce. My crew seemed in no hurry to reengage. As we sat around the low fire in the warm evenings, we saw the flash of artillery against the night sky and the flare of liberated flames. Mischa would shut his eyes and hear the human sounds that went along with them; the cries, the screams, the whimpering and finally, the sobbing of those beyond pain and hope. At night, Mischa told me about this after I recovered and that while I was out of it, he turned on the headset and listened to the static on the line. Sometimes he picked up scraps of conversations, orders, requests. He found the chatter reassuring. We weren't alone, he said. Others were out there.

They took turns looking after me as I sweated through fevers and shook from cold and chills. Sometimes I'd moan and mumble some words, say names that had no meaning to them.

Finally, I lay wrapped in a blanket and slept peacefully.

"He seems a little better," said Yuri, who rotated his left shoulder. He found that the shoulder stiffened up easily and he needed to keep the joint in motion.

"How is your shoulder?" asked Rolf. He squatted on his haunches. For a tall man, he was nimble.

"It is all right. Just stiffens up now and then." Yuri gave them a reassuring look. He didn't want them to think he couldn't do his job or they couldn't count on him when the time came. "Don't worry. It won't hold me back."

"We weren't worried," Mischa said.

"I don't blame you. In your position, I would wonder."

"It's not your fault you got shot." Rolf shifted his position but stayed in the squat.

"Still, I'd rather be here than in hospital. There was one matron there, I thought she was going to kill me."

Rolf and Mischa exchanged looks. "Why?" Mischa asked.

"Every half hour she was in looking at the wound, ripping off the bandages, causing it to bleed. There was no pain medication. When she wasn't doing this, she was trying to force feed me whether I was hungry or not. "Eat, eat," she'd say. "You must get strong so you can get back to the front for the glory of Mother Russia." I thought she was insane. If I didn't get out of there, I'd be a dead man. I was so happy when the doctor said I could go."

Mischa burst out laughing, shaking until the tears ran down his cheeks. He removed his spectacles to wipe his eyes with the back of a sleeve.

"We saw her. The...the...Captain threatened her, said if you weren't looked after properly that she'd hear directly from General Vasilevsky. I think she believed what he said." Yuri looked from one to the other then he too, burst out laughing.

"What are you fools laughing at?" I had one eye open and scowled. "I was sleeping so peacefully."

Mischa bent over me. "Sorry. It's just that Yuri was telling us how he escaped near death in the hospital. And it wasn't from his wounds."

"You're talking nonsense. Get me a drink of water if you please."

Mischa handed me a canteen, unscrewed the top and held it to my lips. I was parched.

"I'll take some tea if you have it."

Mischa set the canteen down and recapped it.

"I remember this Matron. She seemed to take her duties very seriously," I said. The other two snickered. "And you got well, that is the important thing."

Mischa handed me a tin of tea.

"How do you feel?" Rolf asked.

"Better. I think the fever has gone."

Mischa felt my face. "Feels cooler."

I was pleased that the men were concerned about me.

"I'll rest some more. Tomorrow, we'll be on our way."

The others nodded. I took a few sips then handed the tin back to Mischa. I pulled the coarse blankets over my shoulders and drifted back into sleep.

We travelled toward the southern portion of the Bug intending to follow its banks northward toward Brzesc. There was another push on toward Lwow and on through the Janow Woods, then up toward Lublin, then Deblin and the converging Soviet forces would meet up just before Warsaw. And there we would begin to press the Nazis back into Germany, force them to give up the ground they had taken not so long before. I felt a mix of pleasure and satisfaction as the massive T-34s rolled through the small towns and villages. I saw the blank expressions on the faces of the peasants who lined the road. I knew what they were thinking. They exchanged one form of tyranny for another. One oppressor leaves and another takes his place. What could they do? Just what was always done. Give up what they had to, thieve on the side, survive in the only way they knew how. The sight of Soviet tanks and troops brought no joy to the Polish countryside. The communists were despised and feared even more than the fascists. At least, the fascists rid them of the Jews. One less nuisance in their lives.

I sensed a collective moan among the local populations as they returned to something to which they had become inured. That was the practicality of the Polish peasant, to take all of this misery in stride. I didn't feel sorry for them. I thought of their crudeness and stupidity. I thought back to my childhood and the pain I'd endured.

I thought about my family and whether they'd received any help from our neighbours. Neighbours to whom we'd given work and full livelihoods. I pinched the bridge of my nose and slowly shook my head.

We churned out kilometre after kilometre eking our way along the Bug, pausing to rest and take water and on the warmer days, go for a quick swim and a wash. Soon, we would turn due west and head further inland and press on toward Warsaw. The tanks kicked up dust, a skein visible for a distance as the spring and summer burned hot and dry. Dust swirled in through the front slit and as we rode with the hatch open, it drifted down in a cloud. The dust was insatiable, matting our hair, caking the creases in our faces, powdering our clothes. I stripped to the waist to cope with the heat inside the T-34 that reached 40 degrees Celsius and more on some days. We consumed prodigious quantities of water to stave off dehydration.

General Vasilevsky had put me in charge of a tank unit. In all, six tanks were now under my command. We never spoke of Olga. I hadn't heard from her in months. We moved constantly and often weeks went by without me seeing the General, sometimes glimpsed getting in or out of a staff car either late at night or before dawn.

I tried to stop myself from thinking about her. Only in the rare, quiet moments when all of the men fell silent, caught up in their own thoughts, did her presence take hold of my senses. She appeared to me out of the darkness. Through my weariness, she seemed so real, so tangible as if I could reach out and touch her, feel her body in my arms, wrap myself in her heat and sensuality. At those moments, I reached for the vodka bottle. I drank a bottle a day. The General's quartermaster kept me well supplied. When there was little food, there was always vodka and it was distributed liberally to the troops. The men exchanged looks but said nothing. I never appeared drunk or out of control. My commands remained crisp, my actions precise. As the machine guns rattled in my brain and the cannon pounded my head, the vodka kept me removed, helped drain my fear as we hurtled into battle.

The line of tanks halted before a long bend in the road. Scouting reports indicated that German troops had dug in and awaited us. They felt near. We didn't know how near.

"I am going to take a look," I said.

The crews spilled out of their machines and milled around. I had the commanders gathered around me. Mischa hovered near by. The other commanders, young yet grizzled, eyed each other warily. I sensed their apprehension.

"Let me go," Mischa said. "I'll take the motorcycle." Through our long journey, it had ridden with us, strapped to the side.

"Yes, that would be better," said one of the tank commanders. The others nodded. They didn't look like soldiers but rather mechanics, standing in the blazing sun, stripped to the waist, coveralls rolled down, skin glistening with sweat. Among them, I was the darkest and the largest. I grabbed hold of Mischa's arms and squeezed.

"Take it slowly. Don't take any foolish chances."

Mischa nodded and grinned. He removed his spectacles and polished them. His face had a vacant look without them, young, innocent and expectant. As if the best things were yet to come.

"Tovarisch."

"Tovarisch," I replied.

We hugged and clapped each other on the back.

"Go with God," I whispered.

Mischa pursed his lips as if thinking about it. He turned toward the tank. I signaled Rolf and Yuri. They unlashed the motorcycle from the T-34 and lifted it down. One of the other tank men handed Mischa a machine pistol that he slung over his back and placed a helmet on his head. As he kicked the motor into life and revved the two-stroke engine, he fastened the strap under his chin. The road ahead twisted sharply and as he rode off, he raised his right arm in salute, then disappeared from sight.

I turned to the others.

"Let's follow."

The tank commanders motioned to their men, who broke off their muted conversations and gathered around their tanks, ready to clamber inside.

The sun radiated through the trees making shifting patterns on the broken roadway.

Over the years, I dreamed about what happened to Mischa and this is how I imagined it. I imagined that Mischa found himself distracted by the tranquility, the peacefulness of the countryside. Squirrels leapt from branch to branch and he must have noticed bluebirds flitting from tree to tree. He wouldn't have been surprised to see a rabbit burst out of the grass and scamper across the road. It was unusual to see wildlife, most seemed to vanish when the tanks and big guns moved in.

Living in that moment of freedom and serenity, I could understand why Mischa gunned the small engine, lifting up the front, freewheeling down the road effortlessly. A moment later, he must have fought the frontward motion of the motorcycle, squeezed the brakes with all of his strength and attempted to wrestle the handlebars and twist them around. It was likely at that moment that he saw, then felt the blaze of light that brought him into the centre of its flare and onward into oblivion. Then he exploded into a million brilliant colours.

We lumbered on slowly. Mischa disappeared, galloping on ahead. The T-34s plodded some five or six kilometres down the road before we came across the first signs of debris, some metal lying on the road. Rolf had gone up top. With the hatch open, he scanned ahead with field binoculars. Some two hundred metres further up, he spotted a piece of the bike's tail pipe. He called down and I put on the brakes. Rolf signaled the others behind him. I put Yuri in my seat and grabbing a rifle and helmet, went up top. Rolf had dropped to the ground in the shadow of the tank. Others came up, using the tanks for cover. We walked slowly, quietly. I kept my eyes busy, probing the outlying trees, rocks and bushes but kept coming back to the piece of metal. As we came upon it, I recognized it. The metal felt hot to the touch. We crept forward, rounding a corner. There, on the roadway lay a headless torso. I gasped, then sank to my knees. The Russian troops shrank into the shadows of the tanks as they continued to creep forward. I regained my feet. Rolf and I moved quickly up along the side of the road using the trees and brush, until we came abreast of the body. It had been ripped open, gutted like an animal draining its blood into a trough. I felt the urge to vomit but forced my stomach down. A whistle shrilled. We looked over to see one of the other men holding up a pair of twisted spectacles. Seconds later, a mortar shell exploded. The fellow holding the spectacles vaulted into the air. His body cartwheeled along the road until the momentum of the blast dissipated, leaving him lifeless and crumpled. Mischa's spectacles lay where the soldier had dropped them. I dashed over to where they lay and scooped them up. Machine gun bullets pinged off the roadway in front of me and I half ran, half rolled back to cover.

"That was crazy," Rolf said.

"Let's go."

"What about...?" And he nodded toward the body.

"There's nothing we can do for him now. Come on."

I led off through the cover back to the T-34. The Germans loosed their mortars, rocking the ground every few seconds. Back inside the tank, I had to take a moment to control the shaking in my hands, quelling the rage within me. I barked orders into the headset, then swung the T-34 around wide and went off the roadway.

"Hang on," I yelled.

Yuri and Rolf braced themselves as the tank smashed into trees and on to the Nazi positions. The other tanks did the same. I could hear yells and screams. Machine gun fire pinged off the tank's outer shell but we forced the mortars to fall back as the phalange of tanks swept down on them.

"Fire the cannon."

Yuri worked the breech, loading shells firing as quickly as he could set them up. I aimed the tank toward anything that had German insignia and that moved. It could be men, trucks, artillery, I didn't care.

"Keep firing," I roared.

A German stood in front of us with a flamethrower. Nasty tendrils of fire flared inside the slit. I covered my eyes with my arms.

"Machine gun. Shoot the bastard."

The T-34 kept rolling, the flamethrower dropped back. Rolf got him in his sights and fired a burst. A ball of flame caught the fellow's sleeve and within a moment, his uniform blazed. Rolf gave him another burst and the conflagrated figure fell backward to the ground, twitching.

"For Mischa, you Nazi bastard."

I rolled the tank over top of him and laughed crazily. Yuri and Rolf laughed too, hooting like fevered owls.

All around us tanks fired cannon and shot flames. The peaceful section of road and forest that Mischa had admired disappeared. Charred stumps, burnt-out grass, chunks of rock and concrete lay in heaps, dust and sand filled the air like a fine curtain. I walked amidst the devastation. I stepped over bodies and parts of bodies, noticed single boots and pieces of helmets, listened to the moans of the wounded and dying. Blood caked my face. My coveralls were torn and splattered with black oil. Dirt crusted in the corners of my eyes. Never had I been so fatigued, never had I felt like less than a human. I wanted to lie down beside the dead and go to sleep. I could have slept for a month... but there was no time. Yuri plucked at my sleeve. Time to move on.

Chapter 37

Beulah looked at me with her large, brown eyes. Tears squeezed out.
Seeing them, I turned away. The memory had stayed raw, the pain real.
  "I'm sorry about what happened to your friend, Mr. Gold."
  "Thank you."
  "That must have been hard for you."
  I nodded. "Yes. Yes it was. But there was the rest of the war to fight
and I was determined to do my duty and fight as hard as I could."
  "I don't think I could do that," she said.
  "You're wrong," I replied. "If you had no choice, you would do it.
Anyone would."

I became Mordecai the machine, moving through my duties routinely with as little conscious thought as possible. I stepped back from my feelings so they wouldn't interfere with soldiering. There was a mission to see through and I would do it to the best of my ability. Kill or be killed, I told myself over and over again. Mischa's death gnawed at me. I took to staying by myself in the quiet part of the evening, when there was such a thing, and drank vodka to insulate my misery. It didn't work – the ghastly vision of the headless torso leaking fluid into the ditch haunted me. One moment it had been a man and the next, nothing. After a few weeks, there came a replacement. A smiling fellow with blackened teeth named Ivan. He hailed from the Caspian region. Ivan didn't say much. He went about his work amiably and efficiently. Mainly, he smiled at everything and that irked the others, who snapped at him. Ivan shrugged and said nothing. This was his third tank crew. He'd survived the loss of the other two.

Then something happened that turned me away from Russia, turned me away from Olga. I resolved, if I survived the war, that I would find my family then get as far away from that country and Poland and Germany as I could. It was a crisp fall day and we drove toward Warsaw, some 200 kilometres to the west. I felt a sense of calm within myself on that day, the air held still like a deep breath and the sky dazzled blue. Then we heard gunfire, volleys of shots, repeated. I stopped the tank. The volleys sounded yet again.

"Rolf, come with me. Let's go take a look. Yuri. You and Ivan stay here. Keep your wits about you and your rifles ready."

Rolf and I climbed out of the T-34 and dropped to the ground. We had stopped near an apple tree and I plucked one from its branches and took a bite. It tasted bitter and wormy. I spat it out.

"This way," I said, following a path that led down a brambled slope. The undergrowth lay thick and we forced our way through it. We heard more volleys. Something about it didn't seem right. The shots had been fired in unison, in an orderly fashion. I looked at Rolf and he shrugged.

"Hunters?" he said.

"Too many," I replied, "to be a party of hunters."

As we slid toward the bottom of the slope, I heard cries. Cries of human misery and despair. Women wailing. Children crying. Men pleading. Such desolate sounds pierced my soul. Of all the things I'd experienced and witnessed, this remained one of the worst.

"I don't like this," Rolf said. "We should go back. Continue on our way."

I shook my head. "I need to see," I croaked. Some demon possessed me. I don't know why or how but this urge to grope ahead to the source of the horrific baying seized me. I couldn't deny its hold.

"You can stay behind if you wish," I growled.

Rolf spat. "Let's go and get it over with."

We broke through to a clearing, crouching behind some shrubs. There, in a vast field stood a ring of Soviet soldiers with rifles at the ready. Laid end to end, falling where they had stood, I saw bodies, corpses heaped like sticks, hundreds massacred. A line of peasants, for that's what they were, Polish peasants, screaming and begging for their lives. Soldiers pushed and beat them forward, raining blows on their backs and uncovered heads. The soldiers forced the peasants into a ragged formation and then withdrew. An officer raised a baton then sliced it down toward his thigh precisely. Bullets scissored the air and the peasants crumpled to the ground. The officer hurried over. Any he saw moving, he shot in the head.

"Jesu," muttered Rolf. "What in the mother of god…"

"Wait a minute," I said. "Wait a minute."

I stood up. Rolf grabbed my arm. "Are you insane, they'll kill us too. We aren't supposed to be here."

I pushed him off and strode forward. "What is the meaning of this? What do you think you are doing?"

The officer turned toward me, his smoking pistol at his side. He smiled broadly.

"Ah, comrade. A glorious day for the motherland, don't you agree?" Brancovic, the unit's political officer said.

I kept going like a robot. God knows I bore no love for Polacks, no love for any of them. But this? This was monstrous. I stood and gaped at the heaped bodies before me.

Brancovic bragged on eagerly. "A master plan," he said. "Stalin is a genius. A genius. Anyone will think it's the Nazis, don't you see? We bury the bodies in shallow graves. We use German munitions. This is propaganda taken to a whole to new level, don't you agree, Captain?"

I swept my arm in front of me. "This is what you call, propaganda? This?"

Brancovic looked smug and composed. "Of course. "

I stood stunned and inert. I wanted to shoot him, to wipe the far-cical grin off his broad face. His political troops watched me edgily, fingering their weapons. Then a hand gripped my shoulder.

"Captain, Captain. We must get back now. We are needed back at the tank."

All went still. I went to raise my arm but Rolf held me fast. "Time to go," he hissed again. I hesitated. The troops opposite worked their fingers toward taut triggers.

"Think," Rolf said. "Think what Mischa would say. You need to find your family, yes?"

I nodded, suddenly numb and broken.

"I will tell the General about your good work, comrade," I spat.

Brancovic beamed and raised his hand. "For the motherland. Go and be victorious."

Rolf pulled me away and I stumbled behind him not realizing what we had done or where we headed.

It's finished, I told myself. How could I live with this? How could I live in a country, raise a family in a place that thought this made sense? I loved Olga. I wanted her. She left in me an aching chasm yet I knew she'd never leave her father. And I couldn't stay.

The weeks and months fell away. Warsaw had fallen and the So-viet troops and their allies pushed across Germany, heading straight for Berlin. I wanted to drive my tank directly into Hitler's bunker and shove my pistol right into der Fuhrer's nose, then pull the trig-ger. The T-34 had done its job well, bearing up under the battering, the variance in terrain, the pounding of shells, the ricocheting of bullets, the hardscrabble of rocks and trees and other natural barri-ers. The metal behemoth had carried us nobly with only a few minor breakdowns, most of which I had been able to repair. The fighting had been fierce. The Germans were not giving up their territory easily. More and more, however, we noticed the German forces con-sisted of pimple-faced teenagers, fanatical Hitler youth, who fought with a dangerous frenzy, an abandonment that emanated from the belief that they were invincible. The reckless carnage appalled me, but they were the enemy and deserved to die.

"Babies," said Rolf gazing down at the bodies of a squadron we had overrun. "They don't even shave yet."

"Dangerous babies," I replied.

I searched one of the bodies and pulled out a packet of cigarettes, tapped one out then lit it up. "They'll kill you as quick as a cobra and not give it a thought." I held up the pack. Rolf shook his head.

"When will we be done?"

"Soon. When we get to Berlin."

"I want to see it."

"You will."

I drew deeply on the cigarette. It was real tobacco, not the ersatz stuff we were issued. It gave me great pleasure to be smoking the German's cigarettes. I stood up.

"Come on. There's more to do." I clapped Rolf on the shoulder, who stared at me expectantly. Yuri looked on. Ivan stood and grinned. Each with a week's beard and faces crusted with dirt. They could be Neanderthal men.

"We're all tired but we'll sleep when the work is finished and it will be soon.".

The crowds of the 'liberated' never flagged. They lined the narrow roadways, the countryside and the broken streets that had fallen prey to bombs from the sky. They stood shoulder-to-shoulder in mute resignation. The girls no longer pretty and the boys, the few left alive, looked on with hard, hollow expressions. They should have been the victors and triumphant, these German Volkdeutsch. But instead, their pinched, mean faces reflected the fall of a thousand-year empire that had tumbled in little more than a decade. All the promises had been broken, the dreams of glory shattered. And if they had read their history, it was Versailles all over again. And to see this sight, that of mighty tanks bearing down on them, emblazoned with the hammer and sickle as they roared through the countryside, the stoic soldiers of a foreign empire perched atop, expressions calm as they overran the fatherland.

Now we entered Berlin. The time had come. I thought of General Vasilevsky and wondered if I would see him. The mighty German Reich had crumbled just as the buildings around them had been reduced to rubble. The previous three years had seemed both never-ending and somehow in the past, part of a former life. Two days earlier, we had crossed where the Neisse and the Oder connected. There, we'd met up with American troops and exchanged greetings. The Americans gave us chocolate and good tobacco. We gave the Americans vodka. I sat on top the tank with my Kalashnikov cradled in my lap. I smoked an American cigarette, enjoying it. Along the way, we had picked up stray soldiers who needed a lift or had become separated from their units. One of them, an American, lay stretched out asleep on the tank's prow like he was sunning himself on Malibu beach. The American soldier was tall and blond. A fine stubble speckled his chin. He slept with his mouth open and I could see strong teeth, marred only by the yellow of nicotine. The Yank stirred, stretched, yawned, then opened his eyes and blinked.

"Damn. I am on a tank riding into Berlin, ain't I?"

"Yes, you are."

"Thought I dreamed it."

"No, it isn't a dream."

"You speak good English for a Russki."

"I am Polish and a Jew, not Russian."

"Sure thing. What's your name?"

"Captain Mordecai Goldman."

The American stuck out his hand. "Pleased to meet you, Cap. I'm PFC Daniel Ranger." They shook hands. "Been in this conflagration long?"

"This what?"

"This war, Cap. This here damn war."

"I fought the Germans in Poland in 1939. Then I joined the Soviet army in 1941. Long enough, I think."

"You got a girl, Cap?"

"Yes. She's a surgeon in the Soviet army. Her father is an important general, my commanding officer. A great soldier."

The American blew a whistle through his thin lips. "No kidding? A General, huh? I guess that puts you on easy street, don't it?"

"Easy street?"

"Yeah, you know, taken care of, a bigwig to look after you, that kinda thing."

"No, Private Ranger, I look after myself."

"Do you know what you're gonna do after the war, Cap?"

"When the war's over, I'll find my family."

"Where're they at?"

"I don't know. I have to look for them."

"Geez, that's tough. Where do you start?"

"In Poland, my home town, my father's house. Someone will know something and I'll find out what they know."

The American looked pensive, his long face etched in thought, thin lips pushed forward. "I know where my folks are and where my girl is too. We're getting married when I get home."

"Then you know what will happen and what your life will be like."

"Pretty much, Cap. I'm gonna get a job in the local garage and ... "

"Garage?"

"Working on cars and trucks, fixing engines."

"Ah, you're a mechanic."

"Right. 'Cept I don't have my certification yet."

I brought a thumb to my chest. "Me too. I'm a mechanic. I can fix anything... cars, trucks, tanks, you name it."

"No kiddin'. Well, ain't that a coincidence."

I offered the American a German cigarette that was declined politely. The American fished out a pack and shook it. "Have one of mine." I accepted. The American brought out a gold lighter and I leaned in, cupping my hand over the flame. "Good old American tobacco. Best in the world."

I laughed at the young man's enthusiasm.

"I'm sure you are right."

The American rapped the metal surface with his knuckles. "This your rig?"

"Yes."

"Quite a beast. What's it like driving one of these?"

"Very hot and very noisy."

"What's it got under the hood?"

"Pardon?"

"The engine."

"V12 diesel, 1200 horses."

The American let out a long low whistle, blowing smoke. "Wow. That's some kind of power."

"Sure. This tank weighs twenty-five thousand kilos. You need a big engine."

"Ever break down on ya?"

I shook my head.

"Never. It never stops. The men who designed this tank came from Prague so it was a good design and reliable. Not like most things in Russia."

The American straightened up suddenly and let out a piercing whistle. Some soldiers walking by the side of the road looked over.

"There's my unit, Cap. I want to thank you for the lift."

I yelled down into the cockpit and the tank slowed. The American stuck out his hand and I shook it. Then the lanky fellow jumped down.

"See ya in Berlin, Cap. We'll dance on Hitler's grave and I'll buy you a drink in the first bar we find."

"I'll look forward to it."

I saluted. The American effected a salute back, then grinned, showing his long teeth. I banged the stock of my rifle on the surface of the tank and it started up, gathering speed slowly. We had travelled a mere fifty metres when I heard what sounded like a loud pop. I looked back to where the American had been standing, tall and slim, smiling as he was welcomed back by his compatriots, and saw black smoke curling upward. I shouted down for Rolf to stop, then slid down the tank's surface to the roadway and ran back. A crowd had gathered around the soldier's inert body, now curiously doll-like; broken and bent at odd angles. The American's mouth hung open. I was about to say something but nothing came out.

"Must have stepped on a goddam mine, goddam it to hell," said one of the soldiers leaning over him. "Four years and this is how he goes? Goddam."

A gruff-looking man with a cigar butt jammed into the corner of his grizzled mouth pushed his way through. "What's going on, here?"

"It's Ranger, Sarge. Stepped on a mine."

The Sergeant spat the butt out and looked down.

"Sweet Jesus. Look what's happened to you."

The Sergeant stared down at the body for what seemed like a full minute while no one said a word. Then he leaned down and carefully removed the dog tags from around the lanky American's neck.

"All right you men, bag him up. And sweep this whole area for mines before someone else gets blown to hell."

"Right, Sarge," said the first soldier. "Come on guys, let's do this."

The Sergeant looked over at me. "Can I help you?" I shook my head. "You speak English?"

"Yes."

"We've lost too many damn fine men."

"He was my friend. We were going to meet in Berlin for a drink."

"He won't get there but the rest of us will. We'll push the Krauts right into the sea if we have to. Personally, I'd like to put a bullet in Hitler's brain. But then there's no justice in this world, eh, Captain? I am right, you are a Captain?"

"Yes. I command tanks."

"God bless you then, buddy."

The men gathered up the body and I watched as it was wrapped carefully in canvas and then carried away toward a waiting lorry.

The Sergeant removed another cigar from his shirt pocket, stuck it in his lips and began to chew on it with his back teeth.

"So long, Captain."

We shook hands. I trudged back to the waiting tank. It was funny. I was just now hearing the mortar and artillery shells at a distance, as if somehow I had managed to shut them out while I talked to the American.

The American Sergeant's casual attitude toward death angered me. It had been four years and I had held myself in. I hadn't let my emotions out. I'd played the loyal soldier serving the General well. When ordered to take a hill, I took it. The previous winter, I led a breakout group that smashed through the German lines to the west of Warsaw. I'd lost almost a hundred men during that operation but it'd been a crucial part of the General's strategy. It came home to me that war turned existence into blood, piss and shit. The weariness of it, the fact that I'd been filled to capacity with all the blood, piss and shit I could stand unleashed a swell of rage. My boot heels smacked the tarmac and I smelled the diesel oil as it rose off my skin. I felt madness surge through me like an electric bolt. I could have snapped my rifle like a twig smashing it into kindling for the fire. I leapt back onto the T-34 and banged the hood. Rolf engaged the gears and it lurched onward.

Chapter 38

Finally. The Reichstag. Rising out of the mist like a medieval castle. The ring of tanks around the square stood forty deep. Thousands of allied troops, British, American and Soviet milled about, moving lazily in a relaxed manner. We'd heard that Hitler was dead, committing suicide in his bunker along with his mistress, Eva Braun, and his personal staff. Many felt bitterly disappointed. We had wanted to see him humiliated publicly. We had wanted to see him put on trial before the world. I'd wanted a public execution. Death alone wasn't enough when you had the taste of revenge on your tongue.

The city of Berlin was divided into four separate quadrants, each its own unique kingdom. I waited. The others went to the bars and picked up desperate German women, who were bitter yet realistic. They needed to eat. To provide for their families. Most knew their men weren't coming home. Germany had been razed to the ground, brought to its knees then hammered on the skull. The population looked dazed; they staggered as if in a fog and avoided the eyes of the allied soldiers. Only the black market thrived. I could get whatever I wanted in exchange for American dollars – vodka, caviar, British tobacco, chocolate or a woman. Women of all nations appeared as if summoned. Polish, Hungarian, French, Belgian, Czech, they all came to claim some of the spoils. They wanted American soldiers and their American dollars but the more desperate would even go with the Russians. Rolf and Yuri went to the bars while I spent time at Soviet headquarters in the Russian sector. I met with the General.

"So now you can marry my Olga."

"Are you asking me for her?"

The General laughed and lit a cigarette from the stub of the one he'd been smoking. If anything, he'd grown thinner and more translucent. His fingers had turned almost entirely yellow. He poured a glass of vodka and pushed it in my direction.

"It's what she wants."

"I'll go back and see her."

"And then?"

"You know I must look for my family. I need to know what's happened to them."

The General left the cigarette between his thin lips while he rubbed his cheeks with his bony fingers. His eyes had turned yellow.

"Go and see her. Then I'll give you six weeks to complete your business."

"Thank you, sir." I paused. "And what will you do now?"

The General smiled, stretching his thin lips without showing any of his stained teeth. "It's up to the politicians now. As for me, I await my orders just like you." The General blew out smoke, then crushed the cigarette out in the ash tray. Maxim appeared in the doorway. He beckoned.

"Yes, I know. Another staff meeting. How boring. I'd rather preside over a magnificent tank battle, eh?" The General rose, put out his hand.

"Mordecai, one day I hope I may call you son and welcome you to the family. Olga needs a strong man like you. Her strength has been depleted. Be good to her, will you?"

I took it. "I'll do what's best."

The General hesitated, then, after a long moment, clapped me on the shoulder.

"You have six weeks to find your family."

The General strode out of the room without saying anything further. Later, I learned that when General Vasilevsky returned to Moscow, greeted as a hero by the people, he was arrested and sent to Siberia. On Stalin's orders.

I packed up my kit. I had one decent uniform and the rest fit into a small duffel bag. I was catching a flight out of Berlin to Moscow that morning – the fifteenth of June, 1945. I'd been up early and gone round shaking hands with the men, those who fought and served under me. They relaxed and joked. They'd survived and waited for their orders, and tickets home. Rolf and Yuri stood last in the line. They stood kicking at the dust with their boot toes, suddenly looking awkward. A few months ago, they didn't even know if they'd be alive but we had beaten the odds together. We had been a lucky group. Rolf and I embraced.

"This is for you," he said.

I looked down and caught the glint of metal within the roughened palm. A piece of the frame of Mischa's glasses. Rolf had kept it. I accepted this fragment as evidence of a life, of an active mind and a being full of sentiment and emotion.

"Thank you."

From my inside pocket, I removed a handkerchief and carefully wrapped the fragment inside, then replaced it. Yuri and I embraced.

"Tovarich."

"Tovarich. Take care of your shoulder."

Yuri nodded, blinking back the tears that had risen to his eyes. I spoke to both of them.

"Lead good lives. Be well and prosper."

"I hope you find your family, Captain."

"Thank you. With a little luck, perhaps."

With the duffel bag slung over my shoulder, I walked away to where the transport awaited.

Two days later, I arrived in Moscow. After reporting to headquarters, I received the six weeks leave promised by General Vasilevsky. The General had a house on Prospekt Street. A car and driver took me there. The driver's route took me past the Kremlin where, unexpectedly, I felt a surge of something akin to a mingling of pride and fear. The city, indeed the country, continued to bury its dead. Every family had been touched. No town or village could say it was unaffected. Peasant women thronged the streets wearing black headscarves, the widows and orphaned mothers of the war generation. Drunk soldiers reeled on the streets, slept on benches.

The General's house was number forty-eight. It stood as part of a row of cavernous homes surrounded by a rusting iron fence. Only party officials or war heroes might live in such places. The houses looked grand but badly maintained. The facings had faded to grey and the exterior paint peeled badly. I faced a heavy wooden door with a badly tarnished brass knocker and rapped several times. I thought I heard footsteps, fleeting and harried. Flustered hands fumbled with the lock, not the deft hands of a surgeon. The door swung open and I stepped inside. Olga stood within, her hands clasped to her heaving chest. Her eyes clouded with tears. She came forward and ran her hands over me, touching, probing, pinching, all up and down my arms, torso and legs. Finally, she stepped back.

"You're not wounded? You don't hurt anywhere?"

I shook my head. "Not now."

I held my arms out and she folded herself into them like a bird being wrapped in its own wings. I felt her sigh deeply.

"I thought this day would never come."

"You didn't think I'd come back to you?"

"No. No, I don't know. Everything has been so mixed up, so continuous. My work at the hospital, it's been never-ending. I had to stop for a while, I felt I was going mad. And then Papa sent me a wire and told me you were coming to Moscow. I couldn't wait to get here, to fix the place up. It's been a long time since we've actually been here." She looked around. "As you can see, not all the lights are working yet." She looked back at me. "Come. Are you tired? Or hungry? Everything is still rationed but I managed to get a few things, even a decent bottle of vodka. Come."

She held out her hand. I left my kit bag on the floor in the main hallway. She pulled at me with an urgency, a hunger. We went quickly up a flight of steps to the second floor, then turned down a long corridor. At the end of the corridor, she flung open a door and pulled me into a room awash in flickering light. Her bedroom. Large, brocaded pillows adorned the bed. The sheets and blankets had been folded back. She had placed candles around the room, on the tallboy dresser, on the nightstand beside the bed, on her desk.

"This was my room when I was a child."

"I can see you here as you were then."

And I did, looking at her in the soft light that took away the circles under her eyes and rounded the jawline grown taut from fatigue. Her eyes glowed and grew lustrous. Suddenly, she was larger, enveloping me, drawing me to her.

"I don't smell of disinfectant."

"And I don't smell of diesel fuel."

"Are you tired, my love?"

I nodded.

"Then we shall sleep, and when we wake, I shall feed you."

Finally, we embraced. I took her into my arms, feeling her warmth, her vibration making me tingle. She unbuttoned my tunic, pulling my arms out of the sleeves and tossed it onto a chair. She loosened the knot in my tie and while I held my arms out, she unfastened the cuffs, then watched me as I undid my shirt. I balled it up and threw it to the side. Olga's slim fingers went to work on the waistband of my trousers, unbuckling the belt, then sliding the zipper down. I stepped out of my trousers and she took hold of me and moaned low in her throat. I pulled her to me and kissed her – five full years of fury, five full years of fear and passion and hatred unleashed. Olga clung to me, digging her nails into my shoulder blades. She tore at her dress, ripping the buttons, and the dress slid down to her slim ankles. She was naked except for her shoes. I lifted her up and set her down on the bed where I was on her immediately. She took me right away, wanting the hurt and the pain, the sharpness to bring her to her senses. I became a force within her and she rode it to a thundering climax bucking her hips, entwining her legs with mine, raking my back until she screamed at the terror of having lost then regained me. I felt myself transported through a haze of pleasure to earlier days. Her ferocity surprised me as did the sheer physicality of her, the tightness of her thighs, the arch of her back, the tensile force in her arms as she held me to her.

"I missed you," she breathed and I felt the swell of her breasts.

She remained caught in the spell of her passion and as she breathed more deeply she continued to move against me, her face beaded with perspiration. Like a set of pistons, her hips began to pump up and down and again I was surprised, surprised at the depth of her ardour and my response to it. I went willingly, matching her rhythm and intensity. I felt her hot breath on my face. Our bodies went slick with sweat as we moved together more forcefully. The bed rattled, seeming to move across the floor. The walls of the room shook, her head rolled side to side and she gasped, as if fighting for breath. Our bodies jerked harder and faster until Olga dug her nails into my back and emitted a low moan that increased in pitch, transforming into a kind of shriek as I reached under and lifted her to me where, after a long sustained moment, she began to whimper and slowly, I lowered her to the torn and tangled sheets. She covered her face with her hands and sobbed. I lay beside her and took her in my arms, holding her to me until slowly, her breathing regulated and I realized she had fallen asleep.

I existed beyond tired, in some new level of exhaustion, yet I couldn't sleep. My mind wouldn't turn off as I speculated what I might find when I ventured back out into the world. And such a different world it had become. A rebuilding world everywhere, even in the Soviet Union. In the newspapers, I'd read about the amount of money the Americans planned to pour into the rebuilding of Germany, something that disgusted me. Why should the Germans benefit from this goodwill? Are they rebuilding the rest of Europe? No. Only Germany. Why?

And what would I find when I return home? Who would I find? Yes, I was glad it is all over. And this woman lying in my arms. Who is she? Could I make a life with her? She was smart and beautiful and had a good position. I cared for her deeply. For the first time in many years, I began to feel a little bit of peace within myself. Olga Ouspenskaya Vasilevsky. She stirred but did not wake. I couldn't make out her face, she lay so close, but I held her round shoulders, felt her smooth, supple skin. Her firm, full breasts rose and fell with every intake and exhalation of breath. She captivated me and I genuinely admired the General. We fought together these long years and came out as victors. I felt a bond with him. The General had given me six weeks leave to wrap up my affairs, locate my family then report back to headquarters in Moscow. I intended to leave the next day and take the train to the Polish border, these were my drifting thoughts before I fell asleep.

I awoke and instinctively reached out for her but the bed felt empty and cold. The candles had burned down and the room lay in darkness. I heard a rattling noise, then the door to the bedroom opened. A weak light shone in behind her. Olga carried a tray that she set down carefully beside the bed.

"Darling. Are you awake?"

"I am now."

"Oh, I didn't mean to wake you. Not really. But I fixed us something to eat. I thought you might be hungry."

"You're too kind and thoughtful, my Olga."

"I've got some good rye bread and some fish and cheese. And coffee, ersatz, but it isn't bad, not after the first taste. Come, sit up."

I did as I was told. I watched her light several more candles. She wore a light robe but the air in the room was cool. "Come under where you'll be warm."

She clambered over and came under the covers.

"Be careful not to get too many crumbs in my bed. We have enough problems with the mice as it is."

I reached for the tray, laughing.

"As if mice should be our only problem after all we've been through."

I set the tray down in front of us and reached for two plates. I handed one to her.

"I noticed some scar tissue on your thigh. What happened?"

"Never mind doctor. It's all healed now."

"But what happened?"

"Nothing really. Some grenade fragments, that's all. I was lucky. Most of it missed me. The stupid Nazi had terrible aim."

"Were you operated on?"

I took a sip of the coffee and grimaced, then took another. "No, there wasn't time. It happened just outside Warsaw, in the spring of 1944. The tank got stuck in mud. I jumped out to take a look and there he was, perhaps 17 or 18 years old with a potato masher in his hand and a strange grin on his face. He'd pulled the pin and tossed it toward me. I shot him with my pistol but the masher had left his hand. The mud came up over my knees and I couldn't move quickly. Lucky for me, it fell short and the mud absorbed some of the concussion."

"But then some of the metal may still be embedded."

"I dug the metal out with a knife. Don't worry, it was sterilized. It doesn't bother me at all. The leg is fine. I can walk and do everything I did before without any trouble at all."

I fed her some bread.

"Eat and don't worry so much. I didn't tell you when I had typhus, either." I saw her look. "There wasn't anything you could do about it."

"When was this?"

"1942 I think. I can't remember but Mischa was still alive."

Olga chewed the bread slowly.

"Many died from typhus. I saw them brought in. The corpses were buried in lime pits to prevent the spreading of the disease."

"Doses of vodka and tea got me through it. There were no drugs. We were on our own. The men nursed me. They could have come down with it too. But still, they took that chance. Good thing or Mischa would have driven the tank and killed everybody anyway."

We split the smoked herring and ate it silently.

"And then?"

"It was a terrible death. They are all terrible but this was…"

I sighed then threw back the covers and crossed to the chair where my clothes sat in a pile. I searched through the pockets of my tunic, then came back to the bed clutching a piece of metal in my hand. I handed it to her. She turned over the fragment of the thin metal, crumpled and twisted. "I keep them with me as a reminder. I don't want to forget him. He just wanted to get back to Poland and take care of his mother. A man with a good heart. I wasn't just his superior officer but his friend and losing friends can be as bad as losing family, don't you think?"

Olga nodded, holding her face in her hands. "We lost many that came in. Too many to count. I can hear my father speaking in my sleep. He was talking about thousands, tens of thousands, the equivalent of entire towns and villages erased from the earth all at once. How can you prepare for something like this? It's impossible. You start to lose your soul after a while. When you lose the feeling, then you lose your humanity. You cease to care about anything and I found myself having to fight it each day. Each day you become less of a human being."

"What saved you?"

She turned to me and stroked my cheek.

"I'd like to say it was you, my darling and it was, a little. But no, it was just small things. A patient who wasn't expected to live who pulled through, seeing the flowers come up in the spring, startling a pheasant in the woods, knowing that someday it would all be over and my life would resume. I really did think that some days I was going mad and it would have been so easy to give myself up to it, but something in me made me fight it every day. Do I look like a madwoman to you? I fear my eyes have gone hollow and my skin is pinched and vacant, that I have shrunk into a smaller skin. My people needed me, I suppose. It was that simple."

Olga held my face in both hands.

"I waited for you," she whispered. "I couldn't stand it that it was taking so long. I could only bury myself in work, more patients, more operations, more administration. It was almost intolerable. And then finally, after months of not hearing, it's all over and you have come back to me. We will start our life together now. There is no past, only what is to be. I am a little afraid but it also brings me great joy and peace."

I said nothing, but took her in my arms. We lay together on the bed.

"I would like to have two children, a girl and a boy."

I laughed. "Is that all the state permits?"

She slapped at my arm. "Fool. I am being serious. There's no greater gift a woman can offer a man than to bear him children. I want to experience the joy of the innocent and let it take me out of what has been, away from the pain of the righteous. I just want to lose myself in something else."

I inhaled her, her hair, her skin, her breath, all of it.

"No, my darling, it's a wonder."

"You're very quiet. Did you think of our life together?"

"Sometimes. But I had a job to do and most of the time that occupied my mind. There was much planning to do, so many things to think about. But now, I want to put all of this behind me just like you."

"When is your train?"

"Three o'clock." I glanced at my watch. It was a little after six in the morning. "We have a bit of time left." Another leave taking. I had dreamed of her and our reunion. It still didn't seem real. I knew I couldn't live there among communists and I knew she wouldn't leave her father. And so, we remained doomed to be apart. If I felt anything for anyone, I felt it for her. I couldn't say anything. I didn't want to disturb what we had. I wanted to remember her as she was, hold that sense of her in my heart forever.

Chapter 39

Beulah Robinson sat up in the cot holding a cup of tea. Her face remained pinched but the colour looked better, not so sallow. Some brightness had returned to her eyes. "Man, Mr. G, sounded like you really loved that woman."

I nodded. "She was extraordinary. She exceeded me in every way. We were never equals. She had moved beyond me."

"But you left her."

I sighed. "Yes, I did."

"Whatever happened to her?"

"I never found out. So I don't know what became of Olga."

"Didn't you ever wonder?"

"Only all the time. But, times were different. It was difficult to get information – especially if people didn't want to be found."

Olga lay sleeping. Her lips moved as she breathed. I watched her, wondering what she said in her dreams and who she saw. I pulled on my trousers, picked up my shirt, tunic, boots and coat then tip-toed out of the bedroom. On the main floor of the gloomy house, I finished dressing, adjusting my cap while staring into the mirror. I carried my summer coat over my arm and hefted the rucksack over my right shoulder. Gazing around the house, I tried to absorb as much as I could but then my head exploded with details, many of which I wished to forget. I felt burdened and oppressed. I didn't step lightly from the doorway, as if looking toward a shining future, but instead knew I traveled into a murky past. The war wasn't over for me. It would never be over.

The train rattled on its wheels as it carried me west to the Polish border. I reflected on what was going to happen to me. I would hand over my papers and the sentries would see the pass given to me by the General. I wore full uniform and commanded respect. On the other side of the border, barely into Polish territory, lay a small town and once there, I'd look for a man. But then I had a full day's journey ahead of me. The train travelled slowly and made many stops along the way. I pulled my cap down over my eyes and went to sleep, letting the clackety-clack of the train lull me into unconsciousness.

When I awoke, I found a barrel-chested soldier with broad moustaches seated opposite. He watched me warily.

"Comrade Captain."

The burly fellow tipped his hat. I nodded to him.

"Where are we, comrade?"

"About two hours from the Polish border."

"Good."

"You're going home, comrade Captain?"

I nodded. I had no wish to engage this fellow in conversation.

"Me also. I live in Janow."

"You have a long way to travel yet."

The fellow brushed his moustaches with the back of his hand. "We are the lucky ones, no?"

"Lucky?"

"Yes. We're Poles in the Soviet army. We're the conquerors now. It's good to be on the winning side for a change."

The man was clearly a fool but I had no wish to argue with him. "Yes, you're right. We've won."

The soldier reached inside his tunic and removed a flask. He unscrewed the lid and took a deep draught, then held it out in his meaty hand. "Captain?"

I took the flask from him and put it to my lips. The liquid burned my mouth and throat but I swallowed and managed a grateful smile.

"Thank you."

I handed back the flask and as I did, I noticed that it was made of beaten silver and handsomely engraved.

"Took it from a German officer after I put a bullet in his brain."

The burly soldier laughed and slapped his knee, remembering it. "The poor fellow pleaded with me, offered his watch and rings. Didn't matter. I got them anyway." He took another swig. "This is worth a pretty penny, I can tell you."

I stood up. I cared nothing for Germans but the fellow grated on me. "I'm going to get some air. Excuse me, Comrade."

The soldier lifted his cap and scratched at the stubble of his scalp. "Suit yourself, Captain."

Greed, I thought. It's all about greed and money. Not freedom. Not destroying tyranny, but what's in it for me and me alone. That fellow seemed a perfect example of what had gone wrong. I moved through the narrow aisle and stood on the small metal platform between the cars. I lit a cigarette and braced myself against the cold metal rail. The countryside streaked by as Broken images came to me as I exhaled smoke. Brown earth. Ramshackle farm houses, skinny horses and gaunt cows, trees with broken branches, pale sunlight filtered through the patchy leaves of diseased trees. The land was sick as was its people. I too, needed to heal.

The train stopped a short distance before the town of Prodole, just over the Polish border. I stepped off the train on to the platform. I looked behind me and the burly soldier stared at me through the smeared glass. He was saying something. Dirty Jew, mouthed and laughed. I reached for my pistol, unsnapping the holster. The soldier stopped laughing and shrank back from the window. I withdrew the pistol and aimed. Several people close to me stepped away or ducked. A guard sprang forward.

"May I help you, Captain?"

I turned my head toward the guard but kept my eye on the soldier, then slowly lowered the pistol. "It's nothing. A joke."

I re-holstered the weapon and smiled at the train window, giving a mock salute. The guard eyed me warily.

"Back to your station now," I said.

The guard was young and nervous. He licked his lips and gulped. "Thank you, sir." But still he didn't move.

I walked away, aware that the young guard followed me with his eyes as I strode out of the small train station.

The General had given me the name of a farmer, a former soldier under his command. Asking directions from an old man I stopped on the street, I learned that the man's farm was not more than a kilometre out of town. Fifteen minutes' walk, comfortably. A low mist hung in the early morning air but the sun burned its way through. Without it, there remained a distinct chill, but keeping a steady pace kept me warm. I crested a hill and saw a wooden fence held together with baling wire. I turned down a dirt road. Around a bend, I suddenly entered a yard where a brace of chickens scattered. On the property sat a low-slung farmhouse with a thatched roof and a small barn that badly needed painting.

I rapped sharply on the door. I heard a grunt, then a chair scraping inside. The door opened a crack and a lean, hawkish face peered out.

"Yes?" The lean face looked the uniform up and down.

"The General sent me. He thought you might help me out."

"General?"

"Vasilevsky."

"Ah. You'd best come in, Captain." The farmer stepped back from the door as I entered. The room was bare except for a wooden table and three chairs. A woodstove sat in one corner. "How do I know you're from the General?"

I reached inside my tunic and held out a piece of paper. The farmer pulled out a pair of spectacles from his trouser pocket, stepped over to a window and squinted. After a moment, he pursed his lips and handed the letter back. "I'm thinking you're probably hungry."

"Then you're correct."

"I wasn't always a farmer. Before the war, I was the General's adjutant, until I received a serious injury and had to leave the army." He knocked on his left leg. It sounded a hollow *thock*. "I'm here now. My wife died in childbirth during the war. The child died with her. There was no doctor. No medicines."

"I'm sorry."

The fellow held up a reedy hand. "No need. I have made peace with it. I didn't think I would survive the war but I did. I managed to get away to Siberia just before the Germans crossed the border. When I returned, this was all that was left."

He held up his hands as if to measure his meagre holdings.

I wandered restlessly about the room, looking at the objects it held. I was drawn to the fireplace. On the mantel sat a photograph, the glass cracked in its frame. Something drew me to it. I took a closer look. In the picture, I saw the former adjutant and the young woman I presumed was his wife, a pretty, blond woman with a soulful look and shining eyes. Maria.

I coughed then cleared my throat. "And this, this is a picture of you and your wife?"

The fellow set about preparing breakfast. "Yes, that is my Maria. She was beautiful, wasn't she?"

I could barely choke the words out. "Yes. Very. You were a lucky man. Very lucky."

He looked at me sorrowfully. "Yes, but only for a short while."

He reached down beside the wood stove and held up two eggs. "At least the hens are laying. I can enjoy fresh eggs every morning." He placed a large skillet on the stove, spooned out some lard and let it sizzle. Then he cut two slabs of bread and dropped them in the pan. After a moment, he cracked open the eggs. I smelled the aroma and my mouth began to water. I didn't realize I'd been so hungry. The farmer lifted a pot from the stove. "Coffee?"

I nodded.

The farmer poured out a steaming cup full and handed it to me. Then he scraped the bread and eggs on to a cracked enamel plate and brought it to the table. From a trunk, he removed a mess kit and handed it to me.

"I kept mine from the old days," he said almost apologetically. "Are you all right?" he asked. "You look a bit ill."

"No, I'm fine." I looked at him. "What year did your wife pass on?"

"May, 1940. The peace pact was still in place. Why do you ask?"

I shrugged. "It's just that, she looks familiar to me. We may have attended the same school."

The farmer nodded. "That is possible. She was Polish. What town do you come from?"

"Krasnowicz."

"Well, that is something, isn't it? You might have been school mates at that?"

"How did you... er, what I mean is..."

The farmer smiled and put up his hand. "I understand," he said. "She was a beautiful woman and as a girl, well, she must have been an angel. That's how I thought of her, anyway."

"Look, I'm sorry, I didn't mean to cause you any trouble."

"No, no," the farmer said. "I don't mind talking about her. It keeps her memory alive for me. Her parents moved here and opened a bakery in the village. My uncle had owned this farm and he died. There was no one to look after it and so, when I left the army, I came here. I met Maria and I knew from the first moment I saw her, she was the one. I was lucky as you said."

"And her parents?"

"Well the father died during the War. The mother survived but I believe she moved to Warsaw where she had relatives. To be honest, I didn't care for them and them for me. So it was mutual. When Maria died and the child with her, well, that was it. Nothing held us together except the grief of losing her. I know they loved her in their way. Yes, in their way."

The farmer drifted off into his memories. I had now lost Maria twice and it gave me an ache that surprised me, something I'd buried deeply. "I'm sorry," I murmured again.

I sipped the coffee. It was hot but without much taste. The eggs and bread were delicious but they tasted bitter just the same. I choked them down. The farmer watched me silently, perched on a stool with his false leg stretched out in front of him. Finally, I set the knife and fork down.

"That was good. Thank you."

I drank some of the coffee that had cooled a bit.

"You were in the tank corps?" I nodded. The farmer looked bitterly down at his leg. "I wish I … it would have been better than cutting trees in Siberia. After Maria died and the peace pact broke, that's where they sent me. I told them if I could cut trees I could fight. They told me I was needed. The wood was needed for the war effort. Bah." And he spat.

I continued to drink the coffee in silence. The farmer wasn't old, perhaps forty at most. He looked angry and resentful. But then the man's expression softened again.

"I would do anything for the General. And what is it I can do for you, Captain?"

"I need transport."

The farmer nodded. "You have money?"

"Yes."

The farmer pushed himself upright. "Come."

I followed him outside. We crossed the dirt yard where the chickens scattered in front of us flapping their wings and clucking. The farmer pulled a key ring from his pocket, found the one he wanted and inserted it into the padlock on the barn door. The farmer lifted the wooden slat and the door swung open. Weak light spilled in but I caught a glint of metal. Slowly, my eyes became accustomed to the gloom and I took a few steps closer. Before me, sat a German motorcycle and sidecar with twin machine guns mounted on the handlebars.

I let out a low whistle. "And where did you get it?"

The farmer snickered. "I retrieved it from a German officer. I can also give you a jerry can of petrol."

"It is in working order?"

"Of course."

"How much?"

"Five hundred rubles."

I knew its value. Five hundred rubles made up half the back pay I'd been given when I returned to Moscow. "All right. May I try it out?"

The farmer reached into his pocket again and tossed me the keys. I threw my leg over the saddle, fitted the key in the ignition, engaged the clutch and switched it on. The engine sputtered, then roared to life. The farmer quick-stepped to the barn door and swung the other door open. I backed the motorcycle out, turned around and shot forward, scattering the chickens in the yard. I wheeled around, feeling the power of the four-stroke engine. The farmer watched me quietly, leaning against the frame of the barn, his arms crossed, eyes slitted against the rising clouds of dust. I rode from one end of the pen to the other, giving the motorcycle bursts of speed. I wheeled up and stopped in front of the farmer, then cut the engine.

"The Germans make good quality machines."

I reached inside my tunic and removed my billfold. I counted out five hundred rubles and put it in the farmer's hand. From behind me, the farmer lifted out the can of petrol.

"This should give you enough for a week, perhaps more."

"Good." I swung off the motorcycle. I looked at the sidecar and the machine guns approvingly. "Have you got any rounds for these?"

The farmer nodded. "It will cost you another hundred."

"All right."

"You know the war is over."

I looked at him, at the sun-weathered face and the limpid blue eyes. "Not for me, it isn't. I fought with the General for four years. We fought our way across Russia and Poland into Germany, right into Berlin, to the steps of the Reichstag. For me, it isn't over until I find my family."

The farmer raised his hands. "So be it."

I returned to the farmhouse to retrieve my rucksack and stowed it in the sidecar. Underneath, in a gunnysack, lay several hundred rounds of ammunition the farmer had given me and another smaller sack. Inside, I found a well-oiled machine pistol broken down into pieces for storage. A handsome piece of weaponry. I'd also found two sets of helmets and goggles. In the end, the farmer refused the extra money. He banged his wooden leg saying, what would I have done with it anyway? I mounted the machine, kickstarted the engine and with a wave, rode off. The crossing point at the border was not far, about several kilometres. After that, it was three to four hours north to Krasnowicz. After an eternity, and only three to four hours left of it.

At the border, my papers were checked but I passed through quickly. Besides being in full uniform, the General's personal letter dissolved any remaining barriers. Some of the others in line stared at me resentfully as I jumped the queue but when I turned to look back at them, they turned away, casting their eyes to the ground. I assumed most crossing the border were Poles and the harsh reality of their new situation had begun to sink in. They were worthy only of my disgust. And so, I roared past the miserable peasants waiting in their line. It felt good to show them my back.

The day had clouded over and it had begun to drizzle. I roared along the road, passing slow-moving carts and farmers leading horses. As I revved the German engines beneath me, the horses grew restive and skiddish, the farmers tightened their grips on the bridles and cast dark glances at the figure on the motorcycle. I didn't think about what lay ahead. I concentrated on the road and holding the machine to it, as the surface became slicker. I strained my eyes watching for the familiar landmarks and gradually, the scenery began to mould itself into recognizable patterns. The set of the trees against the horizon, the narrow bumpiness of the road, the swoop of the crests of the hills, even the way the clouds hung low in the sky, it all seemed reassuring. I knew the road now. I'd been on it so many times. On family trips, driving with my father and school excursions. I was certain my class must have camped nearby.

It was mid-afternoon when I turned on to the street where the house stood. Pilsudski Street. I wondered if it had kept its name under the Nazis and whether it would be changed back under the Soviets. No doubt tanks and lorries had driven on this street, soldiers had marched with their jackboots and their swastikas here. I saw peasants working in the fields just as before the war. It was as if their lives had been left untouched. A horse grazed nearby, head down into the grass, black forelocks falling across its face. A peaceful scene, yet I didn't feel at ease.

A kilometre went by and I came to the beginning of the long drive that led to my home. My mouth went dry. My heart began to race. I slowed the motorcycle down, bumping along the now-rutted road. I could see that heavy vehicles had travelled here, judging by the deep grooves and pits. At the first sight of the house, I stopped, and letting the engine idle, allowed myself to stare for a long moment. I thought back to my last night and how I had been shot by Colonel Roediger. The back of my head ached at the memory.

I parked the motorcycle around the back and tried the door handle. It was locked. I stepped back and looked up, thinking I saw a slight movement behind some curtains. With a gloved fist, I pounded on the door and waited. From inside, I heard slow footsteps, saw a flash of white hair and waited as someone fumbled with the lock. The heavy door swung open a crack and a thin face surrounding watery blue eyes and a beaky nose peered out.

"Yes?" The voice sounded querulous.

I peered in then took a step forward. The face shrank back. "Pyotr?"

"Yes?"

The fellow allowed the door to fall open. The watery eyes blinked, then blinked again. The frail man took a step forward into the daylight.

"Is it you? Master Mordecai?"

I nodded.

Pyotr turned and called into the house.

"Amalija. Come. Come."

A moment later, the round face of Amalija appeared behind him.

"He has returned."

Amalija hands went to her mouth and tears began to stream down her wrinkled face. She put her arms out and embraced me.

"We thought never to see you again."

We sat in the Goldman kitchen. Amalija had made tea and put out stale bread with preserves. I was shocked to see they had grown old in such a few years. But then I couldn't wait any longer.

"And what of my parents, my brother?"

Amalija shook her head but stayed silent. Pyotr looked into his lap.

"Gone."

"Where?"

Pyotr looked up with a haunted look.

"Oswiecim," he whispered, then turned his face away.

I felt my heart turn to ice.

"A few nights after you left, trucks came in the middle of the night. The Germans put them on the trucks and that was the last we saw of them. The house was taken over by the officers. When they left, we moved in to keep out the thieves. There are a few families living here. They have no place to go," Amalija said.

I nodded. "I won't be staying. I will find them." I rubbed my hands, then took a sip of the weak tea. "And how is it now?"

Pyotr looked at me sadly.

"We are not permitted to own land or hold possessions. We are told it all belongs to the state. There are commissars in every district. Every district has a council and the head of the council reports to the commissar. Children in school are taught the Soviet way. Churches and priests have been banned. When the men go to work, their pay goes to the state. Women must go to work also and do the same jobs as the men. I am happy that I am too old. We are told the state will take care of us and we are not to worry. We received permission to move in here, but we were told this house and the property now belongs to the state."

I drained my cup. "Is there a room for me, old friends?"

"We have kept your room," Pyotr said. "She believed you would come back." Amalija nodded. "I wasn't sure, but she was."

"Good. I'll take a little rest. I've been travelling since early this morning." I stood up and hefted my rucksack over my shoulder, carrying a gunnysack in my left hand. The two Poles looked small and bent. Time hadn't been kind to them.

Pyotr held out his hand. "Please."

Reluctantly, I handed the heavy rucksack to him.

As we climbed the stairs, Pyotr spoke over his shoulder. "There have been enquiries about you over the past few months."

"From who?"

Pyotr's boots made a fearsome clump as we climbed. "A fellow you knew in school. The tall one."

"Ah."

"He has come around several times."

"What did he want?"

"I don't know. Just to speak to you. He was not friendly but ill-mannered. "

"I'm sorry if he troubled you."

Amalija followed up from behind. "I will give him a knock on the noggin if he comes around again."

I laughed. "That won't be necessary. I'll take care of him."

Shadows haunted the corridor. I heard sounds from behind doors and as we passed, each one opened just a crack.

"Don't mind them, they are afraid," said Pyotr as he stopped in front of the door to my old room. "First the Nazis and now the Communists."

"We tried to keep the room as it was," Amalija said, wringing her hands.

"I'm sure it will be fine, thank you."

I took the rucksack from Pyotr's shoulders. "I'll see you in a little while."

I shook Pyotr's hand, who just nodded numbly. I bent down and gave Amalija a kiss on the cheek.

"It has been a terrible time. Every moment I think..."

She stopped and took a gulp. Tears streamed down her ruddy face. "I fear the worst."

"I'll find out, don't you worry. If they are alive, I'll find them."

I went to the window and parted the curtains. Pale afternoon light streamed in. My bed sat where it used to be and the dresser and the night table but that was all. None of my books or possessions remained. An oil lamp sat on the night table, and a soiled blanket lay over the mattress. Yes, I thought, time had not been kind. The interior walls showed grime and needed painting. The windows were covered with the residue of smoke and grease spewed out by men and machinery. God knows what took place in this house, in this room or who slept here in the past six years. Six years gone in a flash. Six years of torment, of death, of killing. Was it over yet? I wondered.

I kicked off my boots, stripped off my tunic and dress shirt, then I stretched out on the bed. The mattress groaned as I sank into the middle but somehow I felt comforted being in my own house after all this time. I felt the spirit of my parents and brother and sister in the walls. As I lay back, a flood of memories entered my mind. Gradually, I drifted off to sleep.

Sometime later, a noise awoke me. I heard harsh voices down below. It took a moment for me to come to my senses. I'd slept longer and heavier than I'd wanted. I heard a deep voice full of anger and the feeble protests of Pyotr. I strapped on my revolver, then went out into the hall. I stood at the top of the stairs and looked down as Pyotr was being forced up backward, stumbling as he went. In front of him stood a tall, powerful figure, followed by three others. I recognized him immediately. The same lank hair falling across a narrow forehead, the small grey eyes. The same self-satisfied expression. I heard each door along the hall open a crack as the hidden residents peeked out fearfully. Pyotr stumbled backwards and fell into my arms. I moved the old man behind me.

"So, you threaten old men now?"

Jerzy stood before me and put his hands on his hips. I noticed his body had thickened. The skin on his face had mottled and gone puffy. The eyes had been reduced to slits.

"So, it is you. I heard that you'd come back."

"Yes, it's me."

I looked beyond him and saw the other three in a line, just as they stood back in high school. I saw them as boys, all together in this house where I helped them with their homework. They had needed my help then. But none of that mattered now.

"I see you've brought your gang with you."

"And an officer in the Soviet Army too, what do you think of that?"

Jerzy jerked his head to the others behind him, who, typically, said nothing.

"You haven't come to talk over old times, I think."

"No, I haven't."

"What do you want? Why do you bother this harmless old man?"

"He tried to stop us from coming in. We have every right..."

"On whose authority?"

"I'm empowered by the state."

I laughed. "Yes? And to do what?"

"You're no longer a landowner. Your bourgeois family doesn't own this property or any other. It all belongs to the people of Poland."

"So, you've finally found your vocation. You're a good communist, are you?"

"Don't mock the state, Jew. I did warn you all those years ago and it has come to pass. The revolution has taken hold, even here."

"Yes, I see what you're saying. I'm an officer in the Soviet army under the command of the most courageous General Stalin commissioned. I fought for Poland against the Nazis and I fought the Nazis again from 1941. I was at Stalingrad and we pushed those bastards all the way back to Berlin. I've killed many Germans and my only regret is that I didn't kill more. And what did you do?"

"I was with the partisans. The Nazis shot my father. He refused to give them fresh milk and cheese."

"I'm sorry."

"I don't want your sympathy. He was a son of a bitch but I buried him properly anyway. That was in 1943. The next day, I joined the partisans and fought with them until the war was over. I was at Warsaw when it was taken. We were there ahead of the glorious Soviet army."

"Okay. So your penis is as big as mine. What do you want? Why were you bothering this old man?"

Jerzy crossed his arms. He still dressed like a peasant, with baggy trousers, loose tunic and worn leather boots.

"I've come to give you a warning. I do this out of respect for our previous friendship."

"We were never friends. You wanted something I could give you, that's all."

He shrugged. "Perhaps you're right."

I formed a fist of my right hand and tapped it into the open palm of my left. "What are you warning me about?"

"You're a Jew and a landowner. Neither are wanted here. You have twenty-four hours to get out. The peasants can stay. This house gives them shelter and the local land committee has voted to let them remain until things settle down."

"And if I don't?"

"We will kill you."

"You will kill me?"

The others shifted uncomfortably behind him.

"Yes," Jerzy replied.

I took a step closer.

"You can try."

The taller man hesitated for a moment.

"You've been warned, Mordecai. Believe me, this isn't something I do happily but a directive is a directive and can't be disobeyed. Do yourself a favour and get out while you can before it is too late."

With a jerk of his head, the others turned and rattled down the stairs in their sturdy peasant boots. Jerzy waited for a beat, then turned and followed them. Pyotr trembled at my side while I silently watched them go. They left the front door wide open.

Pyotr turned to me, his eyes wide with fright.

"What will you do?"

"Nothing."

"But they said… they said you will be killed."

"I don't die so easily, old friend."

"You must leave before they come back."

"I don't think so."

"But there's been enough killing. You've lived through the war. Why take the chance?"

I looked sharply at the open doorways and sensed the refugees behind them listening intently. I stamped my foot and the doors closed abruptly.

"This is my house and I'll leave when *I* say so, not before."

"But… but…"

"Don't worry old friend. Come. It's late. We both need our rest."

I took Pyotr by the elbow and steered him to his room. The older man didn't protest but hung his grizzled head in resignation.

Back in my room, I picked up the gunnysack and removed the well-oiled pieces of metal. I fitted them together and checked the parts. The General's former adjutant had kept it clean and nicely maintained. In the bottom of the sack I found half a dozen clips. I rammed one home, then checked the others. All seemed in proper working order. I wrapped the machine pistol in its oilcloth, put it back in the sack then slid it under the bed. Then I lay down to wait.

The next morning, Pyotr and I pored over a map. He had some news.

"There is a neighbor who lives across the field. He has a cousin. During the War, this cousin delivered clean linens to the officers' quarters of the camp. He spent time in the camp laundry where clothes and bedding were washed for the enlisted men. He says the cousin got to know your brother and that Simmy was still alive in the weeks before the camp was liberated. But that's all he knows."

I seized on this hope. If my brother lived then there was a chance for Papa and Mama too. I decided to scour all of the hospitals in the surrounding towns and villages to look for them.

I spent the morning with Pyotr and Amalija drinking tea and planning my route. Then I helped Pyotr milk the two cows they managed to keep on the property. The cows gave them milk and cheese that they bartered for eggs from a farmer down the road. Because the flour mills had shut down, they were forced to buy bread in town, something Pyotr did once a week. Two zlotys a loaf. They could afford just two loaves a week and rationed their bread use closely. Amalija managed to find beets and onions and occasionally a chicken so she could make soup and used the bones for the stock.

The day passed quickly and by late afternoon, I returned to my room to rest. A long night lay ahead and I needed to remain alert. I managed to get Amalija and Pyotr to stay with neighbours for the evening. The others cowered in their rooms. I left them alone. They were like a small army of ghosts, ever-present and hovering but barely there.

I took the straight-back chair from my room and set it on the landing, where I had a clear view of the front door. I sipped some tea. The house creaked and groaned as if it too had aged since the War began. The machine pistol lay cradled in my lap. I checked the lock, making sure it was off and set to fire. I didn't know the precise moment when I made the decision not to return to Moscow but since leaving Russia, it felt further and further away. It might have been the massacre in the woods or simply Mischa's death. I couldn't see myself going back, but the vision of Olga made me ache. I kept very still in the chair, shifting my weight carefully. I positioned myself in the shadows. She wanted my children and I thought about what our lives might have been like. A dacha in the country, two young-sters, a boy and a girl running freely, laughing and playing in the snow. And what might I have done? I was fed up with the military and had no wish to continue my army career and didn't want a life under the Soviets, not after all I'd seen. And if Jerzy was a prime example of how the proletariat acted, a cog in the Soviet machine, then who wanted it? Not me, certainly. What else? I shook my head and reached for the tea cup.

I must have dozed for a moment. I'd been thinking that if the clock had still been in Papa's study, it would have struck midnight by now. But the clock was gone and the study had been stripped into a bare room with boarded windows and torn curtains. I tried to imagine what it used to look like; all the furniture it contained, the books and mementos it housed, the family portraits, all gone now. Mordecai, I said to myself, you're a grown man now, thirty years old, a soldier who has fought many battles. Yet when you think of these things, you feel like an orphan. You're eleven years old, running through the fields with the Polacks chasing you, screaming for your blood. Because it's dark and you know the paths and you run faster, you get away and vow to take revenge on them. If not them, their sons. Now, the time has come.

Just as I thought this, I caught the low murmur of voices. A stone clattered carelessly across the path. I heard a short, sharp exchange, then silence. I watched the knob turn slowly and almost laughed out loud. The door swung half-open and a tall dark figure stepped inside and swiveled. Jerzy motioned for the others to follow and the three entered behind. They held pistols and wore dark clothing and hats.

For a moment, they seemed unsure of what to do. Then Jerzy took a step forward and made for the stairs, taking pains to move silently.

My voice crashed through the gloom.

"I'm here, my friends."

I heard the scratch of sulphur on wood and a match flared up throwing an eerie light. Jerzy's broad face flickered next to the flame. A flame that was about to be snuffed out. His cheeks and jaw stayed in shadow, the eyes looked ghostly.

"Let's see you," Jerzy said. "Stop hiding in the dark."

I rose from the chair cradling the machine pistol in my arms and began to slowly descend the steps.

"I'm not hiding," I said.

"We told you to leave. Why didn't you?"

"Because I've had enough of orders and enough of tyranny. This is my house and I will leave when I say."

The Luger looked like a toy in Jerzy's big mitt.

"Always the stubborn Jew, Mordecai. You will never learn, will you? Your time is up. It is our turn now."

"Leave before it is too late."

"Too late for who? You think you can get rid of all of us? Don't be a fool."

I fired the machine pistol. It spat bullets. In the twilight I watched the four bodies jerk and groan and cry. They slumped to the ground. The noise rang in my ears and it seemed a long time before the echoes and reverberations faded away. It had taken only a few seconds. Imagine being stupid enough to come through the front door? Holding the machine pistol in front of me, I descended the stairs. I nudged each of the bodies with my boot. They were all dead. I slung the machine pistol around my back. One by one, I lifted their arms and dragged them outside in front of the steps where I laid them out in a row from shortest to tallest, Jerzy being the last. I wanted them found like that.

After that I closed the door, climbed the stairs and went into my room. Without taking off my clothes, I lay down on the bed, the machine pistol at my side, and quickly fell asleep.

Early the next morning, I rose before the light. I packed my things, picked up the rucksack and the gunnysack and went downstairs. I had the impression that some of the doors opened and pairs of eyes followed my progress but I didn't turn around. They lay as I'd left them, lying peacefully on the open ground, their faces full of surprise, the eyes wide open as if wondering what had gone wrong. Except that now, their faces had turned waxy and pale in death. I would let Pyotr and Amalija know not to come back to the house for a while, until the dust had settled.

I went round the back to where I'd left the motorcycle. And just as the sun began to rise, I began the search for my lost family.

Chapter 40

"Jesus, Mr. G., that was harsh."

"You think so?" I asked.

"Yes, I do."

"They had come to kill me, you do understand that, don't you? They wouldn't have shown me any mercy. They came to my house. They told me I had to leave. After all I'd been through and all I'd done, no one was going to tell me what I could or couldn't do, do you see?"

Beulah coughed and the spasm shook her thin frame. "I see that war is senseless, Mr. G and no good ever comes from it."

"You may be right there." I paused. "Do you need anything? Hungry? Thirsty?"

She shook her head. "No, I'm okay."

I looked at her more closely. "You are hiding too."

"What do you mean?"

"I think you left something or someone behind."

She looked at me. "I didn't know what else to do. Where else to go."

"But you think they'll come looking for you?"

"I'm praying they don't, honestly."

"We shall see," I said.

A New Life

For seven days I rode through towns and villages. I slept in farmers' barns and in fields. In towns with an inn, I rented a room. I visited every hospital and clinic I heard about. I circled my way closer and closer to the Russian border, seeing Russian lorries filled with soldiers. No one questioned me. They accepted my authority and rank. I spoke with some of them, shared a tent with a Colonel who had been at Stalingrad. We exchanged stories and drank vodka until late in the night. It was the Colonel who told me about the hospital in Zvia, a small town just shading the border on the Polish side. It lay half an hour away, perhaps less. The obliging Colonel drew me a map. We spoke together of Vasilevsky, of his intelligence and bravery. The Colonel admired him and when he found out that I knew him personally, the Colonel couldn't do enough.

"Can I send an escort with you? Did you need extra provisions? Petrol?" I nodded. "Yes, you shall have it and I offer this gladly for a fellow officer and friend of the General's."

The Colonel loved the military life. He had a wife and three children and seldom saw them, which suited him very well, he said.

"I'm not cut out to be a family man. I support them well. All of my pay goes to them. But I enjoy my freedom."

He knew that he might be recalled to Moscow at any time but he had volunteered for duty in Poland and even requested a transfer to

Germany, where he claimed great things were about to take place. A new Soviet state was being created. The glory of communism had spread around the globe. The Colonel laughed and I laughed with him at the foolish Nazis, thinking they had built an empire that would last a millennium. But the Soviet regime, eh, now that was a different story. I smiled my agreement. When the Colonel slapped me on the back, I did the same, playing the game. All the time, I thought only of my family.

We talked through much of the night. Early the next morning, I got up and washed. The Colonel snored away in his bunk, sleeping off the influence of the drink. My head felt a bit thick but that was all. Hadn't I drunk a full bottle of vodka every day for the previous six years? That morning I made a decision. Enough of that. The drinking had been part of my old life. All associations with the past must go. My new life didn't include vodka.

Zvia was much like many of the towns I'd swept through. The farmers hauled their produce in wagons pulled by slack-looking horses. As I rode into the small market square, sets of curious eyes looked up at the noise. A large church anchored the square. One of the priests swept the concrete steps, mechanically rhythmic, his posture resigned.

"Father," I called over the rumble of the motorcycle engine.

The priest looked up. He set down the broom and ambled over. "Yes sir? I can help?"

"I'm looking for the hospital. Can you tell me how to get there?"

The priest, a lean man of middling years with a gaunt face, bobbed his head.

"Certainly, sir. It is on the other end of the square. You must go around and come from the other side. Then you will see the hospital."

"Thank you, Father. And good luck to you."

The priest looked grateful. "And to you."

I revved the engine and sped off, throwing up a cloud of dust. I followed the priest's directions, exiting at the opposite end of the square and following a narrow road behind. Here, I found stalls that served the market place and stone houses crowded together. At the end of the narrow road sat a small hospital. I noted the hammer and sickle insignia indicating that the hospital was administered by the military. The main building, that sat in a low rectangle just two stories high, looked clean and had been freshly painted. This was the fourteenth hospital I'd visited. Each time, my pulse quickened and I felt a squeezing in my stomach.

I left the motorcycle parked out front and mounted the stone steps. At the main entrance, I straightened my uniform, then marched inside. I found the main desk and announced myself. A small nurse barely out of her teens scurried over.

"I need to see the patient list."

The young woman gulped, then nodded quickly. She went to a desk and picked up a clipboard.

"Here it is, sir."

"Thank you."

I scanned the list quickly but found no name I recognized. I set the clipboard down with a bit of clatter, then rubbed my face. The young nurse picked up the list and set it back down in its original spot. I was about to turn away but stopped.

"Are there any patients you can't identify?"

"Sir?"

"Some you don't know who they are, they have no papers."

The nurse nodded. "Ah yes, I see. There are several. They're in a special ward."

"Did any come from Oswieczim?"

"Oswieczim?" she repeated under her breath. "No, I ... I don't really know. I haven't been here long."

"Where are they, these patients?"

"They're in a special room, on the second floor at the back."

"What number?"

"I ... I can't say really. They're Dr. Butskaya's special patients, you see and, and no one is permitted, I mean, you must have her permission..."

"Young lady. You can see who I am. Now just tell me the number."

"204, sir. You go down the hall to the back stairs, then straight up, sir."

I smiled at her, then leaned in closely.

"I won't tell anyone."

I put a finger to my lips while backing away, then strode briskly down the corridor. I reached the stairs and climbed them quickly, stopping to compose myself before I opened the door to room 204. I saw a large square room, sparsely furnished. Four beds. Three of the beds were occupied; three vacant-eyed men stared at me. I walked to each bed individually and looked down at the occupant. One was an old man with a scraggly beard and a patch over one eye. I moved to the next bed. This patient looked younger and heavy-set. He boasted a thick beard and stared at me with malevolence.

"What do you want?" he sneered. "I have nothing for you. Go away." He turned over and pulled the blanket up over his shoulders. I moved on. The third man was middle-aged and quite jolly.

"Don't mind him," he said. "He's always like this. No one comes to visit him. We think his wife has run off with someone else."

"Shut up, you," called the other from under his blankets. "Say another word and I will come over there and strangle you."

"He always says that too," laughed the third man. "But he knows he would never do such a thing because I am a Party official, just like the comrade officer here. Even if I am the one who has taken his wife, who is to say?"

"I'll kill you, you bastard. I'll kill you," muttered the other from below the blanket. The old man stared straight in front of him.

The fourth man sat in a chair staring out the window and smoking. Smoke billowed up around him. His hair had been shaved recently and grew back in patches. I could see the bones sticking out of his thin shoulders. The knobs on the back of his neck stood out like boils. The man, who seemed quite young, stiffened at the sound of my boots striking the floor, body tensed like a steel coil. Everyone in the room went silent. Slowly, he turned around to face his tormentor. And there he was, staring at me.

I gazed on a pale face where the bones showed through the cheeks. Jutting out of the starched hospital gown were arms resembling twigs and spindly legs that shouldn't be able to support a child, let alone a grown man. My eyes watered over and the sad vision blurred as tears rolled down my cheeks.

"Oh my God. At last," I breathed.

Simmy rose slowly, unsteadily to his feet. I held out my arms. His body quivered. "I'm dreaming," he said.

I brought my brother to me. I felt the sharp angles of his body. Where there had been padding, now there was none.

"What have they done to you, little brother?" I whispered.

I stroked his face, looking for the small boy with the wire-rimmed glasses who had been so serious.

"I survived," he said throatily, his voice rasping and harsh.

"And Mama?"

Simmy shook his head. "They took her on the first day. The gas chambers."

I felt a blow to my chest. I gasped out loud.

"And Papa?"

Simmy held me up.

"Just before we were liberated, he died from typhoid fever. Oh my God, Mordecai, he was so strong. If it hadn't been for him... you have no idea, no idea how strong he was, helping me and others. He was a miracle."

I sank to my knees, wracked with pain, put my face to the floor and pounded my fists. The other patients watched in complete silence, the only sound the dull thud of flesh hitting the hard surface. "If only I ..."

Simmy stared down at me. "There was nothing you could have done," he said flatly.

"I could have killed that little Nazi bastard. We could have gone across the border…"

"We can't change what happened. I'm alive and that's all I know. I don't even know why."

Simmy reached down and strained to lift me up. I looked up at him. Within the emaciated face, his coal-black eyes burned with fire.

"How long have you been here?"

"I'm not sure. Perhaps a month."

"You're very skinny."

"But better than when I first came. That's because of Dr. Butskaya."

"Yes, I see."

I rose and sat down on the edge of Simmy's bed.

"Where are your clothes? You must get dressed. We're leaving."

"Leaving? Now?"

"Yes. Right now."

Simmy spread out his arms and smiled in apology.

"I can't leave. We're to be married."

"Who's to be married?"

"Me and the doctor. Dr. Butskaya."

I jumped to my feet and roared. The others skulked down in their beds. "Are you mad? Don't talk such nonsense."

"I'm not."

"Do you love this woman?"

"No."

"Then why would you marry her?"

"Because I'm grateful."

"Grateful? Then give her a present. Come on. We're wasting time."

"But I must say something to her."

"Leave her a note."

"But…"

"She's a Russian, this doctor?"

"Yes."

"Then she'll take you with her to the Soviet Union. Is that where you want to live out your days, under the heel of communism? Believe me, Simmy, I've seen it close up. You think the communists are any better than the Nazis? You think they don't hate the Jews too?"

"But you fought with them, lived with them."

"War time is different. We had a common purpose, a goal. Now I'm fed up with all of it. Don't you still want to go to Palestine?"

"Yes."

"Then we'll get you there. Now get dressed and hurry."

I glanced at the door uneasily. Simmy started to undress, then stopped suddenly.

"What's the matter?" I questioned.

"I don't have any clothes."

I walked over to the bed of the younger man with the beard.

"You. How would you like to sell your clothes? I have money. Fifty zlotys."

"You can't do that," said the Party official. "I'll report you."

The younger man looked at the fellow with malevolence.

"Go ahead. Take them. I won't charge you," he said.

"I'll report you all," the Party official screeched.

I drew my pistol. I placed the barrel against the man's neck. The man's eyes bulged in fear.

"You won't be telling anyone anything. And if you do, I'll come back and blow your head off, do you understand?"

The fellow nodded quickly as the younger man laughed.

"That was worth it."

Simmy scrambled into the man's trousers and shirt. They were absurdly large.

"Take my jacket too," the man said.

Simmy put it on and it engulfed him like a loose tent.

"I have no shoes, only my slippers," Simmy said.

"We'll buy you shoes. Come on, let's go."

"Goodbye everyone." Simmy waved to his former roommates. "Good luck to you."

"And to you," called the clothes donor, still laughing.

"Bah," spat the Party official. Only the old man lay snoring in his bed.

"Try to act as if everything is normal," I said as Simmy and I slipped down the stairs. "Here, walk on my right and I'll cover you."

We moved past the front desk together. The young nurse glanced up curiously for a moment then bent back to her work. Outside, we stood on the front stairs to the building. Simmy tugged at my sleeve.

"Not so fast. That was a lot for me," he panted. "What're we using for transport?"

I pointed to the motorcycle and sidecar.

Simmy laughed. "Wonderful. Where did you get it?"

"I bought it. That's all you need to know."

"Do the guns work?"

"Of course."

I helped Simmy down the stairs, then supported him as he stepped gingerly into the sidecar.

I handed him a helmet and goggles. "Here. Put these on," I said, while I did the same myself. As I mounted the motorcycle, I heard a commotion at the top of the stairs. I saw the Party official, the young nurse and a severe-looking woman in a white smock.

"She's here," Simmy hissed.

I smiled, revved the motor and as the group reached the bottom, not ten feet from where we were, I wheeled away, spewing dust and gravel.

"Where are we going?" Simmy yelled over the roar of the motor. He coughed, choking on the fumes and the dust.

"Germany."

Simmy looked at me as if I was mad.

"Why on earth would I want to go to Germany after all I've been through the past four years?" he shouted.

But I didn't listen. Once again, he'd become my little brother. Later on, he told me if it hadn't been for the American troops who'd liberated the camp, he wouldn't have made it into hospital. Before leaving the camp, he insisted they bury Papa properly so he could say Kaddish for him. He sat shiva in the camp barracks and wouldn't leave until the time was up, calling upon his deepest reserves of energy. Meanwhile other survivors had already been transported. The Americans fed him and kept him alive until he'd made it to hospital.

In those last days, the Nazis didn't care who lived and died. They only cared about saving their own necks. They didn't even have time to shoot the remaining prisoners, those like Simmy who were too weak to march anywhere. Rumours had spread that the end was near, that the Americans and the Russians were close. The Nazis feared the Russians. In the evenings before the liberation, Simmy and the others heard the guns. Papa was very ill then, very far gone. Simmy would hold him and tell him to hold on, that the war wouldn't last much longer. And then on that last day, a soldier burst into their barracks, screaming. He looked half-crazed, his voice hoarse from yelling. This fellow made them all line up in front. Simmy was on the far right. The guard came toward him holding out his machine pistol. He raised it and went to press the trigger. Simmy just stared at him intently, willing him to die, to disappear into the earth. The bloodshot eyes of the guard clouded, he frowned. He went to press the trigger but stopped. He tried again, but something held him back. He looked from Simmy and then slowly turned his gaze to the others, some forty of them in the barracks where two hundred had once been crammed in. Then slowly, an expression of fear came over the guard's face, as if realizing for the first time his existence was over. That his supremacy had crumbled.

"Remember what I've done for you," he growled. He raised his machine pistol above his head and loosed a volley of shots. Simmy described the inmates as they fell to the ground – all except Simmy, who remained standing, too weak to let himself fall. The camp guard waited a moment, then left, the only reminder of him the door swinging on its rusted hinges. Simmy said he looked out the filthy window and saw the guard running toward a lorry filled with shouting, beckoning soldiers. Simmy turned from the window and went to where his father lay, to tell him the good news, that their torment had ended. It was finally over. Only, he was dead. Papa had held out as long as he could. Seeing Papa's still, emaciated form Simmy wanted to weep, but his tear ducts had dried. Who would have recognized Papa for the prosperous merchant he'd once been?

Now, on hearing we were to go to Germany, fatherland of all his suffering, Simmy questioned me again. "Where in Germany?"

"Hamburg."

"Why Hamburg?"

"You'll see, little brother. Be patient."

Chapter 41

We stopped in a village and took a room in a modest inn. I wasn't refused, although I could see the proprietor and his wife were nervous. They looked at Simmy suspiciously as if he was an escapee from a lunatic asylum but the authority of a Soviet officer kept their tongues still and their eyes averted. Simmy sat on the bed and smoked intensely while I doused my face in the washbasin removing grit from travel. We had passed many vehicles, many military convoys rumbling across Poland.

"Where do they go?" Simmy had asked as we waited for a line of lorries to pass us by and free the road.

"To the eastern side of Germany."

"Why there?"

"It's a new world order, little brother. For her sins, Germany is being divided up. The communists are taking the east. Even Berlin is a divided city, with half belonging to the communists and the other half to the west.'

"Are we going to the western side?"

I nodded but put a finger to his lips. "We'll speak of this later."

And now in the cramped room, Simmy began to realize that time hadn't stood still and that while he spent years in hell, the world had moved on. "Did you have a woman in Russia?"

I gave him a wary look.

"Yes."

"Was she Jewish?" I shook my head. "And she knew you were a Jew?"

"Yes, she did."

"And it didn't bother her?"

I shrugged. "I don't think so. Just as your doctor didn't care. She wanted a man in her bed. If she had taken you back to Russia, you would have disappeared forever."

"She wasn't so bad."

"Even so. I know what life is like there. You wouldn't have survived it."

Simmy stood up, eyes flashing, smoke streaming out his mouth and nose.

"What are you talking about? I survived Oswiecizm. I can survive anything. Don't talk to me about what I can and cannot do."

I reached for the pack of cigarettes, shook one out and lit it.

"Do you imagine that the Soviets are any better than the Nazis?" I asked, blowing out a thin string of smoke. "Just as the occupied territories during the war were dangerous places for Jews, so too is the Soviet Union. The communists hate the Jews, just like the Tsars did. When it is convenient for them, they use us for their own purposes. When it isn't, you have a pogrom, or you're executed or sent to Siberia. And it's *because* of what you've gone through, Simmy, that I say this. How much more could you take? A day? A week? A month? Imagine the rest of your life slaving for the Soviet state. Did you know that our home is now owned by the state? It's not our home anymore. We don't have title to it. Just as if we never existed."

"You were home?"

"Yes."

"What was it like?"

"Pyotr and Amalija were there taking care of the place. Most of what we knew has been taken out and stripped away. The furniture, carpets, curtains, paintings, all looted. Families were living in the rooms upstairs."

"What families?"

"I don't know. I never saw them. They were living like rats, shut away from the light and afraid of everything."

"Why did you leave?"

"I came looking for you."

"We aren't going back?"

"No."

"I would like to see it again, if only for a short while."

"We can't go back."

"Why not?"

"I killed four men. They came to kill me but I shot first."

Simmy's eyes opened wide and his emaciated jaw dropped.

"You killed them? But why? Who were they? What did they want from you?"

I told the story to him. Simmy sat back on the edge of the narrow bed and gasped. "That's unbelievable. But this act, it doesn't affect you? They weren't total strangers. You knew them."

"You know, Simmy, when you fight a war, you don't think too much about whether killing is the right thing to do. You just do it. And when the war is over, it's not an easy thing to switch off. These men were just like Nazis, no better or worse," I said. "Don't you feel the same way about the Germans? If I let you have one of those machine guns, wouldn't you like to kill every one of them after what they've done to you?"

Simmy stared at me, then slowly shook his head. "I couldn't do it."

"Why not? You don't want revenge?"

"No, I don't."

"Are you afraid?"

"There's been enough killing. We don't need any more," he answered wearily. "Killing solves nothing. Did it save Mama and Papa? Did it save Katya and her husband?"

I stared at the floor for a moment, then looked up.

"There was a child too."

"A child?"

Simmy closed his eyes, squeezing until tears came out.

"A child. I didn't know. Where could they be?"

"I fear they're in the ground, just like Mama and Papa."

I saw them again walking in the distance, carrying their suitcases, Katya holding the child…then the heat rising from the road swallowing them up. I pounded my fist on the dresser. Tears streamed down my cheeks until I slumped to my knees, my forehead against the gritty wooden floor, animal sounds keening out.

Simmy edged his way over to me, reached out and stroked my hair. He spoke softly and tenderly.

"What a world it has become, Mordecai. What a fucking world."

Chapter 42

I rolled up my uniform and carefully stowed it in the bottom of my rucksack. Now I wore cotton trousers, a work shirt and a rough-hewn wool jacket. We'd managed to buy some clothes for Simmy that fit him a little better and didn't hang from his emaciated frame. Although tired much of the time, he began to recover his strength, eating more and putting on a little weight. No longer did he look like the dead awakened but now had the appearance of someone who had suffered severe privation. But there were few in the aftermath of the war of whom it could be said they looked shiny and fat.

At this time, the borders between Poland and Germany were virtually non-existent, loose sentry points where guards waved the straggling masses through. As people moved from place to place, many returned home, searching for lost relatives or simply looking for a new life. That morning, Simmy and I joined the throngs that crossed from Poland into Germany. The checkpoint was manned by American soldiers. They nodded and smiled and snapped their chewing gum. My motorcycle drew admiring comments and the Yanks cracked a few jokes about the sidecar and the way Simmy looked on his perch. Nonetheless, we joined the moveable column that undulated into Germany.

"I don't like being here. It makes me uneasy," Simmy said.

"Don't worry, there are plenty of foreigners here too. You'll see the Germans in a different light. Now, they're a cowering, defeated people forced to beg for a handout. They have to scavenge for food and shelter and money. They forced so many to behave like animals and now they're in the same position."

While we sat in a café having dinner, Simmy eyed the waitress. She noticed him and let her look linger on him as she served our food or when she came to clear the dishes. She was young but looked older than her years, with the washed-out, defeated look of one who has been dragged through a mind-numbing existence and had wearily grown used to it. I could see that she must have been attractive once and might still be if she took care. But something in her interested my brother. Perhaps the air of vulnerability she carried about her. At the end of the evening, Simmy nudged me.

"What is it?"

Simmy jerked his head toward the waitress, who watched us silently from a corner. "Do you have any spare money?"

"Why?"

"You know. It's for her. A few marks only." I sighed. "This is how you get your revenge? By sleeping with their women and daughters?" Simmy shrugged but suppressed a smile. "Make sure you tell her that you're a Jew. That she knows she's being screwed by one." Simmy nodded. I reached into my pocket and laid down five marks. "That's all you get."

"Thanks, big brother. I'll see you later." Simmy got up to speak to the waitress. She responded to him and smiled. Then she took off her apron, collected her coat and handbag from behind the small counter and together they left. I watched them with brooding eyes, then sighed to myself. What could I do? The war was over and my brother was no longer a boy.

I found a small flat in Hamburg. I made contact with the United Nations Relief Agency office and they got me a job driving a truck. I delivered supplies to the army bases, food and clothes for the refugees that flooded into Germany on their way to somewhere else.

The UNRA office brought them. It was a clearing-house for the dispossessed and rootless. For several weeks, Simmy took it easy. He rested and began to get well. Often when I came home, I found he'd gone out. I knew he went to bars to pick up German women. Many of them were available for a few packs of cigarettes and some chocolate. On these occasions, Simmy usually wasn't home by the time I left for work in the morning. For weeks on end, we rarely saw each other and I grew agitated with my brother. Finally, early one morning, I caught him as he climbed the steep flight of stairs to the flat.

"You're drunk."

Simmy smiled affectionately. "What of it?"

"It's six o'clock in the morning."

"Is that so?"

"I think you're ready to go to work."

"Do you?"

"Yes."

Simmy was in a good mood. He laughed. "Whatever you say, big brother. I'm ready to start my new life."

"Good. You start tomorrow morning. Make sure you're home this evening and I'll give you the details."

"I just want to sleep today, that's all."

"Get plenty of rest. You'll need it."

I pushed past him into the frigid morning air.

Early the next morning, I shook Simmy awake.

"Come on, get up."

Simmy tried to ignore me and when that didn't work, he rolled over. I stripped the blankets off the bed. Simmy was naked and made no attempt to cover himself up, just blinked sleepily.

"You're no fun, Mordecai. But then you never were."

"Come on, I've made coffee and there's bread and a little jam too."

Simmy set his feet on the cold floor and yawned.

"It's the middle of the night."

I stood at the mirror in my shirtsleeves and put the finishing touches on combing of my hair. A steaming mug sat on the wash-stand near me. I took a tentative sip.

"Bah. This ersatz coffee is terrible. At least during the war, I sweetened it with vodka."

Simmy nodded and then slowly got himself dressed. "And what is it you have arranged for me to do exactly?"

"You'll be unloading trucks at the depot."

"And for this I must miss a date with Hilke? To unload trucks?"

"You'll earn some money and then you can buy this Hilke some nice stockings or take her to dinner somewhere."

Simmy grimaced.

"Why should I want to do that? She's only good for taking to bed."

"Having a job shouldn't stop you from that."

"But it might make me too tired."

"Well. You must conserve your energy. C'mon, let's get going. It's getting late." I watched as my brother put on his jacket and hat.

"This is the beginning of what'll get you to Palestine. You still want to go?"

Simmy nodded.

"Of course. It's been my dream."

"Then you're on your way."

Simmy looked at me curiously. He wasn't confident that unloading trucks in Hamburg would get him to Palestine faster than he would have liked. But he put his faith in my words. He always had.

Several months passed. One day, I received a message that I was wanted in the UNRA office. I drove my truck to the compound and parked it. I went inside the main office and waited in the anteroom while an American secretary typed correspondence.

"Mr. Green will see you now," she said, pointing to the inner office door. I removed my cap and smoothed my hair before knocking.

Mr. Green, a slim man in shirtsleeves and wire-rimmed glasses, sat behind a cluttered desk writing in a file folder. He looked up as I came in but didn't stand.

"Take a seat, please, Mr. Goldman." I nodded. Mr. Green bent back to his folder and continued writing. "Almost finished. Sorry. So much paperwork to do. Now then." He set the pen down. "I have a temporary position for you if you're interested."

"What sort of position?"

"Driving for an American general."

"A general?"

Green nodded and grimaced a smile.

"A rabbi, as it turns out. He's being sent over to investigate the circumstances of Jewish refugees, provide what aid he can and write a report. He wants a driver who is Jewish, understands the military and speaks English and German. You'll be given the rank of Captain in the American army. What do you think?"

"And the pay is in American dollars?"

"That is correct," Green said crisply. Green was a Pole and a survivor of Buchenwald. He'd been a lawyer before the war.

"And I'm just to drive him around?"

"Well, you'll act as a guide and interpreter."

"Do I get a gun?"

Green sighed. "No." He had a sallow complexion and fingers yellowed from smoking. "Well. Take it or not?"

"I'll take it."

Green nodded curtly. "Good. I'll make all the necessary arrangements. This General, Rabbi Newman, will be here the day after tomorrow. I'll see you then at eight o'clock sharp. Remember, you're now temporarily back in the military."

I stood up at attention. "I haven't forgotten what it's like."

"Goodbye Captain Goldman."

Green turned back to his papers. As I left, he lit a cigarette and inhaled deeply, closing his eyes as he blew smoke in a thin stream.

That evening, I told Simmy the news.

"That's wonderful for you, dear brother. You get to drive around with a General while I break my back unloading trucks."

"You're not working that hard is what I hear."

"Who told you that?"

"I have my eyes and my ears."

"I'll beat the shit out of those eyes and ears when I catch them."

I laughed.

"Don't worry. It won't be much longer and you'll be in Palestine. You can take the motorcycle with you. I'm sure it will be of use there… and the two guns."

I had dismantled the machine guns, having stowed them beneath a loose floorboard in my bedroom. I kept them in perfect working condition.

Simmy rubbed his hands. They were sore from the work he did.

"I'm sure Mendel will approve. It will make him happy."

Mendel was an influential official with the Palestine Relief Committee. He recruited refugees who wanted to go to Palestine and arranged their passage by whatever means possible. Still, it required an official exit permit from the joint American-German authorities. Simmy had heard a rumour that a ship would be leaving for Palestine in about three months' time. He hoped he'd be on it.

"Don't make trouble, Simmy, and the Committee will get you on that boat."

"So you know about it?"

"Sure. It's not a well-kept secret. There're rumours everywhere. I hear talk of little else."

"Many want to go. No one wants to stay in this cursed country."

I unbuttoned my shirt cuff and rolled up the sleeve. "I understand."

"And where will you go, big brother?"

I shrugged as I unrolled the other sleeve and prepared to wash my hands in the basin.

"I don't know. Maybe America. Perhaps this Jewish General will give me a hand. We'll see."

I had the following day off. A courier delivered a set of American uniforms to my door. I tried them on. Remarkably, they fit rather well. Clearly, Mr. Green had a good eye. Green, the ultimate clerk, the fixer, the fellow who solved problems that no one else could.

There were men like him everywhere and large organizations that were in disarray found him and his ilk indispensable.

General Newman – Rabbi Newman – was a solidly built man of middling height who wore a yarmulke under his general's cap. He appraised me with grayish eyes.

"Just so you know, Captain Goldman, I'm a combat veteran. I've been banging around Europe since 1941. I don't want you to get it into your head that I rode out the war in a barracks some place."

"Of course not, General."

The General continued to stare at me. "Are you a religious man, Captain Goldman?"

"No sir, I'm not."

"You weren't brought up in a religious home? You never went to schul?"

"Occasionally, but not often."

"Why was that?"

"We weren't like most of the shtetl Jews you've heard of. My family was influential in our town. My father and mother were very liberal. They supported the synagogue but they weren't deeply religious and neither am I."

"Well, that's okay. I'm not here to preach about anything. My mission is to help Jewish refugees in any way that I can. I need to submit a report to the Relief Committee and make recommendations about resettlement in the United States. Your job is to drive me around and act as my guide and interpreter. How many languages do you speak?"

"Five sir. Polish, German, Russian, Yiddish and English."

"No French or Italian?"

"No."

The General eased himself behind the desk in the office that had been assigned to him. "This place is going to get pretty busy in a little while, Goldman. I'm being given quite a lot of admin support. We'll be bustling with clerks and secretaries, all American army, of course. Why don't we take a little drive? You can show me the sights."

"Yes sir."

For some reason, the General wasn't assigned a regular army vehicle but what the bureaucracy thought would be the next best thing, a converted ambulance painted in camouflage colours. As motor vehicles went, it had been properly maintained but looked incongruous.

"It'll do," said the General. "I understand Goldman, that you're also a mechanic."

"Yes sir."

"Well, that may be useful."

I felt fine until I got in behind the wheel. Then the memories of the day the Nazis broke the non-aggression pact came flooding back. In my mind, I saw the distant figures of my sister, her child and husband walking down the road away from me. The sun had been very bright that day, flashing off the pitted surface. I gripped the steering wheel tightly, my arms stiff. I blinked the sun away.

"Something wrong?"

The General's question snapped me out of it.

"No sir."

I turned the key in the ignition and the motor fired.

Simmy and I were having a farewell drink at a local bar called Der Strasse. Simmy was to depart for Palestine early in the morning. I gave him the motorcycle and the machine guns. They would be shipped and labeled as "household" items; donated to the Haganah who battled the British and the Arabs for control of Palestine.

"Are you sure you won't change your mind?" Simmy asked me. He pushed his spectacles up his nose and again I saw the studious youngster of our childhood.

I shook my head. "Too many Jews there."

Simmy snorted. "What does that mean?"

"It means that I don't care for Jewish politics, just as I didn't care for Polish politics or Russian politics either. You put too many Jews together and there's trouble. You think these people you go to help will ever agree on anything? Right now they're fighting the British. When the British leave, then who will they fight?"

"The Arabs, of course."

"Yes, the Arabs," I replied wearily. "And then it will be each other. It's our destiny, Simmy. I want no part of it."

"But just think, it's a chance to build a new homeland from scratch, to participate in the creation of a new country just for the Jews. When will that happen again? Never. We have to take the risk now."

"Good. Good. And good luck with it."

"And what'll you do? You can't stay in the American army forever. This Rabbi General will go home soon."

"Perhaps I'll go to America. Or not. Perhaps someplace else. I'm not looking that far ahead. For now, I do a job and that's good enough."

"We could use your help over there. A man with your experience. Yossi was saying that you'd be very valuable. You know armaments and strategy. You understand what it's like to be in battle, to kill when you must."

"Yes, and I'm tired of it. I've had more than enough. I only wish to kill Nazis and they've gone to ground, those that haven't been caught already and put on trial."

I stared toward the bar. A group of rough-looking men, in threadbare coats and tattered caps, working men, kept glancing our way over steins of beer. They were speaking German, and the biggest of them kept tossing his head back and speaking loudly while slurping his beer, some of which ran down his chin. I could see he was a drunk, and a mean one. So, it didn't surprise me when the fellow kicked back his stool and swaggered over to our table. A large brute with wide shoulders and a thick neck, built like a wrestler. I sighed, put a hand on Simmy's arm to silence him until I could see what this fellow was up to. The drunkard leaned rudely on our table and stabbed a thick forefinger in my direction.

"You fucking Americans think you own the world..."

"I'm not American," I replied quietly in German.

The fellow stopped speaking, looking puzzled for a moment as the question worked through his brain. "Then what are you?"

"I'm a Jew. I was in the Russian army and drove my tank right up into Berlin and was very pleased to see the crushed rabble that had been the *proud German people* ground into nothing. I killed Nazis and enjoyed it. That's who I am."

I stood up slowly and stepped clear. The intruder reared back, surprised.

"Now who the hell are you, apart from being some stupid, drunken German bastard."

The fellow's eyebrows shot up into his cap and he grinned crookedly, then licked his lips. His companions moved in closer, forming a semi-circle around him. I noticed some servicemen also moved in.

"It's all right," I said in a loud voice. "This is just a friendly disagreement between this fellow and myself. What's your name, friend?"

"Rudy. And I hate Americans almost as much as I hate Jews."

I smiled. "Good. I am glad."

The fellow's anger worked itself further up into his face. He lunged forward and grabbed for me. But all he grabbed was air as I easily sidestepped his blow. Rudy pushed himself away from the wall and stood with his fists up, crouched now in a boxer's stance. Still my hands stayed at my sides.

"I don't think you want to do this, Rudy."

"Come on."

Rudy beckoned with his fists and moved between the tables where there was more space. I sighed, unbuttoned my tunic and handed it to Simmy.

"Ten bucks on the guy in uniform," an American voice shouted which, suddenly set up a flurry of yells and calls as bets were exchanged both in English and German. American dollars and deutschmarks exchanged hands as Simmy found himself holding all the money, which in a matter of seconds grew to a fistful. Seeing the action, Rudy smiled and he too removed his cap and jacket and handed them to one of his drinking companions. The man rotated his huge shoulders and twisted his neck around. A malevolent grin appeared on his wide face. He was easily fifty pounds heavier and two to three inches taller. The others pulled away some of the tables and chairs pushing complacent patrons out of the way.

We circled each other carefully. The fellow seemed to have shaken off his drunkenness and appeared to be all business. This was confirmed when Rudy snapped out a left and caught me under the eye, a shot that not only stung but rocked me back on my heels. A cry went up in the crowd. I wasn't hurt but the stinging blow brought me to my senses. I remembered Frederick's hard lessons and steeled myself to fight and get hit. Although the speed of the punch surprised me, I could see that Rudy was solid but slow. He'd obviously boxed before, perhaps professionally. Rudy snapped out another left but I slipped it and returned with a combination to the ribs. Rudy grabbed me around the shoulders and I jerked my head back and twisted to the side, throwing my shoulder up as I took the force of Rudy's big head against my upper bicep. A head butt gone wrong. I punished him with a left to the jaw as the momentum of the butt carried Rudy forward and down. I kept him down by snaking my right arm around his bull neck and punched him in the ribs with my left hand. The grunts became audible now. Rudy wrapped his thick arms around my waist and pulled forward. We crashed into a table with Rudy on top. Even before we landed, I rolled using my momentum and scrambled up quickly, feet in balance, hands poised. As Rudy pushed himself upwards, I gave him a combination to the face, chin and side of the head that forced him back to one knee. Then his left hand disappeared and as he swung around, a switchblade appeared in his meaty fist. I backed off and Rudy gained his feet, grinning wolfishly, flicking at the blood running out of his nose and down his chin.

"And now, Jew, I will cut you into little pieces and feed you to the dogs."

He took a wide sweeping swipe that I dodged. The bar had become an animal pit with the spectators yowling for blood. Rudy feinted again and I moved with him while quickly scanning the space for a weapon I could use. The crowd had closed me in within a tight ring. Rudy lunged, and I sidestepped quickly giving him a shot in the back of the head but he swung around, letting the blade lead as he scythed the air in a wide arc. The German enjoyed himself now, taking pleasure from stalking me. We circled slowly around. We'd completed a full circuit when a wild cry came from somewhere behind the crowd and I saw two of the men sprawl forward in surprise. Rudy half-turned, only to see a bellowing Simmy surge forward with a wooden chair. He smashed it across the bulky German's back. Rudy went down in a heap. I stood there, dumbfounded. Simmy held the remnants of the chair and began swinging and chopping crazily at the crowd, some of whom stumbled backward, falling into those behind them. I grabbed him.

"We'd better go."

Simmy looked at me and nodded.

"I've got your jacket."

And before the surprised onlookers could move, we pushed our way through and out of the bar. We ducked into an alleyway and slumped against a wall, panting and laughing. Simmy dug into his pocket.

"I've got all the money," he cried triumphantly and we both laughed again.

"Come on," I said. "We'd better get out of here. We don't want to get picked up by the MPs. You'll never get to Palestine that way."

Quickly and furtively, we made our way back to the flat. Inside, I poured the two of us some vodka. We clinked glasses.

"You're a madman, Simmy."

"You rescued me," he replied a bit breathlessly after downing the vodka. "And now I have rescued you, big brother."

"Thank you."

"My pleasure."

We sat up the rest of the evening, talking until it was time for Simmy to leave. I drove him down to the pier in the ambulance and we were waved right through once the security guards caught a glimpse of my American uniform.

The ship was a rust bucket called *The Irish Maiden* registered out of Liberia, piloted by a Dutchman and his mainly Greek crew. I saw families gathered on the wharf hugging, kissing and crying their farewells. The past few months had changed my little brother considerably. He'd gained weight and there was life in his face. Simmy now looked forward to what life had in store for him; no longer the burnt-out soul I'd found in the Soviet hospital.

"You be careful in the Haganah, young fellow."

"It's my turn to fight for something now. A Jewish homeland is worth it."

"I hope so. I hope you find what you're looking for, little brother. Maybe a sturdy Jewish wife who'll bear you plenty of children. You'll need help scratching a living in the desert."

Simmy laughed.

"I won't be scratching anything, believe me." And then he went quiet for a moment. "There will be a war and God knows what will happen."

"Then you must be careful."

"I'm not you, Mordecai but I believe between myself and something else I shall be protected."

"What's this something else?"

Simmy shrugged.

"I'm not sure but I'll let you know if I find out."

Simmy glanced at the gangway as the last of the passengers carried their belongings aboard. "I must go now." And suddenly he went quiet.

I held out my arms.

"Come little brother."

We embraced. Although Simmy now stood taller, he still felt frail and skinny. I held him tightly as if he was still the small child with wire-rimmed spectacles and the serious air. We held each other for a long moment, then I broke the embrace.

"You watch out for yourself. Don't be crazy or take unnecessary risks. Build a good homeland for the Jews and one day I'll visit you there. We'll pick oranges and dates together."

Simmy nodded as tears fell from his eyes. He stepped back and held his hand up in farewell, then turned and moved toward the gangway, striding quickly without looking back. I watched him gain the deck, then Simmy turned toward me and raised his hand again. *Dos vidaniya*, little brother, I said to myself as Simmy's figure atop the ship's deck began to fade from sight. Until we meet again. Then I climbed back into the ambulance, swung it around and headed out the way I came.

Chapter 43

Das Vidaniya

January 5, 1948. I stood on the upper deck of the ship, The *General Heintzelmann*, as it steamed out of Hamburg harbour. Five levels below in our tiny cabin, my wife, Esther, lay in bed. She felt ill and we had just got under way. The temperature hovered near freezing and felt colder in the strong winds but I liked the fresh air and inhaled it deeply into my lungs. The *General Heintzelmann* had been a troop ship during the War, transporting three thousand men at a time, carrying them to the European theatre of operations. Somehow, it had managed to elude the U-boats that travelled in packs sinking hundreds of thousands of tons of Allied shipping. Many thousands lost their lives in the icy waters of the Atlantic but this one had survived. That was one reason I felt good about the journey to Canada – to a city called Toronto where I knew no one, had no contacts except through the Jewish Agency.

General Rabbi Newman had offered to sponsor me to come to America. I might have lived in New York where my wife had some cousins but she didn't want to go there. She didn't want to be near her relations, and that was fine with me. I didn't care. It was just the two of us now and together we'd make a new life. I'd had my thirty-second birthday while Esther was just nineteen.

Shortly after seeing Simmy off on the ship to Palestine, I went on leave with Rabbi General Newman who had business in Berlin. I drove the ambulance and then I was given a week to spend on my own. I had wanted to go to Berlin to see if I could find out any news about my family. Number 57 Alexanderplatz housed the Jewish Relief Agency message centre and anyone looking for family came to see if information had been posted about those gone missing. The displaced persons community had put the word out to come to Berlin to seek the truth. The Nazis had been very meticulous in their paperwork and much had been salvaged. Records were kept on everything; names, dates, numbers, locations, even photographs. Many anguished pilgrims found nothing but bitter disappointment but others shed tears of joy and laughter upon finding lost family members. I had no expectations. Once I'd known that my parents had died, there was little else I might look forward to. Perhaps it was morbid curiosity that drew me to the centre.

I'd noticed the tall, blonde girl staring determinedly at the vast message board in the Jewish Relief Agency offices where refugees had left messages scrawled on scraps of paper, pieces of cloth, even food wrappers. She looked painfully thin, this young girl but otherwise, seemed placid, remarkably untouched. I didn't think she was Jewish, with that sharp little nose, the luminescent blue eyes and milky-white skin. I watched her for a moment as she mouthed the messages to herself and then I turned away. I'd already scanned the message board and there'd been nothing there for me. I left the offices and began to wander Berlin.

Later that day, I took some lunch in a beer garden, making certain I spoke brusquely to the waiter, who cowered before me. I strolled along the promenade, enjoying the fine weather and trying to forget who I'd been and what I'd done. Just try and exist in the world, I told myself as I endured the looks of envy and hatred of the Berliners when they saw me in uniform. Any number had confessed to me that they hadn't supported the Nazis. What had they waited for? I would ask myself. All of humanity to disappear or just the Jews? I turned away grimly after one such encounter and saw her standing in the square, hugging herself in her threadbare jacket.

I came up behind her. "Did you find a message?" I asked her in German.

She started, then turned suddenly. As she saw me, her eyes widened in fear but she smiled prettily nonetheless. She shook her head.

"No, I found no one," she answered me in Polish.

"And where are you from little one?" I said in Yiddish.

She smiled more openly then.

"I'm from Sosnovitz, sir."

"Really. I'm from Krasnowicz, very close to there."

"Yes, I know it. I was there a few times."

"And what's your name?"

"Esther. Esther Hellman."

She blushed in front of me.

I put out my hand and she touched my fingers timidly.

"I'm Mordecai Goldman. Tell me, Esther, are you on your own?"

She shook her head. "I'm with a girlfriend. We're to meet here."

"But it's just the two of you?"

"Yes."

"How about I show you around Berlin? I was here in the War."

"Well...I suppose it might be all right."

"You're looking for your family?"

She nodded again.

"My brothers. My parents died before the war in an automobile accident. I was only eleven. When the War broke out, my brothers and I were separated and I had hoped to find them again."

We waited together another half an hour for Esther's friend, Miriam. She didn't show. We spoke easily together. I treated her gently as if she was a fragile child; she looked frail enough. I asked her if she was hungry and she nodded.

"Then come. I know a place to eat nearby and the food is very good." I took her to a small café. A few officers occupied some of the tables. The waiter bustled over and seated us. Esther looked impressed.

"How long have you been in the city?" I asked.

She studied the menu. "A week only. So far, I've heard nothing. Do you think the potato pudding is good? Or perhaps the bratwurst and cabbage?"

I laughed. "Have both if you like. You could use it. You're very thin."

"There wasn't much time for eating when the War ended."

I ordered the cabbage borscht and a dumpling. I asked for some bread and a stein of beer. Esther had a lemonade. When the food arrived, she tucked in immediately.

"Mmm. This is very good," she said.

"Have whatever you like and if you're still hungry, then order something else too."

"Thank you. I'm embarrassed."

"You're hungry. There's nothing wrong with that. Many people went hungry during the War."

"I was luckier than most. At least I didn't starve. At least I didn't end up in a camp and burned in an oven." Her voice hardened, her throat tight.

"Sometimes it's luck and other times, it's cunning that guides a person, the pure instinct to survive."

She hesitated, resting her fork. "I want to tell you what happened to me. I don't know why. I haven't told anyone."

"I'd like to hear it. Don't worry, there's plenty of time. The city can wait for us."

She took a sip of her lemonade, settled herself, dabbed at her lips with the paper napkin, then took a deep breath.

"When our town was invaded by the Nazis, my brothers fled across the border into Russia. They left during the night and when I woke up in the morning, they were gone and I was alone. I packed my things and went to the train station and took the first train east to the next town. It was near Kielce. No one knew me there. I went to the Church and asked the priest to help me. I don't know why I did this but I was lucky and the priest was a good man. He secured new identity papers for me. I was no longer Esther Hellman, Jewess but Oksana Bratsov, a Catholic orphan. I learned the catechisms and all the prayers and by the time the Nazis came, I was transformed. I could walk in the streets. I would see the Jewish families lined up, pushed out of their homes and standing with their belongings and their crying children, waiting for hours to be taken away. I wanted to run, to confess that I was one of them and they should take me too. But I did not. I couldn't open my mouth. The Gestapo set up offices in the town and as it turned out, they were looking for interpreters. I could speak German because my parents spoke Yiddish in the house and I spoke Polish too. They came to me and asked me to work in their office. There were many legal matters that needed attending to. So I agreed. I had little choice. I was fourteen when I went to work for the Gestapo."

"And you were there with them in the office the whole time?"

"Yes."

"And how did they treat you?"

She smiled sadly, creases showing in her thin face. "Very well, actually. They were polite and always called me Fraulein. All the time I was on edge in case I should be found out. That they would arrest me too and I would join the lines of people waiting to get on the next train to the camps. I was afraid that they could smell my Jewishness."

I sat back in my chair and marveled at the presence of mind of one so young, working in the lion's den and never giving it away. "And they never found out about you?"

"No, they never found out. In 1944, in the spring, something happened. For the past year, I had been renting a room in a house near the office where I worked. It was owned by a Polish widow. When I left my home I took some things with me, photographs and papers. This woman had been going through my room even though I hid them very well. One day I was walking home and as I came to the street where I lived the landlady was standing outside. She waited for me. As I approached she pointed and called out in a loud voice, "She is a Jewess, arrest her, she is a Jewess." So, I turned around and walked back the way I came. I went right to the train station and got on the next train that came in. I had a little bit of money and the clothes I wore and that was all. I left everything I had behind. I couldn't go back there. It was too dangerous."

"And how did you survive?"

"I wrote a letter to the officer in charge of the Gestapo and told him that my aunt had become very ill suddenly and I was urgently needed to help look after her. I asked him to give me a letter of recommendation to the officer in charge where I was staying and he did. Then I got another job working for the Gestapo. It was a small town just outside of Zamosc. I stayed there until the Russians invaded. One morning, I came into the office and the door was open. I walked in. The desks had been cleaned out, all of the files were gone, maps and pictures from the walls, books, everything had been taken. It was like they had never been there, and then I knew finally that I had survived the War. I just sat in one of the chairs crying. It was such a relief. Suddenly, the pressure that I had been feeling all those years lifted. Still, I wanted to avoid the Russians since they may not look kindly on me for working with the Gestapo, even though I was still a young girl. I decided that I wanted to find my family. To see what happened to my brothers. And now I'm a refugee like everyone else."

I drained the stein of beer and set the glass down on the table. I looked at her. She was very pretty. Her blonde hair was pulled back severely and tied in a bun but her skin was clear and smooth and her eyes had that lovely shade of blue that made me think of soothing waters.

"I think you've been very brave," I said.

"I did what I had to do to live, that's all. Anyone would've done the same. During that early time when I was leaving my town, I saw my school friends lined up in the street. I wanted to run to them but they warned me away. Because my parents were fair-haired and pale-skinned, I was lucky and the Nazis didn't arrest me. They thought I was Polish and didn't even check my papers. I got on a train that took me away to safety. The rest died. All of them." Tears rolled down the contours of her cheeks and dripped on the table. I handed her my handkerchief. It had been newly laundered.

"Thank you," she said. "You're very kind."

It was a remarkable story of courage and resilience. Such a young girl and yet what an immense presence of mind and determination. To survive in this way. As she wept before me looking so fragile and vulnerable, I told myself, this was an exceptional person. How many could have done the same?

Chapter 44

Two years passed. Esther and I married. At first, I thought of myself as her protector. As time went on however, our relationship became more intimate. It was Esther who made the first move and it was she who said, "I want you for my husband, Mordecai. Together, we can build a new life." I didn't know how to say no.

And now Esther felt dizzy and nauseated and lay in the cabin below while I strolled the deck buffeted by the blustery winds. At last, I said to myself, my life is starting. I looked about the enormous ship and saw other men, inadequately dressed in light trench coats and fedoras they clutched to their heads, while the wives suffered below.

The voyage on the *General Heintzelmann* took ten days. Esther remained ill the entire time. I could barely get her to eat some soup or drink a little tea. She grew even thinner because of the nausea and vomiting.

"Mordecai," she moaned and put out her hand. I took it in mine. "Your hands, they're so strong, so powerful," she said. "How much longer?"

"A few days. We'll dock in Halifax the day after tomorrow. I've heard that the closer we get to Canada, the weather should improve."

"Thank God."

"Come, come. This is nothing compared to what you endured in the War. This is nothing like having to fear the Nazis every day."

"But I wasn't sick and throwing up all the time. I got used to it. This I will never…"

"Don't think about it. Be positive."

Esther laughed weakly. "That's your answer for everything. Are you sure we're doing the right thing? What do we know about Toronto? We don't know anyone there."

I patted her hand lightly. "It's a new life Esther, and a new start. We can do what we want. Be who we want and it doesn't matter. We'll make a good life there, I promise you."

She nodded, drawing breath through her lips then closed her eyes, the eyelids showing violet. "I'm trying to sleep now."

The next day, we went up on deck together. The winds had calmed and Esther felt better. She had been able to keep down most of a meal the evening before and ate a solid breakfast that morning. She seemed excited as the city of Halifax appeared on the horizon. Despite the cold, we and hundreds of other emigrants, new Canadians to be, stared at the shoreline and wondered about our new homeland. I looked about and saw some of the men I briefly encountered from the voyage. Some were Jews but others were Hungarians, Poles, Czechs and even a few Russians. I'd deliberately avoided direct contact with most of them but nodded at one or two. I'd shared a cigarette on one occasion with a Czech fellow who'd served in the British Army. We'd spoken briefly but neither of us had been forthcoming or friendly. The demeanour of the men didn't encourage any closeness or sharing of confidences. We both acknowledged our wives were ill and that we wanted the voyage to end, to get on with what would become the rest of our lives, as if everything up until that point had been a pretense. This Czech fellow had been wounded at El Alamein as the British fought the desert campaign against Rommel. He'd recovered in a field hospital in Algeria and then went back into the desert. He'd been a demolitions expert.

I spotted the Czech, who was gazing toward the shore. He looked up and smiled.

"And so, it's time," he said, sticking out his hand. After a slight hesitation, I took it.

"Good luck to you."

"And to you."

We parted as the Czech turned back to his wife, a short woman with dark hair and a kerchief tied around her head. I turned back to Esther.

"Aren't you cold?"

"Yes, but it's wonderful. I feel well and we're here finally."

She threw her arms around me and gave me a big hug and kiss.

"I'm happy."

"You'll be happier once we're in Toronto and settled in our own place."

"You think we'll have our own place? We won't have to share?"

"We'll find something nice, don't worry about it."

She looked at me uncertainly, then turned back to look at the approaching harbour.

"It seems very small," she said.

"Don't worry, Esther. I believe it is the land of opportunity. We'll build a new life and leave all the shit behind us."

She laughed. "You say the nicest things."

We had one suitcase each and I carried my army duffel bag over one shoulder. Esther clutched her small bag with all of the possessions she could bring. Most had been left behind.

The bitter wind in Halifax tore at our clothing. People clutched their hats and their bags and bent their heads. There was a great deal of snow.

"It's like Siberia," I said as we boarded a bus to the train station. We were to travel to Montreal, then transfer to another train to Toronto. The first train had been late in leaving. Too much snow on the tracks. Crews cleared the snow and to me, they reminded me of the winter campaigns I'd fought and the prisoners forced into labour camps.

"They look like kulaks but this is Canada, Esther, and these men are paid for their work."

She said nothing but clutched my arm tightly.

The train travelled slowly. Inside the compartment it was very warm and crowded. Esther squeezed up against me and let the rhythm rock her to sleep. I tried to look out the window but all I saw through the mist was a barren, snowy landscape and occasionally, small towns and some buildings. Ten hours later, the train arrived in Montreal. We dredged up our meagre belongings and found the train to Toronto. I bought coffee and toast in a small, dreary café. I had ten dollars in Canadian money I'd been given by the Canadian immigration office in Hamburg, and money I'd changed from German deutschmarks, the value of which was very low. I'd saved some American currency, close to a hundred dollars from my army pay. After paying for the coffee, we made our way to the platform to catch the train to Toronto. Esther was bleary-eyed and sleepy, numbed from the travelling and from the cold.

"I don't like it here," she said and shivered inside her thin coat.

"It'll get better, I promise."

"I don't know what I am doing here," she said in a distant voice. "I wish I was back home. I wish my parents were still alive and I lived in their house. I am only nineteen years old, what am I doing?"

She set her small suitcase on the ground and put her face to her hands, her thin shoulders convulsing. I put my arms around her. "I don't speak the language. I don't know anyone," she sobbed in Yiddish.

"Hush now, little one. That will change. It will get better. You'll see. You must trust me and everything will be fine."

I kept my voice low and gentle and after a time, the convulsions eased and she looked up at me with reddened eyes.

"Now dry your eyes and let's get to our train. Only a few more hours and we shall be in a new city that very soon we shall call home, okay?"

Esther didn't say anything but she wiped her eyes with a cotton handkerchief. I put my arm through hers and together we boarded the train, showing our tickets to the conductor. This train was less crowded. We found seats to ourselves and settled in.

"See? This is better already," I said. We sat down and I put my arm around her. A moment later came the blast of the conductor's whistle and the train moved slowly out of the station. This time, we both slept, heads lolling together. And when we woke up, the train had pulled into Union Station. I looked at my watch, almost noon. Everything had been on time. How extraordinary was this place that seemed untouched by the War. I saw no bombed-out buildings, no rutted tracks, no abandoned lorries or tanks. The people may have looked pinched and nervous but overall appeared prosperous, well fed and well dressed. I saw no fear or desperation in the eyes of the Canadians, only resignation and impatience.

The train doors opened and we exited. As we walked slowly along the platform, following the current of the crowd, a short, stout woman in a fur coat and matching hat approached us.

"Mr. and Mrs. Goldman?" she inquired.

"Yes?"

The plump woman put out her gloved hand. I noticed a line of beaded sweat on her upper lip.

"I'm Ruth Rosenberg from the Jewish Agency. Welcome to Canada and welcome especially to our city of Toronto."

I took her hand and shook it.

"Thank you. You are most kind."

Esther took the smaller woman's hand shyly and smiled nervously.

"I've come to take you to your new home."

"Our new home?"

"Why yes. We have an apartment ready for you. I think you'll like it. But if you don't, you can take your time and find something you do like. At least, you will have a roof over your head and you can settle in."

I relayed this information to Esther in Yiddish and she gasped.

"Is this true?" she asked. "Can it be?"

Mrs. Rosenberg led us outside and we found snow piled at least six feet high on the sidewalks. "Is there always this much snow?" I asked.

"We do get quite a lot of snow," Mrs. Rosenberg replied curtly. She took Esther by the elbow as she struggled in her shoes to negotiate the sidewalk. "You'll need to get a proper pair of boots, my dear. My car is just over here." And she indicated a large, dark sedan.

"This automobile is yours?" I asked incredulously.

"Why yes. We all own cars over here."

"What make of automobile is it?"

"It's a Buick."

I nodded.

"A fine machine."

I'd studied American cars and read about them. In Germany, some of the mechanics in the motor pool loaned me magazines they received from the States. "This is the eight-cylinder model."

Mrs. Rosenberg looked at me in surprise.

"Why yes, however did you know? Oh, I forgot that you're a mechanic. Of course, how silly of me." She opened the door and beckoned us in. "Just put your suitcases on the floor. There's plenty of room." Esther sat in the back. I sat up front. Mrs. Rosenberg slammed the door and the engine roared to life. "Ready everybody," she called out gaily. "We haven't got far to go." She pulled the car out into traffic on Front Street and I got my first glimpse of the city. I was struck by the size and height of the buildings, the width of the streets and the number of personal vehicles on the roads. I saw just a few buses and trams. The streets were covered in snow as Mrs. Rosenberg drove slowly. Being so short, she hunched very close over the wheel, practically on top of the dashboard. "Would you like to hear the radio?"

"You have a radio?"

"Oh yes. It's the latest thing." And she flicked the knob and suddenly there was dance music filling the car. Esther looked around bewildered.

I pointed. "Look. It has a radio. Isn't it wonderful?" Esther smiled at my boyish glee.

"It has a heater too."

Mrs. Rosenberg flicked a knob and I heard rushing air fill the interior but all I felt was the cold. "Don't worry, it will warm up soon." Mrs. Rosenberg asked us about the trip and the accommodations on *The General Heinzelmann* and what we thought of the train and had we ever seen this much snow. She chatted in a nervous patter all the way along Front Street to Spadina Avenue where she turned north and announced that we were in the heart of the rag trade, the "schmate" district and further up we'd enter Chinatown. She drove ahead of trams that seemed to glide on the glistening rails like silent mechanical beasts stopping only to disgorge passengers and swallow up new ones. And then suddenly, she turned down a small street called Cecil.

"Practically there," she cried.

A block further along and she steered the car to the side where the curb might have been. Esther still shivered in the back. The car hadn't yet warmed up. Mrs. Rosenberg turned off the engine and stepped out of the car calling, "Come. Come."

We stood on the sidewalk and looked at a narrow, two-story house of pale brown brick with white wood paneling on the front.

"Come. Come."

I took Esther's arm and followed Mrs. Rosenberg as she made her way up the walk and around the side to a door. "This is the entrance to your apartment. You see? You have your own way to get in and out without disturbing anyone. The owner lives on the main floor. Come." She removed a key from her purse and fitted it into the lock. We followed her up a stairway to a door where she fitted another key and went inside. Esther and I stood on the threshold of the open doorway, hesitating.

"Come in," Mrs. Rosenberg urged. "This is your new home. Please. Let me show you." She pulled us in and closed the door. We found ourselves in a large, pleasant room, a living room with a sofa and two chairs. The room was L-shaped and ended in a nook where a family would sit down and eat.

"Look at this."

Mrs. Rosenberg disappeared and we followed her into what became the kitchen. "All the modern appliances. Stove, oven, brand new sinks and a refrigerator." She opened the door. "And you have enough groceries for the next week."

Esther and I looked in the refrigerator and felt the cold air and saw that indeed, there were provisions inside.

"And look here."

Mrs. Rosenberg opened the cupboards and showed boxes and packages of food.

"Now you've got to see this."

She took Esther by the arm and led her into the bedroom, showed her a neatly made bed, two chests of drawers and an extra chair. Mrs. Rosenberg opened a door and inside was a closet. "For your clothes," she said. She tugged Esther forward again and opened yet another door. "This is the bathroom. You have your own and no one to share. You are very, very lucky." I followed them in and immediately went to the sink and turned on the taps. I turned them off, then on, then off before pronouncing myself satisfied. "Bring your things in here and you can unpack in a minute but first we'll talk for a moment in the other room. Then I'll let you get settled because I'm sure you want to rest."

We'd removed our coats and were surprised to discover that the apartment was quite warm. We sat around the small table opposite the kitchen. Mrs. Rosenberg brought out a sheaf of papers that she lay flat in front of her. "Here's the rental agreement for the apartment." And she showed it to me.

"How much is the rent?" I asked her.

"Twenty-five dollars a month but don't worry, the first month is paid and if you need help financially, just give me a call and I'm sure we can do something for you."

"And what sort of people own this house? Who's the landlord?"

For the first time, Mrs. Rosenberg hesitated.

"They're good people and we've used them in the past but if you must know, they're German."

I stood up so quickly that the chair fell over backward.

"Are you mad?" I exclaimed. "Do you know who we are and what we've come through?"

"Of course I know," Mrs. Rosenberg retorted indignantly. "But these are good people. They've lived here since the First War. We wouldn't use them otherwise. Do you think we'd settle you with Nazis? Of course not. The owners are a retired couple who don't need all the space they have and they rent for a reasonable rate. Just look at this apartment, it's wonderful and perfect for you. Now sit down please, Mr. Goldman and let's get to business. You'll need to find work, won't you?"

"I'll make some tea." Esther said in halting English. I'd been teaching her but she was a very intelligent girl and learned quickly. Mrs. Rosenberg looked at her in surprise.

"Why yes, Mrs. Goldman. That would be very nice. You'll find everything you need inside."

As she rose, Esther shot me a steely look and I sighed inwardly. "My wife thinks that I have a bad temper, Mrs. Rosenberg." I sat down heavily. "Perhaps she's right but you must understand. Germans and Poles are not my friends. I killed plenty during the War."

"I'm sure you did, Mr. Goldman. You certainly look capable of it." Mrs. Rosenberg tittered nervously. "But the War is over now and you must get on. You'll want a job and to save some money for a place of your own. Maybe you'll have a family soon? Your wife is a lovely girl and she seems very sensible. I know the two of you will work hard and prosper here, I can feel it. Oh, I forgot to mention, you have your own telephone too. It's included in the rent. The phone will help you when you're looking for a job. But don't worry, I have some possibilities for you and you can start to look on Monday. This way, you'll have all of Sunday to get settled and organized. Now I should tell you that most businesses don't start until nine in the morning with a few that start earlier, around eight o'clock."

I felt surprised.

"In Europe, I started work at seven o'clock and sometimes as early as six."

"Yes, well. Things are a bit different here but you'll work it out, don't worry. And if you don't know, simply ask, people are usually pretty friendly around here."

When Esther returned with the tea things, she found Mrs. Rosenberg and I hunched over the papers. Mrs. Rosenberg also had a map laid out in front of her and was showing me the main streets. Esther set the tea tray down and Mrs. Rosenberg looked up gratefully.

"I know you'll do very well here. Your husband is a strong man and he has a strong woman to help him out." Esther smiled for the first time in weeks.

First thing Monday morning, I got ready. I rose at six o'clock and took a quick bath, careful not to use too much hot water. Then I shaved and dressed and made myself some coffee and toast. Esther was still asleep. Mrs. Rosenberg had given me some letters of introduction and set up a few appointments. She had also drawn out the routes on the map to the places she had recommended. I had appointments at four car dealerships that day, all of them in the downtown area and near each other. I knew already the Canadian currency and how much the pram would cost and had my change counted out.

"Shall I make you something for your lunch?" Esther leaned against the doorway and shivered.

"I didn't want to wake you. Why are you up?"

"I couldn't sleep. I heard you moving around."

I held out my arms and she came to me. I felt her trembling in her nightclothes. "Go back to bed and get warm. I'll be all right."

"What time will you be back?"

"I don't know. After I have found a job. Okay?"

Esther nodded.

"I want a job too."

"First things first, little one. I'll get work and then we'll help you too."

"I can't believe it. We're here. In Canada. It doesn't seem real to me. I was dreaming I was at home in bed at my mother's house and she was going to call me for breakfast. It was a nice dream but that's all it was."

I kissed her forehead.

"Now I want you to go back to bed and get some rest. It's been a long and tiring journey. You haven't been sleeping well. If we're to succeed here, we need to stay healthy."

I kissed her again and went to get my coat and hat. I still had my warm military overcoat. Esther had cleverly removed all of the insignia and it looked quite smart. I pulled on a pair of leather gloves.

"Now, I'm ready."

I touched my pockets where I'd placed the map, the piece of paper where Mrs. Rosenberg had written out the names of the places and people I was to see and my change for the tram. I smiled at Esther, then opened the door to my first day as a new settler in Canada.

I walked up to College Street and waited for the tram. It was bitterly cold and passersby were bundled up. But I didn't feel it. I had felt the cold in 1942 at Stalingrad where the temperature fell routinely to forty below. This, I told myself, was nothing. If I can survive that, I can survive anything. What can they have to frighten me here in Canada?

The first business I went to was Uptown Motors on Bay Street near Wellesley. The proprietor was Sam Samuelson. I told the girl behind the desk who I wanted to see and was asked to wait. About fifteen minutes later, a thin man in shirtsleeves came out. His tie was pulled loose at the collar and he wore pince-nez glasses and had a pencil moustache. It looked like a grease mark above his lip.

"Mr. Goldman?"

"Yes?"

"I'm David Greenspon, the general manager. Mr. Samuelson isn't in yet. Won't you come into my office?"

"Sure."

I rose and followed the harried fellow into a disheveled room where he closed the door.

"Please. Have a seat Mr. Goldman." I sat down. "Have you got your papers and certificates?"

"Of course."

I handed the sheaf of papers to Greenspon who turned a reading lamp on and peered at each one in turn, holding the sheets under the light.

"Well, these seem to be in order. While we're waiting, would you mind filling out an application form? While you're doing that, I'll take these papers into Mr. Samuelson. Take your time and I'll be right back."

I nodded, then read over the form and filled it out. Greenspon came back in leaving the door open.

"Mr. Samuelson will see you now."

I stood up and followed him down a corridor, where Greenspon rapped sharply on a door once, then entered another cluttered room. Samuelson sat behind a large desk with a telephone on either side. A cigar stub was pushed into his mouth and the odour of stale smoke permeated the air. Samuelson was obese, a fat man with wattles below his rounded chin, a mottled red complexion and thick purple lips.

"Mr. Samuelson. This is Mordecai Goldman."

Samuelson said nothing but gazed out at me under slitted eyes. He removed the stub from his lips and spat out a shred of tobacco. I stood before him, gazing calmly. The fat man cleared his throat.

"So, you want to work for me, is that it?"

"I need a job."

"Well, let me tell you, Mr. Goldman," he said with a sneer. "You're wasting your time. I don't hire Greenies like you."

"It was the Agency that sent me here."

"I know that and I'll talk to them. But I've got nothing for you. You can go now." And the fat man waved his hand dismissively.

"So it's like that, is it?"

"Yeah, that's right. Now scram."

I leaned over the desk and seized Samuelson by the collar, bunching it up so that the flesh bulged, and easily pulled him up out of the chair. Greenspon's jaw dropped. Samuelson began to gag.

"I fought and killed Nazis so fat bastards like you could be safe. You make me sick. I wouldn't take a job from you even if you had one, you fucking bastard."

I released the collar and Samuelson fell back into the chair that groaned under his weight.

"You," he sputtered. "You, get out of here…I'll call the police…I'll have you deported…"

"Good." I swept the phone into the fat man's lap. "You call the police and I'll tell them how you treat people. I'm an army veteran and I served in the American army too. What did you do except sit on your fat ass and bleed people for money? Go ahead and call."

I continued to stare at him until Samuelson looked away. Then I snatched my papers off Samuelson's desk and with a withering look at Greenspon, strode out of the room.

Outside in the street, I could feel my hands shaking. Someone touched me on the shoulder and I spun quickly. Greenspon. He swallowed hard.

"I wish to apologize, Mr. Goldman. That was inexcusable. He should never have spoken to you that way."

"I've killed for less."

"We're not at war anymore. I served too, you know. Infantry."

"So why do you work for that bastard?"

"I'm married to his niece and I'm well paid."

"Then I'm sorry for you." I lit up a cigarette.

"Listen, I've got to get back inside but there's another dealership about three blocks from here. Murchison's. Murchison's on Bay. They can probably use a man like you. I know the manager there, Jerry Waldman. Give him this note. Say I sent you." Greenspon quickly shoved a slip of paper into my hand. "I've got to go but I want to wish you good luck."

I narrowed my eyes, then nodded. "Thank you."

I put out my hand and Greenspon shook it. "Good luck to you," he called as he pushed back through the door.

I looked at the note, then dropped the cigarette on the ground and crushed it under my heel. I put the note in my pocket and began to walk north on Bay. Within the hour, I had a job as a mechanic. My starting pay was eighty-five cents an hour.

That evening, I returned home to tell Esther the news. She was excited and happy for me thinking how easy it all sounded that jobs could be had so quickly. I told her I'd take her out to celebrate. We went to a small, crowded delicatessen, Zak's, around the corner on Spadina near College Street. For twenty-five cents, you could have a bowl of chicken soup with matzoh balls and a corned beef sandwich with a pickle. Tea and a cookie came to five cents extra. I felt rich. I still had eight dollars in my pocket after the meal, enough for us to eat the whole week until I got my first pay cheque.

"And how did you spend your time?"

Esther dipped into the soup.

"I cleaned the apartment. It was very dusty and I listened to the radio and I took a bath. Then I went for a walk but it was cold and windy so I came back."

"Did you eat anything?"

"Oh yes. I made some tea and had some bread. It was fine."

"You don't eat enough," I replied, looking at her half-empty plate.

"I'm not terribly hungry. I don't have a big appetite like you." Then she pushed her plate toward me. "Don't let it go to waste, it would be a shame."

So I finished the second half of her sandwich while she watched me, her chin on her hands and smiled. When I finished, I dabbed at my lips with the paper napkin. All around us, patrons spoke in loud voices. The waitress was elderly. She limped. Her hair was a bright orange frizz. A bird's nest.

"So, darlings? Can I get you something else?" Esther looked at her.

"You know, I think I can do something with your hair," she said in Yiddish.

"What? Impossible." And the waitress made a face.

"No, it's true," Esther insisted.

"Darling, how long have you been in this country? Five minutes?"

Esther reddened. "Just a few days."

"Well, trust me. No one can do anything with this mop."

"I'd like to try."

I looked at her, mouth agape.

The waitress shrugged.

"You know what? If you could do something for me, then I've got plenty of friends who'd come too. We all need help. Okay, darling, what's your address?"

And as I watched in amazement, Esther made a date for the waitress, whose name was Sadie, to come over that Saturday to have her hair done. When the waitress looked at me, I just shrugged.

"Just the cheque, I think."

"Okay, there you go. Please come again." She put the bill down on the table. Meanwhile, other customers called for her. "All right. All right, already." She gave Esther a wink.

After she'd gone, I turned to her. "Do you know anything about this business?"

"A little. My Auntie Belle was a hairdresser and I used to spend time with her in her shop. Before the War, of course. It had been a good money earner for her."

"And you think you can do something about it?"

"I don't know but we must start somewhere." Esther chewed her lip a moment. "I'm going to need a few things."

"What things?"

"Combs and brushes, some creams and shampoos and scissors."

"How much?"

"I don't know. Perhaps five dollars."

"Five dollars. That's a lot of money. How much will you charge?"

"I don't know, perhaps thirty-five or fifty cents."

"And they'll pay?"

"Yes, I think so."

I felt in my pocket. I didn't have to take the tram to work. If I left earlier, I could walk it fairly easily. "Then let's go. The sooner the better."

Esther's face lit up and I saw how young and pretty she was, even in the garish light of the delicatessen. I saw something else too. Her spirit, her drive to make something of her life, of our lives, together.

Chapter 45

Sadie the waitress kept her promise and came to see Esther to have her hair done. She was so pleased with the results that she told her friends, other waitresses, family members and within a few weeks, Esther had a steady flow of customers.

"See," Sadie crowed. "I'll get a new husband any day now, just you watch."

When I came home from work, often there were women waiting in the living room or someone coming in or going out. Some of the women brought their children and the odd, occasional husband who cooled his heels listening to the radio or reading the newspaper. I felt pleased and annoyed at the same time. I didn't like coming home to strangers when I was tired and hungry after work, so Esther promised she would try and keep most of the appointments during the day while I was out. The Jewish community congregated in the College—Spadina—Bathurst corridor, many of them recent immigrants. They chatted away in Yiddish just like they used to in the old country. It brought back bittersweet memories for most of them. Esther took to serving coffee and cakes she baked herself. The neighbourhood women liked her. They enjoyed her youth and sweet nature but she was no pushover when it came to money and finances. It was Esther who opened the account at the bank and I dutifully handed over my pay cheque every week. The first week I made twenty-five dollars and it wasn't long before we put money aside.

I had been at Murchison's about six months and was pleased with the work and my new life in Canada. Summer had arrived and the days radiated warmth and bright sunshine. Esther and I went for walks after dinner, sometimes stopping for a coffee or a gelato at one of the Italian sidewalk cafes. The streets pulsed with life. People promenaded with their families and neighbours, talking, arguing, laughing. I felt a calm come over me, a feeling almost of serenity that I'd never known. I didn't fear for anything, wasn't angry or combative. Toronto was safe compared to the war-weary world I'd come from.

One morning, early in June, I had a customer's car up on the hoist. One of the springs had seized badly. I took a hammer and gave the spring a great whack. A tiny shard of metal splintered. I felt pain and my vision went dark. I felt something run down my face and as I fell backwards, I shouted. Within moments, I was surrounded by other mechanics who raised the alarm. The General Manager came running out of his office.

"My eye, my eye," I moaned.

"Let me through," said the General Manager, whose name was Hirshfield. He knelt down beside me and lifted my hand away from my face. He saw blood welling up beneath the eyelid and pouring down my face. "Better call an ambulance and make it snappy. He's got to get to hospital."

In the ambulance my mind raced, as I thought of Esther who knew nothing of what happened.

"My wife. I've got to call my wife."

"Don't worry, bud. There'll be plenty of time for that once we get you to the General."

"What General? General who?"

I heard a caustic laugh.

"He means the hospital. It's called The General, Toronto General, see?" said another voice and I smelled coffee and cigarettes. "Don't worry, buddy, once the doc has a look, you'll be right as rain, good as new." These expressions confused me. I chafed at the straps holding me to the gurney.

"Whoa there, fella. Take it easy now," said the first one. "You're a big strong guy, I can see that. We wouldn't want you breaking the straps now. You've got to keep still or you might hurt yourself even more. Don't worry, we're almost there and Joe's a good driver. He'll try not to hit anything on the way."

I felt the ambulance swerve then screech to a stop. I heard the snapping of the legs of the gurney and felt the contact with the ground as I rolled forward out of the back doors.

"Whaddya got?" said a female voice.

"Work injury. Splinter in the eye. Needs an ock dock."

"Okay, roll him into two," said the nurse.

Again, they moved and I smelled the antiseptic I associated with a hospital, the bleach and chloride odour, the starch and detergent.

"Okay big guy. We're going to shift you on to a bed." The straps came off and I felt pairs of arms tunnel underneath me. "One. Two. Three."

A chorus of grunts and groans as I was lifted, then shifted over. "Healthy specimen. Must weigh at least two hundred. Just our luck."

"All right boys," said the nurse. "You've done your job. It's our turn now."

I felt hot breath near my right ear. "Mr. Goldman? It is Mr. Goldman, isn't it?"

"Yes."

"The doctor will be down to see you shortly. In just a minute, I'm going to clean up your face. There's been a lot of blood. Is there anyone you'd like us to call?"

"My wife," I croaked. "Walnut four two four three four."

"All right. Won't be a minute."

And then I was left alone with sudden fear and panic. In a way, I had to laugh. Six years of war. Some of the fiercest fighting any soldier might see and nothing. Here, in a peaceful and prosperous country, I receive an injury. I worried now what would happen to us, how would we get along? My thoughts went round and round and I must have dozed off.

A hand gently shook me awake.

"Mr. Goldman? I'm Dr. Chesterton. Can you look at me with your good eye?" I opened my right eye and saw a hazy, shadowy figure in a white smock. He had dark hair, glasses and a trim little moustache. "Good. Do you feel any pain in your right eye?" I shook my head.

"I'm just going to shine a light in."

A bright light filled my vision and everything disappeared into it. Then, the light snapped off. "I'm going to look at your other eye now. I shall lift the lid. You might feel some pain but I have to take a look. Won't take a moment. Are you ready?"

I nodded. The light snapped back on. I closed the right eye. From the left, I felt more than saw the glare.

"Mr. Goldman, I'm going to use an eye dropper and shall be putting some solution just to clear the area a bit, all right?"

The doctor's voice was low and reassuring. I felt the wetness and drops rolling down my cheek. Then the light closed.

"Mr. Goldman. You have a tiny metal fragment that has lodged in the eye. It's right in the cornea, I'm afraid and it must come out. That requires an operation. I don't know how much damage has been done frankly and we won't know until afterward and we see how you recover. What do you think about the surgery? We must have your permission, of course."

"Let's go."

The doctor laughed.

"I like that. No hesitation. Umm, we'll wait for your wife to arrive. In the meantime, we'll get an operating room prepared. It shouldn't be long, all right?"

"That's fine, doctor. I trust you. You do what's necessary."

The doctor laughed again.

"Good. I wish all my patients were as forthright. I'll see you in a few moments then." And he patted me on the shoulder.

Esther was beside herself, crying, wiping at her eyes with the heel of her hand, nose running freely. I found myself comforting her.

"Don't worry, it'll be all right."

"But...but..."

"Is it the money? We'll pay. I'll be back to work soon. You'll see."

Esther nodded and pulled a handkerchief from her plastic handbag. "I had wished, I mean, I thought...everything was going so well."

"And everything is and will continue, you'll see. This doctor knows what he's doing."

Dr. Chesterton bustled back in.

"Ah good. You are Mrs. Goldman, then, I take it?" Esther nodded. "Very well, Mrs. Goldman. As I explained to your husband, he needs an operation. There's a nasty metal fragment in his eye you see, and it must be removed."

"And what will happen to the eye? Will he see?"

The doctor pursed his thin lips.

"I can't guarantee anything. There could be some loss of vision. We won't know until afterward." He turned to me. "Now Mr. Goldman, after the operation is over, you will be required to convalesce for at least four weeks. That's to ensure the eye heals properly. It means that you must lie immobilized for much of that time. You should be able to get up and go to the washroom and so on, but otherwise, it's flat on your back until the eye is healed."

"Four weeks. That's a long time."

"Yes," Chesterton agreed. "But it is absolutely necessary or the eye won't heal. There appears to be significant damage. We don't want you to lose your sight now, do we?"

"No," Esther answered and I laughed.

"My wife doesn't want to live with a blind man, you see. Someone who's dependent on her for everything."

"Well. You won't be. I can assure you." The doctor glanced at his watch. "Now then, I'm going to see about that operating room. It should be a few hours anyway. I'd advise you both to get a little rest. The operation itself shouldn't take more than an hour and then another hour or so in recovery. We won't put you to sleep but must freeze the entire area around the eye, otherwise you will feel a great deal of pain and there will be enough of that once you come out of it. All right, then? See you shortly." Doctor Chesterton bustled out.

"I like that fellow," I said.

"Does it hurt?"

"No. There's no pain."

"Well then…"

"What is it?"

"I was hoping for a better time…"

"Time for what? You're making no sense."

"To tell you something."

I became annoyed. "Tell me what? Speak up Esther."

She sniffed into her handkerchief. "That you will be a papa."

My good eye opened wide and began to tear. "It's true?"

Esther smiled through her tears. "Yes, it's true."

"That's wonderful news. Give me a kiss." She bent down to kiss me.

"But now, we have a child on the way and you're injured."

"Don't be so silly. It'll be fine. You'll see. We're blessed."

I lay in a convalescent ward flat on my back for four weeks. Every other day, Dr. Chesterton came in to check on the eye.

"Every day it's looking better, Mr. Goldman. How does it feel? Is there any pain?"

"No. No pain."

"Good. Once we remove the bandage permanently, we shall see how your vision responded to the operation. There was damage but it seems to be healing up rather nicely. I see no reason why you can't go back to work but I'd advise you to take care and always wear safety glasses from now on, okay?"

"I won't fight with you, Doctor. I've learned a valuable lesson."

The doctor smiled. "I'm sure you have. Not the best way to learn it though, is it? Right. I must be off on my rounds. I think you'll be able to go home at the end of this week. Then I want you to come back and see me a week Friday. If everything looks all right, I see no reason why you can't go back to work the following Monday. Is everything all right at home?"

"Yes, fine."

"I hear your wife is expecting."

"Yes."

"Your first?"

"Our first."

"My very best to you both. You're a strong fellow and I expect you'll be back on your feet in no time. It doesn't look like something like this would slow you down much."

"I work hard, Doctor. And my wife does too."

"I know. We're lucky to have you. The country, I mean. Many people wouldn't say that, of course but then they are small-minded. We are a nation of immigrants. I'm one myself, although you might not think so, coming from London. We need people who have strength and courage and fortitude to build this young country. I'm very glad I came here, despite the damned cold winters, and my wife feels the same way, I'm glad to say. It's been a wonderful experience for my children."

"How many children do you have?"

"Three. Two girls and a boy. They range in age from seven to twelve so you see I'm doing my bit to breed a race of young Canadians. And they are too. They ice skate and ski and have virtually lost their English accents. When my relatives visit, they can scarcely believe it. But the way of life isn't stifling here like it is in England and that's what I like about it. You know, a man of my age couldn't secure a position there like the one I've got here. Why, I'd have to wait ten years to become a department head in a major hospital. But here, they just look at you and what you have to offer and if you're capable then you can get the job on merit."

"Then I'm happy for you, Doctor."

"Well, I hope you feel the same way about this country."

"Believe me, where I came from this country is a paradise."

"Yes, well. I was overseas for two years. I was in London during the Blitz. It was pretty grim, wasn't it?"

"You may describe it that way. That would be a charitable view, Doctor. I saw thousands of men die around me during the winter of 1942, Russians and Germans both. Fortunately, more were Germans but if there was a hell on earth then that was it."

"Poor chap, you were really in the thick of it."

"Poor? I don't think so."

"Lucky then."

"Luck didn't have anything to do with it. I didn't think if I was going to live or die, I just thought about what I had to do. I was prepared to die. It didn't work out that way and I'm happy that it didn't. Except for my brother, my family is gone and now we must start again."

"Well, it sounds as if you're on the right track. I must be off now, but I'll be back before the end of the week then we'll see about getting you discharged."

That Friday, the bandage was finally removed and the doctor pronounced me fit to leave. Esther smiled happily now that I was coming home. I put on the clothes she had brought for me and packed the rest in a small kit bag. As we left and said our goodbyes while settling the bill, I didn't mention to anyone, least of all the doctor, that I couldn't see out of my left eye. I saw fuzzy outlines and gradations of light and that was all. But I never told a soul.

Chapter 46

Our son, Reuben, was born healthy and strong-lunged in March, 1949. The winter had broken early that year and I had been promoted to shop foreman at Murchison's on Bay. My pay rose to $1.20 an hour. Between what I and Esther earned with her hair appointments, we had managed to save $2000 and planned to use that as a down payment for a house. I liked the apartment and the area where we lived but now that the baby had arrived, it seemed too small for us suddenly.

"What happened to all the space?" I asked as I surveyed the living room full of baby clothes and blankets and squeeze toys. A playpen had been put into the corner so Esther could watch Reuben while she worked. He never lacked for attention. Every woman who came in couldn't resist picking him up and cuddling him and rocking him in their arms. Esther scheduled her appointments around his feeding times and that became easier as he grew older and didn't cry and fuss so much. From the beginning, he was a good-natured child who slept through the night and ate well. But the pregnancy had been difficult for Esther and the doctor said it was unlikely she'd conceive another child. This came as a terrible blow to her barely twenty-one, denied by nature. She had wanted a large family to make up for the loss both she and I suffered through the War.

"He is our precious child," she would say. "He is our diamond, our golden boy."

And that's the way Reuben was treated, as a very rare object never to be discovered on the face of the Earth again. Esther always felt a pang of concern when the other women picked up her child and held him in their arms, bounced him on a knee or hugged him to an ample bosom. She suppressed an urge to snatch him away but controlled herself not wanting to offend her customers and knowing that her family needed the money they brought in.

Now that I worked as shop foreman at Murchison's on Bay, they had given me the use of one of their cars, an Oldsmobile that had been in the showroom the year before. Esther and I, with the baby in our arms, drove around the city looking at neighbourhoods we liked and watched for the "for sale" signs.

Finally, I found something and took Esther to see it. The house stood two storeys on a nice wide lot on a leafy and quiet street. Arnprior Street. The house had been built by the owner himself, an English plumber who had been very fussy. It was set back some twenty feet from the street and had a lovely backyard where the owner's wife had planted roses and gladioli. I saw the house had been kept immaculately. Each of the three bedrooms, the kitchen, dining room and basement, was spotless. The hardwood floors and banisters gleamed. The owner wanted $13,000. His wife served us tea in the kitchen. The plumber, now retired, had bought a small farm in the country.

"I've had three offers," said the plumber. "But they've all been from Jews and I don't like Jews," he said appraising Esther's blond hair, fair skin and crystal-blue eyes.

I bit my lip.

"I can only offer $11,000," I said as Esther gripped my hand under the table.

"That's fine," said the plumber. "You're a working man, I can tell by your hands. A big, strong fellow with a pretty young wife. This place is perfect for you. Drink up and then I'll show you around."

"Good," I said through clenched teeth.

Within the week, the plumber had his deposit. Five weeks later, we moved in. I wrote Simmy in Israel to tell him of the good news and that if he should ever want to visit or better yet, emigrate, he had a place to stay. I didn't often hear from my brother.

He'd joined the Haganah as soon as he landed in Palestine in 1946 and fought both the British and the Arabs. And now that the War of Independence had ended, he worked on a kibbutz transforming the desert into the Garden of Eden. Or so he implied, albeit not happily. The work sounded dull and the hours long and hard. Simmy preferred to be where the action was. His revolutionary blood demanded it. Unfortunately, he wasn't disciplined enough to join the military, the fledgling Israeli army that had sprung up. Many of the officers had fought with the British in the War and had excellent training. Some too, were even Americans and a few Canadians. But Simmy didn't respond to spit and polish. He wanted action but his superiors considered him reckless and one who endangered the lives of others needlessly. At the kibbutz, he washed out and ended up back where he started, just as he had been in Hamburg. Loading and unloading trucks on the docks in Haifa. They wouldn't even trust him to drive one of their precious trucks, he complained in a letter to me.

Esther hadn't yet lost the fullness from her pregnancy even though Reuben was now two months old, her breasts and hips had filled out. I liked this aspect of her and said so. She'd just blush and push me away while she breastfed the baby.

I went to the bank to deposit my pay cheque during lunch break each payday. One day, about six months after Esther and I moved into the house, the other men asked me to deposit their cheques too. I said, sure, no problem. I took the envelope with the pay cheques. One of the stubs fell out on the floor. I picked it up and couldn't help noticing that the hourly rate was $1.75 while I, the foreman, was being paid $1.20 an hour. How come? I asked myself, why I, who supervised their work, should make less? I went to the general manager, Jerry Waldman, the man who hired me.

"Yes, Mordecai? What is it?" Waldman was a thin man who smoked incessantly. He had a nervous smile and tired eyes.

"How come I'm making less than the other mechanics? I'm the foreman and they're making more than me? Why?"

Waldman swallowed hard and took a nervous drag on his cigarette.

"Listen Mordecai. You know I don't make the rules around here. I don't think it's fair either but it's Murchison, those are his rules so you'll have to talk to him."

"Okay. Let's go."

Waldman didn't want to have anything to do with it but reluctantly, he stood up from the desk, sighed audibly and then opened the door. With me behind him, he walked down the short corridor to Murchison's office and knocked. There was a grunt and Waldman went in.

"Mr. Murchison?"

"Yes?"

He had a well-modulated voice, surprising for such a diminutive man. Murchison didn't glance up from the papers he read.

"Sorry to disturb you but Mordecai here would like to speak to you."

Murchison glanced up and took in the glare coming his way.

"What can I do for you Goldman?"

I stepped forward brandishing the pay cheque.

"Are you happy with my work?"

"Yes."

"You think I'm doing a good job for you?"

"Yes."

"Good enough that you promoted me to foreman?"

"Yes."

"Then why do you pay me less than the others?"

Murchison may have been a small man with thin hair plastered to his scalp and combed over, but he didn't lack in forthrightness. He hadn't been in business for over twenty years without having to be tough, even ruthless.

"I'll give it to you straight, Goldman. You're a good man and work hard but you're not a citizen, see. You're an immigrant and I don't pay immigrants the same as I pay native-born Canadians. It's as simple as that. Take it or leave it."

"So I'm not as good as a Canadian..."

"I didn't say that."

I placed my palms flat on the desk and leaned in toward Murchison until I was inches from his face.

"That is what you're saying. I'm not good enough because I was born somewhere else."

"Don't threaten me," Murchison said.

"I'm not threatening you, Murchison. If I was, believe me you'd know it. Is that what you want me to do?"

Murchison glared at me. "You're fired. Now get out."

"I'm not fired. I quit, you sonofabitch."

I stormed out of the office and gathered together my tools. Then I cleaned out my locker. Jerry Waldman showed up at my side.

"That was pretty harsh," he said.

I turned to him.

"Harsh? No one tells me that I'm not good enough when I'm doing my own work and checking every other sonofabitch who works here too."

Waldman swallowed hard, then pulled an envelope out of his jacket pocket.

"You've still got some pay owing."

"Keep it."

"But it's yours."

"I don't want that bastard's money. Give it to the widows and the orphans, I don't care."

I resumed cleaning out the locker. After I had all my things piled in a box, I left the dealership, walked two blocks further up on Bay Street to Midtown Motors. I went in and applied for a job and started working right away. My starting salary was $200 a week, not including overtime.

Esther shook her head and smiled sadly when she heard the news. Reuben played on the floor in front of them.

"What shall we do with you, Mordecai? Your temper will get you in trouble one day." Then she gazed at her little boy who chewed on a block.

"No, darling, take that out of your mouth, it is dirty." And she took it away. Reuben began to wail at his loss. I went over and picked the child up.

"You're mean to him."

I placed the baby on my lap and bumped him on my knees until the child subsided.

Esther watched me with an amused look.

"I wonder who is the child."

"What do you mean?" My face flushed with anger.

"You know what I mean. Come to the table. Your dinner is ready. The baby and I have eaten already."

I handed her the baby and went to sit down.

"I am making $200 a week. Soon, we'll have enough saved to buy a car. What do you think of that?"

"I think it's wonderful but don't expect me to learn to drive it."

"Why not? You should learn to drive a car."

"I don't want to."

"Are you afraid?"

"No. I don't think I'll need it."

"And how will you carry the groceries and push the buggy at the same time? With a car, it's easy."

"I'll make it easy too. You're going to do the shopping with the car or we'll do it together, that's all."

"That's silly. You'll need it one day."

"I'll always have you to drive me."

"Don't be silly. I won't be around forever. Don't forget I'm twelve years older than you."

"I haven't forgotten," she replied in a coquettish tone. "I married a real man."

Esther had made stew with potatoes and a small salad. I dug in. "You're a lucky woman. That's what I think."

Esther sat opposite me with the child over her shoulder. "Am I? You're very confident."

"I know."

"Perhaps I'll agree with you. This time." And she laughed.

"You make fun of me," I said, forking some stew into my mouth.

"Only a little."

"That's all right then. There aren't many men who'd allow such things."

Esther opened her eyes wide. "This is why I am such a lucky woman, no?"

I looked at her and then at the child.

"If he'll let us, perhaps we'll go to bed early tonight."

"We shall see, Mr. Goldman. You're not the boss of this house anymore. It's your son. We do his bidding now."

I reached out and touched the child's soft head and stroked his silky hair.

"I know, thank God."

I resumed eating, and watched mother and son together as if it was the most entrancing scene in the known world.

Chapter 47

Reuben walked at ten months and spoke at fifteen.

"He's so clever," Esther said.

I worked long hours and saw little of my family during the week. The boy was often in bed by the time I came home. I usually worked a half-day on Saturday. My hands acquired calluses, split nails and grime embedded deep into the grooves of my fingers.

"It's such dirty work," Esther said.

"It's honest work," I replied.

"Yes, I know." She looked up from her sewing. "But it's still dirty."

At Midtown Motors, employees could get a good discount on a car if purchased through the dealership. Finally, I decided I had enough money and picked out an Oldsmobile that I liked. Normally, it would have cost me $3500 but with the employee plan, I paid just $3000. When I drove the car home, it looked shiny and clean and as I pulled into the driveway, I beeped the horn. Esther and little Reuben bolted out the front door to see it. I switched off the engine and stepped out proudly.

"What do you think?" I asked.

Esther ran her hands down the length of the exterior as Reuben imitated her, running his tiny finger along the wheel wells and the fender.

Apart from loving cars and machines, the vehicle gave me a sense of independence and of means. I'd been careful with money and saved assiduously. Anything that could be fixed or repaired, I first attempted myself before paying anyone else to do it. In the evenings and weekends, I'd take in some work at home. If a neighbour needed a minor repair done to his car or someone to look at a toilet or washing machine, I'd do it. If I couldn't fix it, then I wouldn't charge for my time. This kept me busy, on top of the regular work I did. Before I could blink, Reuben had started school and from the very first day, he loved it. He loved to learn and was naturally a helpful child. His teachers were so impressed with his eagerness and intelligence.

"Why, he's reading already," said his kindergarten teacher, Miss Brooks. "Most of the children can't sound out the alphabet. What have you been doing with him?"

Esther shrugged. "Nothing. He does this all on his own."

"Well, he is very, very bright, Mrs. and Mr. Goldman."

On my way to work each day, I took notice of the surroundings. I'd drive down Bathurst Street to Dupont Avenue and from there head east to Bay Street and to the dealership. I left home early, usually around six in the morning so the traffic remained light. I'd noticed a group of small apartment buildings, quadplexes, set off the street, well back from the noise of traffic and pedestrian activity. A For Sale sign had been staked out in front of one of the buildings. I pulled the car over to the side and wrote the phone number down, then continued on to work. During my lunch break that day, I asked the General Manager if I could use the phone in his office, then dialed the number that was on the sign. An elderly woman answered the phone.

"Hello?" she bawled.

"Hello, missus," I said. "I am calling about the For Sale sign on the property on Bathurst Street?"

"Yes, what about it?"

"Well, I'm interested in finding out about it. Can you help me?"

"Just a second."

I heard her put the phone down and then yell.

"Max. Max. Come to the phone. Someone wants to talk about the apartment building. Come. Max. Can you hear me?"

I thought everyone up and down Bay Street would hear her. I heard some wheezing, then a muffled exchange of words. A gruff voice came on the line.

"Hello? I can help you?"

"Yes. I'm calling about the building."

"What about it?"

"Is it still for sale?"

"Of course it's for sale. You saw the sign, didn't you?"

"That's why I'm calling. I'd like to talk about it. I'm working right now, but I can come at six o'clock."

"Six o'clock? Okay. I'll meet you at the building. I'll be out front. What's your name please?"

"Goldman. Mordecai Goldman. And yours?"

"Diamond. Max Diamond."

"Good, Mr. Diamond, I'll see you there at six, okay?"

"Okay. Hey listen, you got a phone number in case I can't make it for some reason?"

I gave him the number at the dealership.

"Midtown Motors? You sell cars?"

"I'm a mechanic, the foreman."

"I see. That's good. I'll see you at six." Max Diamond hung up the phone.

I smiled to myself as I replaced the receiver.

At six o'clock, I drove up Bathurst Street and turned in the driveway of number sixteen forty-one. I spotted a new Cadillac parked and a man asleep behind the wheel. I got out of the car and tapped on the window. The man started, then brought his head up, looked at me and then rolled down the window.

"You Goldman?"

"That's right."

Max Diamond smiled and showed a set of gold teeth.

"I fell asleep waiting. Come on, I'll show you the building, okay?"

Diamond got out of the car. He stood short and stocky with close-cropped white hair and a moustache. He walked with a pronounced limp.

"I got kicked by a horse when I was a kid. Broke my leg and it never healed. That's how I stayed out of the Tsar's army in the old country." And he looked me up and down for a moment.

"Come, it's this way."

He limped around the side to the main entrance and opened the door.

"Each of these buildings has four apartments. They're only ten years old and believe me they're in very good shape. I should know, I built them myself. Everything is practically brand new. These units are all rented and bring in a very nice income, I might add."

"How much, if you don't mind me asking?"

Max Diamond stopped and looked at him before answering.

"You're serious about buying this building?"

"Yes."

"And I should believe you?"

"Of course."

"Are you married, Mr. Goldman?"

"Yes."

"Have you discussed this with your wife?"

"No, not yet."

"Then, believe me, you aren't serious until you talk with her."

"How much did you say the income was?"

"I didn't say."

"Okay, I'm asking you. How much?"

"Six hundred dollars."

I whistled.

"Every month?"

"That's right. Every month. And all of my tenants pay on time. I've never had any trouble. Come, I'll show you the boiler for the hot water and the furnace."

We descended to the basement and went into the boiler room. I noticed that the area seemed clean and well-maintained. The boiler looked new and the furnace did too.

Max screwed up his face into a smile.

"Nice, hah? Wait until you see the apartments. They're bigger than most houses, let me tell you." Then he turned to me. "You said you were a mechanic?"

"That's right."

"How much do you make?"

"Two hundred dollars a week and extra if I work overtime."

"That's not bad." Max looked upward. "Come, we'll look at the apartments. Mrs. Singer is out now so I can show you her place."

Mrs. Singer wasn't the neatest housekeeper. There were clothes piled on the chesterfield and dirty dishes in the sink but I could see clearly the apartments were spacious and modern. Each unit had three bedrooms, an eat-in kitchen, a separate den and the master bedroom had its own bathroom and a walk-in closet plus a built-in rack for shoes.

"What do you think?" asked Max.

I didn't want to look too impressed. "It's not bad," I admitted.

Max chuckled. "I thought so."

"Why are you selling, if you don't mind my asking?"

Max sighed and pulled over one of Mrs. Singer's kitchen chairs and sat down heavily. "This was my first apartment building after I came from the old country. Mainly, I built houses but this building is special to me and I want to make sure it goes to the right person. My wife and I have no children. We have not been blessed in that way. I have a partner but..." and he shrugged, "...like me he is getting older and wants to spend more time in Florida. His children aren't interested in the business, just in taking the money from it. I will sell all the buildings at the right time. Now, I start with one and see how it goes. We have friends in Miami and my wife doesn't like the winters anymore. It is too cold and reminds her of the old country. Miami is warm. You don't need a heavy overcoat or galoshes. It's a paradise and I promised her that we would live there. You're a young man. How old are you?"

"Thirty-six."

"You see? I told you. I can see you know how to look after yourself. You have a young family and don't look like you're afraid of hard work, Mr. Goldman. I have had other inquiries about this place, I can tell you."

"And if you don't mind me asking Mr. Diamond, what's the price you want for this building?"

"Twenty-five thousand dollars."

I let out a low whistle. Twenty-five thousand dollars was a fortune but as I calculated quickly in my head $600 a month should cover the cost of a mortgage.

"That's a lot of money, Mr. Diamond."

Diamond shrugged again. "It is and it isn't," he replied.

I walked through the open kitchen doorway into the spacious living room. It reminded me of the living room of our home in Krasnowicz. Before me stood a bank of windows that looked out on to Bathurst Street. I could see the cars making their way over the rise and down again, people out walking the streets. It was a warm and lovely day. "This apartment feels like a good place to live," I said.

"Of course it's good," replied Diamond coming up behind him. "All of my families in all of the buildings are very happy here. What did you think?"

"Do you have all the bills, Mr. Diamond, so I can take a look?"

"They're at my house. You'll have to come and take a look there. I didn't bring anything with me because I didn't know if you were serious or not. If you're serious there is time to look later. I think that maybe you are serious?"

"I take everything seriously."

"Of course," Diamond nodded his white head. "Doesn't everybody?"

"When can I take a look?"

"Come to my house on Sunday morning. I'll give you the address. By then you'll talk to your wife and see what she thinks and also you can talk to your man at the bank too. Unless you are sitting on that much money?"

I laughed at such a notion. "I sit on nothing. I work for everything I get."

Diamond poked a finger at me. "You're a greenie like me. These Canadians, the ones born here, they're different. They don't know hardship, let me tell you. I was up at five in the morning when I was a boy, working in the fields until I went to school. Right after school I came home and went back to work. These children, these Canadians, have a life that is good, let me tell you." He wrote out the address on a slip of paper and fixed a date for ten o'clock that Sunday morning. Outside, we shook hands and Diamond got into his Cadillac, while I walked to my parked car, thinking hard.

That evening I told Esther of my plans.

"I want to be my own boss," I told her.

"But the money?"

"We'll borrow against the house. "

"But what if it all goes wrong? We'll be out in the street."

"Then we'll start again. Are you afraid after all that has happened to you? This is nothing. You, who were surrounded by SS officers and your life in danger at every moment. We'll be fine."

"I don't want to have any more danger. There's the child to think of."

"We shall always be there to protect him and he'll grow up well. Esther," I took her slim, fine hands in mine, "This city is growing. There's money here and people will need places to live. This building is in a good location and I can raise the rents if costs go up. I'll know better when I look at the bills for water, heating and taxes and so on."

"But who will take care of this building?"

"I will," I replied with a shocked look.

"But you work so hard already, Mordecai. Reuben never sees you. A boy needs his father."

"I'll bring him with me. He'll be my helper and I'll teach him things too."

Esther put her hand on my bicep. "I need to see you too."

I looked at her.

"Do I ignore you? You're my best girlfriend. There's only you and the child. We have no one else. I'm doing this for us. You'll see, it's the right thing to do."

Esther looked at my face, probingly.

"See what the man at the bank says. But you must listen to me. I'll help you and keep the books and look after the money, okay?"

I embraced her.

The man at the bank seemed skeptical at first but I impressed him with my confidence and work ethic. It didn't hurt that the fellow was an army veteran and listened avidly as I described my wartime experiences.

"Mr. Goldman," he said. "We'll loan you the money, but you've got to get this fellow to drop his price because I can't loan you the full amount. Now the government does have a program that guarantees such loans for veterans and the fact that you served in the American forces is very much in your favour, so is your rank. I only made lieutenant myself so in a way you outrank me." The fellow gave a laugh then offered me a cigarette. We shook hands.

I went back to Max Diamond and offered him $21,000 for the building. Max listened, cocked his head, rolled his eyes and then the haggling began. Finally, we settled on a strange number that seemed to satisfy us both: $22,222 was the purchase price. Afterward, Max put out a hand and said, "Mazel tov, you've bought yourself a building and you won't be sorry. Me, I'm sorry but now I'll have some peace in my life from my wife. Who knows, in a couple of years, we can talk about the other buildings but we'll see how things go, yeah?"

I grinned. "Sure."

Then Max poured us each a shot of vodka and we drank.

"*L'chaim.*"

I didn't feel any different than before now that I had become a property owner and in business for myself. When I got up in the morning, I was still a mechanic. And now it meant that I worked even longer hours. I met all of the tenants and looked over the leases, which seemed to be in order. I went over all of the bills and maintenance records. Max passed on the name of the service people he used to cut the grass and shovel out the driveway, but I decided to dispense with all of that and took on those tasks myself to save money. It was costing close to $75 a month for those extras. That money could go right into my pocket.

On the weekends, Reuben helped as best he could and in this way, I got to know my son. Esther still took in customers to do their hair and branched out into nails and make-up. She read all of the magazines and tried out all of the latest styles for her clientele. The women liked to come and forget their families and troubles for a while and enjoy the company of other women. Esther didn't gossip, nor did she talk much. They could confide in her knowing it would go no farther.

I felt too tired to listen when I dragged myself in at the end of the day and didn't care for the nattering of women. I'd eat dinner, listen to the radio and then go to bed, only to begin again the next day. On a rare Sunday, we'd all go for a drive in the country or for a dinner downtown. We'd dress up and little Reuben looked so serious in his white shirt and bow tie and grey short pants. We weren't rich but we had become comfortable. I worked hard but it had been worth the effort. Bit by bit, I began to relax into this life. I thought about those early days at home with Mama and Papa, Simmy and Katya. I could now provide for Reuben and Esther like Papa did for us. But I would never be his equal in so many ways.

Two years later, Max Diamond came to see me at home.

"I want to sell another building, Mordecai. Are you interested?"

I looked at him. We sat at the kitchen table drinking tea Russian style with a slice of lemon and a sugar cube between the front teeth.

"Only one?"

"You want the other two as well?"

"Depends on the price."

"You can afford this?"

I smiled, then took a sip of tea.

"It depends on the price, Max. The building has been doing well. If the other three do as well then it should be okay, I think."

Just then, Reuben, who was now seven, came into the kitchen and climbed on to my lap.

"Hello young man," Max said.

"Hello," Reuben replied. "What are you talking about?"

"Business," said Max.

"What sort of business?"

"Well, your father wants to buy my apartment buildings."

"Will you give him a good price?" the little boy asked seriously.

Max's eyes widened, then he guffawed, which quickly turned into an elongated wheeze.

"He's very clever. What a clever boy." He sipped at the tea. "Of course I will give your father a good price."

So with Reuben sitting on my lap, Max and I haggled until the price was decided. We shook hands at the door.

"You have made my wife very happy," Max said. "Now there is no reason for us to come back in the winter anymore."

"And you?" I asked him.

Max shrugged. "I'll find something to do. I go to the dog races and the jai alai. I play shuffleboard and bridge. You know, it's very quiet. Nothing exciting. And the weather is good for you. No snow or heavy galoshes and coats to wear. Complaints? I've got no complaints."

Reuben stood at my side and Max ruffled the boy's hair.

"Such a clever boy. You're lucky, Goldman. I wish I had children but it wasn't to be. I'll have the papers ready for you in a couple of days."

Chapter 48

When I told Esther about the opportunity, she didn't respond as I thought she would. "Who's going to do the work? With one building you're working all of the time."

"I could quit my job…"

"No, I don't want you to do that. Just in case."

"In case what?"

"In case something happens. In case it doesn't work out. You're making good money now and we need to save for Reuben's education."

Esther had put Reuben in the bath and he sputtered and spat as she washed his face.

"Hush darling, it's so you will be clean."

"I'm thinking," I said. "My brother Simmy."

"Simmy?"

"He isn't happy in Israel. What's he doing? Loading and unloading trucks. The Haganah have no use for him. I'm thinking he can help me with the buildings. He can do my work while I'm away."

Esther wasn't sure. "You think he'll do it?"

"I can ask."

Later that evening, I wrote my brother a letter outlining the proposition to him. I'd sponsor him and he could have a room in my house until he got settled on his own. I figured that my brother could make between $150 to $200 a week helping me with the buildings.

Ten days later, Simmy wrote me back saying that he was coming and couldn't wait to get out of Israel, that his prayers had been answered. It would take about two months to get the necessary papers and then Simmy could leave.

On October 15, 1955, Simmy stepped off an El Al airliner at Malton airport. I waited for him. We hadn't seen each other in nine years. Simmy was now thirty-four. He looked deeply tanned and had filled out. He wore his dark hair long but I recognized the wire-rimmed glasses perched on his nose. I embraced him in a bone-crunching bear hug.

"Let me go you animal," Simmy laughed. He stood back and appraised. "Canada has been good to you," he pronounced.

"I can't complain and I don't think you will either," I replied. "What'd you do with my motorcycle?"

Simmy laughed. "Don't worry, big brother. It was put to good use. And the machine guns too. It's good to be here. I was going crazy in that place."

I clapped my brother on the shoulder.

"Come on. I'll treat you to a coffee before we go home."

"Home has a good sound to it."

I led the way to the car. Simmy whistled when he saw it.

"This is yours?"

"Of course."

"Such a vehicle would cost many fortunes in Israel."

"I know."

I opened the driver's door and climbed in. We drove to Bergman's Delicatessen on Bathurst Street near Lawrence. Simmy had a corned beef on rye with a dill pickle while I just sipped a coffee.

"It was a long flight," Simmy said ruefully. "And there wasn't much to eat."

"You want dessert? Go ahead. Have fun."

Simmy ordered apple strudel and coffee. When the coffee arrived, he stirred in cream and sugar thoughtfully. "So you're a big businessman now?"

"No. I'm still a mechanic but I now own a few properties and they need to be looked after properly. I can't do this myself and still work at the car dealership. Esther doesn't want me to quit my job because the money is good. When there was just one building, it was okay but now with four, I can't do it. I want to spend some time with my family. I need to see Reuben growing up. It's happening too quickly."

"And how is my nephew?"

"He's wonderful. And he does very well in school. The teachers there want to accelerate him."

"What's that?"

"Put him ahead." And then I paused. "You remember? Just like Katya. She was good in school and always ahead of herself."

Simmy grimaced and stared into his cup.

"I remember. That was the only good thing about living in Israel. Every day we existed, it was like we were spitting in the face of the Nazis. But now, it's the Arabs. You know, there will be war soon. I almost didn't get out. Everyone was getting called up. Believe me, the world will be shocked when it happens. But I don't have the stomach for it anymore. It was bad enough in '48."

He took a sip of coffee.

"You know, it was like the war in Europe had continued. The hatred and anger. I had a girl, you know. She was killed. They raped her first and then cut her breasts off..." The corners of Simmy's mouth trembled.

"That was it for me. I never wanted to get involved again after that. When it was over, I swore I had enough. They didn't like that attitude there. It wasn't patriotic. Everything has gotten so political now. And that's why I was banished. I couldn't get a permanent position in the military even though I had been decorated twice. They called me insolent. Ah well, perhaps I was – I drank too much and chased women just like half of the General Staff but for them it was okay."

He rapped his knuckles sharply on the table and some of the other patrons looked over at this tall, darkly handsome foreigner. He took out a packet of cigarettes and shook one out. I offered him my lighter and we both lit up.

"It's peaceful here," I said. "You only have to worry about making a living and that's it. The rest is easy."

Simmy folded his hands together, the cigarette dangling from his lip, his eyes half-closed.

"Sounds good to me, big brother." Then he rubbed his hands together, drained the coffee in his cup and said, "Let's go meet the family, eh?"

Esther hung back shyly when we walked into the house but little Reuben, who was now eight, was less restrained. He launched himself into his uncle's arms, who raised him up to the ceiling and laughed. Reuben clung to his neck while Simmy kissed Esther on the cheek and she smiled demurely.

"Now we're a complete family again," I said.

"I've made a special dinner," said Esther. "Reuben, why don't you show Uncle Simmy his room and then you can come down and eat."

"Great idea," Reuben screeched. He tugged at Simmy's hand. "Come on, I'll show you where it is."

Simmy laughed. I picked up my brother's suitcase and began climbing the steps. My son and brother followed closely.

"This is a nice house, Mordecai. It's quite large, no?"

"It's big enough for four people," I replied. "It shouldn't be too cramped."

"Are you mad?" Simmy exclaimed. "I lived with eight people in a small apartment in Jerusalem. This is a palace."

"Welcome to my palace." I placed a hand on Reuben's behind to help him negotiate the stairs. "Go on, little one."

Reuben turned on me indignantly. "I'm not little and please stop saying that, Papa."

"You're right. You're practically a man, halfway to being grown up. When I was your age, I had a lot of responsibilities."

We made the second floor landing and Reuben led us to the room Esther had prepared for Simmy. The room had a southern exposure and two big windows. The light had faded but the room still looked bright enough without turning on any of the lamps.

"What do you think?" I asked.

"Do you like it?" Reuben yelled.

Simmy laughed again, unable to articulate anything for a moment, then pushed his spectacles up the bridge of his nose.

"It's a wonderful room and I'm sure I'll be very happy here."

At dinner that evening, Reuben kept pestering Simmy with questions about Israel.

"Is it true that the Arabs ride camels and the temperature in the desert is one hundred and fifty degrees and that everybody carries a gun?"

"Reuben," said Esther. "Leave your uncle alone. He's trying to eat his dinner. Give him a second's rest."

"I don't mind," Simmy replied. "Yes, the Arabs ride camels, some of them. But many drive lorries and jeeps and cars too. The temperature in the desert gets very hot during the day, perhaps one hundred degrees but then it's cold at night, sometimes dropping close to zero. And no, not everybody carries guns, only if you're in the army. The guns must be locked up properly in the barracks. Occasionally, you might be allowed to take a gun home but it's rare. A gun could go off. We don't want anyone getting shot by accident, do we?"

"What did you do with your gun?"

"I gave it back. It didn't belong to me."

Reuben looked disappointed, his mouth drooped.

"You mean you didn't bring it with you?"

"Don't be silly," said Esther. "Why would you need a gun in Canada?"

"Your mother is right. Canada is a peaceful country. There is no war, no hostile neighbours to worry about."

"But the police carry guns," insisted Reuben.

"They carry guns to protect us and themselves from criminals but there's not much to be concerned about," I said. "You can watch a little television after supper, then it's time for bed. You have school tomorrow."

Reuben made a face but nodded his reluctant assent. When he was tucked into bed Simmy and I sat at the kitchen table drinking tea. Esther came into the room and sat down.

"He's asleep?" She nodded.

"Excellent," I said. "He has a great deal of energy. It's like a tap you can't turn off."

"He's a good boy," said Simmy. He looked around the kitchen until his gaze settled on Esther. "You've done well here, Mordecai. Krasnowicz seems very far away."

"It is and it isn't. I think about it all the time. Our parents. Katya and Alex and the child. Our uncles and aunts and cousins, goddammit. How can I not think about it? Now they're talking about compensation from the German government. I spit on it. For them to give you money, you must sign a piece of paper, *Wieder Gut Machen*. This piece of paper takes away the terrible wrongs they have done? Never. I shall never take any blood money from them." And I banged my thick fist down on the table.

"All right, Mordecai. You'll wake Reuben." Esther stroked my forearm. "He often gets like this," she said to Simmy.

"He's always been angry, even as a young boy," Simmy said and then he told her the story how, as a twelve year old, I hit the farmer across the head with a two by four and laid him out cold. Esther put her hand to her mouth and then stared at me.

"You did this?"

I shrugged and looked down at my hands.

"They were cheating us. Someone had to teach them a lesson. They never cheated us again I can tell you."

Simmy stirred his tea silently.

Chapter 49

Simmy settled into his new routine, and I started to drop him off at the buildings at six-thirty in the morning before going off to the dealership. Simmy soon discovered that it was far too early to do anything in any of the buildings as most of the tenants were still asleep. Rather, he found a coffee shop just up Bathurst Street a few blocks and he would sit there and drink coffee, smoke cigarettes and read the paper before heading back down to begin his working day. At five o'clock, I'd come back and help him with anything that needed doing or more often, pick him up to take him home.

It wasn't arduous work and in some ways, Simmy found it to be rather pleasant. He came to know the tenants quite well, even if at first they seemed disconcerted by his dark looks and intensity. I treated him fairly and paid him a decent wage, more than he would make otherwise. Quickly, his bank account accumulated money as his expenses were few.

One tenant in particular, he told me, he'd found more than interesting. A young divorcee who worked as a secretary in a law firm. Her name was Rachel Green. She had shoulder-length brown hair, grey eyes and a lithe figure. When she came out of her apartment, he could smell her perfume and hear the silky swish of her underclothes as she walked down the hall to descend the stairs. Simmy's hungry eyes followed each supple movement. In the mornings, he mopped the floor outside her door when she exited her apartment. They greeted each other.

"Good morning Mr. Goldman, how are you?"

"I am well, Mrs. Green, and you?"

"Very well, thank you."

She'd give him a lingering look and a hint of a smile before catching her bus.

"Well, ask her out then," I said.

Simmy glowered. "I can't."

"Why?"

"Because she works in an office, Mordecai and I am just a menial worker."

"What do you mean? You think I don't pay you enough?"

"It isn't the money."

"Then what?"

We were in the car driving back to the house. "It's my position." Simmy looked at me. "I want to be a partner with you. I want to have something too."

"But how will you afford it?"

"I'll use the money I make."

"You mean, you'll pay me with the money I already give to you?"

"Yes. I have one thousand and five hundred dollars saved already. I just need a few dollars to live and this way I can put some toward buying in to the business."

Simmy's ambition surprised me but I understood his need to get on.

"Okay. I'll talk with Esther and see what she says." And then I paused. "You don't think Mrs. Green will fuck you unless you're a partner in the business?"

Simmy smiled. "I didn't say that."

I glanced at him while watching for the traffic, shook my head and laughed.

Simmy took Rachel Green out the next Saturday evening. I let him borrow the car. It didn't take long before Simmy spent more time at her apartment than at home. Days passed and I rarely saw my brother. Each day, I stopped by the buildings and made sure everything was taken care of and I never found anything out of place; the grass had been cut, the halls and stairs cleaned, the furnace checked and I received only the rare phone call about minor problems in the units.

Until one evening when Simmy burst in on us during dinner. Immediately, Reuben rushed over and threw his arms around him. Laughing, Simmy picked the boy up and tossed him in the air. Esther almost had a heart attack.

"Rachel and I are getting married," he cried.

I stood up and looked at my brother sternly, then spread my arms out wide.

"Mazel tov, little brother."

The wedding was modest, attended by a few of the friends we'd made since we moved to Canada nine years earlier. Rachel's parents and younger brother came. The Canadian-born Greens wanted their daughter to marry a doctor, so didn't approve. But then, Rachel had married a doctor the first time and he had turned out to be an alcoholic who beat her. To them, Simmy was an exotic, a greenie. He spoke with an accent. He had served in the Haganah. These things made them suspicious of him.

Rachel and Simmy decided they would live in her apartment and as a gesture, I told them that I'd forgo the rent. They'd save one hundred and fifty dollars a month. We had also decided to allow Simmy to buy into the ownership of the buildings. Rachel had about $10,000 in savings and money from her divorce settlement. This helped secure the partnership. We had more than enough for the two families. We all understood that, some day, when it came to retire, this would be our nest egg, our security for the future.

I worked hard but was pleased that I prospered. Hard work never fazed me. Reuben, now ten, excelled in school and seemed popular with his schoolmates. On the weekends, in the summertime, I took him down to Sunnyside pool with a view of the lake. There, we'd spend the day, lying in the sun and swimming. In the winter months, I taught my son figure skating and cross-country skiing, even snow shoeing. Esther rarely participated in these events. She felt that the time should be special between her two men, that we didn't have the opportunity to spend as much time together as we should because I worked so hard. She didn't mind having the extra time to herself, which she scheduled around her hair and make-up clients.

In the house, she'd converted one of the bedrooms into her work area. She had two chairs and mirrors and lights set up. I'd installed everything for her. To my surprise and great pride, Esther's business also flourished. She had steady customers, many had been coming since she started. She expanded into other areas of hairdressing that I didn't understand, manicures, pedicures, waxes and so on. Her rates went up modestly but steadily as her customers too had become established in Canada and began to prosper. Things got so busy that she hired two assistants, one to handle the bookings and help with the paperwork and the other to help with the hairdressing itself. Her customers seemed very loyal. They just liked her and her quiet manner. And that kept them coming back. She'd listen to their stories and gossip but never judged and never gossiped in turn. She had become a confidant to many of these women, eastern Europeans mainly, most had experienced trouble and heartache in their lives.

I also felt pleased that my brother had finally settled and although I didn't feel as warm toward Rachel as I might have done, I was happy to see that Simmy's wildness had been toned down. Perhaps he'd met his match. Rachel too, didn't mind a drink and smoked as much as the men did. She seemed to genuinely love my brother and for that alone, I was grateful. They talked about buying a house and starting a family.

We'd slipped into a dreamy complacency and when Esther grabbed her abdomen and lurched across the dinner table one March evening in 1961, I felt myself less a man of action than of helplessness. Reuben ran to the phone and called an ambulance. We rode to the hospital full of fear and worry. I murmured to Esther and held one hand. Reuben held the other. She smiled at us both through tears of pain as spasms took hold of her and wracked her slender frame.

I sat in the dreary waiting room of Toronto General Hospital with Reuben on my lap when the doctor came out to speak to us. The doctor was tall and thin and had the pallor of one who rarely saw the light of day.

"Mr. Goldman?" I nodded. He looked at us myopically through his spectacles, then down at Reuben. "Hello son."

"Hi."

"Mr. Goldman, we took X-rays and your wife has a problem with her stomach. Has she had trouble eating?"

"She's very thin. She's never been a big eater."

"I see. She has an inflammation there, part of her stomach is infected."

"How do you treat it?"

The doctor slumped down into the seat beside us, folding himself up like a crane that had tucked in its ungainly wings. He lowered his voice.

"I wish I could say there was an easy way. That we could give her drugs and the inflammation would subside, but I don't think so. I think it will require an operation."

I swallowed hard. "What kind of operation?"

"You're going to hurt my mummy," Reuben shouted.

The doctor looked at him resignedly. "We'll try not to, son. We'll do our very best, I promise."

"Hush now, Reuben. You were explaining, doctor?"

"Uh-huh," and he pushed his spectacles up the bridge of his nose. "We'll have to remove the infected part. That's the best way to stop the inflammation from spreading. But this will affect her for the rest of her life. It will be difficult for her to eat because her stomach will be smaller. Some foods she may not tolerate well. She will have to experiment a little bit afterward."

"This is the only way?"

The doctor nodded, his head bobbing on his slender neck. "I believe so."

"Is she awake?"

"Yes. We've given her something for the pain."

"Then I'll talk to her and tell her what you've said." I hesitated. "You've done this procedure before?"

"Oh yes, many times. I won't tell you it's an easy operation. It isn't. And there is a recovery period, some weeks I should imagine before she can look after herself properly."

"How long will she be in hospital?"

"I'd say eight to ten days after the operation, depending on how well she responds and gets up and about. But everyone is different and some do better than others."

"My wife is strong-willed. I know she'll be okay."

The doctor clapped me on the knee.

"Good. Why don't you and your son go in and see her now and I'll speak with you later." I stood up and Reuben slid off my lap.

"Thank you, Doctor."

Esther lay in bed, a crumpled figure. Reuben looked frightened.

"Mama," he cried and threw himself at her. She raised herself on an elbow painfully.

"Hello, my darling," she told him and managed to snake one arm around the head now buried in her chest. I bent down and kissed her cheek.

"How are you feeling?"

I felt uneasy with her pain and discomfort. I knew how to deal with my own but that of someone I loved was difficult.

"I'm sore," she said quietly. Her voice came out weak and quivery. Reuben lifted his tear-streaked face.

"When I grow up I shall be a doctor and I will fix you up. I won't let you get sick anymore."

"Will you, darling? That's wonderful. That makes me feel better already." She stroked his dark head.

Once Esther came home from the hospital, she required private nursing care for several weeks. She couldn't work and so I had to work extra hours to pay the medical expenses. Rachel and Simmy helped out in the evenings and on the weekends and they took Reuben out so I could spend some time with Esther alone. Gradually, her strength returned and within a month she began to see her customers again. But as the doctor predicted, her appetite never really returned. No heavyweight before, she became painfully thin. After two mouthfuls of anything she felt full. So, like any practical person, Esther adapted. Rather than eating three formal meals, she ate lightly but more frequently throughout the day. She didn't mind cooking for her family but she rarely ate. But in this way, she was able to gain back some of the weight she had lost and even add a few pounds.

And then came the news that Rachel was pregnant. There were congratulations all around. Simmy picked up Reuben and told him that he was going to have a little cousin.

"But it'll only be a baby," Reuben said.

"So?"

"Babies are too small to play with," he replied glumly.

"But in a few years, you'll be bigger and older and you'll be looking after your little cousin, just like your mummy looks after you."

"A baby-sitter?"

Simmy nodded. "Yes, of course."

"I don't want to be a baby-sitter."

"When I was little, your father looked after me, especially when the bad people in our town were after me. Your father wouldn't let them beat me up."

Reuben wrinkled up his brow.

"How did he do that?"

"He just did."

Later on, after Rachel and Simmy had left, Reuben asked me about what Uncle Simmy had told him.

"I'd beat them up. Punch them right in the nose and then nobody would bother me or your Uncle Simmy."

"How?"

"I learned how to box and after that nobody tried to start anything with me, I can tell you."

Esther looked up from her sewing. "That's enough. I don't want him getting those kind of ideas."

"What ideas?"

"That all your problems can be solved with your fists. You must use your brain first."

"Always. But sometimes there's no choice because the other person won't listen."

"Then you walk away."

"What? I never walked away. Never."

"That's you. And that was Europe where things were bad," Esther said mildly. "Here, it's different. There's no violence against the Jews here. It's a peaceful country. "

"Jews are still not loved here." Reuben followed this exchange between his parents swiveling his head.

"Come Reuben, it is time for your bath."

"Awww." That always seemed to be his mother's answer when things got interesting. I thought back to the time Simmy had been stabbed and I went after his so-called friends. I felt happy that Reuben wouldn't experience the same prejudice or bullying. Jews could just be like anyone else in Canada. We'd made a good decision to come to this country.

Chapter 50

The Fifties gave way to the Sixties. Reuben was our precious child, so naturally we put all our energy into him; all of our expectations and hopes. We told ourselves that we worked hard so we could provide for him. So that he might have a better life. He did well in school and formed several strong friendships. Reuben now had two younger cousins and his aunt and uncle had purchased a home just down the block. Simmy and I purchased four more apartment buildings, so now we owned eight. Rachel left the legal firm to keep our books and we hired a full time superintendent and maintenance man to look after the needs of the buildings. Simmy still did his share however. There was more than enough to do between fixing leaky faucets and wonky furnaces and clearing debris after a storm, mowing the lawns, putting out the garbage bins; the tasks seemed endless. We screened our tenants very carefully, but our units rarely became available and we got new tenants purely through word of mouth, never having to advertise.

A couple of years later, we owned ten apartment buildings and at the age of fifty-one, I decided that I didn't need to keep my job as a mechanic anymore. We had enough money put by and the apartments delivered a healthy income that could support all of us. I quit my job at Midtown Motors and went into property management full-time with my brother. Simmy too, had aged well, although he still smoked too much. I'd quit years earlier when Reuben, having listened to a presentation at school, ran home and begged me to stop. I quit that day, cold turkey. It had been over ten years and I hadn't smoked since. I'd put on some weight, it was true, but overall felt much better.

Simmy was forty-seven, his children were growing and Rachel did a good job in managing the books for the company. We'd decided that within five years, we'd retire and sell the buildings, buy a motor home and together, the two couples would tour North America. Eagerly, we set about making our plans.

Simmy brought home brochures and pored over them, looking at the different makes and models and prices of the motor homes, marveling at the different types of accommodations each offered.

"It's like a hotel on wheels," he exclaimed.

Simmy scoured maps and travel packages, making a detailed list of the various routes and sights along the way. Simmy loved his children and although he and Rachel had their moments, they got along well enough. Well enough for him to remain committed to her and faithful.

Our golden child graduated with top honours and was selected valedictorian of his high school class. He enrolled at the University of Toronto in sciences, paving the way to a medical degree. That is, until his second year of university when the beguiling Lila came into his life. She was the daughter of South African Jews who had emigrated to Toronto during the worst years of apartheid. The Freedmans, chartered accountants by trade, managed to do well in their new homeland. They operated a chain of discount furniture stores that appealed to young, first-time homebuyers and those looking for "quality at a bargain price". Lila had spotted Reuben playing tennis with me at Edgecourt Park near her home. Reuben had a fluid and powerful grace and his dark good looks transfixed her.

One day, when we had finished playing, we came off the court laughing and joking together. Lila put on her most dazzling smile and turned it on Reuben like a beacon. It caught my son's attention and I looked on, amused at first, but I could see what she wanted.

"You two really know how to play. I wish I could play as well." And she turned to me. "You're really in great shape. Don't tell me, the two of you are brothers." Reuben laughed and shook his head. He recognized the ploy but her audacity impressed him.

"No, this is my father and I have a feeling you figured that out."

"Whoops. You caught me."

Lila smiled again, showing perfect white teeth. She then introduced herself and her friend Judy, and we all exchanged names. Within the space of a minute, Reuben discovered they were the same age and coincidentally attending the same school where Lila Freedman was taking an honours degree in psychology. When we finally walked to our car, I turned and stared at the slim back of the young woman and knew that I hadn't seen the last of her.

Within a week, Reuben had "bumped" into Lila on campus and not much longer than that, they began dating heavily. I was stunned. I told Esther, who hadn't yet met the girl, but she didn't seem concerned.

"There's nothing wrong with him going out on a date."

"She wants to marry him, I can see it."

"So? Most young girls want to get married."

"He's young. He doesn't know what he's doing or what he wants. He's too young to be thinking about such things."

"You want him only to marry someone who meets with your approval."

"Of course. Wouldn't that be nice?'

Esther turned away from the television set and used the remote control to turn the sound down. "Of course it would be nice, but we can't expect it will go the way we want, Mordecai."

Reuben often hummed to himself or smiled suddenly without saying anything. He took great pains with his appearance, checking his look in the mirror every time he went out the door. He went shopping for clothes, something he normally left to his mother, and dressed carefully, often changing several times before going out. It seemed as if he and Lila spent all of their free time together and Lila had become a fixture in our home on the weekends. Still, the two sets of parents hadn't met. I tolerated this situation but Lila knew that to win the son, she had to woo the father and she set about that task as diligently as if it were a military campaign. And gradually, she wore me down until, even I, the unflinching man of steel, relented toward her. She arranged a dinner at her parents' golf club one Saturday evening.

I didn't like the air of pretension permeating the Cedar Grove Golf Club. I wasn't in the mood to be friendly or charitable when we were shown to our table in the sumptuous dining room by a white-jacketed waiter. The Freedmans resembled their daughter in one way, quick to smile and laugh but with a purpose behind their eyes. Paul Freedman wore a dark toupee that I found ridiculous and Esther attempted to stifle her initial laughter, citing it as nervousness. Margo Freedman was a short, dumpy woman who stood almost as wide as she was tall. That the Freedmans could produce a tall, rangy daughter like Lila seemed astonishing.

"Good to meet you," cried Paul Freedman in his mixed up Polish/South African twang, clasping us both in turn by the shoulders. He stood a full head shorter than me.

"We love your son. He is brilliant, absolutely brilliant."

Reuben flushed.

"Paul please, there's no need, really..."

Lila then took Reuben by the arm and steered him to his seat.

Sitting down to the meal, I wondered how they had come so far. I admitted to myself that my son seemed smitten with the girl and that I could be stuck with these irritating people for a long time to come. This thought didn't improve my mood any nor did it help my appetite. Lila chatted eagerly with her parents and Reuben talked for the entire table. The sets of parents barely exchanged a word. Esther ate very little because of her condition. This had been explained very carefully to the Freedmans, who nonetheless, kept exhorting her to eat more and to try something else on the menu until I banged my fist on the table and growled.

"She can't. She has a stomach condition."

Paul Freedman halted mid-word, swallowed heavily, then said. "Of course. We knew that. But the soufflé is very light, just like a feather. You don't even feel it going down."

"Thank you, no," Esther replied.

After the dinner ended and the tea and cakes had been served, we got up to go. Paul Freedman clapped me on the back.

"I hope we will see a lot more of each other," and he leaned in closer, "for the kids' sake."

I looked down on him and the stupid-looking hairpiece that was the wrong colour and didn't fit properly. "We'll see."

Paul took that as an affirmative. "Good. I'm glad to hear it."

On the way home, no one spoke. It was a warm summer night in early June and I had the car windows open.

"You didn't like them," Reuben said accusingly.

"I never said that," I replied.

"You didn't have to. You made it very clear."

"I don't have to like them."

"But you can make an effort."

"Please, don't argue," Esther interjected.

"I'm going to marry her."

"But you're only twenty-one," I said.

"So? Ma was only nineteen when you got married."

"It was different then. It was wartime."

Reuben didn't reply at first.

"I'm going to marry Lila," he said in a quiet, even tone. "And I want you to be happy about it."

I looked into the rear view mirror and caught my son's intense look. A mixture of pain and joy swelled up in my chest.

"We will, when the time comes."

Reuben's determination to become a doctor melted away. We were shocked when he switched his major from medicine to the study of corporate law. With his marks, he had no trouble gaining admittance. He worked hard, no question. Lila and Reuben announced their engagement at a party organized by the Freedmans at their palatial home in Forest Hill. Simmy and I stood around awkwardly. Rachel seemed enthralled with all of the glamour and the showiness of the house.

"That's a limited edition Picasso print," I heard her whisper to Esther, pointing to the art on one wall. "Must be worth at least $15,000." Esther nodded and smiled.

The Freedman's home had a formal ballroom that held some seventy-five people. The air conditioning went full blast. A trio of musicians shoved off into a corner on a raised platform played some light jazz while the guests circulated. Reuben only had a moment with us, then he gave Esther a light kiss and me a squeeze on the bicep before going off to mingle. Lila had come to claim him, there were some important people he had to meet, associates of her father. Now that he was coming into the family business, it was time to get to know the players. I watched the young woman lead my son away and I felt like spitting on the floor.

"Don't say anything," Esther hissed. She didn't want to be embarrassed or ruin her son's big day.

"I wouldn't waste my breath," I replied.

"It's time to relax," Simmy said. "Let me get you a drink. And you, Esther?"

Rachel watched Simmy disappear into the crowd as he headed to the bar. "He still gives me the hots, even after fifteen years of marriage." Esther blushed and I laughed appreciatively.

"I'm glad to hear it."

"All of my friends are in love with him."

I looked at her. "And why shouldn't they be? He's a handsome young man, much like myself." Rachel laughed throatily and I joined in.

We made it through dinner without insulting anyone. The Freedmans gave a short speech welcoming Reuben to the family. Lila also spoke. And then it was Reuben's turn. The guests turned their attention to the celebrated "handsome young man."

"I want to tell you that I feel at home already and appreciate all your good wishes. I know too that Lila and I will have a happy and fulfilled life together. A man couldn't ask for more in a prospective bride. She is beautiful, intelligent and has a wonderful sense of humour. Her parents have made me feel very special and have welcomed me in their home from the very beginning. I'm grateful to them and extend that warmth back from the bottom of my heart. I love Lila and know she will be my life partner forever..." At that, a sigh ran around the room like a whistling wind, accompanied by a smattering of claps. "But I learned something about gratitude and love and warmth from my parents. I learned to appreciate the sacrifices they made for me, how hard they worked so I could reap the benefits. If I needed help with schoolwork, my father was there. If I needed a lift, he would drive me. My mother has given endless love and affection. Their feelings for me have sustained me throughout my life and for that I can never offer any form of gratitude or repayment except to say that I have learned from you and will teach my children just as well, and they will love you forever as I do. Thank you."

I blinked and felt my eyes stinging. I looked at Esther, barely forty-two years old and the mother of a grown man. She cried. Together we stood up and hand in hand, stumbled over to Reuben, where we embraced, to the applause of the guests.

The wedding represented everything I dreaded; large, loud, ostentatious and expensive. Somehow, I found myself spending more and more. Gifts for the wedding party, the wedding dinner, tuxedos for the ushers, food and liquor. The more I dealt with the Freedmans, the more I realized how they became wealthy; by letting everyone else pay. And yet I couldn't make a fuss. This was for my son and Esther wouldn't hear of it. It cost me $2500 to send the honeymooners to Aruba for two weeks plus a brand new set of luggage that cost an extra $800. Esther and I had married in a quiet ceremony presided over by Rabbi General Newman and a few fellow officers and Esther's friend, Miriam. No other family attended. And as I thought back to that day, I knew it should be different for my son. After all, I had vowed to myself years ago that it would be so.

Within a year, Reuben and Lila moved into a large, four bedroom brick home on Peverill Hill Road. Six months later, Lila announced she was pregnant. We were to become grandparents. We were thrilled. But once the words had been spoken, Lila's mother took over managing all of the arrangements. She went shopping with her for maternity clothes and accompanied Lila on her doctor's appointments and looked for baby furniture and supervised the decorating of the baby's room. Esther was invited to come along on these outings but usually found an excuse not to go. After all, she still had customers for hair and make-up appointments coming to our home, some of whom had been coming to her since Reuben was a baby.

The Freedman's furniture business prospered, as did Reuben's family. Three more children followed within the next five years and between work and spending time with his family, little time was left for us, just the occasional Friday evening dinner and special occasions like certain religious holidays. At Lila's urging, Reuben had become religious and now attended schul regularly. He read Torah and took to wearing a kepah on his head at all times. Simmy and I were astonished at this turn of events.

As we made our rounds checking the apartments, my brother and I talked. Over the years, we had grown closer. Simmy's two children had entered university and he was rightfully proud of them. He still loved his wife Rachel, who had kept herself well over the years. "The flame is still there," Simmy would say. "And it burns hot."

My thoughts turned more and more to my past as I grew older and the love I left behind in Moscow. I thought of Olga Ouspenskaya Vasilevsky frequently and wondered what had become of her, what she had made of her life and whether she had married and had children. The pangs I felt nicked at my insides, small cuts that made me wince. Not once had I said a word about her in all these years.

As Simmy approached his fiftieth birthday, we spoke more actively of retirement. Simmy still avidly researched motor homes and felt that he'd found the one that would suit all of us. It was roomy enough to sleep four and had a good engine and superior handling, so much so that it drove like a large car. On weekends, he spent his time going to dealerships and shows and taking models out for test drives.

As Reuben grew older, I watched as the neighbourhood changed its face and character. Many of the families moved out once their children grew up. There seemed to be more transients, more empty houses or those who rented rooms or flats. The Italians and Portuguese had moved out of the city making way for Orientals, East Asians and West Indians. The main streets were dotted with Chinese and Vietnamese take-outs and roti shops where there had once been pizza parlours and chirascurros serving fresh barbecued chicken and pork. I didn't mind the changes, but Esther was unhappy. She wanted to sell the house and move into a condominium but I wouldn't have it. I wouldn't be cooped up in a high rise. I enjoyed the garden and planted tomatoes, green peppers, cucumbers and lettuce every summer. You couldn't do that in a condominium.

I watched as the demeanour of the neighbourhood kids changed. I'd seen it all. In the Fifties, a lot of the kids looked more buttoned-down; the girls wore skirts and blouses and socks while the boys wore crisp shirts and slacks and black shoes. Some of the boys greased their hair and the girls packed on a lot of eye make-up and had puffy hair-dos. In the Sixties, all of that changed. This was Reuben's era. Hair and sideburns grew long, pants dragged and expanded at the cuff and the overall look seemed shapeless. You couldn't tell the difference between the boys and the girls. I remarked to Esther that they tried to blend together so that they could disappear.

"They don't have any identity," I said. "And they think they're trying so hard to be different. It makes me laugh." I observed the comings and goings as the local high school was just three blocks away and our street became the major thoroughfare for the neighbourhood kids who walked to school. At first, I'd observed this evolution with wry objectiveness, as long as it didn't affect me and in particular, my son. Reuben, to his credit, had remained above most of it. Yes, he grew his hair longer and wore jeans to school but he stayed away from drugs and never disrespected his parents. His friends came from what Esther called "solid homes" where the parents stayed married and worked hard to do their best for their kids.

A week after my sixtieth birthday, Esther and sat down to dinner when suddenly, she grew very pale. She got up shakily. I saw the change in her pallor and also got out of my chair.

"What's wrong?"

"Get me to the bathroom," she gasped.

I supported my wife and helped her to the bathroom where she vomited into the toilet. I saw blood in the toilet bowl. I bathed her face with a warm damp cloth, picked her up and carried her to the couch in the living room. Then I called an ambulance. By the time the ambulance had arrived, I had a small bag packed with some of her things. I opened the door to the paramedics and they came in, briefly examined Esther, who remained conscious but weak, then brought in a gurney. By this time, some of the neighbours had gathered around. It was a lovely Sunday afternoon in May, 1976. We were the grandparents of four young children and Esther was about to celebrate her forty-eighth birthday. Two of the neighbours, the Robinsons, a black couple who lived across the street, appeared on the porch.

Gloria Robinson was a dignified, handsome woman and a retired nurse. Her husband, Lenny had worked for the railroad until he retired. The couple had two sons.

"Mordecai," Gloria said and reached out to touch my arm. "Is there anything we can do? Can we help in any way?"

"Anything," Lenny added. He had an easy smile and a grey moustache.

I looked at them. "You're very kind. I'll take her to the hospital and then we'll see. I'll let you know when I come back. Thank you for asking."

For years, I had worked on Lenny's various cars for no charge. I wouldn't hear of it. We'd been good neighbours for over twenty years.

"You just let us know," Lenny said firmly.

I nodded and then watched as the paramedics lifted Esther into the back of the ambulance. I squeezed Lenny's arm before following. Lenny and Gloria exchanged worried, meaningful looks.

Reuben joined me in the emergency waiting room at Mount Sinai Hospital. He wore expensive slacks, loafers and a suit jacket.

"How is she? Have you heard anything?"

I shook my head. My son slumped down beside me. Twenty-seven years old and suddenly, he looked very worried.

"I'm going to get some coffee. You want some, Dad?"

I nodded and Reuben went off down the hall, relieved to be doing something, his mind and body always restless, like mine. We waited while the doctors took X-Rays and blood and ran all kinds of tests. We were allowed in to see Esther but she remained very weak and had been sedated. After seven hours, Reuben left to go home. I thought back to his desire to become a doctor when he had been little. Reuben couldn't fix his mother then and it looked like he couldn't fix her now.

I sat up all night in Esther's room, dozing in the chair beside her, thinking off and on of all the things we should have done. I'd vowed to retire earlier but had kept going. I had wanted to travel, to go to Israel, back to Europe to see the miracles that had been wrought in the thirty years since I'd left. All of this had been sacrificed to my work ethic. After all, I reasoned, we weren't old and there'd be time. I'd never passionately loved Esther, I admitted to myself, not like it had been with Olga. But Esther had become my lifelong companion;

my best friend, who could speak to me bluntly and whose instincts were usually right. We leaned on each other.

And now, I told himself, is this part of my life coming to an end? I hadn't really thought about it before. I just assumed that if anyone became seriously ill, it would be me. Esther was so much younger but had been frail ever since I'd met her.

When I heard the prognosis from the bright young doctor with the blonde beard, it still didn't quite have meaning for me. How could this happen without our knowing? How had we missed it? But yes, the blond doctor said, they had confirmed the diagnosis that Mrs. Goldman had an advanced case of stomach cancer. Inoperable. There was nothing they could do except give her medication for the inevitable pain.

I sat in the hospital room and held her limp hand. It was spreading very fast, the doctor said, and it might be just a matter of days, perhaps weeks, but no more.

Over the next days, Esther woke up just once. It was late, after midnight. I'd lost track of time. There'd been a steady stream of visitors. Reuben and Lila, Rachel and Simmy and their children, the Freedmans. She had touched my face and I awoke suddenly.

"Don't be angry, Mordecai."

"What? What are you saying?"

"Please, don't be angry."

"I'm not angry."

"But you can be. Your anger can be so hard. Don't let it take you over. Think of me and grow calm."

"Esther...I..."

"I'm leaving you," she whispered. "I'm very tired, very tired." And she closed her eyes. She never regained consciousness.

Chapter 51

"I'm sorry, Mr. G. That must have been hard for you."
  I didn't answer for a moment. "Yes, it was," I managed to croak.
  "Both of us have had it tough, huh?"
  "You could say that. You could say that."

I didn't want a big funeral. I'd purchased two plots in the Pardes Shalom cemetery at the top end of Dufferin Street through the Lebovitcher Society. I gave them a small donation each year. A small group gathered at the chapel; our family, some of the neighbours, a few of my co-workers from Midtown Motors, a number of the long-term tenants who'd come to know me and Simmy and our families over the years and Esther's long term customers, many of whom were heartbroken at the news. It was a long, sad ride out of the city to the cemetery.

Two o'clock in the afternoon of May 21st, Victoria Day. For everyone else, a holiday. For me, the day I buried my wife of thirty years. The cemetery was tranquil in an unearthly way. Ours was the only funeral that day and I looked down over the rolling hills and the lush greenery and felt at peace. I heard the robins and the bluebirds chirping in the trees. An urban paradise. I sighed. Reuben had insisted on a religious service and engaged a rabbi who didn't know us but had spoken eloquently nonetheless. He recounted our early lives as best as he could and the trip on the *General Heintzelmann* across the rough Atlantic and then the disembarkation on to the frigid ground of Canada.

But I'd always felt warm here. I'd chosen a handsome oak casket in the mid-price range, letting the funeral director make me feel just guilty enough to spend $3000. I watched this investment disappear into the ground and kept thinking that Esther couldn't be in there, that I'd go home and there she'd be making my tea and putting out a slice of lemon cake.

Reuben had wanted me to spend the night with them but I refused. I wanted to go home, to the house we had lived in together. It was important for me to feel her presence again before I could finally say goodbye. Everyone looked sad and meant well, giving me meaningful looks and sympathetic squeezes and reassuring smiles. Many cried, but I didn't. They thought I was being brave but I merely felt used up.

I told my brother that I wouldn't be available to help him the next day but on the day following I'd be there. There'd be shiva for one day only at my house. I didn't want a long and drawn-out period of mourning. I kept myself a private man and I'd mourn in my own way, not according to the religious laws or how some rabbi told me to mourn.

"Don't be a martyr," Reuben said.

"I'm not a martyr. I just need to be on my own."

"But this is a time for family. We're supposed to..."

"Supposed, nothing," I replied. "I'll do what I feel is right, Reuben. I'm sorry, but that's what I want."

Reuben nodded glumly. He knew that he'd put a space between himself and us when he married Lila and the gulf would only widen now.

"Okay Dad. We'll do it your way." And he smiled a bit glumly, that reminded me of the way he'd looked when he was a little boy.

"You're not our little boy anymore."

"No."

"You're a father and have the responsibility of raising children. But you'll do well."

"Thank you."

"You're a Goldman."

"I don't know what that means."

"It means whatever you want. It's up to you."

I didn't change my routine. I still rose at four in the morning and made myself a cup of coffee and ate a sliced banana. Then I turned on the news to see what was happening in the world. At five-fifteen, the morning paper arrived. I sat in the den and read the paper for a quarter of an hour. Then it was time to go. By five-forty, I drove into the driveway of the Dante Alighieri Community Centre. The doors opened at five forty-five when I went into the locker room, changed into gym clothes and started my routine. An hour and a half later, I'd be done, and having shaved and showered, I was ready for the day. Then I drove home where I had breakfast; cereal, toast, orange juice and another cup of coffee. I'd pick Simmy up at eight-thirty and together we'd make the rounds of the buildings. Seven years earlier, we'd purchased four more quadplexes, making it fourteen that we owned. A large developer had been after us to sell. They wanted to build twin condo towers and a recreation centre and felt the land we owned would be a perfect location. So far, we hadn't been interested. But a good deal of money lay on the table.

"You smoke too much," I said in August, 1976. "Roll down the window."

"You say that every morning."

"I say it because it's true. The truth of it doesn't change from day to day. Those things will kill you."

"You're a reformed smoker. The worst kind," Simmy answered.

"Maybe so. But I can't stand the smell of it anymore. I don't know how I smoked for so many years."

"You were a soldier and everybody smoked."

"It didn't seem to matter when you could die at any moment. You never knew when your brains would be splattered on the ground or on a comrade's uniform."

"In the camps, we would've killed for a cigarette. I mean it. I'm not afraid of death because I've lived through hell." And then Simmy cackled in a half-crazy sort of way.

"We've each experienced our own part of it," I said. "No one understands what it's like."

Simmy tossed his cigarette stub out the window.

"No, you cannot describe it adequately. It's beyond human language, perhaps even human comprehension, don't you think?"

He went to light up again but I gave him a stern look and Simmy smiled ruefully, then shrugged, slipping the packet back into the front pocket of his cotton shirt.

I turned into the driveway of 1641 Bathurst, our first stop. I drove around the back and parked in a vacant spot.

"We're lucky you and I. We're here and nowhere else." Simmy laughed. As he slid out the door, he reached into the front pocket of his shirt.

I always said that cigarettes would kill my brother. Some eight months later, on a cold February day that had dawned dry and bright, Simmy drove his car on Highway 401, about two o'clock in the afternoon. There'd been a sudden thaw the day before and it had rained. Overnight the temperature had plummeted, causing what the meteorologists called a "flash freeze". But on what appeared to be a bright, dry day, there seemed little cause for concern. Simmy reached into the inside pocket of his coat for a packet of cigarettes. But the packet fell to the floor, and he reached down taking his eyes off the road for an instant; that fatal instant when his new Buick Regal hit a patch of black ice and sloughed around, the momentum coming from the back. Simmy had been in the middle lane. To his left, a tractor trailer, hell bent on making it to Montreal in record time had begun to pull even with him as he went into the spin. The trucker hit Simmy's car at a ninety-degree angle. The burly driver stood on the air brakes with all the strength he could muster but the momentum of the great truck forced it ahead and he drove Simmy's car forward, crushing it against a cement light standard. The twisted metal of the Regal wrapped itself around the standard like a bow. Simmy's car was virtually unrecognizable, a pulverized lump of metal. Ambulances and firefighters came and used the "jaws of life" to pry Simmy out, but he was pronounced dead on arrival at the hospital. Traffic had been tied up for several hours.

I took the call from Rachel at home. I felt the beating of my heart and the sudden dryness in my mouth.

"I'll come right away," I said.

I'm not even sure I hung up the phone in its cradle. Time fell into a vacuum and stretched into an unearthly continuum as I went through the motions that were required of me. I comforted a sobbing Rachel and the two bereaved children. Mechanically, I dealt with the funeral director and made the arrangements for the service and the burial. I spoke with the rabbi. But all along, I felt heavy and slow and dull-witted. First Esther, now Simmy. My shoulders sagged, my face pulled downward by a profound sadness that seeped through my pores. Simmy, such a young man to be taken away, barely fifty-seven years old. Rachel sat in the kitchen, the trip brochures spread out in front of her and sobbed uncontrollably. I sat down beside her and she collapsed against me. What could I do? Nothing, I told myself. There was nothing to do.

I hadn't given up. I endured life's tragedies, its disappointments and brutality and managed to go on, to find some purpose. Shortly after Simmy's death, I, with Rachel's permission, sold all of the apartment buildings to the developer who'd been pestering us and split the money with Rachel, to provide for her and her children. After all, she was a young woman, still in her forties, and her children were going to college. There was more than enough to provide for us all. I didn't need much. My house was paid, my wants few.

And so I retired for good at the age of sixty-five, a relatively wealthy man. Reuben stepped up his campaign to get me to move.

Why should I live there on my own? They had just bought a new house, bigger than the one before. I could live with them. Plenty of space. But stubborn old bastard that I was, I refused. I preferred my independence. Looking after the house would give me something to do.

Still, I rose at four in the morning keeping the same routine. The difference was coming home after the workout. Esther wasn't there to greet me with toast and coffee. I couldn't call my brother up on the phone to talk. And Reuben was Reuben, busy with his own family. They travelled, taking several vacations a year, and the grandchildren were doing well in their education. If Reuben needed help with anything, babysitting, someone had to go somewhere, then I made myself available. I read in the garden and in the summer planted my vegetables and shared the bounty with my neighbours, especially the Robinsons across the street. They were the last family who'd lived there as long as me. Often, they had their young granddaughter over to visit. A delightful, pretty girl with braided hair, she would cross the street and visit with me. I gave her milk and cookies while she chatted on in the unassuming way of four-year olds. Then after a while, I'd take Beulah's hand and walk her carefully back across the street to her grandparents.

"She's a beautiful child," I always said to the Robinsons and they beamed with pride. Their only grandchild. One of their sons had turned out gay and wouldn't have children while the other had skirted trouble all of his life. He'd married the child's mother but they didn't stay together for very long. The mother, Mrs. Robinson confided, had a drinking problem and they were trying to gain custody of the child, so she could grow up in a stable and supportive household. I spoke to Reuben, who recommended a friend from law school and after a year-long battle, the child was placed in the Robinson's custody. They were thrilled and couldn't thank me enough.

"Don't thank me. Thank my son. He's the one with the connections. He's the big shot."

I took as much pleasure in watching Beulah Robinson grow up as I did my own grandchildren. She was a bright and inquisitive child who did well in school and always had plenty of playmates.

The proximity of the high school fomented illicit commerce, impressionable teens becoming tempted by those who had something exciting to sell. Many adolescents who thought of themselves as rebels fell prey to such come-ons. Many just dabbled, but some got hooked.

I'd become the eyes and ears of the neighbourhood. As soon as the drug dealers hit the streets and started to solicit, I called the police. Then, as the patrol cars pulled up, I stood on the curb with a smile of grim satisfaction as the dealers scattered. But I and the police knew that this wasn't a solution to the problem. Still, it enraged me to see these parasites peddling their filth on my street.

"Goddam bastards," I shouted as the dealers jumped into cars and sped off, scattering like frightened vermin.

Reuben pleaded with me to sell the house and move but I always refused. I know he found me frustrating in the extreme but I couldn't help it.

By the time she turned seventeen, Beulah Robinson, so full of promise, became addicted to crack. She had fallen and continued to fall deeper and deeper. She dropped out of school. She disappeared for days on end. She sold her body to feed her habit. When she showed up at the Robinsons, it was to ask for money and clothes. Her grandparents begged her to stay, to get help, to let them take care of her – but the grip of the drug was too powerful.

The Robinsons poured out their woes to me and I listened in stunned silence as a mixture of sadness and rage swept over me.

"This is a war," I declared. "They're stealing our children, these people, these goddam parasites. We must do something."

"What can we do? We're old," bleated the Robinsons.

"But you're not dead yet. Don't act as if you are."

The Robinsons shook their grey heads and walked slowly across the street.

I watched and waited. I noticed that one group of young men came almost every day. They wore baggy clothes and bandanas. Their leader was a young man with a thin moustache and a swarthy complexion. He wore a black bandana, drove a black BMW, and carried a cellular phone. He was never alone, but accompanied by two or three bodyguards. This one never actually did anything, never passed money or drugs but I knew he directed the others. They had bribed some little children to be their lookouts, to warn them in case of trouble.

Each day, I went out and stood by the curb and stared at them, these young men. I made certain they noticed me. The dealers gave me looks but paid little mind. After all, I was an old man, why bother? Until I turned on my heel and called the police, then went back outside and stood on the curb again and stared, particularly at the one with the thin moustache and the black bandana. The police showed up and the dealers scattered. It became a game we played every day.

One morning as I went to put the garbage out to the curb, I saw the young drug dealer. He lounged against his car and watched me approach the curb through slitted eyes. A cigarette dangled from his lips. He wore a sleeveless undershirt that showed the blue tattoos up and down his skinny arms. I ignored him as I set down the bin and the plastic bag I carried and was about to go back when the young man spoke.

"What you playin' at old man?"

I turned and stared at the young man as he sauntered across the street and stood before me, blew cigarette smoke in my direction, then spat at his feet.

"You speaking to me?"

"You know I am."

"So?" And I shrugged and smiled.

"You're fuckin with my business, you understand? Every time you call the cops, it's a hassle. I'm sayin', in case you don't understand me, that you better stop if you know what's good for you. Old man."

I chuckled.

"You think I'm afraid of you? You piece of shit. I killed Nazis, some with my bare hands. I should be afraid of you?"

The young man shifted his weight and smiled, but there was no warmth in his expression.

"Do yourself a favour, if you want to keep on living. Stop calling the cops on us, hear? Or we'll come get you. I know where you live, right?"

"Be my guest. Anytime," I retorted. "You want me to stand by while you sell drugs to children? You ruin lives and I should do nothing?"

"Look. If it wasn't me, it'd be somebody else. So what's the difference? That's just the way it is today."

"And why should we put up with it, huh? From parasites like you."

"'Cause nobody's gonna stop us – including you, you dig?"

"Get out of here and don't come back."

The young man dropped the cigarette butt and ground it under his boot heel slowly.

"You got balls, old man, I give you that, but I'm here to tell you that you're dead." He pointed at me with his finger extended, as he backed across the road.

"Dead, old man. One sorry dead fucker, that's you."

He sauntered over to the black BMW, going slow, fondling his keys and then, glancing back with a squint, started up the engine and sped away.

I stood and watched until the black car turned the corner, squealing its tires. I looked up and thought I saw something at the Robinsons' top window but the curtain dropped quickly back into place.

It's time, I told myself. Time to get ready. I turned and went back into the house.

Chapter 52

Beulah had fallen asleep finally upstairs. I found the key to the cellar and unlocked the door, then clumped down the stairs. I switched on the bare light and picked my way through the lawn furniture, bookcases and ceiling tiles easing to the back where I'd built some shelves for my tools. There was a set of drawers and I pulled one of them out. I felt around for the gunnysack and placed it on the table. I reached inside and felt the well-oiled metal.

I laid each piece out and then practiced assembling and re-assembling with my eyes closed as I'd done so many years ago. I'd kept half a dozen clips and over the years I'd checked each one to ensure the powder hadn't dried and everything remained in perfect working order. I'd done this without Esther's knowledge. Some things had been difficult to let go. After examining each piece carefully, I assembled the machinery and slid the bolt back and forth. It went smoothly and easily. Time for me to get some rest. I knew they wouldn't come during the day. They'd come early in the morning, just as they'd come all those years ago.

I slept fitfully but managed to rest a little. I knew I had to conserve energy and it'd be a long night. I heard the phone ring twice but let it go. I'd slipped some sleeping powder into the soup I'd given Beulah so she wouldn't wake up for a long while.

I awoke as the sun came through the windows. My room faced west, the room I'd taken after Esther and I decided to sleep separately. I hadn't gone into Esther's room since she died except to tidy up, dust and vacuum. Thoughts of Olga kept plaguing me and I'd found myself dreaming of her. I saw us together in her father's house in Moscow and in the army cot we'd shared during the War.

In the bathroom, I rinsed my face with cold water, splashing the fatigue out of my eyes. Then I went deep into my closet and pulled out an old trunk, one that hadn't been opened in years. The locks snapped open and I lifted the lid. I removed the top tray and beneath lay my American officer's uniform but that wasn't what I wanted. I lifted it out and arranged it on the bed. I wanted the next layer down, wrinkled and smelling stale. I spread it out, then went to the mirror holding the pieces before me. Yes, it would do. Very well indeed. I grunted in satisfaction.

I took my meals in the front room upstairs, so I could sit and watch the street. I knew what to look for and it didn't take long to see. The black BMW cruised up the street slowly, carefully. An hour later it came back down. This occurred twice more during the course of the early evening. I felt that whatever would happen, it would be soon. I thought about my options and knew these people, these new enemies, were rash and impatient. They were young after all, and waiting wasn't part of their nature. It was instant this and instant that. I'd show them. I could be patient. I knew how to wait.

I'd found the chair I wanted in the cellar and set it up in a position on the landing that gave me a good vantage point. I sat, elevated, and could see both the front and back of the house. I didn't think they'd troop in the front door as they had before. They weren't that foolish. These were violent people without any moral conscience. I had no illusions about them but also knew they'd be in for a surprise and this pleased me. I laughed out loud. Yes, the joke would be on them.

Darkness settled over the house. I made myself some tea, collected a blanket and took up my position. The tunic and pants hung on me but I felt more whole and collected wearing those clothes. Even the boots weren't too bad. I set the cap down on the floor beside the chair. In my arms, I felt the cold, dispassionate metal. I slipped the safety off. And now I was ready. I turned all the lights off. The house was still.

Stay focused, I told myself. I didn't want to slip off into the past. I didn't want to lose concentration, something all too easy to do at my age. I felt the years drop away and in the darkness I became my old self. The ruthlessness and the rage seeped back into my blood. I bounced my heels off the ground to keep the circulation flowing. My elderly eyes, one still strong, adjusted to the darkness. I had the advantage of knowing the layout. I'd placed glass objects along all of the window sills and chairs in front of doorways as an early warning system.

I dozed off. Shortly after midnight, I awoke with a start. It took a moment for me to collect my thoughts, to remember my surroundings. The cold steel in my hands reminded me. I threw the blanket off my shoulders as I heard the tinkling of glass breaking, not once but twice. I slid off the chair and crouched down by the banister. I heard the creaking of a window as it slid up and the soft step of a track shoe. One, perhaps two in the back I reasoned. I waited. They would come to me.

The intruders moved carefully through the living room around the staircase. One of them went to the front door and opened it. Two others slipped in. There were four. Just as before, I thought. Have they learned nothing? Just four and me? One of the intruders motioned now. I could see they were armed, arms extended out in front of them, letting the weapons lead. They formed a line at the bottom of the stairs and kept their line of sight directly in front of them, waiting to adjust to the gloom.

Heart pounding and throat dry, I squeezed the trigger. I heard a dull click.

"Whazz'at?" whispered one of the men as they dropped to the floor. "Whazz'at?"

I squeezed the trigger again and the machine pistol erupted into flame pouring molten lead into the room, its roar a firestorm in our ears. The intruders, caught by surprise were suddenly afraid as bullets spat all about them, tearing up the floor, the carpet and the furnishings. They scattered around the room, yelling wildly, shooting blindly at whatever they could and imagined what they could not see. Only the one with the black bandanna and the thin moustache kept his composure. He pointed his pistol and aimed at the origin of the flames leaping out in the darkness.

Chapter 53

Beulah

I slept for a long time. Night had come round again. Mr. G, he'd been plying me with chicken soup and tea and grilled cheese sandwiches. I looked forward to it when he came clumping in carrying a tray for me. I hadn't thrown up in a few days and I think my mind slowly started to focus around the edges. I'd been in that fuzzy world for so long. I figured Mr. G was sleeping. Although I felt better, I didn't have any strength. I felt like a little baby in a cradle. I wish I'd had a momma to cuddle me though. But I did have Grammy Robinson, bless her. She gave me everything. She and Gramps never held back and now that my mind had returned, I felt nothing but shame. How could I ever make it up to them? How could I ever thank Mr. G for helping me out these past few days?

Ohmigod. I don't know what happened but I heard it sure enough and it sounded loud. I knew the sound of gunfire. I'd grown up on it. But this was different. A heavy mechanical sound like a jackhammer, busting open the room next door. I heard yelling. I heard screams. Just for a second, I thought I'd dived back into my own nightmare. I rolled out of the cot, braced my hand on the floor and crawled to the door. I wanted to call out, to call Mr. G's name but I couldn't. My throat had frozen.

I used the doorknob to pull myself up. I got the door open. I leaned heavily against the wall 'cause my legs had buckled from weakness but more from fear. I could smell it now too. The bitter odour of gunfire. I almost gagged but somehow I held it together.

"Mr. G?" I called out in a quivery voice. "Mr. G?"

I slid toward the landing thinking that any second, I'd fall over, just crumple up into a heap. I could make out the top of the stairs now.

"Mr. G?" I called out again. "You there?"

Someone moaned. It came out like a soft sigh, like a wave of relief. I saw something on the landing. A chair knocked over. And a figure slumped against the bannister.

I reached for the light switch. With trembling fingers, I turned it on. And then, it was like, holy shit, I never witnessed such a horror. In all the things I'd seen and all the crazy shit I'd done.

"Mr. G." I bent down toward him. A red stain had spread down his chest. He wore something old and grey and smelly. Some kind of uniform. I looked down the stairs and saw them. Four dudes with guns sprawled out on the floor. They all looked dead. And Mr. G, he looked at me and smiled. Can you imagine, he smiled at me.

"It's the first time I've been wounded," he gasped.

I plucked at his belt and began to unbutton his tunic. He pushed my hand away.

"Don't bother, Beulah. It won't do any good."

We heard the sirens in the distance now. Someone, even in this neighbourhood, had called the cops. I looked down the stairs.

"They're all dead, huh?"

"I sincerely hope so," Mr. G said. "Otherwise," and he pointed to his belly, "this wouldn't have been worth it."

Tears sprang down my cheeks and I felt an overwhelming pain rise up inside me.

"Mr. G. You crazy old man. What did you think you were doing, huh? What was this for?"

"I did it for you. And for them." He pointed toward the door. "They'll get the message now. They'll stay away from here. You don't have to worry."

"Save your breath," I said. "Help's coming. Should be here any minute."

He smiled again, then grimaced.

"Too late. I've seen these wounds before with my own men."

"Don't say that. You're not going to die, you hear? I won't let you." He panted heavily now, gasping at each breath.

"Upstairs," he breathed. "On the dresser. A letter. Please, give it to my son."

"Okay."

Then Mr. G began to struggle, moving his legs under him, pushing his back up, bracing against the bannister.

"Whoa there. Where you going?"

"I must drag the bodies outside."

"You aren't dragging anybody anywhere. Now sit back down and rest for a minute."

"You don't understand. I must show them. Let this be a warning to the others," he gasped.

Then the cops burst in and all hell broke loose.

I sat on the stairs, a blanket around my shoulders watching as they carried the bodies out. The four gangbangers first, then finally, Mr. G. I held the letter in my hand. The cops had bagged it first as evidence. I told them to call his son. I just knew his name, that's all. Reuben. They tried to talk to me but I didn't want to say anything. I told them my grandparents lived across the street and I wanted to go there.

A while later, Mr. G's son showed up. He looked like Mr. G might if he'd been forty years younger. But something was missing. Strength maybe. His face looked grey and his eyes had swelled. I could barely see myself. A cop had gone over to him and whispered something. Then Reuben looked over at me with a bewildered expression. He looked like a lost little boy. I held up the letter. He came over, his lips trembling.

"*Thank you,*" *he said in a tiny voice. I'd read the letter and I felt sorry for him and deeper, sicker at what I had done. I hadn't brought the gangbangers to the neighbourhood and I know that Mr. G provoked them. But it was because of me he did what he did, crazy old fool. All I could do was make sure he hadn't died for no reason. I had to get myself straight or die trying.*

My Dear Son,

How can I explain this to you so that you will understand? It's possible that I can't. You mustn't feel sadness or anger. I've brought this on myself. Pride can get the better of us even when we are old. I had to prove something. I was angry, just as I was angry sixty years ago when I returned to my home in Krasnowicz. I have never told you this but shortly after the War, I shot four men in my house. They had come to kill me. The four were boys I had gone to school with. I had helped them with their homework. They befriended me because I was good in school and they couldn't afford to fail their studies. Today, when you read this note, you will know that I have killed again. Again, I was angry and wished to rid the world of a scourge. I've seen a beautiful, young girl destroyed because of the drugs these vermin sell. Are they any different from the Nazis? I'm not so sure. I raised you to be civilized. I wasn't so fortunate. I became a man in terrible times. These past years have been difficult for me. I've lost your mother and my brother and many years ago my parents, my sister, her husband and child to the camps. The anger and the bitterness still burns in me. I also said goodbye to someone I loved very much. Someone I knew in Moscow during the War. It is time now for me too. Sometimes, you can live too long. And so, my son, you must know that your mother and I called you the precious one. I'm very proud of you and I hope you will understand someday. That it was not only time to say goodbye but time to say Dos Vidaniya. *To everything. To the world. To you and your family. To hatred and love. Hold me in your thoughts. Dry your tears.*

Dos Vidaniya *Reuben, precious boy. We shall meet again.*

Your loving father.

About the Author

W.L. Liberman believes in the power of storytelling but is not a fan of the often excruciating psychic pain required to bring stories to life. Truthfully, years of effort and of pure, unadulterated toil is demanded. Not to sugarcoat it, of course, writing is a serious endeavor. It is plain, hard work. If you've slogged away at construction work, at lumberjacking, delivery work, forest rangering, sandwich making, truck driving, house painting, among other things, as I have, writing is far and beyond more rigorous and exhausting. At the end of a long, often tedious, usually mind-cracking process, some individual you don't know pronounces judgment and that judgment is usually a resounding 'No'. This business of writing is about perseverance and stick-to-it-iveness. When you get knocked down and for most of us, this happens frequently, you take a moment to reflect, to self-pity, then get back at it. You need dogged determination and a thick skin to survive. And an alternate source of income.

W.L. Liberman is currently the author of eight novels, two graphic novels and a children's storybook. He is the founding editor and publisher of TEACH Magazine; www.teachmag.com, and has worked as a television producer and on-air commentator.

He holds an Honours BA from the University of Toronto in some subject or other and a Masters in Creative Writing from De Montfort University in the UK. He is married, currently lives in Toronto (although wishes to be elsewhere) and is father to three grown sons.

Lightning Source UK Ltd.
Milton Keynes UK
UKHW021836180920
370162UK00009B/165